# The Drowning Guard

*A Novel of the Ottoman Empire*

## ALSO BY LINDA LAFFERTY

*The Bloodletter's Daughter*

# The Drowning Guard

### A Novel of the Ottoman Empire

## LINDA LAFFERTY

**lake union** publishing

Text copyright © 2013 Linda Lafferty
All rights reserved.

Printed in the United States of America.

Published by Lake Union Publishing – Seattle, Washington

www.apub.com

ISBN-13: 9781477805299
ISBN-10: 147780529X

*To my first editor and the love of my life,*
*Andy Stone*

*Note to Reader:* Please refer to glossary provided at the back of this book for an explanation of Ottoman and Turkish words from the nineteenth century.

# The Drowning Guard

## A Novel of the Ottoman Empire

# Prologue

*May 1826*

The oarsman's lantern threw shadows against the side of the Royal Launch as he maneuvered the boat into the deepest waters of the Bosphorus, halfway between Asia and Europe.

The wind blew warm from the west, through the Straits of the Dardanelles and up the waterway to the Imperial City of Constantinople, where Sultan Mahmud II's favorite sister lay sleeping, her night's lover condemned to death.

The launch, painted bright blue to ward off the evil eye, had higher sides than any of the Sultan's *kayik* fleet; it was meant to carry cargo across the Bosphorus, between Europe and Asia. Tonight its cargo consisted of three: the oarsman, a condemned man, and the janissary who must kill him.

The janissary's freakish size—he was the giant of the Ottoman army—meant that no other guards were needed to subdue the struggling victim. Ahmed Kadir was known to be neat and efficient, for no one could overpower him. Except for the oarsman, there was to be no witness.

But even this early, an hour before dawn, there were a few who had seen the launch set off from docks on the the Golden Horn, heading towards deeper waters with a battered prisoner and the giant soldier. The chestnut vendor uttered a prayer to Allah and fed a whining cur a burned nut from his blackened hand, just to feel the presence of life in the dark belly of night.

The water lapped against the hull of the boat as the prisoner pleaded for mercy, stinking of urine and fear as he invoked the name of the Virgin Mary to comfort him in his last hour.

The janissary studied the Eastern waters that flowed from the Black Sea and saw the blood streak of dawn on the horizon. He cursed himself for allowing time to escape as the prisoner babbled prayers to the Christian God. He preferred to do his work in the dead of night and return to the harbor of the Golden Horn unnoticed.

"There is no mercy I can give you; you are condemned to die by decree of the Princess Esma Sultan. Not to carry out this order would mean my own death."

The prisoner craned his neck, covered with savage bites and bruises, looking up at the guard who towered above him. The janissary noticed a series of long angry welts along the man's back—the marks of a savage flogging.

"In the name of Jesus Christ," the man whispered. "Hear my confession and give me a quick death. They say that you strangle your victims rather than have them face the nightmare of drowning in a sack."

The janissary threw a quick look at the oarsman whose face was drained of color. This was his favorite boatman, one who clearly hated his work.

"I am of the true faith of Islam," pronounced the janissary loudly, a gust of wind snatching his words. "How could I absolve you of your Christian sins when I pray to the God of our Prophet Mohammed?"

The man winced and gagged. The janissary grabbed him by the shoulders and held his head overboard as the prisoner retched up a cream-colored fruit, wrinkled purple skin still partially adhered to the meat.

"I gave her no pleasure," gasped the man through the dripping spittle. "That is why I was beaten, I am sure. I die a virgin as I was meant to be, a priest to the Holy Byzantine Church."

The janissary felt the weight of the man's head in his hands, holding him like a tired child as he vomited one last time into the salty water. The condemned man had come from the landlocked provinces and this would be his first glimpse—and last—of the terrifying sea.

"What was your Christian name?" whispered the prisoner, his face just inches from the water. "Before you send me to my grave, tell me your name."

"I was born Ivan Postivich," said the janissary, his mouth next to the prisoner's ear. "I forgive you only if you can forgive me for what I am about to do. But Allah will never forgive me. And your Virgin Mary spits on my soul."

With that, the janissary dipped his fingers in the saltwater and made the sign of the cross on the condemned man's forehead. Looking him in the eye, Ivan Postivich placed his huge hands around his prisoner's throat, his thumbs on either side of the man's Adam's apple, and snapped his neck as if it were a brittle branch.

Without a word to the oarsman, Postivich hauled the lifeless body to the middle of the boat and stuffed it in the sack filled with stones. His hands looped a knot in the bag and pitched the body overboard, the tea-colored water parting with a heavy splash. As the depression in the water quickly healed, the bag disappeared in the depths. The guard made a quick motion to the oarsman to return to shore.

A diminutive eunuch stood at the Imperial Docks as they reached the Golden Horn. As always, he kept his distance from the vessel, as if by proximity he would be cursed by its mission. Postivich could never quite make out the features of the eunuch's face, recognizing him only by his crimson tunic, starched white turban, and preternaturally pale skin.

"What news to report to the Sultaness?" the eunuch called.

The janissary cursed under his breath, his words obscured by the waters lapping against the pylons of the dock.

"Tell her—this one was different. He died without a word."

# Part I
# Drowned Men

# Chapter 1

The Bazaar of old Constantinople rang with a dozen languages and the savage barking of mongrel dogs. Amber-skinned North Africans bartered with sailors from the Far East, who cursed and spat in disgust on the azure tiles of the marketplace. Armenians cried out the virtues of their carpets and offered sweet apple tea to blue-eyed Englishmen, their northern skin burned red under the harsh sun of the Near Orient. Portuguese and Italian merchants tried shouting to make their language more intelligible to Asian ears as yellow and green African parrots, chained to their perches, mimicked the screeching.

The Jewish street sweep, whose family had escaped brutal persecution in Spain and fled to the relative sanctuary that the Muslim Sultans provided, leaned on his broom and smiled crookedly at all those fortunate enough to live and breathe in the most cosmopolitan city on earth.

By now, in the late spring of 1826, the old Greek residents had grudgingly accepted a peace with the Sultan's army of Janissaries. It had been four years since the last uprising had been savagely crushed, and the Orthodox Patriarch dragged from his pulpit, a rope around his neck, to answer for conspiracy against the Otto-mans. The Greeks' staccato voices mixed with the Serbo-Croat pidgin of the crowd, rising to the sky along with Ladino, Turkish, and the lilting strains of the Ottoman language of the elite, edu-cated in the Topkapi Palace.

Noisy vendors hawked their fiercely colored spices—green hennas and saffrons—their silver teapots, and lapis opium pipes. Red glass hookahs hung from rawhide tethers under the awnings. The tang of tobacco laced the air, mingling with the aroma of fish frying in olive oil and garlic.

On the Meydan, the square in front of the Bazaar's maze of tents and stalls, an English slavemaster was unloading his wares. Three young women—black, amber, and white-skinned—crawled awkwardly out of the donkey cart, their wrists chained together.

"Come on, hurry up then," grunted their master in a Cockney-accented English. He inspected their meager clothing and removed their veils, rubbing one's cheek with a spit-moistened thumb to remove a smear of dirt.

He tapped the girls firmly in the small of their backs with his fist to make them stand straight.

"Smile," he whispered. "Smile or get a good lashing from James R. Rickles."

A group of men gathered, leering and pointing. They rubbed their genitals as they exchanged lewd remarks in a stew of languages.

The Englishman knew that these were not buyers. He ignored them, his eyes searching for a likely customer.

"Is that one really a virgin?" shouted a man in a tunic and crimson sash. He wore a fine linen turban.

The slavemaster smiled and addressed him in a guttural Turkish laced with very bad French. "This one here? The pretty white girl?

She was captured in Chios during the last uprising and knows no man. Barely fourteen. She would bear strong, fine-boned children in your harem and pass along her comely looks."

"I want to inspect her."

The three women cowered as the man approached; the chains jingled with their terror.

"Well, go ahead. See that she is still intact. Can't do better than my goods, guaranteed!"

The man ran his fingers slowly over the girl's breasts, pinching them around the nipples and then dipped his hands under her tunic. He pressed his ear against her belly and groped between her legs as if he were milking a cow.

Tears rolled down the girl's cheeks but she said nothing.

Suddenly she gasped.

"You satisfied now?" said the vendor. "No more than a sample there, sir. Move your hand away. You might damage the goods with all that handling."

The buyer removed his hand and grasped her cheeks.

"Tell her to open her mouth."

"Open your mouth, love. That's a good girl."

The prospective buyer stared into the girl's open mouth. He wrinkled his nose at her breath.

"Her teeth are not good. They smell of rot."

"Too much of that honeyed baklava the Greeks cook. Feed her yoghurt and make her chew mint. Chases away the smell."

The buyer sniffed again at her mouth, unconvinced.

"You could pull her teeth," suggested the vendor. "For what you want, she doesn't need a tooth in her head, now does she?"

Those in the crowd who could understand him laughed.

"How much are you asking?"

The slavemaster smiled and whispered in his ear.

"What?" said the Turk, outraged. "For that I could buy a Circassian!"

"That's my price. And not an *akce* less."

The man spat on the ground. "I waste my time with you, Englishman. I will buy my slaves elsewhere, where foreign thieves do not try to rob me."

With that, the Turk disappeared into the crowd.

The Greek girl smiled sadly. The other girls kissed her wet cheeks and mumbled comforting words in a mix of languages.

"Enough of that!" grumbled the vendor. "And you do have bad teeth, you Greek dog. You've cost me a sale!"

The girls straightened their backs and looked glumly at their worn sandals and now tears trickled down all three faces, speckling the dusty cobblestones at their feet.

A Venetian ambassador and a Russian diplomat conversed in French as they walked along the great blue Bosphorus, their ivory-inlaid walking sticks clicking against the paving stones of the one good road that led to the Bazaar.

As they approached the slave market, the Venetian pulled at his collar and wrinkled his face in disgust.

"They treat these poor women as if they were nothing more than cattle at a fair," said the Russian. "Deplorable."

Suddenly, a black lacquered coach, with a crimson crescent moon and star emblazoned on the door, clattered over the stones. The horses' hooves struck sparks as the turbaned driver reined them adroitly through the mob.

The crowd knew the carriage of Esma Sultan, favorite sister of their glorious Sultan Mahmud II. They were quick to stand back and make way, staring at the fine black horses in their gold-studded harnesses. The curtains were drawn, but everyone knew the Princess reclined inside, spying on the crowd through a peephole.

The driver tightened the reins, as the matched pair of horses pranced in excitement.

The slavemaster opened his eyes wide as he saw a small panel slide open.

An exquisite white hand, filigreed in twisting strands of red henna, reached out, a ring with a ruby the size of a quail's egg glittering. In the outstretched palm lay a silken pouch that jingled with gold coins.

The driver took the money and threw it at the vendor.

"Send those women to Esma Sultan's palace immediately."

"Which palace?"

"On the Bosphorus. And see that they are delivered . . . undamaged or I will deal with you personally."

The vendor inspected the pouch and grunted in satisfaction.

"Of course, guv'nor. You can count on it. Tell the—er, Sultaness —you can always count on James R. Rickles, that is."

Then he approached the driver and looked up with a conspirator's glance, beckoning the driver to bend near him.

"She want any more?" he whispered. "I can always find plenty more."

"Get out of the way, infidel swine!" shouted the driver. With a snap of his whip, the horses took off, leaving the Englishman coughing in the dust.

"Fair enough," said Rickles, straightening his coat in indignation. "It is no secret what she is up to now!" he said in a low voice. "At least I am not selling her a lamb for slaughter."

*Like those young men she seeks,* the slavemaster thought, but did not dare say.

No one said a word. To criticize the Sultan's favorite sister was high treason, punishable by decapitation.

"She is hunting for young men Christian to take to her bed," shouted a dervish, spit flecking the side of his mouth. "She is the whore of Constantinople and the Sultan is the pimp who indulges her!"

"Shut up, man," warned the vendor. "You want your crazy Sufi head poking off a bloody stick at Topkapi? The Sultan's Solaks there are just waiting for an excuse to take you away!"

"The Sultan be damned for his sins! Allah shall have his revenge!" shouted the dervish.

The Englishman backed away as the Solaks seized the ranting Sufi and dragged him away.

"Why does she not take a Muslim lover, one of her own kind?" whispered the Venetian diplomat to his Russian counterpart. "Surely he would do as well and be more to her liking, circumcised and what not."

"You have not been amongst the Ottomans for very long, my friend. A fellow Muslim is untouchable, protected by the Sheriat and Koran. It is only the 'infidels' she seeks."

"Surely Muslim men can have sex as easily as any Christian!"

"It's not the tryst," said the Russian grimly. "It's the murder that will follow."

The Venetian ambassador turned to him, eyebrow raised.

The Russian nodded solemnly.

"By morning, the poor man will be lying at the bottom of the Bosphorus."

With that the Venetian ambassador made the sign of the cross and kissed his fingertips as he watched the black coach disappear into the dusty warren of roads that flanked the raucous Bazaar of Constantinople.

The day after the drowning, Ivan Postivich was ordered to stand guard all morning and afternoon outside the Royal Audience Chamber. His muscles had grown stiff from the effort of the execution and then standing motionless on guard for hours on end. He could not understand why he had been summoned to the inner confines of the palace, when his usual post was in the gardens, watching the palace walls.

When he prepared to leave at supper for the janissary barracks at Et Meydan, the Sultaness's private guard told him to remain. Esma Sultan had demanded an audience with him that night.

Ivan Postivich's eyes widened and he challenged the Solak guard, his voice gruff and savage.

"I am a janissary! Why would Her Highness want the stench of a soldier's body in the Royal Audience Chamber? I will answer to her brother, our Sultan Mahmud II, who will understand a military man."

"The Princess Esma, the Royal Sultane, has summoned you," snapped the guard. "And do not think our Sultan concerns himself with your pride. He holds you in no high regard. Has he not stripped you of your cavalry command and assigned you here?" He flashed a tight, mocking smile. "What is a Kapikulu cavalry-man without a horse?"

Postivich had to fight to control his anger. The loss of his cavalry command was the deepest wound of his life. The unfairness—the shame—that had brought him to this very moment was almost more than he could stand. But wounds are a soldier's life and he knew he must bear this one.

With an angry wave of his hand the guard dismissed the janissary to the company of the Head Eunuch. This servant was nearly as tall as Postivich himself and held his head proudly erect, in the manner befitting a confidant of the Royal Ottomans. The bare skin of his arms shone in the torchlight, glossy like a black viper newly shed. "You shall be prepared for your audience. I am Saffron."

Ivan Postivich was led to a courtyard fountain where the Head Eunuch supervised his washing by grunting now and then with satisfaction or swinging a copper lantern towards a neglected square inch of dirty flesh. The night spun away each time the eunuch focused light on the janissary's newly white skin, the filth rinsing off on the cobbled stones.

Postivich bit his tongue as the eunuch handed him a sponge, insisting he scrub again. The janissary understood the rituals of bathing before entering the royal chambers; he had been raised in a Sultan's court at Topkapi. But bathing before seeing a woman—this he had only done before sex as was mandated by the Koran and the Prophet Mohammed. A man's bathing and circumcision honored Allah; that women were spared a soldier's stinking body and a filthy foreskin was an unintended consequence.

Ivan Postivich dried himself with a fine linen sheet. He tossed it, damp and wrinkled, back to the Head Eunuch.

"Does your mistress require such standards of cleanliness of all her male visitors?" growled Postivich.

"My mistress's requirements are none of your business, janissary," said Saffron. "Watch your tongue tonight or you will leave bound in a sack."

The janissary was finally ushered into the Royal Chamber a little after midnight. Hundreds of lanterns glowed in the darkness of the domed room. Candles from an elaborate French chandelier flickered, lighting vividly colored tiles and casting shadows on the thick velvets of the divans and cushions. The chamber was vast, with intricately carved moldings, perforated cornices rising in white plaster and pearl alabaster. Sandalwood incense burned, a heady scent that spoke of the furthest reaches of the Ottoman Empire.

The Head Eunuch shoved the janissary to his knees as he stared at the opulence of the cavernous room.

"Approach the Sultaness," he hissed. "Or I sharpen my sword against your neckbones."

Postivich shuffled forward, his knees scuffing the straw mats laid over priceless carpets. It was a long, humiliating journey to the divan on which the Sultaness reclined, her head listlessly raised from a pillow to watch him approach.

She was indeed the sister of Mahmud II. She had inherited her high cheekbones and auburn hair from her Christian mother, but her aquiline nose was pure Ottoman, a gift of her father, Sultan Abdulhamid, and his forefathers. In the capricious candlelight, her eyes looked black, but were in fact the deep brown of mahogany. Below them, shadows of blue showed through her translucent skin, the telltale signs of fatigue and illness.

The Sultaness raised her chin as he bowed, his head touching the floor that smelled of lemon blossoms mixed with the faintest odor of sweating feet.

"Stand now, janissary."

Her voice was low and authoritative. It was also female and its register was foreign to a janissary who had lived only among fighting men for the past two decades.

The janissary rocked back on his heels and, keeping his head lowered, raised his body on his massive legs. The Princess must have been impressed with his height as it uncoiled above her, but she showed no sign of it.

"Tell me. Did you—drown a man last night?"

Postivich raised his eyes to meet hers.

"As you ordered, Sultane," he said. "I followed my orders explicitly. The man was put to death."

Esma Sultan took a deep breath and held it and looked beyond him, into the shadows where the candlelight did not flicker.

"What did the infidel say?" she finally whispered.

*Infidel indeed,* he thought. He could smell her now, a scent masked by the sandalwood and lemon oils, the musk of her woman's body. Despite the danger, despite the knowledge that this woman was the Sultan's sister, he felt himself aroused.

The only women he had seen unveiled in the years since his circumcision had been prostitutes. His body was conditioned to the only response it knew.

He cursed the Ottoman emperors, one by one, back to Mehmed the Conqueror, for his body's mutiny. That an unveiled woman—Sultaness or otherwise—dressed in a gauzy linen tunic, should address a janissary was surely against the Sheriat, the rules of Islam that govern even the Ottoman sultans, with its holy word.

"Speak, I say! What said the infidel in the moment of his death?" As she spoke, he could see the outline of her breasts, trembling.

Ivan Postivich spoke clearly to the mosaic floor, not daring to raise his eyes, for fear he would falter. As he began his story, he thought of the saltwater on his fingertips and the sign of the cross he had drawn across the prisoner's forehead. He could not comprehend the gesture that came so spontaneously to his hands just before he snapped the stranger's neck.

None of this would ever be known to anyone, he promised himself. This much of a gift he would give the dead man who had extracted his Christian name.

"Very little, your Sultaness. Only a few Latin words offering up his soul to his infidel god."

He portrayed an uneventful execution, a stoic, silent prisoner. As he spoke he contemplated his words and story as one with the mosaic floor and the geometric figures on the rugs. *Simple, but perfectly matched*, he thought, never daring to look straight at the Princess's eye. A pattern of facts that made a perfect, elegant design, one piece fitting into the next.

"Are you sure you have told me every detail?" Her arched eyebrows now diving low over her eyes. Her eunuchs and the other Janissaries who guarded her palace were far more subservient than this giant of a man.

The soldier shifted his weight on the cool floor and wondered at how the palace locked out the cruel heat of summer and the suffering of the world.

"Look at me, janissary," commanded the Sultaness, her dark eyes boring into him. "Tell me the last words of the drowning man!"

Postivich raised his eyes reluctantly and again felt his organ quicken under his tunic and sash. He cursed himself for his impulses and stared into her eyes in defiance.

*Eyes of death*, thought Ivan Postivich, though he registered the handsome beauty of her lineage. *This Ottoman whore commands me to grovel in front of her and tries to intimidate me with her imitation of a man's authority! I am not one of the Christian boys she finds for the night, but a janissary with rights guaranteed by the sanctity of the Sheriat. Should she lay a hand on me without just provocation, the Janissary Corps would burn her palace and sever her brother's head, just as they did his cousin before him.*

Ivan Postivich thought of the man he had drowned last night. The man's last words haunted him.

*What was your Christian name?* He saw the condemned man mouthing the words inches above the sea where he would lie for eternity. These last cries, these last seconds on Earth would remain his secret and Allah's. This murderess would never hear the story of the humiliation of her victim, his body's stench of terror before death. The humiliation and agony would be drowned in the depths, as was the man.

The janissary fastened his gaze on the finest work of Persia's blind weavers who created this miracle under his feet, as he remained silent.

The Sultaness let the silence draw out, staring at a small ruby, the shape of a teardrop, in the palm of her hand.

"Bah!" she uttered suddenly, clutching at the jewel savagely and then flinging it into the dark recesses of the room.

*An Ottoman plays with precious jewels and men's lives as if they were a child's toys,* thought Postivich.

"You bring me nothing! You are useless to me. You, like all Janissaries, are corrupt and faithless to your Sultans and the Ottoman Empire you profess to serve!"

Ivan Postivich smiled inwardly, a warm satisfaction spreading through his body.

"Your Sultaness," said the janissary, his eyes lowered. "I have searched my mind for more observations and have found none. The prisoner surrendered himself to be placed in the cloth bag, the stones piled over his feet. He did not even twist in the bag as we heaved him over the side. He seemed resigned to his fate and the protection of his Christian god."

The Princess pursed her lips, which without paint looked

bloodless. The brightness of her eyes, within black kohl rims, sought him out, like night creatures.

"No screams. A cry for a loved one, perhaps? A regret, a confession? Did he not beg for my mercy, as they all do?" she pleaded, her voice ragged in desperation. "You lie, janissary!"

"He disappeared silently into the Bosphorus, the water closing over him like the lid of a coffin."

The janissary's defiance made her eyes flick suddenly towards the soldier, and the muscles tighten around her jaw. For the first time that night, she stopped to observe him as a man. Light brown hair and broad Slavic bones. This man was a giant compared to the other Serbs and Croats and Greeks who surrounded her as Janissaries. He was even taller than the Head Eunuch. She could not see his eyes with his head bowed to the floor.

She knew they must be blue. Blue like her own mother's eyes.

"He was stoic as befits Your Highness's"—the janissary hesitated, if only for a second—"standards."

She focused her eyes on the strong chin of the Serb.

She remembered now, the day the Pasha had delivered him to the Topkapi. The lad was a carefully selected slave from the *devshirme*, the "gathering" of Christian youth, taken from their homes to serve as Janissaries, years after the practice had officially been abolished. Pasha Imad had picked this one out, a boy of only seven, having heard tales of a young boy, already a giant, and his beautiful sister. He had been delivered to the Sultan's palace as a gift from the Pasha, when Esma Sultan was still a girl. She wondered if he had been one of her father's "favorites" when he was but a child.

"Standards?" she said, quickly. "Is a common janissary now to appraise the tastes of the Sultan's favorite sister?"

Ivan Postivich felt a cold shock seize his spine, despite his newfound pleasure in antagonizing this woman before him. The Ottoman Princess was looking at him now, not as an unknown soldier who had carried out a nightly chore, but as a man who had made an observation in her presence—a judgment. His choice of words could cost him his life, but a growing anger replaced his fear when he thought how she had made him a murderer. He suppressed the great urge to spit in her face.

"Speak, janissary, or have your tongue cut from the back of your throat," shouted her personal bodyguard, moving towards him with vengeance.

"Do not touch him, guard. Let him speak," she commanded sharply.

"Your Princess," said Postivich, his gaze returning to floor again, "I confuse high Ottoman with the barbarous Slavic tongue of the army. I—"

"You have been brought up in the palace since you were a boy. You speak Ottoman as well as I. You think I don't remember you as a child, you colossal fool! I have seen you play *cirit* and polo on the imperial grounds—you were the Pasha's gift to my father long before you rode your horse on campaigns as a Kapikulu cavalryman. Speak now or suffer before Allah."

Ivan Postivich straightened his bowed neck and forced himself to breathe. His next words could be his last and he chose them as carefully as weapons on the battlefield.

"My tongue is clumsy with the language of Allah and the Sultans. My race is not worthy of the language of imperial divinity, O Sultane."

The Princess's eyes sparkled in amusement and the hard gleam of the huntress receded into the black depths. She relaxed her rigid back against the velvet draped divan.

"The Persians would murder you for what you have just said," she mused. "They claim their own tongue cleaves to Allah's ear." Satisfied with his quick answer, her lips curled, almost imperceptibly, up towards her high cheekbones. "But you have won your life with your agility in Ottoman, and recovery. Your grace belies your size. Who would guess an oafish giant astride a mare could avoid the cirit spear with such grace?"

Postivich did not answer. His silence at the compliment amused her. She was accustomed to the fawning slaves and foreign ambassadors who indulged her, hoping Esma Sultan would speak favorably to her brother. This janissary was different.

"I have marveled with the rest of the Topkapi Court at how you could swing under your horse at a gallop to avoid your opponent's *jereed*," she continued. "The Horse Master taught you well."

"The Horse Master was a gifted man," replied the janissary. "He spent great effort and time in my instruction and I will never forget him. He and your cousin Selim III were great men and I mourned their passing."

Praise for the current Sultan, Esma's brother, Mahmud II, was conspicuously absent from his utterance. The cavernous silence of the great hall magnified the insult, but Postivich's lips pressed tight refusing to say more.

"I see that you are uncomfortable in my presence," said the Sultaness, her smile and the memory of the janissary's war games fading now. "I give you leave to go."

Postivich bowed, backing towards the door.

"Wait. I've seen your shadow many nights now, janissary, through the lattice to my gardens. What fate has placed you so far from your *orta* to serve me?"

He swallowed and answered.

"It was the Sultan's wish."

Esma Sultan looked at the giant thoughtfully.

"What is your name?"

He hesitated, wondering if giving the Princess his name would mark his fate.

"Pasha Mustafa named me Ahmed Kadir, Sultane."

Despite having been given the name at seven years old, after his circumcision, Ivan Postivich had never accepted it, though no one knew him by any other. His true name had been discarded as a matter of course, as had his religion, family, and foreskin.

"You do not look an 'Ahmed.' Perhaps the Pasha had run out of names when your turn came," she smiled. "No. You are not an Ahmed, I am quite sure of it. I shall call you—'Biscuit.'"

Her freckled handmaid, hidden in the corner until now, laughed, suddenly filling the cavernous audience chamber with the sound of startled birds.

The Sultaness turned towards her and raised her chin at the janissary, her face full of mirth. She looked no longer an Ottoman ruler, but a woman.

The janissary had no time to react, for two bodyguards seized his arms and pulled him away like a prisoner. They led Ivan Postivich, twitching with indignation at their touch, through the mother-of-pearl doors that led out of the Princess's private council.

One of the guards who had seized his arm roughly now released Ivan and gave him a hard shove that sent his great body stumbling across the mosaic floor into the hall, shaking the wooden grille with his thunderous footsteps. He heard the startled cries and then a titter of laughter from the Princess's harem just beyond the intricately carved screen.

"You are lucky you still have breath, janissary," said the turbaned guard, spitting on the polished tiles. A young page scurried and wiped the floor clean with a lemon-scented rag.

The guard looked at the boy in disgust, his thick lips curled up under his black mustache. He had wanted the satisfaction of seeing his saliva glisten at the janissary's feet.

"Speak an opinion to the Princess again and you will be feeding the fish of the Bosphorus with your pagan Christian flesh, you Serbian dog!"

The guard stalked off to return to the Princess's inner chamber.

Postivich felt a tug on his sleeve and saw the other guard motioning him to a far corner of the room under an enormous palm tree.

"That you should arouse a princess's regard enrages his Turkish soul," whispered the fair-skinned guard, his mouth working quickly over the words in Serbo-Croatian. He gave a furtive look at the dark screen, knowing that the harem sat listening but would not understand the guttural dialect of the Janissaries. "You should know that a janissary has no eyes or ears, and only a tongue when the Sultan wills it."

"Every night she sends her servant, the small white eunuch, for details of the murders," whispered Ivan. "This night there were none to give him."

"Then next time, invent them, my friend, and spare your miserable life."

The guard turned and disappeared through the doors towards the royal council chamber.

Ivan Postivich walked to the outer courtyard of the palace. He heard horses clattering on the stones and saw fine Turkish and Arab steeds come through the palace gates. The lead rider was a grizzled old man with hide as tough as an elephant's. He led a string of three ponies on each side. On their backs were ragged children riding bareback, their naked heels clapping at the horses' sides, making them prance and crow-hop. One black mare reared high, pawing at the night air, and her rider slid off her back to a volley of profanity, whistles, and laughter.

A Solak captain approached. The children slid off their mounts, naked bellies buffing the sheen on the well-kept horses.

"Old man, did you not receive the news? Esma Sultan is not well—there is no game tonight. Return to the stables and take these filthy urchins with you!"

The head groom signaled to his squad of children.

"Remount your horses. We will return to our beds early tonight," he smiled. "Go on, move the horses out of here before I get kicked by that blood-cursed stallion!"

Postivich watched the children throw their gangly legs over the bare backs of the animals and pull themselves up. They laughed as their horses pranced and bobbed, eager to return to the stables. He smiled at their skill and ease, born from being raised in the stables of Esma Sultan.

"What game would they play at this hour?" asked Postivich of the Solak.

"You ask too many questions, janissary," growled the Solak, who waved him through the palace gates. "You are dismissed."

Until that night, Esma's attendant Bezm-i Alem had not seen this giant called Ahmed Kadir, except from a distance. He was a man from Serbian stock who had emerged as the *corbaci*, the captain of the Kapikulu Cavalry, forswearing his religion, his family, his past, even the possibility of marriage, to serve the Sultan.

Bezm-i Alem had watched him from the walls of the palace on sleepless nights, as he accompanied his victims, the blue boat emerging from the mouth of the Golden Horn into the Bosphorus. Only on moonlit nights could she see him and his doomed charge, but more than once, even on the darkest nights, she could hear the death wails of the men, carried on the still air across the water.

Those moments haunted her and she found herself crying silently at the cruelty. Nothing in her own painful life had made her cry since she was a little girl, but somehow these innocent men's deaths moved her more than she could stand. She was glad that no one witnessed her tears, for they would surely have been construed as weakness—a dangerous defect in the Ottoman world.

The servant girl knelt on the cool tile floors of the harem and prayed to the Virgin for the men's souls. She could never reconcile Esma Sultan's kindness to women with her inhuman cruelty towards men, and realized she was powerless to change her mistress.

The thought of the drowning guard who sent these men to their death filled her waking hours and dreams at night. How he must hate the woman who had damned his own soul in her foul service!

Nazip had attended Esma Sultan in the audience chamber. The Sultane had forbidden Bezm-i Alem to enter, though she had pleaded to have a closer look at the man who had so captivated her imagination. For once in her indulged life with Esma Sultan, the Ottoman Princess had denied Bezm-i Alem's request and ordered her to remain with the other women of the harem behind the screen.

"I do not wish you to see him, ever," she commanded. Bezm-i Alem nodded, her jaw clenching until her teeth ached. She longed to know this giant of a man, this Serbian rebel who had incurred the wrath of the Sultan himself, but she also understood she must accept the order of Esma Sultan.

Nazip was standing, in rapt attention in the shadows of the room, near the serving tables. She was there ostensibly to serve the mistress, but Bezm-i Alem knew this was a favor shown to her by Esma, to see and hear the giant speak.

Every woman of the harem peered into the audience room, hidden behind the filigreed wall screens, eyes pressed against the carved porphyry.

"He is as large as the great plane tree at the Hippodrome! Surely no Turk nor Arab has a stature to match his," gasped Leyla. "He is a freak of nature!"

"Shh!" Bezm-i Alem admonished, waving her hand, but not willing to move her eye from the curlicued hollow of the screen.

Bezm-i Alem drank in every feature, studying his large-boned Serbian face and the fierce blue of his eyes as he listened to Esma's words. He curled his lip like a dog in an inaudible snarl, remaining silent, enduring her presence only because he was forced to do so or die.

If not under the vigilant eye of the Solaks, Bezm-i Alem felt sure he would leap for the Sultane's throat like a wolf. Instead he bowed his massive head and studied the floor. The harem girl noticed how he challenged Esma Sultan, subtly but clearly, despite their great discrepancy in station.

Bezm-i Alem wondered how he must feel, the deaths of so many men on his hands. The Sultan had assigned him to Esma Sultan's palace, so there was no recourse. He had somehow dishonored himself and had fallen from favor at Topkapi, or so the rumors in the harem had it. He had been stripped of his command of the Kapikulu Cavalry Orta and even denied the right to ride his own horse. Bezm-i Alem—indeed the entire Court at Topkapi—missed his skill on the cirit field, watching him rein his great grey mare in pursuit of his opponent, rising like a tower in his stirrups to hurl his jereed at the retreating rider, then, atop his galloping mare, circling the Hippodrome in a victory lap. He inspired legions of young riders, made old men break into toothless smiles, and moved ambassadors' wives to clap their gloved hands in muffled delight.

Now he faced Bezm-i Alem's mistress with smoldering hatred. And she, sensing his displeasure, engaged him far longer than she would normally deign to speak to a man. Perhaps she enjoyed his suffering—this game appealed to her.

*Show caution, mistress!* Bezm-i Alem thought. *He will leap for your throat, my Sultane. He still has the heart of a Serbian rebel and his rage must strain his will.*

The one-eyed cook had saved the drowning guard some stewed lamb simmered in paprika. The old Greek focused his eye on the giant, muttering to himself and spitting twice on the filthy floor. Ladling the lamb into a terra-cotta bowl, he whispered, "Did you drown another one tonight?"

Ivan snarled at the words and grabbed the cook's arm. "Your business is to cook," he hissed.

The Greek's green eye stared back at him through a blurry haze of cataract. "And your business is to murder innocents." He set the bowl in front of the janissary and turned back to his oven.

"And how, cook, would you handle your post, if the Princess commanded you to carry out the same order?" growled Postivich, dipping his crusty bread into the stew. He hunched over his food, his hands glistening with grease as he packed the bread into his mouth with his open palm. A killing always made him ravenous, and he had been offered nothing to eat at the palace. "Come, you tell me what you would do, cook," he said, pointing to his bowl for more stew.

"I would sooner die as a man without blood on his hands than to kill night after night, a butcher of men."

"Cooks have big dreams. That's why they remain cooks."

"And your dreams at night, Ahmed Kadir?" said the cook, slamming his ladle down on a dirty rag. "Do they come to visit you in your dreams?"

"Who?" asked Postivich, looking up at the cook sideways, his chin still tucked over his food.

"The drowned men. Do they beg you to spare their lives? Do they ask you to give last messages to their parents, their wives, their loved ones? Do they curse your newfound Allah as they evoke the true Christ's name?"

Postivich swept the bowl off the table with the back of his arm. It shattered on the floor. The men at the back table playing dominos stopped and looked up from their game.

"No one visits me," he growled. He grabbed the cook by the throat and the other Janissaries stood and moved towards him, one drawing his scimitar.

"Release him, Kadir," ordered one with a silver-edged dagger in his hand.

Postivich eyed him and grunted, his grip loosening on the filthy wattles of the Greek's throat.

"I sleep like a suckled babe every night, cook," he muttered, shoving the Greek hard against the wall. A chip of loose plaster broke off and sent dust spinning in the dim light. "It must be your good cooking," he said.

He nodded to the small group of men and they relaxed their grips on the daggers.

Ivan Postivich left them and made his way back to his bunk.

Esma Sultan could not sleep. The breeze coming off the Bosphorus was cooling and she could smell the jasmine and lemon of her gardens. She usually slept peacefully after her evenings of passion, exhausted physically. Her two favorite harem girls would wash her, dry her with white linen, and anoint her body with fragrant oils, as they begged her to recount in detail her moments of ecstasy, her ploys, and conquests.

The men working in the palace and the gardens would shudder at the women's laughter and turn away, saying a quick prayer to Allah.

But this night had been different. Esma Sultan had performed her ablutions quietly and her dark looks had forbidden any trespass. The harem girls had kept their eyes fastened on the mosaics of the bath and not dared to speak, except to offer her tea and refreshment.

*This had been the first one to refuse her.*

Her nose wrinkled in disgust as she thought she smelled a foul undertone to the wind off the Bosphorus.

She threw a gauze sleeve over her mouth and nose as the breeze stirred the linen curtains. Her stomach rose in her throat and she gagged.

She recognized it as the smell of Death.

The favorite sister of Sultan Mahmud II, Princess Esma Sultan had never been denied anything. She kept palaces at Macka, Eyup, and Sultanahmet in addition to her sumptuous residence at Ortakoy. Last night's Christian man, obtained in Bosnia on one of her slave raids, had entered the palace gates, neither surveying the unparalleled garden with its fountains nor raising his eyes to the formidable entry with its fluted columns and cornices. He had seemed blind to the lush tapestries and rugs that lined her inner chamber, and the jewels that adorned the Princess's head, neck, arms, and hands.

"Why have you summoned me?" he said through a slave girl interpreter.

"Sit down, subject. Have you washed?"

The man stared at her pointed silk tasseled shoes, and began stuttering in Serbo-Croatian.

"Yes, Princess. I supervised the washing myself," said the ivory-skinned eunuch at her right.

"Was he given food and drink, Emerald?"

"He refused both. His belly is as empty as a dried gourd."

The Princess cocked her head.

"Have you not tasted the fresh figs from my own garden?"

"I have no appetite," answered the man, his eyes fixed firmly on the floor. He looked up briefly, imploring help from the slave girl, but she stared blankly back at his pleading eyes.

The Princess studied his face. It was finely molded, an almost noble look on the head of a peasant. He had been acquired five days before. His sisters, both beautiful and fair, had been sold to a Pasha for a good sum.

"You are not as fair as your sisters. But you are comely." Her finger stroked his cheek. She turned his head with a pivot of her wrist, as if she were examining a pet.

The man raised his head suddenly. "You have news of my sisters?"

"Of course. But I will only exchange news for something of value to me."

"What do you want?"

"You will take a bite of the fig I offer you from my own hand and I will tell you of your sisters."

She nodded to Emerald who disappeared down the hall.

"They are alive, then."

"Wait. I will tell you after you are refreshed. You must also drink some tea. Then you will hear all I have to tell on the subject."

The Princess clapped her hands, her eyes never leaving her guest's face.

Emerald reappeared with a harem girl, each bearing a tray. One contained three large purple and green figs, along with a silver knife. The other held an ornate silver tea service.

"Now admire the beauty of the most magnificent fruit in all Constantinople." Esma Sultan cupped her right hand and placed the fig in her palm. With her left hand she slowly turned the fruit by the stem, making it pirouette.

"See the marvelous fig, how the skin begs to wrinkle from its own weight, so ripe for eating." The Princess sliced the fig into quarters, the creamy rose-color flesh exposed against the dark skin.

She flicked a look at her red-haired handmaid and nodded, initiating a secret ritual between them.

"Take this," said the Princess, holding a piece between her delicate white fingers. "Open your mouth."

The man hesitated and then dropped open his jaw. She tucked the fruit inside and then, before he could draw back, slipped a finger into his mouth, and let it linger against his tongue, before she slipped it out, slippery with the juice of the fruit.

"Good," she murmured and the freckled harem girl who had delivered the tea tray laughed.

The man looked around stunned. He stared at his slippered feet and the rich silk tunic in which the eunuch had dressed him. The billowing white pants were sashed at the waist with a maroon and gold corded belt.

"Your sisters were sold to a dear friend of mine, Pasha Mustafa Efendi. He will treat them well and their lives will be much easier than what they knew in their village. I suspect they will become fat and content within a year's time and bear him strong Muslim children."

"They are a part of his harem?"

"Yes, of course. They will convert to Islam and learn the Koran. He will see that they are taught calligraphy and embroidery. They are still young enough to learn well. They will speak Ottoman and learn verses well enough to recite to the Sultan, my Angel brother."

"And my mother?"

The Princess frowned. "I told you I would give you news of your sisters. You must satisfy other wishes to hear of your mother's destiny."

Ivan Postivich had lied to the Greek cook. He found it more and more difficult to sleep and this particular night was the worst he could remember.

The room was fetid with the smell of sleeping men. Their bodies gave off the odors of sweat and passion, five having stopped at a brothel just before curfew. Despite the Koran's commandment to wash before and after sex, the Janissaries, native to Wallachia, Greece, and the Baltic territories, were sometimes too drunk and exhausted to carry out the ritual ablutions. Their snores carried the stench of rotting teeth, and a stifling acrid odor filled the barracks.

Postivich left his cot and threw on his tunic, slipping his long dagger under his waistband. He closed the door behind him and was greeted with the fresh breeze coming off the water.

"Where go you, janissary?" questioned the sentry.

"A night errand," Postivich replied.

"Business or pleasure, Janissary Kadir? Are you doing the Sultane's bidding?"

"Pleasure. I need to visit the brothel."

The sentry leered at him. Ahmed Kadir had special permission to come and go at all hours as the Sultaness's trysts were erratic and unscheduled.

"Pick a sturdy one, Ahmed—a fat one with a strong back. The weight of your body could crush the delicate girls," said the guard, waving him on.

Ivan Postivich had no intention of visiting a brothel. His only wish was to breathe fresh air that did not carry the mingled stench of murder and sex.

For most, a walk along the Bosphorus long past midnight was a dangerous proposition. The waterfront was home to thieves who had immigrated on the ships that passed through the Golden Horn each day.

But no one dared approach the dark silhouette of Ivan Postivich, his giant shadow preceding him, the moon at his back.

A pack of dogs circled him, silent in the dark, as he strode the path towards the harbor. The dog packs of Constantinople were notorious, claiming their territory and killing strays that wandered within their limits. But Postivich bent down to pick up a rock from the ground, and the pack ran whimpering for cover under the blanket of night.

He walked the shore of the Golden Horn below the high walls of the Topkapi Palace. He heard nothing, but knew that the sentries watched his every step, each passing the word in whispers and clucks of the tongue to the next, as they checked his progress around the perimeter of the fortress. At last he came to the palace limits and into the harbor. Here there were signs of life.

He bought some chestnuts from a vendor, the chalky taste of the outside skin cleaning his mouth of the greasy lamb he had eaten earlier.

"Ahmed Kadir," whispered a voice from the rocks.

Postivich turned towards the voice and shouted down. "Who calls my name?"

"It is I, of your own name, Ahmed—the oarsman," said the voice coming closer.

Postivich spat out a piece of chestnut shell, deliberating. Cracking another between his fingers, he pried out the soft meat.

"What are doing out at this hour, oarsman? Surely your mistress will call you tomorrow to row her in the Sultan's procession for Friday prayers."

"Yes," answered the oarsman, stumbling through the darkness on the rocks. He made his way towards the light that spilled from the chestnut merchant's lantern. "But sleep will not visit me tonight."

The young man's body was now visible to Postivich, narrow-waisted with a hairless chest and muscles cut deeply into his arms and legs. He saw the wide-eyed fright that was concealed by day from the world and especially from Esma Sultan.

"I cannot sleep," whispered the oarsman, "when the Bosphorus stinks of death."

"Your words could be your own death," cautioned Postivich. "Speak no more, the shores and even the waters have ears."

"They have heard me cry, then," he replied. "For I cannot face Allah laughing at the death of dozens of men."

Postivich picked at a bit of chestnut in his teeth. He looked over his shoulder towards the water and the grief-stricken man.

"What then, oarsman, do you plan?"

"My name is Ahmed," he said. "Surely you can remember the name that is the same as the Ottomans have given you! Why will you not speak it when we are intimates in murder?"

"I despise my own name, oarsman. Do not curse yourself by having me utter it. What do you propose then, as you make your way to the mosque to pray on the morrow?"

"I have no plan but to confide in Allah of my horror."

"Allah surely sees all that man does, before a man even sees it himself."

"Then twice is his suffering," muttered the oarsman.

"And your mistress?" said Postivich, looking out to the deep waters of the Bosphorus. "You think Allah sees her?"

The man stared down at his frayed sandals, his own fine clothes for the Royal Barge laid out in his bedroom chamber in the outer court of the palace. He was favored by the Sultan and his sister for his beauty and strength at the oars and was rising quickly through the lower ranks of the Ottoman navy, though he still had to perform the vile task of rowing men to their death.

"Allah sees all," the oarsman said. "No Sultan or Ottoman is above his judgment."

"That is inconvenient for all of us then," whispered Ivan Postivich. "For Allah seems to offer no recourse."

"In my heart, I seethe with loathing for the deeds I have committed. I see the men I have transported to their death in my dreams, struggling against the knotted bag at the bottom of the Bosphorus. How can Allah not answer with his own sword of revenge for the innocent? I shall have my revenge one day in a manner that will cripple the Ottoman rule."

"You do not speak as one who sleeps under the roof of the palace," said Postivich, wiping his hands of the charred bits of chestnuts. "But for all I know you are a spy for the Princess, searching for those disloyal to her. So I shall say to you, oarsman with the unlucky name of Ahmed, 'Long live the Sultan and his favorite sister.'"

With that, the janissary turned to continue his walk, the oarsman protesting his innocence and agony in his wake.

"You shall see how earnest my confession is," hissed the oarsman from the rocks. "One day, I shall redeem my soul and that of this Empire!"

Ivan Postivich turned and looked down at the defiant eyes of the Turkish sailor.

"Then Allah be with you to guide your soul," he said, registering the oath as truth. He walked on, leaving the young man at the edge of the Bosphorus.

As Postivich returned to the barracks on the edge of the massive drilling grounds of Et Meydan, he heard the raucous laughter of Janissaries coming from a tavern. He saw a piece of parchment nailed to the door, flapping slightly in the light breeze.

It was a crude picture of a janissary—made obvious by the exaggerated white sleevehat—and, beside him, the Sultan, attached to a leash. And below the drawing, in crude capital letters:

YOU SEE HOW WE USE OUR DOGS. AS LONG AS THEY ARE USEFUL
TO US AND SUFFER THEMSELVES TO BE LED, WE USE THEM WELL,
BUT WHEN THEY CEASE TO BE OF SERVICE, WE CAST THEM
INTO THE STREETS.

Postivich knew that a similar paper had been found on the
Topkapi gates and the Sultan, furious with the insult, had ordered
the artist to be found and beheaded. The Aga of the Janissary
Corps had summoned his troops to the Topkapi walls and made
the announcement, even though it was rumored he sneered at the
Sultan's command, knowing that the loyal brotherhood of these
soldiers was far stronger than an Ottoman ruler's decree.

Postivich avoided taverns; they were hotbeds of mutiny and
defiance. The Sultan himself was known to frequent them in disguise to flush out the ringleaders and agitators who threatened his
regime. It was Sultan Mahmud II who had stripped Postivich of
his command after the border campaigns, suspicious of the huge
soldier's power over other men.

The public display of scorn for the all-powerful Sultan flapped
insolently on the tavern door.

The Sultan's procession to Friday morning prayers was an event
the chestnut vendor looked forward to every week. Everyone gathered along the shores of the Golden Horn to see the great Sultan's
kayik cut through the water, accompanied by the fleet of his
entourage. He sat bejeweled on cushions, his aquiline nose jutting
into the wind, face immobile—imperial grandeur incarnate.

As Mahmud's subjects gathered to watch this convoy, the chestnut vendor's business was good. Men and boys stood in line to buy nuts hot from his fire.

The women stayed close to their men, but their eyes were trained on a single kayik, flying fast across the water. Near-naked men, their legs and loins wrapped in gauzy white breeches, rowed the Princess Esma Sultan across the Golden Horn to the Aya Sofya. The men's skin was oiled and their muscles gleamed in the sun. The Princess reclined under an awning, joined by her two favorite handmaids, the freckled Nazip and always veiled Bezm-i Alem, the "Jewel of the Universe."

It was rumored that Bezm-i Alem was so beautiful that if any man gazed upon her unveiled, he could never love another woman. Still the other women of Esma Sultan's harem laughed barefaced at the sun and exchanged whispers at the beauty of the oarsman, who pulled the kayik gracefully across the water.

It was treason to criticize the Sultan or the Sultan's favorite sister, so knowing looks and gasps at the bare faces and necks of the women sufficed to convey how the Princess's court brazenly disregarded the word of the Prophet. Esma Sultan's lack of morals was notorious and made clear yet again each Friday before prayers.

But today the Princess appeared with her face covered in blue silk. Had there been a death in the Royal Family? Some favorite niece or nephew? Or had the Sultan drowned one of his once-favored wives?

The chestnut man chewed pensively on one of his wares and wondered what the sudden change might portend.

Ivan Postivich sat on the edge of his cot, inspecting his saber. There were nicks and scrapes that could not be repaired, and he considered each with a flash of memory.

In the Sultan's service, fighting the Greeks in Peloponnesus or the Russians in Wallachia, he had nicked and scored his sword a dozen times. He remembered the sound of a skull cleaved in two, the blade sinking into the brain as swiftly as a knife into a melon. He had fought off starving looters who had tried to rob the Sultan's shipment of French champagne and fine brandy, his sword slicing into the backs of their thighs as they ran, attempting in vain to flee their death.

Indeed, the fame of Ahmed Kadir had reached the inner court of Topkapi and inflamed the jealousy of the young prince Mahmud, long before he became Sultan. The paths of their lives ran surprisingly close. The sultan and the soldier were of the same age and the soldier was trained and educated within the palace.

Even as a boy, Ahmed Kadir worked with the wildest of horses and won the grudging respect of the Turkish Master of the Horse. It was his skill in the war game of cirit that had won the highest praise, for despite his size Ahmed Kadir was agile as an acrobat on his horse, ducking the pointed spears that whistled over him.

"He climbs around on a horse like a monkey hanging from a tree!" marveled Sultan Selim III, watching a cirit game. "What agility he has!"

"Truly an ape," muttered Mahmud.

The Horse Master cleared his throat and addressed Selim III, turning away from the young prince Mahmud.

"Ahmed Kadir will one day become a great cavalryman, my Sultan, and though he was born in the northlands, he is Turkish in his instincts. He will save his horse and stand on the field if he thinks there is an advantage in fighting on foot. The infantry respect him as much as the cavalry—he will inspire the Ottoman armies on the battlefield and win many battles, if Allah wills it. He is a leader, and the soldiers look to him to follow."

Mahmud remembered these words when his cousin Selim was butchered by rogue Janissaries who attacked the Topkapi. At that time Ahmed Kadir was only a boy himself, and his orta was on a foreign campaign in the borderlands of Wallachia, fighting the Russians. It was only a faction of the soldiers who supported Mahmud's half brother, Mustafa IV, in the struggle for the throne and carried out the assassination. Still when Mahmud closed his eyes, he saw the Janissaries who searched the Topkapi to kill him as well. Mustafa was eager to spill the blood of any male relatives who might threaten his claim to the throne. Mahmud would never forget the terror of his narrow escape. His mother, Nakshidil, hid him in an oven as a servant distracted the Janissaries. Mahmud had trembled in fear, stifling the urge to sneeze as the ashes filled his nostrils. Outside the oven doors he heard the shouts and heavy footsteps of the Janissaries.

Years later, soon after he became sultan, Mahmud thought hard about the power that Ahmed Kadir could one day wield over the Janissaries. He remembered his cousin's murder and trembled at the memory of those footsteps outside the oven where he cowered in terror. By that time, Ahmed Kadir had proved himself on battlefields and campaigns far from Constantinople. Now, Mahmud's own Grand Vizier boasted of the giant's fearless attacks, riding his grey-dappled mare into battle as he dodged the arrows and javelins of the opposing army with breathtaking agility. And as the Horse Master had predicted, Janissary Kadir left his horse with a groom and led the infantry into the last decisive battle against the Greeks, his sword slashing through the enemy like a sharp scythe through hay.

"Bah," grumbled Mahmud, when the Grand Vizier came to tell him how a cavalryman had handed his reins to another man and joined the infantry. "Our Ottoman army needs reform, Vizier! A Kapikulu cavalryman joining the infantry at a whim? The man is mad! A dismounted cavalryman brings disgrace upon the Ottomans!"

"The man is a hero, my Sultan, and it is this willingness to lead that has won him the respect of the Janissaries. The Aga of the Janissaries holds him in the highest regard."

The Sultan rose from his throne and paced the carpeted floors.

"The Aga is a fool who indulges slovenly conduct on the battlefield! I shall order a complete reform of our military and their tactics," he said. "No Topkapi-trained cavalryman shall ever again descend from his horse! We will fight in regiments, with order, not like a pack of mongrel dogs who mount and dismount capriciously."

The old Vizier looked aghast at the Sultan at the thought of reforming the Janissaries. The Corps was created by the first Sultan of Constantinople, Mehmed the Conqueror, and without them, there would be no Ottoman Empire. The Aga himself had a palace that rivaled the Topkapi.

"But, my Sultan, that is exactly how your honorable cousin Selim III was murdered, instigating reform. The Janissaries will rebel and storm Topkapi, just as they have done before. You put your life in jeopardy!"

Mahmud dismissed his remark with a wave of his hand.

"My honorable cousin did not play his move with wisdom. He did not have the strength and will of the citizens. He tried to reform them with a timid hand—I shall crush them with my fist!" The Sultan's fingers tightened in a ball, the knuckles white against his ruby and emerald rings.

The Vizier bowed his head

"You are absolutely correct, O Sultan. The Janissaries have become a barbarous lot—the merchants in the Bazaar hide their daughters from the Janissaries' groping hands and people flee the bastinado, which they use too freely to club the innocent. But we might work within the ranks to root out corruption. If we were to infiltrate the ortas with disciplined leaders who believed in the spirit of the Corps—the tradition of honor and defenders of the Faith—we might yet stay the wave of corruption and their assault on the common people. Let us enlist those whom the men admire—this giant, for example, and lead them to more honorable ways of serving their Sultan as was the case with your ancestor Mehmed I or even Suleyman the Great!"

"Let them lie with the Devil! The more corrupt and menacing they become, the swifter the day will arrive when the Ottoman people will stand by their Sultan to stain the Bosphorus red with janissary blood. These thugs will not suffer reform and their arrogance will bring about their own demise. I will not spend another moment considering their future, other than their death!

"We will form regiments, not ortas, with our new corps, and we shall have more discipline like the European armies," said Mahmud, rubbing his hands enthusiastically as he imagined the future. He looked out over the Bosphorus towards the Sweet Waters of Asia. "I shall stand proud to see an Ottoman army drilling to Western marches and wearing new uniforms that reflect our dignity and my sovereignty!"

"But my Sultan—" began the Grand Vizier.

"Silence! Our new army will be the pride of Constantinople. I shall speak to the English and French ambassadors this very afternoon and begin immediately to study the problem."

"But, Your Highness, I only wish to defend you and your harem. The Janissary Corps has existed for over three hundred years. They will resist imitating the armies of the infidels and become rebellious. The Ulema could side with them, accusing you of fraternizing with the pagan enemies of the Prophet—"

"Enough! I shall reform these bloody brutes and we shall have discipline. Send me this Ahmed Kadir immediately."

The Grand Vizier left the throne room stunned. What had begun as a report of the glorious Janissaries' feats in the Western provinces had ended in a tirade by the Sultan. What had provoked such wrath in his master? Still, he suspected Mahmud would have to obtain a fatwa from the Mufti to conspire further, for the Janissaries were protected by the Sheriat as interpreted by the highest Muslim Imam. This would take time, and perhaps the Sultan would come to his senses.

He sent a page to run to the barracks and fetch the soldier, Ahmed Kadir. Then he hurried off to consult the military officers and the Aga on the decision the Sultan was threatening to make.

Several hours later, Ivan Postivich entered the Topkapi Court, his skin rubbed raw by an overzealous servant in the royal *hamam*. His blue tunic was spotless and starched as stiff as felt. He bowed to the new Sultan, the third he had known in just three decades. This one had been a boy let out of a Topkapi cage for equestrian events and cavalry drills, an arrogant, terrified youth about the same age as Postivich.

The Sultan asked to examine Postivich's sword.

The Sultan's smooth hand ran over the blade, his fine white fingers settling momentarily into the grooves etched in battle.

"This is the sword of a true Ottoman warrior," the Sultan had said. "Your feats as a corbaci of the elite Kapikulu are legend."

"The Ottomans have made me what I am, my Sultan."

The Sultan narrowed his eyes. He studied the giant who stood before him. This man was becoming a leader of other men. And any leader other than the Sultan was dangerous, especially when it came to the volatile and powerful janissaries.

"Yes. The Ottomans have made you who you are, janissary. And I will make you who you will yet be."

Two days later, the Sultan's private guard arrived to escort Postivich to the Sultan's favorite sister's palace, stripping the janissary of his command of his cavalry orta.

"This is your new post, Ahmed Kadir. You shall guard the honor and life of Esma Sultan. The Sultan fears for his sister's—habits," he said. "Already there have been insults shouted at her by a man at the Galata Bridge, a man whose head now mourns the loss of his body. A madman—a Bektashi Sufi."

"I am a warrior—the corbaci of the cavalry orta—not a palace servant!" protested Postivich. "I was not trained as a palace Solak! I have my horses to attend to and I must train the new recruits in cirit and polo. I shall go insane if I spend hours groveling on the floor to please a princess's fancy. Let me fight the Russians or send me to reclaim lands in the west from the Greeks!"

"You know what you ask is impossible. The Sultan himself has assigned you to the Princess's guard."

But even the Sultan did not understand the fierce competition for the Princess's care and trust. The established guards had barely let Postivich enter the outer courtyards of the palace, growling that the Sultan's sister was in their care and not a janissary's concern.

The Sultan's Grand Vizier—allied closely with the Aga of the Janissaries—came to check on Ahmed Kadir's new post. He appeared murderously angry to see the giant standing guard outside the palace's walls in the shade of lime tree.

"Have we pulled our best soldier from the battlefield to stand and match his shadow with that of fruit trees?" he bellowed. "Why do you stand on the streets, Kadir?"

"The choice is not mine, sir," answered the janissary. "This is my assigned post."

The Vizier ordered the Solak commanding officer to present himself at once, his curses sending the harem girls and servants scurrying through the corridors.

Within the hour, Ivan Postivich had been installed just outside the Royal Audience Chamber doors. The palace guards were forced to acknowledge that he was a member of their force, although he was not a Solak and did not belong to their orta. Even the Turkish guard, who hated all the Janissaries, was forced to accept Ahmed Kadir's presence. The chief minister had assigned him a more respectable mission—to inspect every male visitor for weapons and to study their faces for signs of treason or murder.

But with time there was another duty for which he would become known—the Princess Esma Sultan's personal murderer. Her drowning guard.

# Chapter 2

The first light played on the wet cobblestone streets of Constantinople, fresh and cool from the early morning washing by the Jewish street sweep. This was the cypress-lined road that led to the royal palaces and the Pashas' *yalis* on the Bosphorus and the Golden Horn, the one fine stretch of street meant to impress ambassadors and other foreign dignitaries visiting the capital of the vast Ottoman Empire.

The rest of the byways of Constantinople were a maze of narrow winding passageways, hard-packed dirt that turned into mire with the seasonal rains. It was there in the tangle of alleys that the wild dogs slept in the daytime. The wood-shingled houses with their windows jutting over the streets provided shade for the pack who were desperate to escape the fierce Turkish heat. The mongrels whined and yelped for scraps and fought each other over the carcasses of dead horses or mules that died in the streets. No one carted away the dead animals, as everyone knew the dogs would pick clean the bones overnight, leaving the morning streets tidy with their scavenging.

Ivan Postivich approached the janissary barracks at Et Meydan from this tangle of ancient roads, just as the muezzin began the call to prayer. As he entered the gates, Postivich could see the morning fires of the soup cooks flickering. White peacocks screeched in the trees in the courtyards of the Mosque of the Conqueror, mocking the messenger in the minaret, who summoned Constantinople's faithful to begin their day by worshipping Allah.

The winding road led into the dusty acres of Meat Square, where the military cooks toiled. Lingering in the air was the sweet metallic odor of bloody meat mingled with the stench of rotting offal, for Constantinople's slaughterhouses were located beside the janissary soup kitchens.

Row upon row of huge bronze cauldrons glittered in the sun. Each pot was flagged by a greasy silk banner with the insignia of a particular orta—bears, scimitars, horsetails—flapping in the morning breeze. The soldiers ate communally from the huge kettles, as Janissaries had done for over three hundred years. It was here that Ottoman Sultans' victories and deaths were decided, wars planned, and revolutions staged, contemplated democratically over the hot pilaf pots of the Janissaries.

*La ilaha illa 'Llah*
There is no god but GOD

As the call of the muezzin echoed, Postivich knelt down on the stones and prayed, tucking the long sleeve of his janissary cap behind him. Thousands of men were roused from their blankets and a sea of turbans faced southeast towards Mecca and the rising sun.

Postivich never thought of Mecca. Instead he thought that by facing the City of God he was able to keep his left ear towards his homeland in the north. It was then he would remember.

*"Hide him, oh God, hide him. In the pantry, behind the apple basket."*

*"He won't fit, Mother. He's too big!"*

*"Make him fit or you shall have no brother."*

*His sister Irena hid him behind a woven reed basket and then pushed the door closed.*

*The reeds stuck into his skin as she shoved him in further, trying to make the wooden latch swing down and hold the door shut.*

*He stayed still, quiet and dumb with pain, his scratched limbs contorted and cramped.*

*"We have come to see all the Christian boys," said the Ottoman-accented voice.*

*"They say the devshirme is no more, that the Sultan needs not gather the Christians. Why do you come to this house, janissary?"*

*"You have a son. One the Sultan must see."*

*"Oh," his mother laughed, straining to convince them. "If I had a son, I would have better fortune. I have only my daughter here to help me with so much work since my husband died."*

*From the darkness of the cabinet, the boy heard the strange pitch of the Ottoman language being spoken for the first time. Understanding nothing, he marveled at the sounds, wondering whether they could really understand one another.*

*"We know of the girl," said the corbaci. "But first, the son."*

*"I told you. I have no son."*

*"The neighbor across the way has told us that you have a boy, a giant boy of seven, unlike any in the region. We will take this one to the palace at Topkapi. He will become a great janissary some day and serve the Sultan."*

*Ivan Postivich heard his sister give a little cry. His heart beat quickly in the dark and he wondered if he would suffocate in the strong smell of ripe apples.*

*"That bewitched old woman would tell the Sultan's army anything for a loaf of bread," said his mother. "She has visions, you understand she is a half-wit and—"*

*"Search the house," commanded the officer.*

*The cabinet door was flung open and the boy heard his mother scream as he squinted in the sudden light of day.*

Ivan Postivich rose from his prayers, remembering. He rubbed his back as he straightened. He decided to forgo his morning ration at the soup pot and walk to the stables to supervise the feeding of the horses before he returned to his cot to rest.

The cavalry stables were located just above the River Lycus, at the edge of the city. Ivan Postivich breathed in the good smell of horse, the sweet hay mingled with the salty sweat of fine animals who had carried him into battle. The cool air from the river below carried away the stench of the slaughterhouse and brought with it the freshness of the Sweet Waters beyond.

A horse meant more than the Koran or the Bible to Ivan Postivich. It was a horse that had given him comfort when no religion could. He entered the stables as one of the faithful—here amidst the sweet smell of dried grass and the earthy musk of horse dung, he felt sanctuary.

As a seven-year-old child, lonely for his mother, sister, and homeland, he had cried into the rough coat of his first horse, Dervish, a small Anatolian crossbreed. Young Ahmed Kadir—Ivan Postivich no more—had plenty to weep for and the shaggy Turkish pony seemed not to mind his tears.

Only a week before, a janissary had taken the terrified boy to an immense stadium, the Hippodrome, where he had waited in the bright sun for an eternity. At last, a man in a tall turban approached him with a sharp knife. Bewildered and still not speaking either Ottoman or Turkish, Ivan was made to understand that he was to lie very still. The man removed the boy's trousers and grasped his penis, stretching it thin like taffy. The man spoke some unintelligible words, with just a few that the boy recognized as a prayer from his recent studies of the Koran.

The janissary accompanying the boy bent down and spoke to him in Serbo-Croat.

"As the most important part of your indoctrination to the Holy Faith of Islam, you are to be circumcised on the very day that the young prince Mahmud II celebrates the same glorious rite of manhood. Glory be to Allah, and to our Sultan!"

And then his world exploded in pain. Despite his tears, the janissary and mullah made the incoherent boy recite the introduction to the Koran, correcting his pronunciation until the sura was intelligible to Allah.

As part of Ottoman tradition, Sultan Abdulhamid had paid for the circumcision of all the young boys of Constantinople, from the ages of seven to thirteen so that they, too, could join in the citywide celebration of Mahmud's entry to manhood. The young prince was not present, of course, as he had already had the circumcision performed in the privacy of the Circumcision Hall of Topkapi.

These were the shaming secrets the boy whispered to the Turkish pony as it poked its nose deep in the hay, looking for the greener bits. The boy's penis still ached, the pain exacerbated by the resumption of his equestrian training only a few days after the circumcision. Ivan Postivich's sobs were barely audible above the systematic chewing and snorting of the horses; and this same comforting sound obscured the approach of the Turkish Master of the Horse.

The boy raised his head from the pony's neck and saw the dark green robes of the Master of the Horse just beyond the ropes of the paddock. His heart thumped as he imagined the stern master's anger when he discovered his pupil crying like a Christian girl.

The Master of the Horse, who had no time for emotional children, wisely decided to walk on.

*A lonely boy seeking comfort in his horse is not a vice,* he thought and never said anything to the boy. His wisdom paid off. In the years to come, there was no keener pupil than the young Ahmed Kadir, and no rider who had finer intuition and control of his horse. The boy had lived and breathed horses to quiet his grief and even preferred to sleep in the stables on a bed of straw, instead of in the dormitories with the other cavalrymen.

Now, as a thirty-six-year-old veteran of many battles, it was the stable that gave comfort to him again, although he knew he was forbidden to ride the cavalry horses by the Sultan's decree. The Turkish Horse Master was long dead, but the casual kindness he had shown a young boy remained etched in the janissary's heart.

"*Merhaba*, Ahmed Kadir!" cried the stable boys, throwing down their three-pronged pitchforks and clamoring to embrace him. "You have returned to us, old man!"

"I'm only visiting the horses, to see how they fare," said Postivich gruffly. He told himself he must be careful not to show how much he missed the stables and what shame the Sultan had brought him by removing his command.

The Turkish crew was taken aback, not knowing what to say. They wiped their noses on their sleeves and fidgeted, picking their dust-crusted eyes with dirty fingernails. Ivan Postivich could not bear to see the disappointment in their faces, for the common Turks were as sincere in their friendships as innocent children.

"But how does life greet the dung-chuckers?" Postivich joked, relenting a little, for he had known the Turkish stablemen for more years than he had known his own mother. "Do the horses still provide you a livelihood?"

"Graciously by Allah's permission, we have a life's work ahead of us for the horses never hesitate in providing us occupation!" answered the head groom, overjoyed that the corbaci of the Kapikulus could still see his way to jest among them. "They oblige us with their fruits that are our labor, one ripe horse apple after another!"

Ivan Postivich laughed despite himself and greeted the stablemen, embracing them as they slapped him on the back, over and over again. For the first time in many weeks, Ivan Postivich found himself content as if he had feasted on warm baked bread on an empty belly, for there is nothing more beautiful than a Turkish smile looking upon an old friend.

"Your mare is just here," offered a groom, proudly. "I have brushed her already this morning. Your polo horses are grazing by the Lycus, growing fat on the early summer grass."

"Let me see Peri, my only wife," said Postivich.

The dappled mare lifted her head and snorted. She sniffed at Postivich, her soft nose wrinkling as she nibbled on his tunic. Then she lifted her head high and curled her lip up, showing her teeth as if in disgust.

The stable boys laughed, slapping their dirty thighs.

"See what an intelligent animal she is, Ahmed Kadir," said one. "She is a good judge of character! You shall never have a harem, for not even one woman can abide you."

"As a janissary, I can never have a wife, you bastard of a whore!"

The stable boys jostled each other, grinning. With the exchange of insults, all was right again in their world.

Ivan Postivich ducked under the rope and entered her stall. He threw his great arm around the mare's massive neck and haltered her nose with the palm of his hand. Drawing her head down, he whispered close to her ear, "We shall ride again, Peri, I swear to you. Don't fall in love with another rider or I shall have to murder him."

"What do you say to your horses, Corbaci?" asked the head stableman. His black eyes shone with admiration for there was no cavalryman he liked more than Corbaci Ahmed Kadir.

"You must speak to a mare as a woman," teased the janissary, knowing the Turkish pride as lovers. "And you speak words of love in Serbo-Croat, not a rube's tongue like Turkish."

"Women have always loved me for my tongue," retorted the head stableman, grinning so wide his mustache spread, a bushy caterpillar inching across his face. All the stable boys laughed and the horses snorted and stamped, startled at the sudden outcry. The dust from the hay spun up in lazy clouds in the fresh light of morning. The Turks smiled and drank in the cool air and thanked Allah for such a day. The day was glorious simply because Ahmed Kadir was in the stables again.

Later that afternoon, Ivan Postivich stood beside an enormous potted palm in the palace of Esma Sultan, pinching his belly in boredom. There was a thin layer of loose flesh over the once hard muscle. Fat, thought Postivich in disgust, earned by standing guard in the palace. He had never been fat in his life, and now, at thirty-six, he was hardly more useful than the palm tree that leaned over him—a large decorative ornament in the royal palace.

He missed the brush of the grass under his boots, the Macedonian dust that filled his mouth with acrid grit, the taste of earth on a summer's day. His legs and groin were often stiff at the end of the day from riding, but his body conformed to the saddle so that the horse was almost an extension of himself. Years of campaigns had made him one with his horse, a centaur wielding a yataghan sword, curving murderously over his enemy. He remembered his tongue during battle, fat with thirst, and the concave of his hollow belly, empty, arching back to his spine.

But an empty stomach meant a clear mind and a light body, the essence of a cavalryman. His body was made for war; the Master of the Horse and Pasha Efendi had recognized that immediately.

On campaigns, he ate and drank when he could, much like a camel. The Kapikulu corbaci withstood the pangs of hunger more easily than someone half his size. His muscles were as hard and long as the blade of his sword and when he was not mounted, he made good time with his long stride, leaving huge prints in the dry dust. He lusted for combat, to fight to the death against another man.

Ivan closed his eyes and breathed the humid air of the palace. It was tame and spoiled, pregnant with the ladies' perfumes and oils, decadent with the scent of jasmine and lemons. His nose longed for the acrid smell of sweat, the hot stink of battle.

"What are you dreaming of, giant?" asked a voice from behind the harem lattice.

"Nothing," muttered Postivich, studying the filigree of the screen. He, like all men, had always dreamed of the wonders that lay behind the harem walls.

"Thinking of supper, perhaps," said the voice again. Postivich could make out the shadow of her hair shifting over her shoulder. Long yellow hair, like those of the women that lived in the north of his homeland.

"Or perhaps dreaming of your woman," she teased.

"I have no woman."

"What? A man of your size without a woman?" she paused. "Or you prefer the young boys?"

"I prefer to perform my duties to the Sultan without insults," he replied looking away, and straightening his back.

"Careful, O gentle giant," warned the voice. "As long as I am within the great Esma Sultan's harem I shall command your respect. The Princess would be angry if she heard your tone with me.

"She might impale your head on a stake at Topkapi, to amuse the crowds with your big, round Serbian skull," she said. "The Turkish boys would steal your lonely head to play with and kick your skull about the streets of Constantinople, playing keep-away from the dogs. But they will complain because your Christian nose is so big, it will stub their toes and they will run home to their mothers, crying."

Postivich laughed in spite of himself.

"I'm sorry that my words were clumsy," he said. "I ask forgiveness, madam."

"Clumsy. It seems you have used that excuse before," came her reply. "I don't know how many times our Sultaness will accept that as an excuse."

"Who are you?" said Postivich. He moved quickly towards the screen. "How do you know of my conversation with Esma Sultan?"

"Stay back or I'll call the Head Eunuch," hissed the voice. The hair rippled like a golden wave behind her. He could not make out her face in the shadows.

Postivich plunged his fingers through the perforations of the screen, his great hands tightening around the lattice.

"Ahmed Kadir, you risk both our lives," she whispered in the Serbo-Croat of his homeland. "Move back."

"I knew you were from the Northernlands," he said, switching to his native tongue. "I could hear it in your Turkish."

"Stay back," she repeated from the darkness, and then whispered. "I only approach you to warn you. Do not trust those who come as friends and try to gain your confidence. Listen to my mistress and you will know the secrets of the Ottomans, but never forget she is one herself and will never forfeit her divine right. Yet she might protect you when you least expect it."

"She is a murderess," snarled Ivan Postivich. "She sends innocents to their death. She will find a way to murder me as well when it pleases her."

"Not all is as simple as Good and Evil," answered the voice. "In time you will learn how intricate they weave the tapestry of the royal Ottomans. To unravel it, you must know which thread to pull."

With that, the harem girl's slippers rasped across the mats and Postivich could hear her steps disappear down the corridors beyond the elaborately carved screens.

Mahmud's own doctor, Stephane Karatheodory, was summoned to the Princess's chambers, parting the phalanx of hysterical harem girls with an agitated wave of his hand. The women fluttered away like frightened pigeons, but only a few paces, their fine silks still rippling as they lighted once more, hovering over the ailing Esma Sultan.

"Get them out of here!" commanded the Imperial physician, his Greek disposition piqued by the ignorance of the harem. He addressed the Head Eunuch sternly. "And do not let more than one attendant and guard in this room at a time."

As he approached the Princess's bed, he was struck with the aroma of jasmine, roses, and lilies. Every inch of the royal chamber was lined with vases of flowers in various states of bloom. Harem attendants wiped the floors with concentrated perfumes that emitted such a heady scent that the Sultan's physician gagged.

The doctor, an erudite man who was said to have the command of eighteen languages, shook his head at the ignorance of the Princess's court. He sneezed into his handkerchief and cursed vehemently in Greek. Flowers, courtiers by the dozen. It was no surprise that the Princess was bedridden and failing by the minute.

"She refuses nourishment and has not slept in three days," pronounced Nazip, wringing her freckled hands. "We have tried preparing all of her favorite dishes, even pigeon in spices, but she will not even look upon food."

"What did you eat Sultane, three days past?"

The Sultane raised her chin from her pillow. "Very little. The last I remember eating was a bite of fresh fig from the garden. Oh, by Allah's name?! What is that hideous stench?"

The physician raised his eyebrow and looked around.

"I smell nothing, your Princess, but the lingering closeness of your court. On the contrary, I smell the overpowering fragrance of the flowers. Open the windows at once!"

"She says she smells death, everywhere, sir," whispered the slave girl. "We have brought every sweet-smelling flower of the garden to her room to ease her mind. She will not abide the breeze from the Bosphorus."

The physician considered her words, blinking like an old turtle.

"I presume your tester took a bite first to ensure the figs were not poisoned?"

The Princess turned her head back into her pillow. "I was entertaining. I fed the fruit to my guest first."

"And is he well now?"

The harem girl turned away, her hair sliding across her shoulder.

"He has since left us. I do not know his whereabouts," muttered the Sultaness. "Do not mention him again, physician."

The old doctor studied her face, half turned to him. He noticed a yellowed bruise on her bare shoulder and various other welts that inflamed the white flesh along her neck. He was a wise man and did not inquire further, having heard the rumors of the immoral conduct of Princess Esma Sultan.

He had been present at her birth, overseeing the midwife's work. She had been a squalling infant from the first, colicky and fussy in her mother's arms. But her standing as the favorite child of Sultan Abdulhamid allowed her education and privileges normally given only to Ottoman princes, never women. Her loyal friendship with her half brother Mahmud had sealed her position from the moment of her cousin Selim III's death.

Even a physician could not touch an Ottoman princess without express permission and close supervision. He asked for her to spit on a little golden plate, then to describe her symptoms and the hours of their occurrence. Her eyes were clear but haggard, shadowed by blue half-moons.

As he studied the spittle on the plate and watched her listless eyes, he noticed a spasm along her right eyebrow, a nervous twitch.

"I ask permission to examine you, Esma Sultan. Ready her under drapery, eunuch."

Stephane Karatheodory stepped beyond the drawn curtains while Esma Sultan undressed and was swathed in linens.

"You may approach, Doctor," said the Head Eunuch. "We will observe you."

Karatheodory laid his hand gently on the Princess's arm and raised her palm to his eyes where he could better examine it.

The doctor felt how she flinched when he touched her white hands, drawing them quickly back into her wide sleeves.

"Greek! You must give me notice before you touch my hands," she warned.

"I beg your forgiveness," said the doctor, waiting for her to return them to his outstretched palm, like a beggar supplicating. When she finally extended her left hand, he studied the white moon in her thumbnail and the newly applied henna on her wrist. Her skin was cool and damp, a pale blue white. With the supervision of two eunuchs, and wild-eyed scrutiny from the patient herself, the physician probed the Princess's abdomen. There was no evidence of pain from the pressure of his fingers.

Princess Esma pushed his hand from her belly, agitated at his touch. She threw the linen sheet over her nose, her eyes rolling back in her head.

"The stink of rotten flesh haunts me," she cried. "How can you not abhor it? Are you all fiends? My tongue can taste the stench, it is so thick!"

The old doctor said nothing.

"I dream of the Bosphorus choked with flesh. Heads bob in the current like melons thrown into the sea! Angels plunge into the brine and though they flap their wings desperately, they cannot lift their souls to heaven."

The physician waited, silent. When she seemed a little calmer, he whispered to her. "We must speak in private, Esma Sultan."

The Princess looked up from her pillow, creasing her brow. But she waved away the guard and her handmaiden, though the Head

Eunuch Saffron refused to leave, folding his massive arms over his chest in a stance of defiance.

The Greek physician nodded and waited until the other servants had left the great room.

"When you were born, it was the worst year of the Angel of Death," he began. "A third of Constantinople died from the plague and there seemed to be no hope for any of us. You were born, a blessing, a girl. You would not have to compete with your brothers to be Sultan. The harem rejoiced at the birth of a beautiful daughter they could bathe and spoil."

"What good is it to be a mere woman?" cried Esma, throwing her head back on the embroidered silk cushion. "To be married and remain behind a harem wall? It is to be held prisoner from womb to grave and never be truly born. And if it were not for my husband's death, I should live the same fate."

"Yes. It is highly unusual for a princess never to remarry, especially more than a decade after the loss of her husband. You confound all of Constantinople."

"I would rather have my head on a stake gawking at the fishmongers outside Topkapi than to ever take another husband."

"A daughter is spared the ugliness of a man's world," replied the doctor, scratching at his beard. "That was Mohammed's command, was it not, to remain sequestered from the rougher, more brutal sex?"

"You dare quote the Prophet to me, you Greek? Our Prophet demanded men's respect of women, not sequestration! Besides . . . I saw, old physician. I saw enough brutality for a lifetime."

The doctor considered.

"Perhaps you should tell me what you saw."

The Princess covered her mouth with a kerchief but spoke through the cloth, her voice muffled.

"I saw the murder of my uncle, Selim. He took refuge in the harem and the murderers dragged him out to the courtyard and butchered him under the lime tree. They hacked him to bits with their scimitars. The blood splattered and puddled, clinging to the leaves where I used to play."

"You indeed saw too much, Princess. A woman should never see these things. She hasn't the constitution."

She raised up on her pillow, supporting her weight on her forearm.

"The constitution? Your words mock me and all women! I watched an old slave woman save my brother in an oven when they came to murder him. There is my constitution! When they learned of her cunning, I watched three of the animals rape her, to pay for her loyalty to the Sultan's family. A servant woman who saved a male Ottoman! No assistance from men, no protection!"

"All of the Ottomans seem doomed to suffer," mused the doctor. "But I come to you to heal your condition."

The doctor hesitated. "If you belonged to my religion, I would tell you to confess your sins against God to the Patriarch priest. Then you would at last have rest in your confession and be at peace with God."

A great silence filled the immense room, so that even the old ear of the doctor heard the wooden rakes of the gardeners outside the palace window, scratching at the fallen leaves in the courtyard.

"You dare prescribe your pagan rites to an Ottoman Princess!" said Esma Sultan, suddenly sitting up in bed, a cobra ready to strike.

Karatheodory realized he had gone too far, but he was too old and respected to fear the Sultan's sister's wrath.

"I have only speculated what I would prescribe were you of the Holy Byzantine faith," replied the doctor calmly. "Since you are not of my church, I can only suggest that Allah will decide your destiny and cure you of the headaches, dreams, and sleepless nights; these visions of dead men choking the clear clean waters of the Bosphorus. I have potions that will induce sleep and a headwrap soaked in soothing lavender oils to ease your headache. But I can only treat the symptoms of your disease. There is something that haunts you that I as a man of physical healing, cannot reach."

"You are too old to cure anyone," pronounced Esma Sultan, turning away from the man. "You are dismissed to drink the spirits in the tavern that have polluted your mind so as to render you decrepit and useless to the Ottoman Sultans. I shall tell my Angel brother so!"

The physician nodded that he understood and a guard instantly appeared to escort him to the palace gates.

It had been days since Esma Sultan had left her bedchamber to walk in her gardens or visit her beloved library. Bezm-i Alem and the other harem women took turns bringing the Ottoman Princess sherbets and fruitwaters, offering barley water and honeyed baklavas from the Greek cook, Maria. Nazip offered her the opium pipe, which she took at first, until she became sickened by the drug. Esma Sultan swore she smelled dead bodies, foul with rot. She retched silently into a copper bowl by her divan while Bezm-i Alem pressed damp cotton cloths to her forehead.

The harem woman gathered flowers from the Princess's immense gardens and sent boys to the Bazaar to buy even more from the vendors, but nothing could ease her anguish. Every vase, even the most precious enamel vessels from Topkapi, burst with pungent blooms. The harem sniffed the air like dogs, trying to discern any aroma but the cloying sweet fragrance of the myriad bouquets, while Esma Sultan raged at their ineptness and pressed lemon-scented linen handkerchiefs to her nose, barely breathing.

Ivan Postivich could not bear the soft life of the palace and thought only of battle and the weight of his sword in his hand. He pictured the cirit games, staged somehow without him, and wondered how his favorite mare, Peri, fared under the hand of another rider and groom.

Mahmud was sly, thought Postivich. He preferred to kill a janissary slowly with idleness and seclusion rather than have him die in a war that would bring honor and martyrdom. Postivich sat on a cool marble bench, planning how he would change his life to make himself a soldier once again.

Every night before dinner, if he was not required to stand duty, Ivan Postivich wrestled, challenging not one, but two men at once. He did not lack opponents. Hundreds of Janissaries proved eager to fight together to defeat the renowned giant warrior. The merchants, saddlemakers, butchers, and cooks stopped work to watch the evening games, and the pistachio and chestnut vendors did brisk business among crowds of Janissaries, ravenous before their evening meal.

At first Postivich lost every match, often in less than a minute. Two men could work together to pull the giant down and pin him, as they did over and over again. He grunted, face down in the dirt, under the weight of the men, his spit turning the dust to mud under his chin.

"Kadir! You thick-headed Serb! It is impossible!" the soldiers howled. But they watched in eagerness and exchanged bets as to how long he would stand. It was the very thin chance of victory and the big heart of the warrior that they were willing to gamble on, for Ahmed Kadir embodied the legendary spirit of the Janissaries, even if he lost, time and time again.

Young men from Postivich's old cirit and polo squads stood before an open barrel of crude olive oil, rubbing down their former corbaci before each match. They good-naturedly sponged the oil over his skin and leather wrestling pants until he glistened in the sun like an immortal god.

"How a jereed would slide past you now!" the young cavalrymen joked, though they knew the pain their old captain felt at being stripped of his orta command and mount. Although wrestling was one of the foremost war games, it could not compete with the noble thrill of dodging spears on a galloping horse. But being still young, they had faith in justice, and believed with one heart that a day would come when the giant would fell the two opponents on the wrestling ground, and their warrior would stand victorious. And they hoped that they would see Ahmed Kadir astride his mare again, leading them into battle.

One day, after weeks of competitions that left Postivich's body sore and bruised, the crowd of Janissaries erupted in a fierce roar of cheers that sent the pigeons flying in great circles over the Bosphorus and the Golden Horn. Ivan Postivich had pinned two men at once, locking his trunk-like legs around one and crushing the other in his sinewy arms. The gasping opponents writhed under him, spitting and cursing. Postivich lifted his leonine head to the crowd, his hair matted in sweat and grease, grinning through the still-rising dust.

"Long live the Giant! May Allah protect Ahmed Kadir!"

The cheers of hundreds of Janissaries reached the courtyards of Topkapi, where the Sultan raised his head in alarm.

"What is that cry?" he asked the Grand Vizier who walked at his side in the inner courtyard, under the plane trees. He looked over the wall and saw the birds of Constantinople swoop overhead, still frightened by the roar.

"Send a servant to find out why the pigeons circle the city. Is this a cry of mutiny? Secure the port and harem! Bring me my sword!"

Shortly, a page, still gasping for breath after his run to Et Meydan, asked permission to approach the Sultan.

His head still lowered, sweat glistening on his upper lip, the page reported:

"The giant Ahmed Kadir of the Kapikulu cavalry defeated two other Janissaries in wrestling, pinning them for over a minute on the ground!"

"The shouts we heard were congratulations on a victory in sport, Sultan," said the Vizier in relief. "You can rest calmly now for there is no conspiracy! Simply strength of the giant who lifts our army's hearts in a harmless pastime."

The Sultan rubbed his black beard with his thumb and index finger, pulling at it brutally as he contemplated the news.

Postivich began walking the streets of Constantinople at all hours of the night. He filled a saddlebag with heavy rocks in order to carry more weight and tax his body, as if in battle. Each night he walked farther and farther around the Imperial City, coming back as the muezzins called the faithful for morning prayer. He found that he needed little sleep; his body thrived on the rigorous exercise, clearing his mind.

The wild dog packs of Constantinople began to shadow him. They prowled at his side, sensing his strength and urgency. Though he threw sharp rocks at them and cursed in Serbo-Croat, they only whined and cowered, and soon were at his side again, trotting along in the darkness.

The fishermen and prostitutes would point at the dogs as they loped down the streets to join the pack and say, "The giant must be near, looking for battle that the Sultan denies him."

And thus Ivan Postivich—janissary Ahmed Kadir—slowly became a legend throughout the Royal City of Constantinople.

# Chapter 3

After many sleepless nights, the Princess sat up straight on her divan. The two harem girls had fallen asleep beside her on the floor, their heads across their folded arms, their long hair spread over them like a shawl.

The Princess stared past the flickering candles to the windows that opened onto the Bosphorus.

She could hear some incomprehensible sound, like the howl of a dog, but more human in pitch. A howl of pain, terror. As it came closer, growing louder, she watched the girls to see if they woke. Neither stirred, even as wind from the Sea of Marmara filled the open window, billowing the muslin upward towards the high ceiling.

The Princess knew she could scream. Her screams would shatter the silence and bring legions of sentries, eunuchs, and harem girls to her side in seconds. There were guards just outside her window; wouldn't they have heard the hideous cry from the waters below?

Esma Sultan did not—would not—scream. In her veins ran Ottoman blood, shrewd and cold as it was noble. Her mother had taught her always to be in command, never to let her inferiors see weakness.

*You must rid yourself of weakness, daughter. Even the subtlest whiff of doubt will send your enemies an invitation. And the handmaidens, slaves, and sentries who surround you will spread the word if they suspect hesitation or cowardice. An Ottoman is strong. Or strangled.*

Esma knew now that the stench that gagged her was not detectable by anyone else in the court. The doctor had all but declared it was imaginary, a creation of her fancy. She had seen the two harem girls exchange looks, and then drop their gaze to the floor.

*Fantasy. Weakness.*

So they might consider these sounds to be the same. She would not permit that to happen.

The doctor had asked her of her troubles. What kind of doctor asks a sick patient of her thoughts? The doctor's job was to cure her, not question her. She had no one to answer to but Allah himself—she was an Ottoman. Her nostrils flared in contempt at his boldness.

The strange sound over the Bosphorus grew in volume and clarity, not so much a howl now as a wail.

And now she knew that sound.

It was a drowning man's last gasps, cursing as his fingernails clawed at the coarse hemp bag in the depths of the Bosphorus. In the candlelight, she could see a drowned man's eyes staring cold and glassy through the billowing fold in the curtain.

Esma Sultan fought the scream that climbed to her throat.

*I will not show weakness,* she told herself. *I cannot—*

The entire palace was awakened by her wail, pitiful and violent, helpless in its terror.

"What is it, Your Highness?" shouted the head guard, racing into the chamber, flanked by two other sentries.

"Bring the Topkapi doctor at once!" cried the Sultaness. She covered and uncovered her mouth, touched her throat and gagged.

Nazip brought her rosewater in a golden cup, her hand trembling, splashing big drops on the bed linen.

"I want him here at my bedside before this hour is over, do you hear me?"

"Your Sultaness, he shall be here immediately," promised the guard. "I shall send our fastest runner to the Gates of Bliss."

"Send for Ahmed Kadir," commanded the Turk, over his shoulder. "While I am attending the Princess, we must have all sentries and reinforcements posted outside this door."

A fast-running boy was sent to the fort to fetch the janissary. As he raced to the gate of the barracks, a sentry called from the wall, "Ho! Who goes there?"

"I've come from the palace of Esma Sultan to bring the giant Ahmed Kadir," gasped the runner. "If you will tell me where to find him, I'll wake him. He must come with me at once!"

"You do not know his nightmares or you would not dare to wake him," said the gate guard. He motioned to another guard to take his position. "I'll fetch him myself. Allah be with me!"

The guard entered the barrack, a lantern held high. Among the many sleeping men, one shadowed figure loomed huge, contorted with fitful sleep. The great body shifted restlessly, the mouth agape, dry lips moving in agitation, mumbling in Serbo-Croat, fingers digging feverishly at the straw ticking of his cot, sweat trickling across his temples.

"Wake up, Giant," said the guard, shaking Postivich's shoulders. "You are wanted in Esma Sultan's palace. Immediately."

Postivich's eyes flew open and he lunged violently, his massive hands grabbing for the guard's throat. The guard smacked him hard in the forehead with the hilt of his sword and Postivich fell back onto his cot, grunting in pain.

"You are not an easy man to wake," grumbled the guard, pulling his tunic straight again on his shoulders. "Next time I'll protect myself with the sharp blade of my sword."

"You summoned me, Princess?" said the doctor, his face blue in the candlelight of the royal chamber. His hair curled up in grey wisps under his turban.

"I wish to speak to you in private, doctor," said the Princess. "Guard, see that all my court stands at least ten paces from my closed door. Fatiya—close the windows and latch them. Then let the water run to all the fountains."

The doctor watched the handmaiden hurry from one window to another, shuttering the audience room.

"Bezm-i Alem. Stay at my side. The rest of you, out of my bedchamber," said Esma Sultan.

When the door had closed behind them, Esma Sultan addressed the doctor.

"You told me that if I were a Christian of your Church, I would need to seek confession and absolution from a priest."

The old man sighed, closing his eyes in resignation. "Yes, Your Highness. But you rebuked me for my error. You are of course of the Holy Muslim faith. I was foolish to mention—"

"No," said the Princess, waving her hand. "I am interested. Your faith and the prophet Jesus was a step towards the perfect word of Mohammed." She cleared her throat and reached for a glass of lemon-scented barley water.

"We value the primitive but crucial stepping stones you placed before us to pave the road to the True Faith. Jesus was a valuable prophet and earns high regard in the Koran. But I am curious about your priests. Does it really soothe the worshippers tormented by demons, these confessions to a stranger?"

"In most cases, the priest is known to the worshipper. But it is true that a Christian can go to a priest he does not know and confess in order to obtain absolution. A cleansing of sins is extended by the power of the Church and Jesus Christ."

The water began to trickle through the nickel pipes and spill into the fountains.

The Princess nodded, considering.

"And there is relief in speaking of such things that worry the soul?"

The old man nodded. "Yes. Absolutely." The doctor's watery eyes studied her as she contemplated her fingertips. He dared not speak too hastily.

"Doctor, I shall consider these things you have told me."

"Princess," began the doctor, "if I can help you in any way, perhaps bring the Prelate of the Ecumenical Church here—"

"Silence!" screamed the Princess, her hands flying to her neck. She darted a look at the door. "Old man! Do you really presume I would let the leader of the infidels attend me?"

"Forgive me," stuttered the doctor. "I thought—"

The Princess's eyes bulged and she began to gag.

"It's that stench again."

The doctor remained silent, observing her.

"You are dismissed, doctor. I shall consider your prescription. But never mention your pagan church in my presence again!"

"Your Highness," he said, and he rose to leave her chamber and return to his warm bed at Topkapi.

The Greek physician's words ran through Bezm-i Alem's mind all night. In a dream she saw the clarity of his counsel, the depths of his reason. To speak aloud of the atrocities, those that weighed so heavy on her mistress's mind and kept her hostage from sleep, this might indeed be the cure for her illness. God or her Allah or simply the clear night air would hear the words she spoke and chase away the djinns of the dead, may their tormented souls rest in peace at last.

Esma Sultan would rather slash her wrists and rinse her wounds in vinegar than speak a word of confession to any priest. But what if it were not a priest at all, but the only man who shared and understood the horror of the murders himself who listened to the Sultane's sufferings? Not a man of the cloth or a mullah, or Imam, but an ordinary man, even the man whose very hand had committed the murders in the name of the Ottoman Empire?

Bezm-i Alem sighed. If she were to make this suggestion Esma Sultan would suspect it was because the harem girl longed to see the drowning guard, feel his presence and hear his voice. All of the harem stood transfixed behind the porphory grille when the giant entered her palace. She knew Esma Sultan could feel the women pressing close to the perforations, not daring to blink as they spied on Ahmed Kadir.

*No,* thought Bezm-i Alem. *I have never given her bad counsel. She knows I am worthy of her deepest trust.*

Yet Bezm-i Alem feared that even in her illness and desperate search for a cure, Esma Sultan would balk at speaking of the condemned men, her used lovers. Such a stain on her soul would not be so easily coaxed into the light, no matter how it tormented her.

Bezm-i Alem decided to approach her after Nazip and the harem women had bathed her. She waited until the opium had cast its spell knowing that all things were possible then, especially with the help of the eunuch Saffron.

*In her desperation, she will know he is the only one she can speak to, the only one who shares her burden. She will listen. I know she will. She must.*

*As long as the treacherous white eunuch Emerald does not interfere, all things are possible.*

By the next night, Bezm-i Alem had convinced her sick mistress of her plan, for there was no closer confidante to Esma Sultan than the harem woman.

"I am dying, Bezm-i Alem. The nightmares eat my soul, the stench suffocates me. Soon there will be no air left for me to breathe."

"Let me send for the one who knows best of the drowning men, O Sultaness," said Bezm-i Alem. "He alone can understand. And like you, he is Muslim."

"I can speak to no one of these men. Can you not understand?" said Esma Sultan. Her hand reached for the silver pail to retch. Bezm-i Alem took it from her, holding it.

There was nothing more to bring up. Esma Sultan lay back white-faced against the cushions.

"Please, Esma Sultan . . . just speak to him. Of anything! I will not see you die, my friend and mistress. Grant me this one wish."

Esma Sultan opened her eyes, staring at her beloved friend. She nodded her head, weak as a kitten.

Ivan Postivich's eyes were still swollen with sleep when he arrived at the palace.

"Ahmed Kadir," said Head Eunuch Saffron, obscured in the shadows just beyond the gate. "The Sultaness requires a private audience with you immediately. I will supervise your cleansing."

The Solak took a step back to allow Postivich to pass.

"Another audience?"

"Yes." Saffron studied the janissary. "You have heard that the Princess is very ill."

"There has been rumor of it in Et Meydan. "

"Solak!" commanded Saffron over his shoulder. "Return to your post. If I see you eavesdropping on us again, I'll have you suspended from duty and scrubbing dirty tiles of the hamam with your damnable beard!"

The guard bowed and began walking back to the great doors of the audience room. Saffron watched him carefully until he was well out of hearing range.

"Odors that no one can smell and sights no one can see," said Saffron carefully. "She is left gasping and cannot draw breath."

The janissary walked with the eunuch to the communal fountain. He cupped his hands and splashed water onto his face. The water, icy cold from the enormous ancient cistern under the palace, chased away the sleep, stinging his face.

"I don't understand," said Postivich. "If she sees visions and smells imaginary odors, what can I do? I can fend off intruders, kill thieves, and protect her harem, but my sword is powerless against the ghosts that haunt her."

"Be careful what you say, janissary," said Saffron, black eyes glittering in the lantern light. "Your tongue can save you or destroy you. Your prudence and wit will determine which. If she speaks, listen, and you will profit. Don't underestimate her influence over her brother, the Sultan," he added, quietly. "You may ride in the cirit games yet, Corbaci. But first you must learn to indulge Esma Sultan."

Saffron did not stop to hear the janissary's response but made a sharp, hissing sound through his teeth that brought two pages scurrying to him for orders.

Postivich removed his shoes and washed his feet in silence. When he was finished with his ablutions, the eunuch gave him a fresh pair of silken slippers and a laundered tunic. He helped wind a new turban around his head. Postivich could feel the strong fingers of the enormous man gently creasing the fabric and adjusting the fit. He had not felt the hands of another dress him since he was a young boy in the northern country. The gesture seemed oddly familiar and comforting.

"It is your duty to serve the Ottoman Empire," said Saffron, accompanying Postivich to the doorway of the audience chamber. "That service includes protecting the health of the Sultan and his family. I trust you will do everything in your power to see that the Princess's health flourishes once more. For this, you will be richly rewarded."

Saffron's eyes locked fiercely with the janissary's, an intensity in the stare that Ivan Postivich had seen in men's eyes on the battlefield. Saffron nodded to the guards to announce their arrival to the Princess.

# Chapter 4

The Princess reclined on a blue silk divan, her eyelids swollen and heavy. She barely raised her head to watch her Head Eunuch and the janissary enter the room. She waved the eunuch away, and, without a word, he disappeared down a corridor.

Postivich could see silver hairs mixed in with the Princess's dark auburn tresses; her face was dry as thin parchment. Knowing the Ottoman loathing for grey hair—even warrior Sultans would color their beards—Ivan Postivich knew she must not have been out of this inner sanctum in days.

"Nazip," she called, her voice a whisper. "We must have the utmost privacy. See that no one lurks." She motioned to the janissary. "Sit."

Ivan Postivich looked down at the finely woven Egyptian mat that lined the room. "If the Princess does not object, I prefer to stand."

"The Sultan's sister insists you lower yourself at once!" snapped Esma Sultan, her voice regaining strength. "Your freakish height disgusts me." She coughed and coughed, then spat into her linen handkerchief. Her handmaiden rushed to her with a cup of mint tea on an ebony tray. The slave looked up at the soldier, her eyebrows raised. Her wide hazel eyes implored the giant to sit.

Ivan settled down on the mat, sitting cross-legged in front of the gasping Princess. He prayed that she would gag on her own spittle and die on the spot. It would be justice for the Ottoman witch. He wanted to see her bones settle on the floor of the sea, picked clean and white by the fish of the Bosphorus.

"Do not test my patience again, janissary," warned the Princess. He returned her stony gaze for a second before dropping his eyes. He could smell the secret sweetness of the ancient pharaohs in the delicate weave of the mat. Egypt, too, was subject to the Ottoman dynasty.

The water filled the fountain and flowed into the bowl beneath. As the water wept over the rim and the room filled with the echoes of its plashing, the Princess began to speak, her words clear only to the keen ears of the janissary, and not any others who might be listening, unseen.

"I have been ill for over a week now," said the Princess. "I have a sensation that someone is watching me. One or many." She looked at the janissary who still studied the matted floor.

"I smell a foul odor, more hideous than can be imagined," she said and then hesitated. "The smell of rotting flesh." She turned her head and looked over her shoulder, as if she expected to see someone there. "I dream of legions of men with dead eyes staring up at my palace from the water below my palace walls, their eyes clouded with death. Out of their backs sprout the wings of angels, but their flesh is too foul with rot to lift from the waves and the beautiful wings tear loose from their shoulders and fly away on their own, leaving the corpses to be picked clean by the scuttling pinchers of crabs."

Ivan Postivich turned away in disgust, thinking of the men he had drowned in sacks, fodder for the creatures of the seafloor.

"My visions displease you, Corbaci," she said, accepting a damp cloth wrung in cool cistern water from a handmaiden she had summoned with a gesture, then banished with a wave of her hand.

"It is not for me to judge an Ottoman princess's thoughts," he answered. "You say you are ill. It is the fever that delivers these nightmares."

"They come without fever, even without sleep. My brother's own doctor has come to study my symptoms," she said and then fell briefly silent. "He has treated the ambassadors of Europe and the Court of the Topkapi. My Angel brother has pronounced him expert in the realm of medicine."

"What has the doctor determined?" ventured the janissary.

"He has given me curious advice. He believes there is something diseased in my spirit," said the Princess, her fingers stroking her temples. "Even the most erudite of Greeks still cling to their pagan beliefs. He told me that were he experiencing the same symptoms, he would go to a priest."

*A priest!* Ivan Postivich thought. *You who have murdered your Christian lovers would confess to a priest of the Holy Byzantine Church?* Surely he had heard wrong, her words obscured by the waters of the fountain.

"I told him that his infidel ramblings would not be tolerated in my presence," she added quickly. "But because this doctor is known throughout the Empire as having the power to cure, I have decided to pursue his suggestion . . . on my own terms."

"What terms are those, may I ask, Sultane?"

"I want you to bear witness to my story; you to hear my memories."

Ivan Postivich could not help himself. He raised his head and stared at her, his insolence betraying him. His eyes flashed wide in astonishment and anger.

"Why me?" his spread hand flew to his breast, indicating his insignificance. "I am only a guard to your Royal Highness, no holy man am I! I am soldier, a man of horses, swords, and battle. Could you not speak to your attendants? The Head Eunuch Saffron who serves you night and day? This trusted servant who wrings her hands in worry over your health?" he said, gesturing to the red-haired woman. "Surely you will find more willing and sympathetic ears than mine!"

"No. These are stories they will not understand. I need someone to hear who can—judge me. A stranger who can hear and cannot, even if he tries, deceive himself and thus deceive me. You, Ahmed Kadir, do not like me. I know this. Everyone who surrounds me is subservient to me. They will listen to my story and proclaim my innocence, because they cannot imagine otherwise. And I will die by their deception, for they will not hear and know the truth.

"You, janissary, have learned to hate me because of the work I cause you to do. Some day, I will have to answer to Allah for the acts of my life. I think you will serve very well in the meantime, schooled in your own pagan beliefs and our true Islamic faith. Perhaps if I speak, the *efrits* that haunt me will leave me in peace."

Ivan Postivich looked over at the fountain and listened to the rhythmic splash of water.

"You forget, Sultane, that I, too, have blood on my hands—a stain that all the water of the Black Sea cannot wash clean. How can I be your confessor when I have carried out the murders of innocent men? It is by my very hand each of them has died."

"That is why it is you who must listen. Allah sees all. You have seen only the worst—men sinking to the bottom of the Bosphorus. But you have not known my life. I was once an innocent child—you must know that."

"I will listen," agreed the janissary. "But as Allah is my witness, you will murder me in the end for the hatred I feel."

"I will not touch you, Janissary Kadir. You shall be under my personal protection as long as you remain in my guard. No matter what you decide, your life is secure. I promise you this much. I ask you only to listen, you need not comment.

"If you do not consent, I will speak to my brother who indulges me more than any wife, and he will have your head impaled upon my garden wall for insolence. But if you listen, and listen with your heart and soul, I will grant you freedom from my palace guard to return to the Janissary Corps and the war campaigns that you thirst for."

She smiled languidly and said, "I have my spies, even among the fishmongers, prostitutes, and chestnut vendors. Even midnight's mantle cannot hide your wanderings—you are known as the 'dog warrior' who invades the neighborhoods of Galata, raging for a fight. The Pasha Efendi judged you well—you shall return to the war campaigns of the Ottoman Empire if you grant me these nights to listen to my story. You know nothing of me, nothing of my life. You must know everything if you are to understand me."

Ivan Postivich could think of nothing more repugnant than to hear the Princess's tales, but to refuse her would be suicide. In response he only nodded, his jaw clenched.

"When I close my eyes, I see blood. Red. A dark flowing crimson. Ottoman blood. I see my dearest cousin, Sultan Selim, butchered at the hands of Janissaries like you. His mouth is agape, his tongue is stuck to the skin at the corner of his mouth, drying there like parchment. Dirt and leaves cling to his face, sticky with blood, and I know the Janissaries will return to claim his head and impale it. But now they scour the Topkapi for my youngest brother, Mahmud.

"I know that it is my half brother Mustafa who has caused this, or more likely, his mother, Ayse, who thirsts for power.

"I stand over Selim's mutilated body and wipe the leaves and dirt from his mouth. I try to tuck the tongue behind his teeth again, for his expression is not becoming an Ottoman Sultan. But he will not submit and the tongue lolls back out like a panting dog.

"The rebel Janissaries and my half brother Mustafa will leave me in peace, I know this. An Ottoman princess, barely past puberty, is not a threat to power and I am only a curiosity. Because of my birthright, I am untouchable. It's my male relatives they seek.

"Mustafa will surely drown most of the wives and concubines to rinse the seed of my cousin from their wombs forever. How he can ever face me or the other women of the harem again is something I cannot fathom.

"They have murdered my cousin! He was the most gentle of the Sultans, preferring music and poetry to warfare. It was precisely these gifts that marked him as vulnerable.

"In the harem we had long heard the rumors, long sensed the unrest. We might not have our freedom, but we had our eyes and our ears. And our spies. We knew the Janissaries were angry with

Sultan Selim because he looked to the armies of the West for inspiration and knowledge. And we knew to fear the sullen power and murderous nature of the soldiers."

Postivich met her gaze, but did not let even a flicker of a response reveal his feelings.

"We knew that Mustafa would seize on that savage unhappiness to incite revolt. And we knew it was not really Mustafa. Not slow-witted Mustafa at the heart of plot, but his mother, Ayse, who dreamt of becoming Valide Sultan once her son ascended the throne.

"I hid and spied on the day that fifty thousand Janissaries stood in the courtyards of the palace, immobile as stone, waiting for their pay. And when it was late, their silence turned to anger and they returned to their barracks, their hearts full of murder.

"My cousin Selim refused to hear the din of mutiny as the Janissaries kicked over their copper pilaf caldrons and beat them with sticks. But the women of Selim's harem knew what would come. They knew too well that their fate was tied to the Sultan's. Their knees were worn raw from praying to Allah; their voices rasped through the night beseeching help from heaven.

"When the rampage began and death finally came, I alone would touch the Sultan's body. His harem women wept and trembled in fear of the djinns of death and they dared not go near the corpse. Instead, they huddled in the far reaches of the Serail, terrified of the death that they could not have escaped no matter what they did.

"But I knew I would survive. I had seen barbarous acts and I would live through them while others suffered and died.

"I was born an Ottoman princess.

"Turkish blue is my favorite color, the fierce color of the sky, the color of freedom. My young eyes would seek a world beyond the gates of the Serail, my cheek flattened against the perforations of the grille, to see a slice of the heavens beyond our small world. That patch of sky was a precious jewel, but my mother or our eunuch would snap the jewelry case shut as soon as I began to reach for it.

"'Esma Sultan! You must dress for your music lesson.' I can see my mother giving a withering look at the eunuch Jonquil as she brushed past him to the entrance of the harem. Despite the elaborate screen that blocked the passage, I had trespassed too close to the outside world. 'Come here at once. A man might see you as he passes the courtyard to have audience with the Sultan. There will be a scandal.'

"I lived, of course, with my mother, whose shadow was as far reaching as the tallest plane tree of the courtyard. From my birth, I had the honor of being Sultane, daughter of the Sultan, and with my passage through my mother's loins I immediately outranked her—because Ottoman blood ran through my veins. She would never forgive me. Had I been a son, I would have moved her closer to the throne with the possibility of being queen mother or Valide. But her labor pains counted for nothing—for I was born female.

"Some mothers counted girls as a blessing, knowing that they were much less likely to be murdered in the struggle for the throne. My mother considered me a bawling insult to her status.

"The music lessons, I thought, were part of her revenge. The violin and I were never well matched and I cursed it as a bedeviled invention of the West, brought to us by the infidels. My fingers were clumsy, the strings bit my soft fingertips and made them bleed. Still I was made to learn—to the great frustration of the maestro—because every member of the Imperial family was obliged to master an instrument.

"'Why must I torture my hands with this wretched instrument?' I cried. 'I am not musical—even my father proclaimed this when he heard me at the recital.'

"'You are lucky your honorable father saw humor in your performance and not the obvious shame you brought his honor,' my mother replied. 'If you repeat that incompetence, he will find his own daughter disgraceful to the Serail and to his name.'

"My mother threw back her long chestnut hair in disdain; it was the hair that had bewitched a Sultan. My own hair was much darker than hers, though not without the same glints of red. My mother had the beauty of a goddess, even now as she aged— approaching thirty. The Sultan still called for her, despite his two hundred other women.

"I continued to be a disappointment to her. 'You are suited neither for music nor for feminine pursuits. Your father will see this and you will be married off to some old deaf pasha who cannot hear your torturous music or see your pitiful needlework.'

"She scowled at me as if I could not possibly be her daughter.

"'The other wives and consorts laugh at you.'

"'Let them. I don't care that they do.'

"'No, my daughter. When they laugh at you, they are mocking me. You are my handiwork, embroidery by my own hand. I will not let you fail me.'

"With that she made an angry gesture to shoo me back into the recesses of the harem, to our apartments where I would change into my tutorial clothes: my cloak and a *yasmak*, the translucent veil.

"Jonquil escorted me to the music room where he would remain while I played my instrument. I removed my yasmak while the tutor bowed his head. The maestro was under the eunuch's strict scrutiny as he corrected my finger position and lifted my chin.

"'You must feel the music, Sultane. It is in our Turkish souls—your brother, Prince Mahmud, can play magnificently, tempting the very birds to fly nearer and light to listen. You must not treat the instrument as if it were a mere piece of wood. It has a soul that can be touched by a skilled hand.'

"He was right, of course. I think now that I should try playing again, after all these years. I think I understand what he meant much better now than I did standing in that music room, taking pleasure in the pain on his wrinkled face as he endured my ear-splitting notes.

"I did understand vaguely what he meant of 'soul.' At least I did when I heard my own brother play in the harem. His music filled the corridors with the strains of heaven.

"Perhaps it was because he had seen his own mother, Nakshi-dil, die of a broken heart. He had a new mother now—foreign born, French-tongued, assigned the same name as the woman who had died. She nurtured him now, and saw that he understood the passion of music. She attended my lessons quite often and encouraged my study, as disappointing as I was.

"One night, after a concert in the harem, my little brother found me sulking on a cushion in the corner of the great hall. He sat next to me, under the watchful eye of my mother and Nakshi-dil, and lifted my chin.

"'Esma, why are you so sad tonight? Didn't you enjoy the music? I played the violin expressly for you—I thought you'd recognize my voice in the melody of the notes.'

"I smiled and touched his hand, as it lingered on my face. He was several years my junior and loved me like a goddess.

"'My dear brother, I thought I heard your whisper in the music. But the sweet sound only made me sad. I realize that I will never, ever play the violin the way you do. You caress the strings as if they were—'

"Here I stopped, lowered my head and blushed. Mahmud looked up at his beloved stepmother, who was hurrying towards us.

"'Your blush brings our mothers rushing to separate us,' sighed my brother, though I could tell he was pleased that he had caused the color to rise in my face. 'You have forfeited our few remaining minutes together but I gladly trade them to see the red blood stir in your veins.'

"I looked up, shocked at his words and at his daring to pronounce them under the roof of the Serail. He was only allowed to play with his sisters and female cousins because he was considered still an innocent child. But already he was developing the passions of a man, and he was practicing them on me. Perhaps that is why he, like my cousin Selim, was locked in the Cage of Princes, and only released for Topkapi ceremonies and performances.

"'Remember, Esma. We are only half brother and sister.'

"As he rose to greet his mother and my own, I felt his warm breath exhale in a sigh. I recovered my composure and spoke as a princess should to the favored Nakshidil. I knew that she woke every day with the bright hope of some day seeing her own son as the successor to the Ottoman throne."

"So your brother was in love with you when you were only a child. Is that why he indulges you so?" asked Ivan Postivich.

"Love?" She laughed and threw a pale hand over her eyes, remembering. "What is love, janissary? Such an ignorant word, so silly a passion. There is no such luxury as romantic love in the Imperial Harem, let alone for a princess and prince who share the same father. But my brother cared for me and understood my tempers and ambitions, just as I understood his. It was the same with cousin Selim, who was older and first to ascend the throne, but in so many ways, more tender and compassionate. Still, all of these human emotions must vanish when a prince becomes a sultan. They must, as it is said, 'Else an Ottoman prince is butchered under the falling leaves of a lime tree.'"

Esma Sultan yawned deeply, covering her mouth with a delicate white hand, streaked with shadows of blue veins. She stood up and walked to the windows to see the first light of dawn creeping through the bottom of the shutter. She opened the heavy wooden shutters and the rising sun flooded the space where she stood. She took a deep breath and smiled.

"Why do you smile, Sultane?"

"I smile because all I smell on the morning wind is the taste of salt and my jasmine from the garden, still wet with dew. Speaking to you has temporarily overpowered the efrits and djinns that come up from the waters to haunt me, janissary. I think myself capable of rest until evening falls again."

Ivan Postivich shrugged, examining his coarse, scarred hands. He couldn't understand how his company could have kept the murdered souls at bay. The Sultaness wrinkled her forehead as she looked out over the Bosphorus.

"I wonder if the pagan rites of Christianity may have some superstitions that are useful to the Faithful," she murmured. "Perhaps the old doctor is correct in his remedy."

"I am no priest, Esma Sultan."

She turned again to the janissary and lifted her chin.

"I think you have done your work for today. I will allow you to return to the palace barracks. You are to be relieved from your regular duties. I want you to come at midnight each night, to accompany me through the dark hours when the smell is so overpowering. I shall sleep during the day—I shall instruct Saffron to see that your schedule matches my needs."

The giant rose, his gaze fastened not on the Sultane but on the far side of the room.

"Before I leave, Sultaness, I have one favor to ask you to quench my curiosity."

Her eyes hardened and he noticed a quickening of the muscles around her pale lips.

"Speak, janissary. But do not tire me with requests."

He walked over to the east wall of the room.

"This—" he called over to her, pointing to a painting of horses and riders on a gold background. "Could you please tell me about this painting?"

Her mouth relaxed and she smiled, her face suddenly younger in its softness.

"That painting once hung in my father's chambers at Topkapi." She walked towards it, her silk slippers rasping on the mat. "He gave it to me on my eleventh birthday on one condition. Upon my death, I must return it to Topkapi as it is an Ottoman heirloom. It is precisely what you think it is—a polo game."

The giant nodded, studying the painting.

"The Master of the Horses told me of paintings like these," he said. "I never thought I would see one with my own eyes."

Esma Sultan cocked her head and looked at him with interest.

"Yes, it is quite magnificent. Do you notice anything unusual about the players?"

"A light hand on the reins, perhaps. Youth and delicacy, but exhibiting confidence. These beardless ones must be Janissaries."

Esma Sultan laughed. "O, ignorant janissary! Half of them are women!"

Ivan Postivich opened his eyes wide, looked from the Princess to the painting and back to the Princess again.

"Women on the polo field?"

"Yes, of course," she said. "The love of the horse is in our Turkish blood. Don't look so astonished, it shows your ignorance of our history—you bring shame to our Topkapi tutors who educated you. Before the Prophet, Turkish women were known for their horsemanship, praised in art and legend. This is the work of a Persian master who painted the Sultan's harem at play. It is believed to be Princess Shirin and her ladies."

"It is truly magnificent," said Ivan Postivich.

"It is a treasure," murmured the Princess. "Nothing less."

She regarded him again. "It is perhaps my most prized possession. Curious you would notice it among all the treasures in this room."

She gestured to the exquisite Chinese vases and fine English porcelain, the jewel-studded snuffboxes, pure gold sabers, ivory chests, inlaid tables and the solid gold spittoon she kept near for special visitors.

"Horses," he said, turning back to the painting. "That is what I know best."

She nodded. "It is good to know one true thing."

The Princess rang a small gold bell. Immediately the doors were open to the Head Eunuch who rubbed the sleep from his eyes and straightened his tunic to greet his mistress.

"Escort the janissary to the barracks, Saffron. See that he is treated first to breakfast in the gardens and then relieved of all duties except to be at this very place at a quarter to midnight tonight. Assign him a eunuch to serve him with a company of pages."

"Yes, my Sultaness."

"And open all the shutters to my bedchamber but bring me a dark veil to shade the light from my eyes. I am ready to sleep."

Without another word, the Princess clapped and Ivan Postivich was led out of the chamber and through the grand hall to the garden.

Saffron received Postivich in the courtyard adjacent to the fountain. The janissary studied the eunuch's face and saw none of the hostility of their first meeting, but no sign that the man liked or respected him. Still the janissary had made his mistress eager for rest for the first moment in over a week, and for this, the servant was immensely grateful. This showed in the relaxed folds around his lips and eyes. Still, he did not utter a word.

What was missing in the eunuch's demeanor was more than compensated for by the sumptuous service lavished upon the soldier. A young mulatto eunuch brought a gold encrusted pitcher and poured lemon-scented water over his hands, splashing into a mother-of-pearl bowl. A small parade of servants—the tablakars—entered the courtyard, balancing the wooden trays on their heads. The plates were laden with palace delicacies. The Princess's own dining maids served the food, their waists adorned with white napkins, the ends tasseled in gold embroidery.

The significance of such service was not lost on Ivan; nor was it on the serving girls. This treatment was reserved for members of the royal court or the most esteemed guests.

Ivan dined on *kaymak*, the thick rich cream spread over *simit*s, a bread baked in a ring. An exquisite salted white cheese was laid out on fine china, covered with a linen cloth perfumed in rosemary and lemon. Stuffed mussels, blue-silver caviar that mimicked the White Sea in its translucence and small fish cooked in pools of golden olive oil were arrayed in dishes with silver edges, covered in white cloths embroidered in gold thread.

Plates of *tursu*, pickled vegetables, were arrayed in front of him to tempt his appetite. There was no beverage served, and the meal gave him a great thirst. A servant brought water from a palace cistern, icy cold in a silver goblet.

"Have you eaten your fill?"

Ivan Postivich turned to see a pale ghost of a man in a white turban and scarlet tunic addressing him. He was short and somewhat flabby, with rounded breasts that strained at his starched tunic like those of a fat woman.

Ivan Postivich's gut tightened as if someone had punched him. He recognized this white eunuch who waited on the docks after the drownings.

"My name is Emerald," announced the eunuch. His teeth shone like yellowed bones between his pale lavender lips. His skin was as pale as scar tissue.

"I will be your personal servant while you serve our Sultaness. Please, come. I will show you to your quarters."

Ivan Postivich was shown to a long row of rooms at the edge of the palace that housed the Solaks of the Sultana's guard. He removed his shoes and was given bloodred slippers to pad across the stone floor.

His cot was neatly made, the room immaculate, the windows admitting the sweet air of the adjacent gardens.

"You should sleep during the day. I will come to fetch you each evening, at which time I will supervise your washing in the hamam. You shall be presented to the Princess at her biding after that hour."

"Your name?"

"My name is Emerald," he repeated. "Like the precious stone. If you need me for anything, you should send a page to fetch me. They are always within hearing range of these quarters. They will bring you food and drink and anything else you wish, except for women or boys. There is no fornicating within the palace grounds without express permission of the Princess. Those who disobey her are to be beheaded."

The janissary considered this.

"And with her permission?"

Emerald's mouth stretched into a leer. "There are great festivals of indulgence. All of Constantinople is agitated with shock and envy at her entertainments—as I am certain you well know. There is not a European ambassador in the city who would not pull out a good tooth to be invited."

Postivich noted French accents in the eunuch's speech. "Where were you apprenticed?"

"In the Topkapi itself. I was a boy in Selim's court and was taught Ottoman, French, Persian, Arabic, and English. I accompanied Princess Esma Sultan to her palaces and served her through her marriage. Her husband died seventeen years ago, when she was only twenty-five."

"Pity."

The eunuch lifted his eyebrow and touched his tongue to his lip.

"May he dwell in Paradise with Allah and be recompensed with virgins of exquisite quality for what he has suffered here on this earth."

"What did he suffer?"

"An untouchable Princess who ordered him from her bed, slapping and biting him on their wedding night. She bloodied his nose with a kick when he kissed the coverlet to approach her."

"Banished from his own marriage bed? Did he not demand his rights as a man to claim her?"

"An Ottoman princess is above all men, except her brother. The poor Pasha built his own residence at the edge of Constantinople, so that he might not suffer the disgrace of the bruises from his wife who scorned him. The harem whispers he died without carnal knowledge.

"But enough gossip of the palace. You must rest so that you are ready to serve the Princess at midnight."

Bezm-i Alem spied through the perforation in the ornate marble grille. She did not trust this white eunuch, Emerald.

*Who has assigned this contemptible little beast to Ahmed Kadir? Esma Sultan scorns Emerald and only permits him to enter the palace under orders of Topkapi. When he leaves she demands that lemon oil be rubbed on every surface he has trodden or touched.*

*Does the Sultan have a hand in this?*

She wanted to warn the corbaci, but could not think how to approach him. One of the women in the harem had told Esma Sultan that Bezm-i Alem had spoken to the giant through the screen.

"You may never speak to him again!" she screamed and slapped the young woman across her face. Bezm-i Alem stared at her in wonder, for she had not struck her since the harem girl was a small child.

Bezm-i Alem raised her hand to her cheek. She said nothing but simply studied Esma Sultan's face, trying to understand.

When the harem girl saw the anguish in her mistress's eyes, Bezm-i Alem knew how much she was loved and what price Esma Sultan would pay to keep her safe in the harem. But Bezm-i Alem also saw how much Esma Sultan valued the corbaci—was it just the restful sleep he brought her?

"If my brother the Sultan learned of your interest in the giant, he would kill him, as he has despised the janissary since he was a child. He knows nothing of you now. Would you jeopardize your freedom and the life of the corbaci so foolishly?"

Bezm-i Alem could not go against the Princess's command. Still, she wished she could warn Ahmed Kadir of the treachery of this strange white eunuch who attended him.

# Chapter 5

The janissary slept fitfully through the day, the heat making him sweat his sheets. Others joined him later in the morning, unwinding their turbans and folding them carefully at the foot of their mats. These were the men who had similar shifts to his, for there were servants and Solaks afoot in the palace at all hours of night and day.

At the muezzin's call, twice more during the day, Ivan Postivich dragged himself from his bed and prayed towards Mecca. He bowed his head and lay prostrate on his old woolen prayer rug that scratched mercilessly at his knees as he prayed to Allah. As he recited his prayers, he noticed all but one of the Janissaries in the same position. That one seemed to sleep on, making an exaggerated snore, a mockery to the muezzin's call to prayer.

No one disturbed him.

The men whispered their prayers, hoarse with weariness, but devout. They stumbled back onto their mats and within seconds were sound asleep.

Ivan Postivich rose an hour before sunset. He was immediately greeted by a page who promptly hissed to another down the corridor. Within moments, Emerald appeared with towels and suggested he visit the hamam, where he could bathe and be massaged while he took a light meal.

The hamam was empty. Ivan could hear only the splash of water from the fountains. He stripped off his tunic and untied the sash that bound his billowing pants. A page whisked away his clothes to be laundered, while Emerald laid out a fresh uniform and starched white-sleeved felt hat.

He prepared a coarse hemp bag, rubbing oily soap over the inside weave. He filled it with water until the suds inflated the sack

"I will bathe you, sir."

The janissary lay on the warm marble stone while the eunuch rubbed the bag over his flesh, wringing the suds over the giant's body, massaging his shoulders and legs. His body was soon encased in a billow of rich lather squeezed from the sack. The eunuch's soft hands soaped every centimeter of the janissary's skin, reaching into even the soft, intimate crevices with expertise and without hesitation.

The eunuch then rinsed the man's body with water from a silver pitcher. Then he pulled a long razor from a crimson sheath and honed it expertly against a leather strop.

The janissary watched his back and forth motions with a wary eye. There was something sinister about this diminutive eunuch that he did not trust.

"Lean back and allow me to shave you."

Ivan Postivich locked eyes with the eunuch. One quick move with the sharp edge could be his death.

The jannisary jutted out his chin and exposed his neck. The eunuch smiled slowly, exposing his yellow teeth, and lowered the blade next to his wet skin.

"Do not worry, Ahmed. Should I as much as nick your skin, the Sultaness would have my head mounted on a stick at Topkapi. This shall be the best shave you have ever experienced. Relax with faith in Allah."

A young page asked permission to come in, carrying a teapot and some sweetmeats. Emerald nodded to him to prepare the tea, while the janissary dried himself and rested, reclining against the marble wall.

"When you have rested and been oiled and massaged, I will order your dinner. You can take it in the janissary hall, adjacent to your quarters, or under the lime trees in the garden."

"Sit, eunuch," said the janissary, his mouth full of pastry. "I'm a soldier and not at ease with so many waiting on me."

"I am your personal servant while you attend the Sultaness."

"Then sit, I order you."

Emerald smiled and sat across from the janissary, who drank his tea in the flickering candlelight of the hamam. Ivan motioned to the page to serve tea to the man who had just bathed him.

"Most gracious of you," said the little eunuch, as the page ran to fetch another cup. "Are you aware that this is not the hamam of the palace Janissaries?" said the eunuch.

"Yes, I was surprised you brought me here."

"This hamam is only for the Sultaness's most honored guests. She prescribes a very strict bathing before anyone can enter her inner rooms."

Ivan Postivich tore at another pastry and chewed thoughtfully.

"Did she bring the men I have drowned here?"

Emerald looked up at the vaulted tile ceiling, seeming to study the drops of condensation crawling slowly to the lip of the cobalt-blue tiles before falling in an erratic patter into the pogol below. For a moment, Ivan Postivich thought the man had not heard him.

"Yes. Always," answered Emerald in a soft, high voice. "They must perform the ritual ablutions twice. They are made to soak their privates in buckets of warm seawater before lying on the belly stone, so as to drown any parasites that cling to their infidel bodies. All cleansings are supervised by the Head Eunuch."

"The Sultaness is fastidious about the purity of her lovers," said the janissary.

Emerald raised his fingertips in the air, cautioning the janissary to say no more. He darted a look at the page who was returning with the cup.

"You may go now. I will ring the bell if I need more assistance."

The page bowed his head and left the steaming room.

"I must warn you to be careful what you say in others' presence," said Emerald, wiping the steam from his temples with a linen cloth. "They are paid to have sharp ears and good memories."

He opened the end of two pipes that let a splashing stream of hot water into the bathing pool.

Ivan Postivich grunted. He leaned back against a cool white marble column, enveloped in fresh steam.

"He would bring no news to the Sultaness," said Postivich. "Esma Sultan knows too well how I feel."

The eunuch's eyes widened. The janissary could see the rings of white outlining the pale blue orbits of his eyes.

"You have criticized her Royal Highness to her face and still live? You must have unique kismet in this world!"

"She knows I loathe the blood I have on my hands in her name."

Emerald contemplated this as he opened a bronze pipe to wash the remaining soap from his hands.

"You were brought up in the Topkapi as a boy, I know. I remember a tall lad wrestling a grown man in the training grounds and winning the match. 'The giant' he was called, but the Sultan Selim III later referred to him as 'Biscuit.' That was you."

Ivan Postivich looked away and grunted.

"How can it be that a man of your rank and education could be asked to serve such a duty for the Sultaness? Were you not commander of your cavalry orta?"

Ivan Postivich hesitated. He detected a disingenious note in the eunuch's words. Surely everyone in the Topkapi Court knew the story of the corbaci's demotion.

"The Sultan Mahmud saw fit to relieve me of my post in the Janissary Corps when I returned from the Northern Wars, having served the Ottomans well and brought great honor to Topkapi."

The janissary threw his head back and finished off his tea. In his big hands, the porcelain cup looked tiny and fragile, like a girl's toy.

"This is how the Ottomans reward their faithful soldiers," he said, "by letting them serve their blasphemous sisters."

Emerald suddenly sucked in his breath as if the giant had sunk a fist in his soft belly.

"What is the matter, eunuch? You must know that I hate the Ottomans. I am still a janissary at the core, even if I am one of the Kapikulu elite. You will not find a janissary who admires the Sultan in all Stamboul."

"You honor me with your confidences, but I will again warn you not to utter them in anyone else's company," said the eunuch, his face hardening under the folds of fat. "You might consider withholding them from me, as well. I am sworn to be a faithful Ottoman servant."

The janissary looked the man in the eye. "If I were concerned for my life, I wouldn't speak of them in front of you. But I am not afraid of death or the Sultaness. I am weary of the vice of this regime and the sins committed in the Ottoman name. I am a janissary, meant to protect the Empire and fight the infidels who threaten Constantinople, not a butcher of poor men who entertain an Ottoman whore."

Emerald lit another lantern in silence.

"I prefer to think that you honor me with your confidences, rather than believe you tell me them as a death wish," said the eunuch, illuminated in the glowing flame of the lantern. Ivan Postivich could see that the muscles in his jaw were clenched. "For surely, what you say is high treason against the Ottomans whom I serve."

"A janissary is not known for his subordination and discretion."

"And so there have been many assassinations of Sultans at the Janissaries' hand. 'Long live the brother,' has rung in my ears now twice in a lifetime."

Ivan Postivich grabbed a towel and wiped his dripping face.

"I am not a revolutionary, and it is only under duress and imperial order that I am an unwilling assassin."

"I have seen your face many nights," said the eunuch, through the steam. "It was I who stood in the shadows on the docks and carried your confirmation of death to the Princess."

"Yes. I recognize you."

"I made the report these many nights, repeating your words. May Allah cleanse my soul with the tears I have shed in shame."

The janissary stared at him and wondered if he was telling the truth.

As if he sensed the janissary's doubts and sought to quiet them by sharing his own story, the eunuch went on. "I was born in the northlands and, like you, was captured at a young age. After my castration, I was sold and taken to Stamboul. I was made to memorize passages of the Koran in both Persian and Ottoman in order to prove my faith and worthiness to Allah.

"I delighted in my faith, for after my capture and my castration, I had only this one refuge, for Allah does not indulge such atrocities, but will punish justly those who brought me such shame and robbed me of my manhood."

"How is it that you are so educated, eunuch? You speak like a prince."

"That is the gift of His Highness, Sultan Selim. Under his direction, I was taught foreign languages, algebra, music. It delighted Selim to see his servant master the skills many of the princes and his rivals could not. I was his pet," said Emerald, lowering his eyes, the blond lashes fluttering.

Ivan Postivich understood the particular honor to which the eunuch referred.

"I was second only to his favorite cousins, the Princess Esma Sultan and her brother Mahmud, who also received the finest tutoring as children. But it was I who shared the Sultan's bed more often than the women of his harem.

"But my greatest delight was the reading of the Koran, for I believed that now I truly served Allah, being so close to 'his shadow on earth.' The night he was murdered, I licked his wounds in immeasurable grief and wailed to Allah for his revenge. The butchers later carved his body into pieces, taking his head and impaling it upon the palace wall and flinging the rest of the mutilated corpse over the walls of Topkapi to the crowd below.

"There was only one other member of the court who dared to return to watch his blood dry on the courtyard stones—Esma Sultan. A child, yet she stood under the lime tree, oblivious to the terror and striking at her handmaidens who beseeched her to hide from the Janissaries.

"We shared that horror then—and now I dread the nights of the new moon, knowing I will be sent to fetch news of men's murders."

"Why does the moon figure into this wretchedness?"

"She is a woman and controlled by no man, but the rhythms of nature still mandate her womanly ebb and flow."

"She is a witch, for no human woman could be as cruel."

The eunuch tipped his teacup into his fleshy mouth, masking his expression from the janissary.

"This sin would never have been suffered under Selim, for he honored the teachings of the Prophet. But everything turned on that night, even the destiny of the Sultaness I now serve. Still, control your tongue before it moves falsely again. I have known the Princess these many years. Esma Sultan is more dedicated to goodness and the Koran than you suspect."

"Dedicated to goodness! She defiles herself and the Ottomans and then dispatches men to their deaths. How could a murderess be accused of benevolence!"

"You have a supreme death wish, my friend," said Emerald, rising. "I have been with her since I first came to Topkapi. You, I suspect, will come to know her better and will see what a complicated woman reigns here. Perhaps you will hesitate in your judgment as time passes.

"So, until you have that knowledge and can better know her, I will keep your words in my ears and heart. You are a man of desperate mind to risk the wrath of Esma Sultan, even if you proclaim no fear of death. Still, I will see who will ultimately win, under the judgment of Allah. Come, let me dry your back and prepare you for a good supper."

With that Emerald closed the tap on the pipes of the baths and whistled for the page to assist him in the cooler rooms of the hamam.

# Part II
# Sophie

# Chapter 6

At midnight, Ivan Postivich was admitted to the exterior apartments of the harem, where the Princess stood, her hennaed hands twisting the curtains at a great window that overlooked the Bosphorus.

"Your Highness summoned me," he said, approaching at a walk, barely imitating a bow as he reached the fretting Princess.

"Of course, you fool," she said, dismissing his words with a flick of her palm. Heavy ruby bracelets clattered on her wrist. The calm and easy manner she had possessed when he left her at dawn had vanished. "No man dares enter the Royal Harem without the express consent of the Sultaness."

"I don't know about the men who are admitted to your harem."

She whirled around to face him.

"Are you clean?" demanded the Sultaness. Ivan Postivich noticed beads of sweat on her pale forehead. "Tell me, Saffron, has the janissary been washed thoroughly?"

"Emerald performed the prescribed ablutions himself," responded the Head Eunuch.

She sniffed the air. "There is an acrid odor of man about him that is foul. It pollutes my harem with its stench."

"I can take him back to the hamam again, myself, Your Highness—"

"No, leave him here! I will endure his presence and disgusting odor. Light incense! Bring us mint tea to cleanse my throat. Sit, janissary."

Ivan Postivich crossed his legs upon an enormous silk cushion.

"I have dreamt again and smell the rotting flesh," she said, her white hands pressed against her cheeks, making a temple over her face. "Men's jaws opening wide, exposing rotten yellow teeth that crumble as they scream to me, with no sound issuing from their stinking mouths."

The Sultaness gasped as she covered her nose and mouth with a linen handkerchief scented with lavender oils. "Can you not smell it now, the vile odor of rot?"

Ivan Postivich sniffed the air, placing his hands on his hips. He drew an exaggerated breath, his great chest expanding. He smiled slowly as he exhaled.

"I smell nothing but the sweet feminine aromas of talc and jasmine. Perhaps a pot of musk. The warm smell of bathed women, hungry for a man between their thighs."

"Your impertinence is astonishing," said the Sultaness. Suddenly she gagged and crumpled her face into her fists. "I cannot abide a minute longer this hideous stench! Perform what Christian miracles you have done this past evening. Take away the demons, janissary, I command you! "

Ivan Postivich watched the Ottoman Princess in amazement. He relished this moment, to have the Sultan's sister beg succor from one who had been taken as a slave as an innocent boy. A born Muslim, an Ottoman princess, pleading for the solace of confession, that holy ritual of Christianity.

"I perform no miracles and I am no longer a Christian. I was circumcised and converted quite thoroughly as a young boy, made to renounce my faith, my homeland, and my family. Last night, I merely sat here as I do now, listening to you, as a servant to an Ottoman princess. If there was a miracle to cure you, it was Allah's gift, for I am not capable of the deed."

The Sultaness removed her hands from her face and straightened her spine. She would show no further signs of weakness.

The Head Eunuch knocked and entered with two Circassian slaves, golden curls brought up into twisted braids atop their head, where crimson caps perched.

One served the tea with a flourish, pouring from a great height above the cup. The other presented a cup to the Sultaness, after first testing it for poison.

"No," said the Sultaness, peevishly. "Serve my guest first."

The surprised slave took the cup to the janissary, who examined her fair face with a man's hungry eyes. He took the cup without ever looking at it.

"She pleases you," said the Princess, observing his rapt attention.

"Of course," said Postivich, his eyes still fastened on the beauty of her face and bare throat. "I am a man; how would I not be pleased with an attractive woman? Especially one without a yasmak to obscure her beauty."

The slave blushed but showed her pleasure at the attentions bestowed upon her by the Sultaness's honored guest with a dimpled smile.

"A veil is an invention of man to protect what he feels is his property. None of my slaves wear the yasmak; we show our faces to Allah without shame."

The janissary could not keep his eyes off the girl.

"That is all, Leyla; you are dismissed for the evening," snapped the Sultaness. "We must have our privacy."

"Leyla means 'black.' Why do you call her that, when she is so fair?"

"'Black and abundant as the night' seemed to me a good way to name a blond Circassian. We enjoy our whims in the harem."

Postivich shrugged. He did not understand women's silly entertainments, nor did he care to discuss them. He only thought of the opportunity to lay his rough hands on the young woman's creamy skin and ravish her. What they did in their leisure time was of no importance to him.

The Sultaness studied the janissary's reaction. She combed her auburn hair with her jeweled fingers.

"I see your disdain so plainly, Ahmed Kadir. You despise me and you loathe the attention women receive in my palace, when you feel women are only on earth to please men. You are a fool."

Ivan Postivich sipped his tea, looking deep into the cup. It was true—Esma Sultan toyed with her power, pretending women were equivalent of men. Her behavior was blasphemous and an affront to Allah, who decreed that man, in Mohammed's words, was the protector sex of the women.

"What do you wish to tell me tonight, Sultaness?"

Esma Sultan looked at the fine porcelain teacup, contemplating. She slowly lifted her gaze to the janissary's eyes, her own eyes tawny in the flickering candlelight. She licked her lips before she spoke.

"I will tell you a tale that will comfort me. A time of innocence and childhood."

Ivan Postivich felt a sudden stab as a fleeting memory of his own short childhood raced through his head.

"I will tell you about a little girl, a long time ago in the harem. Her name was Sophie, and she was admitted to the Serail when I was about nine years of age."

Then Esma Sultan looked about, as if surveying the room for spies. She clapped her hands and Saffron appeared.

"Secure the doors and open all the fountains. I want no one to overhear our conversation, Saffron."

The Head Eunuch nodded deeply and backed away from the Sultaness, his head still inclined. Soon a plashing of fountains, both inside and outside the palace, could be heard.

"My tale is for you alone, Ahmed Kadir," she said. "The Sultan's ears are everywhere, especially in my palace."

"Sophie could not speak Ottoman, or Arabic, or Persian, when she arrived, only a guttural tongue of the Northern Provinces. At first, I thought she could not speak at all, but could only utter nonsensical sounds of grief as she rubbed her knuckles into her green eyes to wipe away the tears.

"I judged her near my age, perhaps a few years younger. My mother explained that she was brought from lands far to the north in a trade to please my father, the Sultan. She was to remain under the supervision of my mother and receive the same education as a princess.

"She was the most beautiful creature I had ever seen.

"'You must be kind to her, Esma. But beware of becoming her dear friend. It will only sadden you.'

"I did not understand my mother's words. I was greatly entertained at the thought that this yellow-haired girl would become my playmate and sleep in the same room as my mother and me. I sat next to her as she lay exhausted from tears and I stroked her golden head, murmuring Ottoman lullabies to soothe her fears.

"'Don't cry, *kucuk*,' I said to her, for she was indeed smaller and younger than I.

"Though she could not understand a word of Ottoman, she raised her head and stared at me. I think she saw there was kindness in the harem and she would no longer be handled by the rough probing hands of her male captors, whose fingers touched her childish genitals to assure themselves she was a virgin and could be admitted to the sanctity of our harem.

"This was a time of innocence, when I did not understand the true purpose of a harem. It was a child's paradise, where I was spoiled and pampered and indulged beyond all shame.

"Despite my mother's admonitions, Sophie and I grew to be dear friends. She was more family to me than my cousin Hatice, sister of Selim. He was rumored to be the next Sultan after my father, and I relished the thought of my good, gentle cousin one day ruling the Empire. It seemed so distant a hope, though, for at that time, he was kept locked away in the Cage of Princes. We were only able to see him on feast days, and I looked forward to those opportunities to see him seated at the right of my father.

"But his sister Hatice was petulant and lazy. I much preferred the companionship of my new little blond sister.

"She escorted me everywhere, my Sophie, acting as my handmaiden, albeit a spirited one. The most cherished of our outings was in the security of the Imperial coaches, escorted by the eunuchs. We were allowed to watch through the perforated boards of the carriage the cirit and polo games where my brothers would ride against the Kapikulu."

Esma Sultane smiled wearily at the janissary.

"That is where I first saw you, Corbaci, and your accomplished feats on horseback. You were the youngest of all the players, but the Horse Master thought you capable. I was one of the many Ottoman princesses peeking out from behind the heavy velvet curtains of the Imperial coaches, as young slaves fanned us with ostrich and peacock plumes in an attempt to cool the stifling heat. Outside the coach, we were flanked by dozens of Solak guards and two eunuchs were positioned against the carriage door."

Ivan Postivich suddenly sat erect.

"You watched the matches?"

"Yes, cirit and polo were our favorite entertainment. There was nothing that could calm the soul of my dear companion like the sight, even the smell of horses. Though we were never allowed to leave the confines of the coach, she pressed her eyes and mouth against the grille of the laquered coach and drunk in the odor of the animals, intoxicating her with their scent.

"She cheered the Kapikulus faithfully, which infuriated me as it clearly was treason to favor anyone but the Ottoman court. Still, despite my berating, she thrust her small white fist in the air when your orta scored, and she talked incessantly about the horses and the riders' skills for days after.

"It was the first time I ever heard her utter a word about a man, except in terror.

"I learned I could soothe her with legends about horses and so every night, I would have a new tale to tell to lull her to sleep. She preferred stories about women, so I sought in our Topkapi libraries for stories of equestrian feats. I ordered my tutors to scour all Constantinople for accounts of women and horses to indulge my little friend. Books and parchments arrived as presents from Persia, Egypt, Afghanistan, from noblemen wanting to curry favor with the Sultan by satisfying the whim of his favorite child.

"I read Sophie tales from our great Turkish poet Dede Korkut. Sophie's favorite was the story of the Prince Bamsi Beyrek, the son of Prince Bay Bure, who came to claim the hand of our dear Princess, Lady Chichek. But it was not the royalty who would capture her attention, as she begged me to skip over those parts. Instead she waited for me to arrive at the part about Princess Chichek's handmaiden who challenged the prince to three duels: archery, wrestling, and horsemanship, before he had the honor of meeting the Princess.

"I would imagine the horse races and archery on horseback between the woman servant and the prince and Sophie would clap her hands in delight. The nameless servant held her reins in her teeth, commanding her horse entirely with her seat and legs as she threw the cirit jereed. It was not until the third competition that the woman finally met her shameful defeat, according to the poet—when wrestling, the prince seized her breast and pulled her under him, pinning her and winning the challenge."

The janissary laughed, and then bit his lip to contain his mirth. Esma Sultan watched him, her eyebrow raising high into an arch.

"Sophie hated the ending of this tale, so I would repeat the parts where the handmaiden followed the creed of ancient Turks, devoting themselves to the cult of the horse. I wanted her to think well of the Turks, her captors. Only with the stories of the horse could I see her fear and hatred of us melt away.

"'Of course, Sophie,' I would say, 'you know the ancient creed is that a Turk is born in a hut, lives in freedom, and dies on horseback on the prairie.'

"'Freedom,' she would whisper as she fell asleep against the cushions.

"Seeing how she reveled in the ancient legends of the horse, I ordered the eunuchs to find wooden carvings for her of horses in the Bazaar, so that she might play on the tiles of the Serail and lose her fear of men and her adopted homeland. Indeed as she played, a eunuch could finally approach her without instilling terror and she would simply dismiss him from her thoughts, her fingers playing dreamily on the smooth wooden replicas of her beloved horses.

"The ancient stories of Scheherazade clearly captured her attention. I told her the story about the two Sultan princes and a princess who were set adrift on the river by their jealous aunts and how all three grew up to become skilled archers and equestrians. In the end it is the skill of the princess and her wisdom that saves her brothers' lives and finally leads to joining their long lost parents at the palace.

"She adored the stories from ancient times when Turkish, Persian, and Arab women rode horses as warriors. I would list them on my fingers: Zenobia, wife of Odenath, the king of Palmyra, rode with her husband to battle against the Persians and the Goths. Zaydi chieftain Sharifa Fatima, daughter of an Imam, conquered San'a. The kings of Persia employed female bodyguards. The great poetess El-Khaansa, during the lifetime of Mohammed, laid down her quill and earned a reputation as a warrior. And the Prophet's youngest wife, Aisha, rode in front of her army, screaming death cries as she descended into the field of battle.

"'But why then do we remain here, like caged animals?' Sophie asked me. 'If women can ride and fight, why can't we? Why can we not ride the plains and live and die in freedom as our sisters before us?'

"I had no answer for her.

"'It is my father's wish,' I said, choking on the words. 'You must not question the Sultan, little sister.'"

"But I would not allow her passion to be smothered entirely. She was as rebellious and spoiled as any princess and I indulged her. In the early morning I would run around the corridors of the Serail, chasing Sophie who wore pretty nightclothes as long as she was allowed, despising the billowing pants that the ladies of the harem wore during the day.

"The slaves would have to corner her and pull her night-clothes from her, while she kicked and wailed in protest. One morning, she ran so fast that she eluded the servants. Her blond tresses flew loose as she careened naked around the marbled hall. I ran after her, tears of mirth streaking my face, calling, 'Stop the nightingale! She has flown from her cage and refuses her new plumage!'

"She raced around a corner and flew straight into my father, the Sultan. He gasped in surprise, his breath gone.

"I threw an arm around Sophie and shoved her behind me. Ever since her captors had touched her so intimately, she was terrified of men. She trembled against my back.

"'Dear father, it was an accident. Sophie meant no harm.'

"Before anyone could speak, my mother was at my side. She threw a wrap over the naked girl. 'Esma and Sophie, come with me to our apartments.'

"My father recovered his breath and smiled, though sternly. 'Wait! Let me see the little nightingale who has come to live in my palace.'

"My mother narrowed her eyes at me in a look I only came to understand years later. She would always blame me for this chance meeting, even if little Sophie was already property of my father.

"'Come, Sophie!' I urged. 'Greet my father, the Sultan.'

"Sophie approached him, head bowed. He touched the blond curls and she drew back, her little body trembling uncontrollably.

My father seemed not to notice but reached out and slipped his bejeweled hand under her chin to raise it."

"'Her age?' he inquired of the Head Eunuch, not taking his eyes off the girl.

"'Not far past eight years, my Sultan. Perhaps nine.'

"'My little nightingale, I am pleased to have you in my harem,' said my father, dropping her chin after a gentle caress. 'You must learn to dance well.'

"As he turned to leave, he addressed my mother quite formally.

"'And Saliha. See that you govern the royal Princess with a firmer hand, that she does not fly about Topkapi screaming at the top of her lungs like a barbarian. I have left her in your care to teach her a woman's graces.'

"My mother dropped her gaze to her feet. 'Of course, Your Highness, my Sultan. I will see that it never happens again.'

"'Still, I admire the spirit of our Princess Esma, for she has the Ottoman strength and fire in her veins. Perhaps she will instill the same joy and energy for life into little Sophie.'

"My mother bowed her head. 'As you command, O Sultan.'

"As my father turned to walk down the corridor, he said, 'And see that the nightingale is fed more. She is indeed birdlike—she could do with some fattening.'

"Life changed after that day. I was no longer allowed to play boisterously in the courtyards of the Serail and my mother admonished me for high spirits of any kind. She glared at Sophie, blaming the little child for her reprimand and fall from my father's favor.

"Every day, Sophie's command of Ottoman grew, for she was a clever girl. She was commanded by the Valide Sultan to come and pronounce the new words and phrases she had learned that day. In fact, the Sultan's mother took a keen interest in Sophie following that collision with her son. She saw that Sophie began dance instruction and supervised her lesson each morning.

"When I was ten years old, my father the Sultan gave me a royal party with shadow puppets, jugglers, and actors. The actors, the *zuhuri kolu*, brought painted backdrops that they tied to the plane trees of the courtyard. They played both male and female parts, and their bearded faces behind their fine gauze yasmaks made us howl in laughter, most unbefitting royal princesses.

"But most important of all, that which kidnapped the collective breath of the rest of the court and Serail, was the present my father the Royal Sultan bestowed upon me—the gift of my own palace on the Bosphorus.

"It was this very palace—and though I have acquired many since then, this remains my favorite.

"'Your intellect and social graces shall embellish the Ottoman Empire,' proclaimed the Sultan. 'Your tutors and even the Pasha Efendi insist they have never seen a quicker student in languages, philosophy, calligraphy, and the study of the Holy Koran. You set high standards for your male kinsmen who shall one day rule in my place.'

"This remark had a very strange effect on the court. Of course my mother was delighted that I should have my own palace and be the favored daughter of the Serail, but to suggest that my intellect and achievements were above my brothers, Mustafa and Mahmud and even above that of Selim, was an insult—and a dangerous one.

"My mother, from whom I inherited any wit I can claim, laughed and encouraged those around her to do the same, raising her white hands and clapping.

"'Oh, our glorious Sultan! You bestow such courtesies on the Princess Esma. You are so kind not to mention her clumsy fingers on the lyre or how her chin fights the violin that the music tutor has slaved to teach her. And dancing—oh, now there's an art where she shall not excel!'

"I watched the others laugh, and closed my eyes—in hope that my mother's comments would shield me from the jealousy that could rage like a fire through the Serail. I drew a quick breath, and raised my head, smiling.

"'Ah, Saliha,' replied the Sultan. 'You shall not let me sing praises to another woman in your presence, even if it be your own daughter.'

"This stung my mother; she had not been called to the Sultan's bedchamber in over two months. Still, she smiled sweetly, as does a dog when it has been kicked but crawls on its belly for the love of its master. She waited for my father to continue, bowing her head in respect.

"He called me to him and lifted my chin. 'Come here, kucuk, my little one,' he said. 'You shall have a private audience with the Sultan.'

"I crawled up onto his knees and I still remember the softness of his ermine and velvet robes. It was rare indeed that any of the children were invited onto his lap.

"'If only you were my son,' he whispered, in my ear. 'You would have far more than a palace.'

"Then he raised his hand, a sign that he spoke publicly and the Royal Scribes sharpened their quills and took down his words.

"'I speak as your Sultan—this Princess is the rose of the Ottoman Empire and whoever follows me shall show her the same favor as I do or suffer my curse from the grave.'

"My cousin Selim dropped his head at the words, as if the Prophet himself had spoken, and my half brother Mahmud locked eyes with me, with a fit of trembling. He was only a very young boy and my father's thundering decree had frightened him, especially as he had always been afraid of djinns and efrits.

"My father set me down to play with the other children, gesturing to my mother that he was finished with the audience. He showered the children with gold coins, thrown carelessly to the floor. We ran about snatching the coins and colliding with the knees of the stately adults, which made us silly with mirth. I caught Sophie's hand and we ran and hid in the trees, giggling and dropping nuts onto the eunuchs' turbans.

"Even though now I had my own palace, my mother and I spent little time there. I preferred living at Topkapi, in my Royal Apartments. My mother, though proud of my new home on the Bosphorus, loathed time away from the Sultan and the Serail. I suspect she thought her absence from the Serail as being not unlike banishment to the Palace of Tears with the harem women no longer in favor.

"For Sophie and me, the Topkapi was our own special world. I was the Sultan's pet and Sophie was mine. Together we would race through the corridors and courtyards—sometimes escaping the endless surveillance of the servants. We would explore every corner, finding hidden passageways, some so dusty that we knew no one had ventured there for years. We found our way to places we knew we should not be—and we held our breath in fear of discovery and the unpleasant consequences that would be certain to follow. These were special times—just for Sophie and me.

"We loved to play in our 'throne room,' a tiny clear space deep at the heart of a huge bush that grew in the gardens of our courtyard. We had discovered it during a game of hide and seek and we went there often to be alone with each other.

"In the loam we uncovered miraculous glowworms in the deep earth. The glowworms pulsed blue light, and if you squeezed them, the luminous liquid would color your hand with magical light that glowed in the dark. We would scare the old kadins and eunuchs, waving our hands in the darkness of the Serail corridors, making the old Valide scream witlessly of peri spirits haunting Topkapi.

"We would smother our mouths with the harem cushions, to keep from laughing aloud and being discovered.

"One day we were there, digging for buried Byzantine treasure with golden spoons we had pilfered from our dinner trays. A eunuch had been beaten for their disappearance—no one would dare accuse the Sultan's favorite daughter. But the golden spoons bent and warped. They were useless for digging.

"Sophie began scrabbling at the earth like a dog, until her fingers hit an old rotted plank. Together, we dug with our hennaed hands, packing black earth under our fingernails, until we had uncovered a trapdoor and pulled it open.

"The hole beneath was deep and dark and the ladder leading down looked ready to collapse. It took several days before we were ready to descend, every night saving candle stubs to use to illuminate the dark tunnel when we finally set out on our adventure.

"'Let me go first!' squealed Sophie, lowering her foot gingerly onto the top rung of the rotted wooden ladder.

"'No!' I insisted. 'I am the Ottoman. I will lead the way.'

"I pulled her up by the starched collar of her blouse—she was light as a hummingbird. She cursed me in a peasant tongue as she lay sprawled in the tangle of underbrush.

"'Stop your barbaric babble!,' I commanded. 'You'll have the Solaks here in seconds!'

"This was the only way to quiet her. She knew my threats were harmless, but the idea of the guards seizing her made her plunge her dirty fingers in her mouth in fear.

"I closed my eyes in the darkness as I descended the ladder, not daring to light my candle until my foot felt the damp earth at the bottom. Rats scuttled away from the light, baring their yellow teeth from the edges of the rotting timbers that lined the corridor. Sophie was right behind me, her eyes wide and wary, though I could see not a trace of fear. Again and again, she pressed against me trying to squeeze ahead.

"Eventually, the passage angled upward and narrowed. The walls that now pressed close against us were no longer dirt. They were smooth stones. At last, I spied a tiny point of light ahead of us in the darkness.

"I hurried forward, with Sophie close behind. The passageway ended at a blank wall. The point of light was a hole, barely the size of my finger. I pressed my eye to the hole and found myself looking down into my father's bed chamber.

"I was struck with horror at the sight before me: my father, naked, crouched on all fours over a raven-haired beauty from our harem, the seductive, empty-headed Aygul.

"My father's pale skin sagged at his abdomen and the folds of his buttocks were like the wrinkles of the elephant in our Topkapi zoo. The Head Eunuch stood over him with a golden platter and linen towel.

"'May I attend you now, O Sultan?' whispered the eunuch.

"My father rocked back, his buttocks sitting on his spindly legs, his organ slipping out withered and spent from between Aygul's thighs.

"A few drops of thick liquid dripped from his penis onto the golden plate, which the eunuch had quickly extended. The eunuch motioned and a page appeared with a bowl of water, rose petals floating delicately against the glass.

"My father grunted as the eunuch dipped his sponge into the water and gently cleansed my father's body.

"Aygul raised her hips in an arc, desperately trying to conserve my father's seed so as to conceive an Ottoman prince.

"I forced myself away from the hole in the wall, desperate not to have seen the sight that was seared in my mind's eye.

"'What did you see?' Sophie whispered.

"'Nothing that you need to view,' I answered. 'Do not question me again about it, or I shall have you beaten.'

"Silently we made our way back to the gardens adjacent to the Serail, hearing Emerald call us to prayer."

"Now listen carefully, janissary, for I am telling you secrets of the harem that no man should know. The baths of the Serail were a place for congregation and gossip. The women spent hour upon hour in the hamam, relaxing in the steamy rooms or cooling in the tepidarium. They brought their favorite servants to comb their hair and massage their bodies with scented oils. There were hampers of delicacies to snack on and pets to amuse us during the long, idle hours.

"But it was not all pleasure in the hamam. The Valide herself made sure that we obeyed the holy word of the Koran and tradition in our ablutions. Our attendants scrupulously removed all body hair on a weekly basis. The Valide's cane would poke at a concubine to have her lift an arm or expose her private parts to assure there was not a strand of hair that had gone unplucked.

"As I attended the depilatory rooms, I wished that Sophie could join me. But young as she was, she had not the slightest sign of puberty. She was growing taller, but her body remained that of a child. As the Sultan had ordered, her thin hips were learning to swivel and dance to Persian and Ottoman songs of love, but the women laughed to see a slight child imitate the moves of a woman.

"When I returned from the baths, Sophie begged me to let her stroke my clear skin, pink and hairless.

"'Your skin is as soft as a newborn,' she marveled. 'I, too, shall attend the hamam and have my hairs removed and be like my sister Esma.'

"I laughed and pinched her cheek. 'You are still a child, Sophie! You won't be a woman for years to come! Isn't that right, Mother?'

"I turned to engage my mother in this joke, but she furrowed her brows and turned away from me, focusing on her embroidery. The distraction caused her to prick herself with the sharp needle and she pressed a large red teardrop of blood from her middle finger, staining the white linen.

"It was about this time that I began to learn the secrets of the Serail. As a child I was blind to the intrigue and gossip, preferring to run wild in the gardens and climb the plane trees in the courtyards. But as I grew older, my mother felt it was time I understood politics and she slowly revealed the world of the harem to me, day by day.

"I had not realized the serious purpose of the call from the Head Eunuch that the Royal Sultan was approaching. I knew as a toddler that my mother would scoop me up when she heard that call and hurry to our apartments where we were confined until the Sultan had left the Serail. I had imagined that he inspected the quarters, making sure that all was safe and comfortable for his harem.

"Now I learned that these visits were to see his concubines or wives in their quarters.

"'What does my father do there?' I asked. 'Might we go and visit?'

"My mother smiled wryly. 'These audiences are quite private, my child. Your father would be furious if you were to appear. A woman, even a royal princess, only sees the Sultan upon his request.'

"I also learned that the eunuchs were not as chaste as the Sultan would have wished. I once watched a fat concubine being pressed against a column in the hamam by a eunuch. They were in the shadows of the cooling room and were not aware they were being observed.

"I studied the anatomy of the eunuch very carefully. I had examined the tiny male parts of my little cousins, fascinated. They were so minute and harmless. Nothing like the wrinkled penis of my father that I had spied on that day with Sophie.

"The Ethiopian eunuch, though, had an enormous penis, the scars of his castration were a milky pink against his skin. Still his organ was erect and he pushed it again and again between the concubine's thighs.

"The eunuch appeared to enjoy himself and the concubine whispered words of encouragement and joy. Together they rubbed their moist bodies against one another until a rivulet ran down the woman's thighs.

"I sought out my mother to discuss this. Her hand flew to her mouth and she laughed.

"'I have heard of this eunuch,' she said. 'They say that despite his castration he can make love like a bull. You are certain of what you saw?'

"'Of course,' I answered, irritated that she would question my veracity. For me, so young and innocent, my observations were scientific and I considered myself a young scholar. Besides, though I could never confess to her, this was not my first, but second encounter with lovemaking.

"The next day the hamam was full of mirth and the fat concubine left the baths early, blushing with embarrassment. Not a week later she was married off to an old Pasha and left the Serail for good, though I heard she made complaints about his sexual abilities in comparison with the eunuch's and was soon divorced.

"Sophie begged me to tell her the story of the eunuch and the woman in detail. Her eyes widened as I told her about the length and width of the man's penis and how he had shoved it over and over into the woman's thighs.

"'But why would she endure this?' she said, making a face like an old wrinkled fig.

"'She appeared pleased,' I said, reflecting. 'She even encouraged him.'

"'It cannot be!'

"'Sophie!'

"She raced away and climbed one of the highest plane trees in the interior courtyard, into branches so thin that even I was afraid to follow. I paced around it, looking up at her.

"'Come down, Sophie!'

"'Not until you admit you are a liar.'

"'I am *not* a liar,' I shouted up to her through the leaves. 'I am an Ottoman princess and sworn to truth and the code according to the Koran.'

"'It is only the Muslims who would behave in such a disgusting manner,' she said. She looked out over the Bosphorus and then turned her head north towards her homeland. 'I know that our men would never behave in this way. I have seen my brother naked and never did his penis grow. All Ottomans are beasts, savage and filthy.'

"I realized that we could be overheard easily and hissed up at her. 'I command you as your Princess Esma Sultan to descend from this tree immediately. If you do not, I will call one of the Solaks to fetch you. He will handle you roughly, that I can promise.'

"Sophie's eyes widened at this threat. Except in games, I had never threatened her, but she was well aware I was the Sultan's favorite child. The thought of a man touching her horrified her and she began to shake, making the leaves around her tremble.

"She slowly descended, branch by branch, until she lowered herself onto the cobblestones of the courtyard. Her eyes looked at her bare feet, for she had removed her slippers to climb the tree.

"'And here are your slippers, you silly girl!' I said, throwing them at her. 'It is you infidels who are ignorant fools!' One of the red silk slippers caught her in the cheek, and her hand flew to her face.

"Her eyes flooded with tears and I rushed to embrace her. 'Do not cry, little sister,' I said, my hand stroking her blond hair. 'I did not mean to hurt you.'

"'It is not the slippers that sting,' said Sophie. 'It is the beastliness of men and the helplessness of women.'

"I considered this, looking at the wall around the Serail and envying her the view she had just enjoyed of the Bosphorus beyond it.

"'I know!' I said, and pushed her from my arms so that I could see her flushed face and swollen eyes. 'I know what I will do! I will ask my father to release you from the Serail and you shall come with me to live in my new palace!'

"'What?' said Sophie, rubbing her eyes.

"'You and I will live in the palace and we shall have no men to encumber us. We shall choose companions to visit us and I shall have my own Serail.'

"'Women do not have Serails. They are a man's domain, even I know this. Do not tease me.'

"'Listen to me, Sophie. I shall have my own harem and women will live a life of joy within my palace walls. I have studied the Koran and there is nothing that forbids a woman from having a Serail, I am quite sure of it. I shall speak to my father on Friday, before we attend the noon prayers.

"'It shall be wonderful! I will have my own harem and the finest library in all of my father's Empire. I shall fill the palace with terrariums, aquariums, telescopes, and books. It shall be a refuge for us women and a place of knowledge and study. The only men we have will be there to serve us!'

"'And horses?'"

"'I shall have my own stable that will exceed any in Constantinople.'"

There was the faintest edge of light in the sky outside the windows of the palace. Esma Sultan took a breath and looked sharply at Postivich.

"You laugh at me, Kapikulu," said the Princess. "You have the barbaric gall to mock an Ottoman Sultaness, you Serbian animal!"

"I have not laughed," said Ivan Postivich. "I just cannot imagine an Ottoman princess as innocent as you say."

"You are laughing inside—two ignorant girls, how could they not understand that men are the more powerful sex with their magnificent weapon, made holy in Allah's eyes by their circumcision."

The giant said nothing.

"That is the view of a man. You have forgotten that I was raised in a harem, where caresses and intimate touch were restricted to other women. Your hands have touched your own genitals so much, you glory in their wonder. Why should a Princess, the Sultan's favorite daughter, elect to flee such an honor?"

Esma Sultan rang for Nazip to bring tobacco and opium. The slave girl mixed the tar-like black drug into the tobacco and packed the bowl. She inhaled first, as someone must test anything that would pass an Ottoman's lips.

After a few moments, she passed the pipe to her mistress and another slave lit it.

Esma Sultan drew deeply on the pipe and closed her eyes.

"So did you succeed in rescuing the young Sophie from the horrors of men?" asked Postivich.

"After a fashion," replied the Sultaness, her eyelids drooping. "Leave me, Biscuit. I think sleep will claim me after all."

The huge man stiffened at hearing the hateful nickname from his first days at Topkapi.

"Come back tomorrow and I will tell you more of the story."

# Chapter 7

When Ivan Postivich left the Princess, it was still an hour before sunrise. He could hear the crickets sear the night with their passionate hum—a frenetic energy that was infectious even for those whom sleep had evaded.

He felt no need for his bed as yet. Instead, he walked the fragrant gardens of the palace.

He had thought he would have heard tales of horror by now—the depravities and sins of the Princess who sought to comfort herself in confession, feigning contrition. Instead her stories were almost innocent and allowed him a glimpse of a sensitive, spoiled child who was favored above all others by the Sultan Abdulhamid.

When would she tell him of the seduction and murder of her Christian lovers? What did the story of a servant girl, enslaved and educated in the Royal Serail have to do with her murderous deeds? Her tales seemed unrelated to the deaths of so many men.

As if an Ottoman princess could ever be innocent—or youthful innocence mattered now. He was tired of girlish tales, told by a murderess.

He wondered idly if there had been incestuous love between the ruling Mahmud II and his half sister Esma, even though Islamic law strictly forbade it. Perhaps it was simply the love of his father, Abdulhamid, for Esma Sultan that had persuaded Mahmud to adore her and indulge her every wish.

And if the Sultan Mahmud II had ever loved her erotically, Ivan wondered if he still did. The Princess was certainly older than any of his wives or the young boys he kept as lovers. Still, Postivich could sense something powerful and compelling that made Esma Sultan attractive, not simply as a woman, but as a ruler. He understood that Mahmud recognized that and was attracted by his sister's regal bearing and her favored standing with their father.

As Postivich contemplated the politics of the Ottoman court, he heard a quick hiss from beyond a thick stand of bush. He pulled his dagger, his muscles tensed, ready.

"Who spies on Ahmed Kadir?"

"I am no spy," whispered a voice. A blond head emerged from the bushes. "I am Abdul Recid, of the Janissary guard. I have business to discuss with you. Put away your dagger; I am one of your brothers."

The janissary had removed his cap and had it tucked under his arm. Postivich recognized him as the soldier who refused the muezzin's call and snored during prayers.

"The Corps wants to know if you are with them or not," said Recid. "The New Guard—those infidels dressed up in the fancy costume of Western lackeys—were drilling in the Et Meydan military fields. The dog of a Sultan has thrown his final insult to us and Mohammed's holy Muslim state. He swears he will reform us in the image of European swine, and the Janissaries will be no more!"

Ivan Postivich listened quietly, knowing that there certainly were palace spies. "You speak treason, janissary," he answered. Then he whispered urgently, "Are you sure of what you say?"

"I saw the drill myself, this morning. It is the first step in the destruction of the Janissiary Corps, I swear upon Allah's sacred word. The talk in the taverns is of rebellion—the Sultan has proclaimed the changes in our uniforms were approved in the fatwa from the Mufti, but our brothers refuse to wear them. There is talk of storming the Topkapi—"

"Silence, soldier!" hissed Postivich. "Remember where you are. These are the palace grounds of the Sultan's favorite sister. You speak of mutiny as if there weren't a hundred Solaks within a sentry's call. You will lose your head for such talk."

"I will not be silent in fear. Your orta would surely pledge their blood to defend the traditions of the Janissaries and not play the Sultan's puppet, if they had your leadership. Without it, they may waver and ride against the Corps. Come back, Ahmed. Join us."

Ivan Postivich's heart leapt at the mention of the orta. His mind flashed on the days of battle, defending the kingdom of the Ottomans. This is what a janissary gives his life for—the honor of battle in the name of Allah. Not to play nursemaid to an ailing Princess.

"Surely not all the Janissary Ortas have pledged mutiny?"

"Only a handful will likely remain faithful to the Sultan. Of course the Solaks of the Sultan's bodyguard. The rest of us who are in Constantinople, more than thirty thousand, will force the Sultan to retract his scheme to dishonor the Janissary forces with the infidels' trappings."

Postivich listened, but the image of the resulting slaughter made him stiffen in revulsion. Janissary against janissary; yet another Sultan slaughtered. This would be the third Sultan's death in his lifetime and his stomach hardened at the thought.

"I must consider what you say. That path is surely a bloody course. Thousands upon thousands will die."

"As you please, Corbaci Kadir. But remember if you are not with us, you are against us, and your head shall scream for its shoulders. I will return in a few nights for your decision, for we want to know who is the enemy of the Ottoman Janissaries."

"I thank you for your trouble," said Postivich. "You should return to the barracks now or your absence will be noticed."

"One thing more," said the soldier, pulling Postivich closer. "Beware of the white eunuch who serves you. He is more crafty than you realize."

Ivan Postivich could smell garlic and fish on the janissary's breath, but the words he spoke were so earnest that he did not pull away.

"An eye to him," warned the blond soldier, touching his temple and then disappearing behind the thick hedge. In his wake, the jasmine flowers trembled, emitting a sweet scent.

Postivich stood amidst the heady flowers of Esma Sultan's gardens. He remembered the blood and corpses in the streets of Constantinople just five years earlier in the purge of the Greeks. Many innocents had been killed who were neither soldiers nor traitors to the Empire, merely recognizable targets and easy victims of the Janissaries' wrath. Postivich had seen Greek women and even young girls and boys defiled by the marauding soldiers, hungry for the blood and plunder of victory. He hated the baseness of the men who raped and killed. The centuries-old Ottoman army had been reduced to savagery akin to the dogs who roamed the streets of Istanbul.

Man eat man.

Kept idle without war, purpose, or honor, the Janissaries would turn on their master himself, and rip his corpse apart.

Bezm-i Alem walked the perimeter of the gardens, hoping to catch a glimpse of the drowning guard as he left the palace. Instead she saw a furtive movement from the corner of her eye. A fair-haired man moved quickly to hide behind a thick stand of calla lilies and rosebushes where the moon would not illuminate him. Bezm-i Alem acted as if she had not seen him and stopped to smell a rose in the moonlight and then passed on, her heart beating in her throat. She retreated towards the Serail in slow, measured steps, until she was beyond his vision. Then she circled back crouching in the darkness and waited for the corbaci to emerge from the palace.

When the giant stepped into the garden, the man hissed and whispered his name. Bezm-i Alem stole closer to them and knelt behind a broken fountain. Although she could not hear all of their conversation, she heard most of the fair-haired man's words.

He spoke of treason, of revolt, of murdering the Sultan. This was the gossip that the palace kitchen pages brought back daily from the market, of another janissary revolt like the one that resulted in the murder of Esma Sultan's cousin Selim III. This beardless man was a conspirator looking for allies.

And he meant to draw the corbaci into the plot.

She leaned her cheek against the cool smooth stone and listened. The stink of the dying water lilies and the still water made the girl fear the djinns that haunted pools of calm water, but she struggled to overcome her dread.

It wasn't clear to her whether the giant was in favor of the revolt or not, though he had more grievances against the Sultan than most. But Bezm-i Alem knew the Janissaries demanded loyalty from their brothers; to stand against them was as dangerous as treason against Topkapi. It was not clear who was fomenting the revolt. The Janissary Corps was like a great serpent coiled tight. It was difficult to find its head.

The slave girl hated this fair-haired stranger in the darkness. He would draw the corbaci back into the fray, into the deadly plan that would seal his destiny. The Sultan would have a legitimate reason at last to hunt him down and kill him if he were to breathe even one word of treason. Perhaps Topkapi had sent this man as a spy, she thought, to have Ahmed Kadir agree to help the Corps. He would be seized by the Solaks and hanged from the great plane tree in the Hippodrome, as a warning to the rest of the Janissaries.

She was sickened by the call to war, to death. Would there never be peace, a moment for life without the smell of blood and terror in this Empire? The Empire reeked of death, of hate and revenge, of one man thirsting for the blood of another. The ground had been torn open, red and gaping with new graves, while the women wept and saw no benefit or honor in their deaths—only the abyss of a painful absence that lasted a lifetime.

The harem girl wanted to protect this giant who stood in the darkness, who would surely be pulled into the plot and, in turn, murdered.

Then she thought of the Bektashi Sufis. They spoke of peace and the union of the faithful with Allah, yet were an integral part of the Corps. If the Janissaries are plotting a revolt, the Sufis would know. They would also be in danger, as the Janissaries' counsel and spiritual leaders.

Bezm-i Alem vowed in darkness to consult the Sufis. Perhaps these Bektashi could intervene in the kismet of the drowning guard.

The next morning was Friday, and the great majority of Istanbul attended the Friday Mosque. Ivan Postivich set off towards the reddish dome of Aya Sofya, rising high above the city.

Today the Sultan was to attend prayers in the Aya Sofya, instead of his preferred Fatih Mosque. The Aga of the Janissaries had called out reinforcements for this special visit. As many as two thousand Janissaries would stand guard outside the mosque as part of the royal procession. An order had been delivered to Ivan Postivich that he should join this troop. At many official occasions, he was called to stand in the front rank of soldiers, his towering presence lending prestige to the event, impressing visiting dignitaries.

The muezzin's call echoed through the streets of Istanbul.

*God is most great. I testify that there is no god but Allah. I testify that Mohammed is the Prophet of Allah. Come to Prayer! Come to salvation! There is no god but Allah!*

Postivich took his position among the Jannisary ranks outside the mosque, awaiting the arrival of the royal family. Standing just outside the portals of the Aya Sofya, he could soon see the straight lines of Solaks, the Sultan's private guard, preceding the Sultan on foot. No one could enter the mosque until the Sultan and his court had been admitted and were settled in their own private section.

The selamlik, the royal religious procession to the mosque, was a public spectacle repeated every Friday. Given the growing discontent within the Janissary ranks, this particular selamlik was laden with tension, as the Janissaries stood, silent and grim, immobile as stone outside the mosque.

The Solaks looked warily at the ranks of Janissaries, having heard the mutterings of unrest in the army that was stationed beyond the Topkapi walls. No violence was conceivable within the sacred walls of the Aya Sofya, as the sanctity of Allah was utmost. Nevertheless, the Solaks' eyes shifted uneasily under their white-plumed hats, their hands at the ready on their sharp daggers.

The Sultan was preceded by twenty horses, led by the spahis of the feudal lord cavalry, for at these moments no one was able to ride except the Shadow of God on Earth himself. The horses wore headstalls encrusted with diamonds, sapphires, turquoise, and pearls; leather saddles were covered by rich crimson velvet. Two pages hurried ahead carrying a golden bottle of scented water and a jeweled bowl, in order that the Sultan might wash before entering the mosque.

Postivich studied the one mounted horse in the distance, the sun sparkling off the silver and gold tack. It was highly unusual for the Sultan to ride anything other than a pure white stallion, but this one was dappled. He opened his eyes wide in disbelief against the fierce Turkish sun.

The Sultan rode Postivich's own mare, Peri.

Postivich lunged forward, but a strong hand gripped him, and then another and another. Someone grabbed him from behind, whispering harshly in his ear.

"Don't move. The Sultan hopes to incite you to treason so he can rid himself of you. Do not fall fool to his plan. When the time is right, we will stand shoulder to shoulder. This is not the time, brother."

Ivan Postivich nodded and the hands one by one released him. He choked back the bile in his mouth and watched the Sultan approach the mosque.

"The time shall come soon enough," whispered the voice in his ear.

Before dismounting, Sultan Mahmud II surveyed the phalanx of Janissaries. He reined his horse savagely so that Peri reared, and he was almost thrown. Recovering his composure, he heard a few laughs from the Turks who loved the unexpected, especially in their rulers. Mahmud used his crop to slash at the mare so that she jumped and kicked out, clearing a wide space around the Sultan and causing mutterings in the crowd.

He rode up to Postivich and said, "Oh, giant. I see you have not schooled this mare well enough for a Sultan. The old Master of the Horse would look at you in shame were he still alive. She will either obey her rider or become meat for the dogs of Istanbul."

The janissary opened his mouth to speak and shut it again.

"What is the matter, Kadir? Have you lost the command of the Ottoman tongue? The same as you have lost command of your cavalry orta, perhaps."

The mare began to neigh wildly, looking around for the other horses of the Kapikulu Orta.

"No, my Sultan. But I am forbidden to speak while I am posted on duty. Forgive me as I perform my guard dutifully, saving you from your enemies."

The Sultan eyed him to see if there was insolence about the man, but he stood as still as the Aya Sofya itself. Mahmud II grunted and wheeled the mare around to address the ranks of Janissaries, his dark beard shining in the morning light.

"My loyal Janissaries," he shouted, "defenders of the Ottoman Empire, the Koran, and the Sultan himself. We come to pray to Allah for the favor of his blessings. Come, enter the holy mosque of the Aya Sofya, the site that the Great Mehmed the Conqueror did wrest from the infidels and make sacred unto Allah.

"We pray to strengthen our holy Ottoman Empire with a common cause—let us worship Allah together in peace and in the brotherhood of our faith. A curse be on the head of any man who betrays the trust of God and the divine right of your Sultan and dares to incite insurrection within the shadows of Allah's sacred walls."

He eyed Ivan Postivich, his lip curling under his mustache.

Mahmud dismounted, leaving the dancing mare to a groom. He performed the perfunctory ablutions, the pages holding the heavy jeweled pitcher above the Sultan's hands and feet.

The Sultan entered his special place of worship, surrounded with latticed screens, high above the floor of the mosque. Once he was settled, the rest of the faithful entered below.

Ivan Postivich broke ranks with the call to mosque and strode up to the groom holding the mare.

"Stand back, Ahmed Kadir," warned a solak from the Topkapi.

"I want to see my mare."

"This mare belongs to Topkapi. You are not to approach any closer by orders of the Sultan."

Ivan Postivich called out soothing words in Serbo-Croat. The mare twisted her head away from the groom and whinnied at him, the whites of her eyes showing.

"Leave, Kapikulu," ordered a Solak, raising his scimitar. "Your devil Christian tongue is blasphemous in the environs of the holy mosque."

"They were Christian hands that built this palace to God, you ignorant Turk!" growled Postivich. "You are not fit to scoop the dung of my mare. May she make your wait tedious with her excrement!"

Postivich looked down on the Sultan's guard, a withering regard that made the soldier swallow in shame.

"I shall not pray for your miserable soul, Solak," he said. He turned and walked back to the courtyard of the mosque.

Before entering the holy place of Allah, the soldiers removed their shoes. There were rows of fountains outside the mosque where Ivan Postivich bathed his hot feet and dusty hands and face in preparation for the morning prayers. Beyond the plashing of the fountain, he could smell the boiled meat and vegetable broth served to the poor and ailing of Istanbul, just beyond the steps of the mosque. Crowds of the poor lingered close to the soup kitchens as the Turks took care of their less fortunate citizens, serving thousands of meals a day for those who could not feed themselves.

Entering the Aya Sofya was a holy experience in itself, thought Postivich. Throngs of devoted Muslims knelt shoulder to shoulder under its roof and the universe under the enormous dome was a vortex of light, surely shining from Allah himself.

As he knelt and prostrated himself in prayer, Postivich could not help but look around the walls and see the mosque for what it had originally been—the great Byzantine cathedral of the Aya Sofya of Constantinople.

His gaze traveled up through the vast space. Though the lower walls had been painted long ago after the fall of Constantinople to the Turks, the Muslim artisans had left one small fragment of original art high up on the vaulted ceilings

Two small winged angels offered something to a figure that he imagined might be the Virgin Mary, with only the very tip of her extended finger and a piece of gold halo still visible, the rest having been covered with a thick wash of plaster. As the janissary lowered his forehead to the floor, he considered this.

The Koran and the laws of Islam did not allow any figure of man or beast to be depicted in art, let alone in a mosque. But somehow the Turkish craftsmen had not obscured the two angels in this holy place of worship.

Ivan Postivich thought of the generations of Christians who had knelt on these very floors, worshipping their God. It struck him as curious how a sacred place could be sacked and conquered and on the same ground, within the same walls, another place of worship could be so easily consecrated, awash in the suras of the Koran.

Were not the ghosts and saints of the past hovering above the heads of the Ottomans now? Did those spirits condemn the Muslims? Or did they allow them peace as they honored the tradition of worship, in a different tongue, another religion?

Did not the Koran call Mary a "saintly woman"? Was Jesus not called a prophet? Perhaps the relics and bones of the holy saints would rest content with these honorable references and suffer the Arabic and Ottoman words of the faithful who prayed above their dusty remains.

But then even the Byzantines had incorporated pagan art into their cathedral to their Christian God. Next to the janissary rose the worn and ancient pillar from the Temple of the Sun in Athens. Justin the Conqueror had no qualms about introducing a treasure of beauty, crowning it with an intricately carved capital, supporting Christian walls with the glory that was once Greece.

Ivan Postivich was strangely at peace with the mixing of cultures and religions. Still, as he stared at what he imagined to be an obscured image of the Virgin, he felt a stirring deep within him that had nothing to do with the chanted prayers of the Koran.

He wondered what had happened to his sister.

He knew from the Janissaries who had been posted in the outer provinces that his mother had died not long after his circumcision, though she had been in the grave for nearly two years when the news finally reached him. It was said by a neighbor that she died of grief. He wondered if his sister had lived and of her fate. His eyes blurred with a haze of tears.

Without even realizing what he was doing, he rolled back on his knees from his prostrate position, glanced up again at the two angels and crossed himself.

When he realized what he had done, it was too late. The sea of men, wave upon wave, were so perfectly synchronized in their worship and he was up on his knees, his fingers touching his lips as he executed the genuflection that had been so natural until he was snatched from his village.

The janissary at his right glanced up at him. He gave an inscrutable look and then closed his eyes and pressed his forehead to the cold marble floor, praying towards the Mecca.

Postivich lowered his head to the ground again, a giant man trying to cover his mistake, pressing his palms to the floor—a heathen, among thousands of the faithful.

Esma Sultan gave Bezm-i Alem a withering look, her dark eyes scrutinizing the young woman's face. The harem girl jutted out her chin and held her mistress's eyes, refusing to succumb to humiliation or regret.

"What notion is this, to visit the Bektashi tekke? What plot is afoot, Bezm-i Alem?"

"I only wish to consult a Dede. Have you not said that the Sufis incorporate a universal love of mankind and womankind alike? That women worship alongside men and are regarded as equals. I want to see this order, hear their prayers. I want to learn how they are so different from the Sunnis and Shia."

"They will not allow you this. They guard their rituals from outsiders. You will learn nothing."

"But a Dede might speak to me. Especially were you to accompany me as the Sultan's sister. They could not refuse me if I carried your blessing."

Esma twisted her mouth into a knowing smile, much as an indulgent mother would do when scolding a pampered child.

"You hide the truth, Bezm-i Alem. You are searching for something else, not simply the knowledge of the Bektashi and their rituals."

"It is the corbaci," the harem woman admitted.

Esma Sultan drew a deep breath and let the air escape slowly.

"I suspected as much. Go on."

"Last night another janissary spoke to him in your gardens about . . . a rebellion against Topkapi."

Esma Sultan raised an eyebrow, then shifted her gaze to the windows that looked out over the Bosphorus.

"Of course. It was only a matter of time before that nightmare repeated itself. My brother does nothing to avoid a certain massacre. I suspect he welcomes the conflict. He has always hated the Janissary Corps. He will not stop until the streets of Constantinople are streaked with their blood."

"The Janissaries are counting their allies and ortas who will stand against the Sultan. Esma Sultan—are you in danger?"

"No," she said quietly. "I am the favorite daughter of Abdulhamid, and were I a male, the Janissaries would kill my brother and would install me immediately as Sultan. But as an Ottoman woman, all I have is my immunity to the Janissaries' seething hate of Topkapi."

Esma Sultan tapped a ruby ring with her fingernail and then studied her hennaed hand, twisting and turning it in the late afternoon light.

"Yes, you have my blessing. Consult the Dede," she said at last. "See what you can discover from the Sufis."

"O, thank you, Sultane."

"But on one condition," she said, watching me carefully. "Saffron must accompany you or else you may not leave the palace."

Saffron sat erect and silent across from Bezm-i Alem in the coach. They swayed with the motion of the carriage, as it rocked and creaked over the rutted roads. He avoided the young woman's eyes, but instead focused straight ahead.

Esma Sultan's eunuch was known for his impeccable manners and his fierce devotion to her. Bezm-i Alem was certain that he did not approve of this expedition, to see the Bektashi tekke. His mission was ostensibly to protect Esma Sultan's harem woman but he knew he was also to be a witness for Esma Sultan and see that Bezm-i Alem did not say or do anything untoward.

A bent old woman, her head uncovered, opened the portal of the circular tekke. She was dressed in faded blue and her grey hair was braided down her back.

"*Merhaba*. It is an honor to welcome emissaries of Esma Sultan to our tekke," she said, smiling through broken, brown-stained teeth. She showed her guests the tiled footbath at the entrance and they removed their shoes, performed ablutions, and slippered their feet.

A ritual was underway in the great round courtyard, where men and women alike swayed like wheat undulating in a breeze, dancing to the musicians, who in turn moved to their own music. They seemed unaware of each other, bound only by the rhythm of the music.

"What are they doing?" Bezm-i Alem whispered to Saffron.

"They are in communion with Allah."

Bezm-i Alem stared, her eyes drinking in the sight and marveling. She watched as their bodies rose and fell to the music, mystical in its tones.

"Come, let us follow our hostess," said Saffron, pulling the young woman from her reverie.

Bezm-i Alem could barely tear her eyes away from the spectacle. She had seen the Sufi whirling dervishes, but this dance was different. It was a gentler, more intimate movement and the dancers' faces emitted a glow of joy, not the frenetic frenzy of the dervishes she had seen in public.

"You will meet the Dede in the communal dining room," said the old woman, as she bowed. "We have prepared a repast for you."

The long table was laden with food. Whole roasted chickens, lamb kabobs, chicken pilafs, lamb cooked in eggplant, stuffed grape leaves. Luscious salads with cheese, ripe tomatoes, sweet cucumbers, and fresh mint leaves gleamed in dressings of golden-green olive oil. Sugared almonds and dried quince filled crystal glass plates.

But the dish that drew Bezm-i Alem's eye was the raisin and pomegranate studded zerde nestled in a brass bowl. A rice dish cooked with honey, rosewater, and cinnamon, zerde was a festive dish, usually only for weddings and formal celebrations. The Sufi hostess smiled, her tanned face wrinkling in dozens of deep creases.

"We the faithful feed the poor every day in our refectory. They are served grains and soups, fruits and bread, but for you, Bezm-i Alem, we have prepared a special feast."

"To honour our esteemed guest," said a man's voice. A small elderly man entered from an adjoining room. He wore a green cape, faded to a silver sheen. He was supported by a cane and hobbled slowly towards the group.

"It is a great honor to welcome you," he said. "I am Dede Mustafa."

"Esma Sultan sends her greetings to you, and in her name I thank you for your hospitality." Then Bezm-i Alem whispered, "I've come to ask you some questions in private, Dede."

"Of course, as you wish," he replied, his fingertips touching each other in a peak. "But could we tempt you with some of our Bektashi delicacies? Some wine, perhaps?"

Bezm-i Alem opened her mouth behind her veil, the cloth sticking to her lips as she gasped.

*Wine?*

Esma Sultan's reputation was known throughout the Empire, her indulgences and vices. But here, in the tekke, the spiritual lodge of the Bektashi, what blasphemy, offering her intoxicants, which the Prophet has expressly forbidden. This Dede must think her as the emissary of the evil himself.

Saffron moved close to Bezm-i Alem and whispered in her ear, under the folds of cloth.

"The Bektashi drink wine. He does not insult you or Esma Sultan in his offer. These are the Sufi ways."

"Thank you for your gracious offer," Bezm-i Alem said, recovering her composure. "Just a little barley water would be appreciated. And, of course, how could we refuse such a bountiful meal?"

Bezm-i Alem reclined on cushions, served by the unveiled woman, who smiled as she accepted small bowls of pilaf dishes and meat. The harem woman rarely ate meals in public and resented the inconvenience of pushing food up behind her veil. Too often the cloth retained the odor of the meal, scenting the air she breathed for hours later.

But she refused to remove it.

The Dede sat across from her on the cushions, enjoying a cucumber that he peeled with a knife and ate like fruit.

"Our tekke serves four hundred people a day," he said. "No one is turned away hungry. Ever. And that is thanks to gracious benefactors such as Esma Sultan who support our lodge and give charitable alms to allow us to help our fellow men and women."

Saffron nodded to Bezm-i Alem as the old woman gave her a cool glass of barley water.

"Dede, you have lived many years under the Sultans and always the Bektashi have been brothers and spiritual leaders of the Janissaries," she began.

Saffron suddenly stiffened.

The Dede pulled himself up straight against the cushions. His relaxed, affable face tightened and he clapped his hands three times. The old woman came running from the refectory, wiping her wet hands.

"Ayla, tell Abdul to secure the entries. See that no one enters or disturbs us. Ask the musicians to continue playing until after Bezm-i Alem leaves."

Saffron lifted his eyebrow in wary approval, but his shoulders remained tight and his eyes alert.

"Forgive me, Bezm-i Alem, for the interruption, but the mention of the Janissaries at such tense times can be quite dangerous."

Bezm-i Alem was aware of Saffron's deep and steady breaths as he stood next to her. He fastened his gaze at the main entry.

It was the mix of cultures and faith that made the Bektashi so appealing to the Janissaries, the Dede explained. Through the devshirme, boys from all over the far reaches of the Ottoman Empire, from Egypt to the lands of the Balkans and to the border of Russia were gathered and brought back to Constantinople to train as soldiers and serve the Sultan. Some came quiet and shaking, other shrieked and cried, some died of grief. No matter their emotional state, those who lived would all become Janissaries or be sold as slaves.

Boys were taken from their homes, their culture, language, and their faith. They longed for traditions, these Christians, of the Blessed Mother, who would love and protect them, as their mothers had. Their souls cried out for a woman.

Bektashi tradition revered Fatima, the daughter of Mohammed, as well as the Virgin Mary, giving the lonely boys the comfort of a blessed mother in a strange land.

"Many are drawn to our mysticism because of the similarities with Christianity," the Dede said. "They find comfort in the confession of sin, drinking of wine, and sharing of bread. Dispensation from the five prayers also appeals to those who are at war and cannot face Mecca on their knees, evoking Allah's name."

"But then," Bezm-i Alem ventured, "do you have influence with the Janissaries if you are their spiritual advisor?"

Dede Mustafa's dark eyes glinted with understanding.

"If you mean do we have the power to intervene in their course of total and inevitable destruction, the answer is no. This is their kismet and the Sultan's. We cannot intercede in fate," he said, shrugging his shoulders and lifting his open palms up to the sky. "Even if it means great suffering for all."

His quiet words and gesture conveyed his absolute understanding. There was no point in pursuing this line of questioning and possibly endangering the Dede and his tekke.

"Saffron, would you advise the footman that we are ready to return to the palace?" Bezm-i Alem said, rising. Then she took Dede Mustafa's hand in hers. It felt warm and soft, much softer than her own.

Bezm-i Alem thought of her father who had died when she was an infant. She had never experienced kindness from a man.

Dede Mustafa did not draw away his hand, but she felt his fingers moving tentatively against her palm, exploring her grasp.

His eyes opened in surprise. Bezm-i Alem wondered if it was because she had touched him, or if he felt the contrast of his supple skin against her callused hands, certainly not the hands of a harem woman. Surely he would wonder what caused her to have the rough skin of a farmer, and the daring to thrust her hand in his.

He studied her face and looked deep into her eyes.

"I see you have an unusual kismet," he said slowly. "I will not forget your visit to our tekke or your concerns. You have my word on this. May you go in peace and with Allah's protection, blessed be in the name of the Prophet."

That night, as he was admitted to the interior chambers of the Sultaness, Postivich sensed a brooding darkness in the mood of Esma Sultan. He remembered how she had smiled just two days before and he realized with surprise how much he craved to see her lips arch up again, lifting his heavy spirit.

But tonight was different. She was looking out the windows, her eyes searching for the first sliver of new moon. As he entered he brushed shoulders with Emerald, the eunuch, who wore a stiff mask of hatred and fury.

The little man said nothing but hurried down the corridor.

"It is the Sultan's moon," she murmured, as Postivich entered. "A thin-bladed scimitar carving a swath across the universe."

Ivan remained standing, waiting for an invitation to sit.

"Walk with me in the garden, tonight," said Esma Sultan. "I cannot bear to be confined to this room on such a beautiful night."

The Solaks hurried ahead to take their positions at regular intervals around the garden. They whistled to the sentries on the palace walls to alert them that the Princess was now outside and they should be even more alert for assassins.

Two young girls ran ahead, lighting torches and lanterns. Servants fluttered through the corridors, carrying linen, shawls, and flasks of lemon and barley water in case any should appeal to the Sultaness. The head of the female orchestra was alerted so that music would be at the ready. The boatmen were roused from their mats, for it was entirely possible that a midnight sail would be required.

The palace was in an uproar at the whim of the Sultaness. Nothing was simple in a royal Ottoman household.

The Sultaness waved away offers of music, refreshment, and handmaidens.

"I want the Solaks to keep their distance from me," she warned Saffron. "I want to speak to Ahmed Kadir in privacy."

"Of course, Your Highness," said the eunuch, bowing. "But for your protection, I shall accompany you—"

"You shall do nothing of the kind, Saffron!" she snapped.

The tall man bowed again, backing away.

"I will clap my hands if I need assistance," she said, a little more kindly. "Please keep a distance of twenty paces or more. Come, janissary. Do not be so heavy-footed and slow."

Postivich was surprised how long and quick her stride was.

As they descended into the gardens through an arbor of jasmine and sweet vine, Postivich said, "Forgive me, Sultane, but you seem preoccupied."

She did not answer until they reached a large fountain, illuminated by flickering torches. Dipping her fingers into the rose-petal strewn waters, she finally replied.

"I have reason to believe that there are spies in my palace, Janissary Kadir. Spies from the Topkapi who desire your death."

"It seems I am not considered a friend of the Ottomans," he said, sitting across from the Princess on the rim of the fountain. He watched her chase a petal through the ripples of the water with her hand. "And why do you concern yourself with what spies tell your brother?"

The Princess looked at him through the soft light of the lanterns.

"I have promised you protection, and I will use all my power to keep my promise. Such is an Ottoman's word."

She hesitated.

"I do not know how I feel about you, Ahmed Kadir," she said. "But I have placed some trust in you, for there is a curious truth to your hatred of me. You came to me in loathing and disgust. There was honesty there. I can still see it in your eyes. The moment you decide to betray me, I will see it."

"How can you be so sure?"

"Your blue eyes are the same color and depth as my mother's. I could always judge the truth of what she said by their reflection. I could detect a lie by the way the color changed quickly, like a cloud passing over the waters of the Bosphorus. Eyes like yours cannot betray me, even if they try."

Her own eyes now sought him in the darkness, and he looked into their depths.

He reached out to her cheek, with the same impulse and instinct that had made him cross himself earlier that morning. His fingers brushed her skin and he cradled her fine chin in his palm.

She did not pull back, but closed her eyes. He gasped as a chill rushed up his spine, and seized him by the throat.

"Stop, Ahmed Kadir. Put your hand down at once," she whispered.

"Only if you command it," he said.

She turned away from him, leaving his hand empty in the night air.

"I do command it, if only for your sake. Your impulse is not worth your death."

He dropped his hand to his side, struggling to keep his body under control. Once engaged in a battle, he could not easily disengage. His whole body trembled and his mind could only focus on reaching for her and pressing her soft bosom hard against his mouth. He realized he did not know how to make love, only to seize a woman and satisfy his urges quickly and violently.

"Tonight I want to tell you more of what happened to little Sophie."

Ivan Postivich watched her hands continue to toy with the petals. He did not care about the little girl in the harem; his body was tense with lust and a woman's words now were like nagging flies, bothersome and an unwanted distraction from his physical needs.

She lifted her chin to see that he was listening, as if she were unaware of his impulses.

He suspected she toyed with him as she moved a short distance away on the rim of the fountain.

"I did what I said I would do," she began. "I asked my father for Sophie's release from the Serail—to become my servant forever."

"You cannot imagine how hard it was for me to see the Sultan, my father, in private. The women of the Serail are at his disposal and pleasure. Should he want to visit his children, he will visit the Serail himself. To request a private audience with the Royal Ottoman Sultan, as a young woman—impossible!

"This is where my association with Emerald began. He was one of the many young eunuchs who supervised and served us. I knew he also served regularly in the men's hamam, serving my father, brothers, and cousins. I took a chance and asked him.

"'Emerald. I must ask you a favor.'

"'Your desire is my command,' he replied.

"He was an ambitious man from the start and my father's favor towards me had ignited his interest.

"'I want you to request a private audience for me with my father.'

"He raised his eyebrows and his thick lips parted. 'How am I to do this?'

"'When you are attending my father in the harem, you will ask him gently if he would consider it. Tell him—tell him there is a secret that I cannot share in front of my mother. He will respect that, I should think, and it will make him curious.'

"Emerald nodded, though his face showed great doubt. 'And if he should judge me impertinent?'

"'You will simply say that you were forced to do so by my royal hand, his favorite daughter! He will absolve you of all.'

"The eunuch nodded again, but he looked at me still in doubt. 'Sultaness—I shall carry out your order, but you may learn a difficult lesson.'

"'What is that?'

"'A father's love may be unconditional, but a Sultan's is not.'

"With that he bowed, asking permission to leave.

"Despite Emerald's warning, he did deliver the message to my father in the hamam. At first, the Sultan's annoyance was clear and Emerald feared for his head. But then the Sultan decided he was delighted that I was coming to him for what he supposed was advice.

"'She would have made a stately prince,' he told the Vizier, in front of the eunuch. 'She knows what gossips the women of the Serail are, and comes to me for wisdom. Had she been born a male, she would have governed this Empire with an iron fist.'

"So there was great confusion and disappointment when the Sultan heard my request.

"I was far too big to crawl up in his lap now. I stood straight and bowed low, as I had been taught by my mother.

"'Speak, my daughter,' he said. 'You have been granted your private audience.'

"'But the Solaks,' I complained. 'And the Great Vizier. I requested to speak to you in private.'

"'How little you know!' he roared laughing. He gestured to his Great Vizier who nodded to indulge him, though I could see that the Vizier was not happy about my presence in the throne room, reserved for men only. 'Speak, Esma!' my father commanded. 'I am very busy today with ambassadors from France and Russia. I cannot make them wait much longer without risking war.'

"'I want you to free Sophie, my Sultan father,' I blurted out.

"'What?'

"'If not free her, I want you to give her to me as my handmaiden.'

"My father drew a great breath, and for a few seconds I thought he would fail to expel it. He finally smiled and looked at me as he always did. To him I was a charming, precocious child. Merely a girl, like a pretty charm on a bracelet.

"His eyes looked old but delighted to find innocence in my own.

"'Haven't I given you enough gifts, daughter?' he asked, his voice soft. 'Sophie is part of my harem, Esma. You must not ask me for that which I cannot grant.'

"'She is my friend,' I told him. 'And she is terrified of this place.'

"'Then we must make her feel at ease. You women in the harem should comfort her for I only want harmony in the Serail. I shall talk to your mother about this.'

"This was the last thing I wanted.

"'But you are the Sultan! It is within your power to release Sophie! I beg of you, reconsider. I could buy her from you, father!'

"I was thirteen years old and, despite Emerald's warning, I had mistaken the Sultan for a father who would indulge me everything. What I learned that day was that my father had granted my indulgences only to please himself. He had given me a palace and parties and fine clothes because it gave him pleasure.

"To lose a beautiful virgin in his harem would give him no pleasure at all.

"'Esma, it is time you grew up. My daughter, a harem is not something I barter with, not even with my own blood. By Mohammed's word, I have pledged to care for these women. No harm shall come to Sophie. She will be well cared for and one day have the riches and prestige your mother now enjoys. Her future is immensely better than it ever would have been in the wild regions of the North. Now you must run along, back to the Serail. Emerald, escort the Esma Sultan back to her apartments.'

"That night Sophie was moved from our apartments to the Valide's wing.

"'It will be better this way,' said my mother, trying to comfort me.

"I looked into her clear, blue eyes and saw a shadow pass over their depths. I knew she was lying. But I knew, she too had come to love Sophie, despite her efforts to distance herself.

"A week later, a special feast was celebrated in the Serail. I was to be seated on the right of my father, along with all the other royal princesses and Valide. My brother Mahmud and cousin Selim sat at his left.

"Several women from the harem played the old Turkish music that is rarely heard today. Their fingers on the sitar were graceful and their music full of emotion, bringing tears to the eyes of many who listened.

"Next there were dancers. It was rumored that my father preferred the lascivious dancing of young boys to that of his harem, but I was to learn that my father liked both sexes, and, despite his advanced age, was eager for new conquests. He was a Sultan who loved arts, dance, music—anything that expressed grace.

"The old Valide Sultan, my grandmother and mother of the Sultan, supervised the dancers. She had impeccable standards. It was she who chose the silks and bodices they would wear and sniffed the perfumes to find the most sensuous. She attended the dance practices daily and had harsh words for any girl who did not put forth her best effort.

"The girls had practiced hour upon hour. The best could undulate their breasts at the same time they performed rhythmic pulsations with their bellies, even while curling and unfurling their hips.

"I was shocked to see what Sophie had learned. Despite her slight girlish body, she had mastered the Turkish dance with a style all her own, which astonished us all.

"Perhaps it was because her hips were still slight that she could angle and pivot them, canting them this way and that with an innocence that the bigger girls couldn't. Her bodice was stuffed with cotton gauze, draped discreetly with silk, for her breasts were no bigger than walnuts.

"She was meant to show her fine promise tonight for the years to come when she became a woman.

"The most lascivious dancer was a Circassian beauty named Rushdah with violet eyes and high firm breasts. She was eighteen and danced with a knowing look, clear and direct, even over her yasmak. At the end of the dance, she saucily removed it in front of the Sultan, keeping his eye until she was ushered out of the room.

"The Valide watched her dancers with pride, sliding a glance towards her son every now and again. It was her job to ensure that there be as many heirs as possible for the throne. She noticed how my little brother, Mahmud, eyed Sophie, who so recently had been a playmate—before his circumcision.

"The Valide Sultan laughed with delight at his interest, for she had been demanding of Sophie and was happy to see this little peasant girl would some day turn into a beautiful woman with the graces of a worthy concubine or even a wife.

"Still, Mahmud was only a boy, and third in line for the throne. First was his cousin Selim and then his half brother

Mustafa. It was highly unlikely that young Mahmud would ever reside permanently at Tokapi and enjoy such a fabulous harem.

"Both the Valide and I were wrong that night. She was wrong about Mahmud and I was wrong about my father and his love.

"'Hatice! Come to me, my daughter,' cried the Sultan, though she was not really his daughter; she was my cousin, sister to Selim. 'It is your turn to play my favorite.'

"I stood stunned, my hands heavy at my side. I could neither lift them to my mouth nor could I disguise my expression of astonishment and horror. Was I not his favorite, always? Yet this was my cousin and my father had always treated his nieces and nephews with indulgences, even if Selim was housed in the Top-kapi Cage most of the time. Even my father who dearly loved his dead brother's son, could not willingly invite a rebellion, so he kept his nephew secure in his prison except for special events. He knew how to rule his Empire and he knew how to control his family— just as he was now teaching me a lesson in the meaning of love and power.

"'Esma, close your mouth this instant. You look the fool,' whispered my mother.

"'Come, Hatice. Sit at my side,' said my father. 'We will watch another dance. You and I shall pick the best of the dancers, my dear.'

"Hatice was a silly girl and the unprecedented praise went to her head. What she did not think about was that the decision she made would decide the destiny of the concubines and the Sultan's favor. She thought of it only as a game and an event that would bring her pleasure.

"She would decide which dancer would sleep in his bed.

"The dance kadin clapped her hands and reassembled the dancers. Within seconds, the music resumed and the dancers whirled across the floor. Hatice, clapped her hands along with the music, and my father nodded his head.

"'Come closer, dancers,' he said, for aged as he was, his eyes had grown weak. 'Let me see your graceful moves at closer proximity.'

"The dancers pressed close to him, so that he could examine the sinews of their bodies and see the beads of sweat on their abdomens. The Circassian woman, Rushdah, flexed her muscles and with a quick jerk of her hip, flicked perspiration into my father's face. Her impertinence was rewarded by a slow smile, as the Sultan took his white handkerchief and slowly drew it across his face, lingering on his lips.

"He dropped the kerchief at her feet, signaling his desire for her to visit his bed that night.

"Hatice looked up in dismay. 'Was I not to decide a beautiful dancer, Uncle?' she asked, her voice shrill with disappointment.

"'Forgive me, daughter. I forgot my promise.' He waved for his servant to provide him another handkerchief. He handed it to my foolish cousin.

"'It is true, I have kept you from your pleasure of choosing. You shall double my pleasure!' laughed my father, and he nodded to the young princes, Selim and little Mahmud, that this was how a royal Sultan behaved.

"She received it with great enthusiasm and looked about the room at the dozen or more dancers. To be favored by the Sultan was the most fervent wish of a member of a harem; to be ignored for very long could mean banishment from Topkapi and an unknown destiny.

"I could see each one of the young women widen their eyes in supplication to the Princess. *Please, please,* their eyes whispered so loud that it seemed there was a chant as loud as the muezzin's from the minaret. Fortunes and futures could be decided if the Sultan enjoyed their company in his bed. If not favored, sooner or later the girls would become more menial servants, doing laundry or merely serving food for the rest of their lives.

"Hatice threw the handkerchief far into the room. It fell on the back row of dancers, at Sophie's feet.

"'She is the best, father,' said my cousin. 'None of the others has the grace of our Sophie.'

"There was a murmur within the harem and the Head Eunuch struck his staff twice on the ground to silence the women.

"The Sultan nodded. 'I will listen to the wisdom of the Princess Hatice. Sophie, pick up the handkerchief, my child.'

"Sophie remained still as stone, looking at the piece of white cloth as if it were a venomous serpent.

"'Do as you are told,' commanded the Valide, vexed at the girl's hesitation.

"Sophie bent down and picked up the handkerchief with trembling hands. She tucked it into her bodice, cloth against rustling cloth. She ventured a look at me, furtive and horrified.

"I stood aghast, my heart beating in my throat and temples. My mother motioned me to remain quiet and for the first time in my life, I did as I was told.

"'No, father,' I whispered to myself, for I could do nothing. 'Not her.'

"In my dreams, I saved her. I rescued Sophie, before my father could touch her and I brought her, still a child virgin, to this very palace, where she and others like her would be protected from probing hands of unwelcomed men. But these were just a child's dreams and I was forced to grow up very quickly after that night.

"My mother stroked my arm and tried to smile, though she, too, was touched with emotion and thought Sophie, at age ten, to be far too young to entertain my father.

"The reaction in the Serail was mixed. The women, especially the older ones, had seen all sorts of behavior in their years at the harem and the decision was only a momentary diversion.

"'Sophie's hips are too small to give a man pleasure, and her breasts are like rosebuds. He shall grow impatient with her.'

"'The Sultan will appreciate this. He takes young boys no older than Sophie as lovers. A small breast and slim hips will please him.'

"'She has not started her menses. He should let this closed bud bloom and then enjoy her nectar.'

"'Still the sainted Aisha, wife of the Prophet, was betrothed at age six. Mohammed took her to his bed when she was nine. If this is right by the one who gave us the Koran and God's word, it is example enough for the Sultan. Who has the right to criticize the Prophet?'

"My mother started to answer, then pressed her lips tight. Her eyes sought Nakshidil's. Some silent message was communicated between the two, though neither spoke a word.

"And so the talk drifted on until I could hear no more. I remained alone in my royal apartments, in the bed where my adopted sister normally slept with me. Late that night, as I lay crying on my cushions, Emerald knocked at my door.

"'Your Royal Highness, I bring you this,' he said. 'I come at great risk under the order of the Prince Mahmud and am asked to bring your reply.'

"I admitted Emerald into my apartments and opened the folded and sealed Italian paper with the stamp of the Ottoman prince."

*My Dear Sister,*

*I, too, am horrified at Sophie's destiny, as is my mother who calls the Sultan's decision barbarous. She will not be comforted by the story of Aisha, and says that what the Prophet did does not excuse our father.*

*She pronounced such blasphemy that I dare not write of it in fear that my mother will be executed as an infidel. She, unlike the others in the Serail, still harbors her pagan faith, though she knows so many passages of the Koran and says her prayers five times a day and in all other ways, acts as a faithful servant to Islam. She is so educated in so many matters, but childlike in her devotion to the infidel's creed.*

*I have heard of your pleas to our father and think of your courage. I know Sophie is a sister to you. My mother has shared a secret sura with me, one we were forbidden to read in our Koran studies. She refers to it as the "Forgotten Verse of Women" although it is from Mohammed's mouth—she says that Mohammed loved the goodness of women as much as men's and it was his ambitious followers who destroyed the balance between male and female. These words trouble me just as much as her devotion to Mary, for surely she will go to hell.*

*"These are the exalted Females, and verily their intercession is to be hoped for." She has embroidered this verse onto the handkerchief I enclose and begs you to give it to Sophie.*

*I cannot deny her anything. I love her with all my heart.*

*Your adoring brother,*

*Mahmud*

"I knew that Mahmud was secretly in love with Sophie. His young heart ached with love and he was wretched, thinking of his father touching the object of his devotion. Yet, there was nothing he could do.

"My brother would be cursed with his obsession for Sophie for the rest of his life.

"I woke up the next morning with the songbirds singing in the trees next to my window. The air seemed soft with spring and I thought perhaps my father would hear my reason in his sleep and consent to allow Sophie to mature and delay her appearance in his bed.

"But as I approached the hamam, I immediately saw that I was mistaken. Sophie was conveyed by the Valide herself, who would supervise the day-long ritual of bathing, depilation, and henna tattooing that was compulsory before a visit to the Sultan's bedchamber. Her face was painted and her eyebrows were extended over her nose to look as if they met in the middle, as is the style of beauty in the Serail.

"As Sophie was being bathed, the Valide spoke to my mother.

"'This is an indulgence on my son's part,' she complained. 'Let me sit there next to you, for my aged legs bother me. I'm far too old for this nonsense.'

"The Valide lowered herself slowly to the marble bench while the servant girls served iced lemon-barley water to the two ladies.

"'I was thirteen when the Sultan's father first took me to his bed. But this was different. I had already had my fourth menses. Sophie is just ten and not yet a woman.

"'This is a waste of my son's seed. The girl cannot conceive a child! It is merely an indulgence,' she repeated. 'Haven't I been a good mother in procuring the most beautiful women of the Empire? Why does he choose this yearling to take to his bed?

"'What spills on the sheets could have been better used on one of the older girls. This girl steals my son's virility and my grandchildren!'

"The old woman rubbed her aching hands.

"'Have you spoken to Sophie about her expected conduct tonight?' asked my mother.

"'No. I ask that you perform that task. I fear I might frighten her with talk of her duties in the bedroom. You and Esma are family to her, it will be better for you to tell her. Please remember to tell her not to touch the scar on the side of his right thigh. It still pains him from time to time. Ah, but here I am telling you something that you know better than I! You see, I really am too old to oversee my son's harem.'

"My mother bowed. Yes, she would prepare Sophie."

Ivan Postivich could not sleep that day. He felt some sense of bother, like a worm digging deep in his soul, that left his mind unquiet and incapable of taking his rest. He blamed the boys who swept the rooms as if it were they who disturbed his sleep. He cursed the straw mattresses, he cursed the heat. Sweat beaded on his forehead and ran rivulets into his eyes, stinging them with salt.

He could not stop thinking about Sophie. He arrived early in the audience hall and paced the tiled passage, waiting for Esma Sultan to call for him.

Esma Sultan saw the harrowed look on his face when he entered. He sighed and bent down on his knees to approach her.

"Stand, Corbaci Kadir. I cannot abide seeing you crawl to me like a insect."

Ivan Postivich nodded and rose to his feet.

"I have been busy all day, making preparations for my brother the Sultan's birthday celebration. It shall be a fête to equal no other. Ah, and the cirit—"

Ivan Postivich's eyes opened wide. "Cirit?"

"Ah, now I have your attention. Yes, a game of cirit amongst the Kapikulu Cavalry to start off the festivities."

Esma Sultan watched the drowning guard's face fall as he realized he could not ride.

"What would you give to play again?" asked Esma Sultan.

"Forgive me, Sultaness. You play with me, like a cat with a mouse."

"Anything is possible if I will it," she answered, her eyes lingering on his face. She looked up at the painting of the Persian princess and harem girls playing polo.

"Do I bore you with my stories of little girls?" she asked.

"No," he said quietly. "No."

Esma Sultan drew in her breath and slowly exhaled.

"I am pleased. I cannot say why, but as I unburden my memory of such miserable memories, I breathe more calmly and sleep as if I were a child again."

She then took a sip of barley water and continued the tale of Sophie.

"When Sophie emerged from the hamam, her wrists and hands were colored with fine, curving lines and dots of henna. We dressed her in silks and braided her long blond hair with pearls, pinning it up with clips of sapphires and diamonds.

"Every now and then, her body shook and the pearls clicked against one another. She was beautiful, but she was still very much a child.

"'Esma, send the servants away and open the fountain. I must speak in confidence.'

"I ordered the eunuch and slaves attending us to leave. Knowing that my mother must speak of the Sultan's bed, they complied quickly. I opened the fountain pipes myself, so that no one could eavesdrop on our conversation.

"It was then I gave my mother the embroidered handkerchief. She clasped it to her heart and praised Nakshidil as if she were her sister.

"'This shall give all of us strength,' she said, tracing the delicate threads of the linen.

"She sat beside Sophie. 'Calm yourself, daughter,' she said. 'It is really not bad and the old Sultan does not linger in finishing his task. It will be over before you can recite the full rosary.'

"'Mother!' I exclaimed in horror. 'What blasphemy! Say a prayer to Allah before you are cursed forever.'

"My mother's eyes flashed at me and I could see their depths. How could I have lived my life with this woman and not known?

"She smiled wearily as if relieved to finally share her secret.

"'Esma, I was cursed when I was kidnapped at your age from my home in Circassia. I have brought you up to be a good Muslim and an Ottoman princess, but you must grant me the comfort of my own religion. And this girl is being forced to become a woman before her time, which is a sin in the eyes of any god. She shall take her religion in her heart to comfort her, or she shall die of shame. If you love me and you love her, you will allow us to speak to our God of birth and baptism.'

"I, who was brought up reciting sura after sura of the Koran by heart, merely gaped. I was torn between my love for Sophie and the religion that was as much a part of me as my bones and blood. I could not believe that my mother still clung to a pagan faith and I was embarrassed for her ignorance, but hungry for the secrets she had buried so well in her heart.

"'But Mother! You will not enter heaven!' I wailed.

"'What heaven does the Ottoman faith promise for woman? I shall die a Christian as I was born and another woman, the Virgin—be she virgin or not, for certainly I do not care—shall comfort me in death in a way that no man could.'

"Without hesitating further, my mother took Sophie's hand.

"'When you enter the Sultan's room you must remove your clothes slowly and gracefully, taking time to turn so that he may see you entirely. His eyes are weak so stay close to him but not so close that he grabs you.

"'When you are finally undressed, bow and kiss his feet. Linger there, for he has a weakness for that touch, and you will make quick work of his arousal and pleasure. He may beg you to move up his body, but ignore his pleas until he takes you by the hair.'

"Then my mother went on to explain to Sophie how she should proceed in the Sultan's bedroom. She explained secrets no child should ever know.

"I heard her say, 'You are to take it in your mouth.'

"I stood as still as marble, repulsed, fascinated.

"'At this time, you are to move it between your lips as if you were savoring a sherbet. This will quickly arouse him, so the ugly deed will finish more quickly.'

"Sophie was pale, but she listened, unblinking. I stared in horror, marveling at her composure and her concentration on my mother's words

"'I know this will repulse you, terrify you. You must begin the rosary in your heart. This is your silent strength that will see you through this hour.

"'Imagine the Holy Mother above you, forgiving and blessing you, for she loves most dearly women in desperate need.

"'And you will endure, Sophie. We all do. I will bathe you myself when you return.'

"I covered my mouth. I whispered 'Allah,' as my stomach convulsed and then stared silently at my own mottled vomit on the marble floor."

# Chapter 8

The janissary listened to Esma Sultan's tale and although he was aroused, he was also bewildered.

"And so women of the Royal Serail approach the Sultan like whores in a brothel?"

Esma Sultan lifted her chin, her eyes challenging him.

"Did you not expect it? They are slaves, after all, no matter how many jewels they possess or how many eunuchs serve them. Slaves to men. My knowledge of sex before this moment was confined to gossip—and watching the eunuch and the fat woman in the hamam. I could not imagine my little friend Sophie subjected to such filth at the hands of my own father."

Ivan Postivich grunted. "What happened to the girl, then?"

Esma Sultan lifted an eyebrow.

"At last I have your attention, Biscuit. Sophie just stared, wide-eyed, as if she had realized the horror in her nightmares already. She nodded and did not cry at all as my mother finished her instructions. Then my mother did one more thing to amaze me.

"Kneeling on the carpets of our apartment, my mother sought a crack in a loose tile near the fountain. She tugged at it, bringing up crumbles of clay and mortar. In the space beneath the tile, she found a small piece of red silk. Untying the bundle, she picked up a tiny crucifix dangling on a pure gold chain.

" 'This is for you, Sophie,' she said. 'I no longer need it to remember my faith. But you may.'

"She replaced the tile and dipped her fingers in the fountain, scrubbing away the dirt on the tips of her snow-white fingers. Then she held up the white linen handkerchief from Nakshidil and spoke in Serbo-Croatian so that Sophie could fully comprehend.

" 'Long ago, the faith of the pagan Arabs, Persians, and those of this land embraced women and their gentle natures; some deities were female. Mohammed spoke highly of women. He honored them and made the Arab men pledge to protect them.

" 'The Prophet was born in Mecca, but they rejected him there. He fled to Medina, forming his own religion and followers. But his heart always belonged his his homeland.

" 'With his success in Medina, the Prophet longed to persuade the people of Mecca to leave their worship of Diana of the sun and of Al-ilah, the moon, and embrace Allah. The Arabs of Mecca were steadfast in their adoration of the female and especially the three stars that accompanied the moon, the three gentle daughters of Diana and Al-ilah. It was the star Al-Lat who interceded for them in their prayers to Al-ilah.'

" 'The crescent moon and the star,' I thought. It was at that moment that I realized there was some bone of truth to my mother's ravings. The sliver of moon and its adjacent star are the symbols of our land, even today, despite religion's every attempt to purge them.

"My mother turned towards me with those clear blue eyes of hers. She saw that I was beginning to understand her at last.

"She continued speaking to Sophie, although I knew now that she was speaking for me to hear as well. 'The people of Mecca cast Mohammed out, for he was provoking unrest. He was banished from Mecca and settled in Medina with his followers. Still he could not abide the loss of his homeland and longed to bring the people of Mecca into the fold of his newfound religion, so that they might hear the word of the true God.

"'It was then that Gabriel came to him and spoke words that praised the deified women. The angel said'—and now my mother read the words embroidered on the handkerchief—'*These are the exalted Females, and verily their intercession is to be hoped for.*'

"'When Mohammed spoke Gabriel's good words to the people of Mecca, they rejoiced, for it seemed his faith embraced their own sacred daughters and Diana herself. Had not an angel of God pronounced as much? They feasted and kissed the earth, swearing their allegiance to him, for this prophet had surely spoken the words of Allah himself. An old man, too crippled to prostrate himself, took dirt in his fists and rubbed it over his chest, declaring allegiance to Allah.

"'When the Prophet returned to Medina and told his men about his encounter with Gabriel and the words spoken of Al-Lat, they were aghast. They had pledged themselves to Mohammed the Prophet, and the one God Allah, but the idea of women interceding in the matters of men challenged the patriarchy. Before the appearance of Gabriel to the Prophet, there had been no talk of a goddess that would come between them and Allah, the Father. What talk was this of heavenly women, of intervention? Surely the words that Mohammed had heard were a trick of the devil and not the words of God's Angel, but of Satan himself.

"'What happened then is unrecorded. But it is clear that men's pride and outrage eroded the word of Gabriel. We believe the men who surrounded the Prophet convinced him to retract his own words, despite his deep love of his wives and women of the world.'"

Esma Sultan turned and smiled in scorn. "The pressure of politics can change the course of history, and even the word of God.

"'According to my mother, very little time passed before Mohammed retracted his words. He declared he been tricked by Satan, for how could women ever be elevated to a status equal to the male? Women were clearly to be governed under the rule and guidance of men.

"'The new converts in Mecca must now obliterate these verses from their hearts and creed and forget the gentle star of Al-Lat. There was no God but God and the female deities must be purged. The people, having bowed to Mohammed's god, were obliged to accept his retraction, for they were now of the Faithful and had sworn allegiance to the new God. These words extolling the virtue of women were struck forever from most versions of the Holy Koran, and only whispered from mother to daughter, passed generation to generation. And the holy hadiths, which recorded Mohammed's life and included the verses, were scorned as blasphemous.

"'It was that day that ambitious men pulled a dark veil around womankind, rejecting the word of Gabriel and their own Prophet Mohammed. The Prophet ensured that women's security and some legal rights were respected in the Ara world. But Mohammed could no longer laud the shining star of Al-Lat and the intercession of womankind. The old ways and customs were buried under the new code of Islam, Woman subject to Man's mercy and patriarchy, forever more.' My mother allowed herself a weary smile.

"'These words, that could have given such comfort to all womankind were branded as "The Satanic Verses" to drive away any man or woman who would dare embrace them. Yet it is this very comfort and wisdom that we so urgently seek, when men take our sons to the battlefield and carelessly spill the lifeblood of our wombs in hatred and violence.

" 'What irony that Gabriel—that same angel—had announced great tidings six hundred years earlier to Mary of Bethlehem. But now the men of Medina swore it was Satan who had spoken through Gabriel's voice when the Prophet first heard the suras that praised women as men's equals. Perhaps only a woman can really hear and receive with glad tidings an angel's good news.

" 'And the faithful still circle the great moonstone of Mecca to this day.' "

Ivan Postivich tilted his head. He clenched and unclenched his hand in the silence.

"But what of Sophie?" he said finally.

Esma Sultan nodded.

"My mother pressed the handkerchief into Sophie's hand, closing her fingers around the girl's little fist.

" 'Take these words, my child, and remember the truth. For we women are here to comfort you and intercede as best we can. You are one of us, now.'

"And so Sophie was escorted to my father's bedchamber a little past midnight. She appeared calm and clear-eyed. As she was led away from the Serail, I placed her favorite horse carving in the fold of her tunic and looked away.

"It was the last time I saw her beauty."

There was a long moment of silence.

"I grow tired, Ahmed Kadir. Such sorrow wearies me."

"Shall I go, then?"

The Princess smiled thinly.

"It is nearly morning. I think the end of this story will have to wait for another night, for I find I do not have the courage to finish it now."

She looked at him carefully, studying his eyes.

Ivan Postivich said nothing but returned her gaze. *Such eyes*, she thought. *The blue of freedom.*

"I promise I shall finish the story of Sophie another night. I will find the time, even though we have to prepare for the celebration of my Angel brother's birthday, an elaborate day and night of feasting and sport.

"I just cannot bear to tell you now, when it is such a soft night. Now you must rest, or else you will not be your best on the cirit field on Friday."

The corbaci's eyes flashed.

"Cirit? But the Sultan has forbidden me—"

"He banished you from your orta to my palace. But I command you to play cirit Friday for the honor of his party. Hundreds of guests will attend and you will have an eager audience for your games."

Before he could answer, the Sultaness clapped her hands and the Head Eunuch appeared.

"See that Ahmed Kadir is escorted to his barracks after refreshments. Have Nazip prepare a jasmine bath for me. Good night, Ahmed Kadir. I look forward to the match two days hence."

That night, Ivan Postivich dreamt of Peri. He rode her on the battlefield, dodging the arrows of an opposing army as they charged into the fray. Her neck bulged, muscles taut. He smiled down at her pumping hoofs, graceful but strong, covering the ground twice as fast as any other steed.

And then an arrow plunged into her heart and she faltered. She rolled on the ground and his foot was caught under her as she gasped and whinnied in pain.

He looked up and saw the Sultan, his hands covered in blood, preparing another arrow—this one for the janissary's heart.

"Ahmed! Ahmed Kadir! Wake up!"

The janissary jumped to his feet, lunging at the voice.

"It's me, Recid. Calm down! You wake the palace with your shouts!"

"I was—dreaming."

Recid grunted. "Your nightmares frighten the entire city. Hear the sentry call?"

A Solak appeared at the door.

"What is the cause of these screams?"

"It is nothing, only the giant dreaming."

"Wake him more quickly next time. His shouts have disturbed Esma Sultan."

The Solak left and Recid clapped Kadir on the shoulder.

"Perhaps she is not able to concentrate on her lover."

"What?" said Ivan Postivich, pushing the soldier's hand away. "What do you say?"

Recid wrinkled his forehead.

"Calm yourself, giant. I only jest. Does the Sultaness herself interest you now or is it that you don't want to drown a man tonight? Is that what you dreamt of?"

"No, I dreamt of—dying horses."

"Horses," said a janissary in the adjacent cot. "My mother spoke to spirits. Horses are spirits when they come to you in dreams. A spirit is trying to warn you."

"The Sultan's hands were bloody. He tried to kill me. I was pinned under my mare."

The Janissaries were all listening now, for dreams were significant.

"Have you made a decision, Ahmed?" whispered Recid.

"I need more time to consider."

"Our men grow weary. It is dangerous for all of us."

"A few days will not change our destiny. I need to think."

When Ivan Postivich arrived at the hamam for his bath, Emerald brought his afternoon tea and a light repast. He greeted the soldier with a broader smile than normal.

As the corbaci reclined in the cooling room after his steam and scrub, the eunuch spoke, his fat pink tongue licking his lips in enjoyment of the news he was about to impart.

"I suppose you have heard what has happened in the market today?"

"I hear nothing, if it is not from you. What news?"

"The Princess Esma Sultan has decreed that slave women shall not be inspected at random by the prospective buyers and that decorum should be afforded each one of them!"

The janissary laughed. "They are slaves, aren't they? Surely the buyers will want to inspect their teeth and gums, their legs and feet, their virginity—or the buyers will not know what they purchase."

"Exactly! But the Sultaness has declared their inspections an affront to the Koran and urged that the Ulema must declare such treatment against the teachings of Mohammed."

"It is true that the slavemasters treat the women like cattle," said Postivich, glowering. He had always imagined the fate of his sister at the Muslims' hands, the rough dirty hands that would have probed her. "She surely does rule this Empire through the Sultan's ear."

Emerald smiled. "Yes, the hand of the Sultan moves under her own, and her decisions are absolute. The Janissaries patrolling the market could not contain her. She kicked over the crates upon which slave sellers display the females and bloodied a man's eye who dared to raise his fingers above a young girl's knees. I witnessed it all, and thanked Mohammed I was not cursed by her wrath.

"She also bought over forty Greek slaves herself this very day and has freed them on the instant. Many have begged to stay in her harem and join the others who now wander freely about the palace."

"Are you saying that all those women in the Serail are not the slaves of Esma Sultan?"

"Some are, some are not. It is impossible to remember, for so many have been given their freedom, but few ever leave. They love the freedom to wander the palace grounds without yasmaks, without husbands who demand their submission, without beatings and scorn. They indeed enjoy their lives there. You have heard the music of her female orchestra? It is said that Esma Sultan has the finest female musicians in all the world. A prince of France has argued that the beauty of Constantinople is not the Aya Sofya, but the harem of Esma Sultan and the Sultaness herself."

Emerald sat back, thoroughly satisfied, sipping his tea.

"You are proud of your mistress," observed the janissary. "Yet what say you when she orders an innocent man to be drowned?"

The smile slid from the eunuch's face and he set his teacup down on the porcelain saucer.

"I cannot question the decisions of my Sultaness," he said, stiffening. His easy manner disappeared, and Postivich was struck by the sudden transformation and the ugly mold of his fleshy face.

In the silence, the janissary heard the hiss and creak of the steam in the pipes in the adjacent room.

"But she has not drowned a single lover since you began your evening visits," said the eunuch, recovering his composure. "I thank Allah for your presence."

"You think I am responsible for her not committing her murders?"

The eunuch nodded.

"You cannot dispute that the new moon is upon us and not one lover has she taken to her bed. And from the palace spies, I know that you and she are chaste."

The janissary snorted in astonishment.

"Chaste! Of course! I do not crave drowning! By the Prophet's word, why would I pronounce my own death sentence?"

"It is not your choice, janissary. If she wanted you, she would have you."

"Don't be so certain, eunuch. I know of one who refused her, though his life was not spared."

Emerald's eyes bore into the janissary, the faded blue taking on a fierce glitter.

"Who told you this?" he demanded, his voice surging with rage.

Ivan Postivich realized too late that he had spoken imprudently. He had nearly shared the secret of his last victim's words.

"It is gossip in the whorehouses! The women swear that she has been refused and laugh at the insult. They say she is the woman who offered love at her cup and found a lover who was not thirsty."

Emerald clenched his teeth, a glint of spittle forming at the side of his mouth.

"Tell me which brothels and they will have their wagging tongues cut from their mouths. The brothel shall be burned to the ground before morning!"

"Come, Emerald! I don't think the Sultaness would be charmed by the murder of women on the claims of idle gossip. After all, she is the champion of womankind, as you have it. Besides, would you want Esma Sultan to hear such stories? It would only enrage her and drive her to more murders."

Emerald drew in his breath and exhaled in hissing frustration.

"You are too wise to be a mere janissary, Kadir."

*And you are too proud and vengeful to be a eunuch*, thought Postivich.

Each night Bezm-i Alem paced in slippered feet beside the screen. When she thought she was not being observed, she pressed her eye against the filigreed carvings to watch Esma Sultan and Ahmed Kadir.

The marble felt cool and smooth against her cheekbone. She blinked, looking through the perforations, noticing how the drowning guard sat closer to her mistress now, as a confidante would, and nodded his head.

Bezm-i Alem began to hate her mistress and the spell she cast on the Ahmed Kadir.

The harem women had observed the Princess's trysts for many years now—sometimes the men were afraid and had to be tantalized to perform. Many others were aroused immediately, making quick work to take her to the mats, divan, or bed.

But this man listened. He had grown relaxed, his big shoulders dropping low, his gaze steady on Esma Sultan's face. She served him tea herself now, dismissing Nazip and Leyla as she herself fussed with the pot. She took time to taste to check its flavor and heat before handing it to him.

Bezm-i Alem watched as he accepted the cup and their fingers touched. The harem woman dug her fingernails into her palms to think he might be her mistress's next lover.

Ahmed Kadir was a Muslim. Surely he is protected by the Sheriat. Still, the treacherous Emerald would inform the Sultan, who held his sister in legendary esteem.

*Mahmud II looks upon our corbaci with scorn, what fate would become him if the Sultan's rage was provoked? I must warn the corbaci. I do not care if I incur the rage of Esma Sultan—I shall risk all to save him.*

Esma Sultan sent for the janissary an hour earlier than usual. Far from being agitated by her eventful day, the Princess was calm but invigorated.

"Ah, good! You are here."

"You sent for me, Sultaness."

"Yes, but I could not be certain if you would be here or in town still. In a tavern or perhaps a brothel."

The janissary answered cautiously. "I avoid each lately."

"Wise, perhaps. The taverns are cesspools of traitorous gossip and the brothels are full of disease. Perhaps you would like one of the girls from my harem to share in your pleasure?"

Ivan Postivich hesitated. Of course he wanted a night with

one of the beauties of the Princess's harem. But he wondered what price he would pay.

"I hear that you disrupted commerce in the slave market this morning."

The Sultaness raised her head and allowed herself to smile. The janissary was suddenly overcome by the warmth of her beauty as her face was transformed by the simple smile. He marveled at how the rare blade of muscle and bone formed on a woman's face, particularly this woman with a lineage of the most beautiful women of the Ottoman Empire.

"I indeed did pay my respects to that illustrious place of business and the swine who wallow there, making brisk money from women's bodies."

"And how many of the forty slaves have returned to their homes in Greece?"

"Ten, I believe. There are others undecided, but at least fifteen have begged to stay in the harem."

The janissary snorted.

"What troubles you, janissary?"

"With respect, I will not bother Your Highness with my opinion."

"Speak, I command you." The smile was gone. The Sultaness had returned.

"I find it impossible to imagine that a woman who has been taken roughly from her homeland, her own religion torn from her, would not choose to be liberated and return to her family. Why would a woman or a girl child choose to remain in the land of her captors?"

"Because I am not a man and I am not a captor. On the contrary, I am their savior in this world of men's abuses."

"You underestimate the pull of religion and homeland, Sultane."

"And you, Biscuit, underestimate womankind."

Postivich bridled under the nickname and bit his inner lip in frustration.

"I will finish my story tomorrow night, Ahmed Kadir, and to ward away the evil perils that prey on the heart's sadness, I shall show you a secret."

"Is it a good secret?"

The Sultaness's eyes softened and she shook her head. "You shall judge for yourself. It will be a surprise to you. But first I will finish the story of Sophie. Tonight I must attend the new women of my harem."

The forty slave girls crowded in Esma Sultan's hamam. Their eyes were wide with astonishment and a few among them—the youngest girls—trembled and cried, for they were not sure what had happened to them. Who was this Ottoman Princess who had her own harem?

Most of the women were Greek from the raid in Chios, and so the Greek-born among the harem comforted them in their own language. They bathed them and dressed them, anointing them with aromatic oils of lavender, rose, and lemon.

The cooks, chief among them Greek Maria, worked hard to make them comforting foods from their homeland. The kitchens' aromas spilled over and filled the entire palace with what must have been the smells of Constantinople more than four hundred years before, now confined to the Greek sections of the Galata neighborhood. Maria, ruddy with sweat and beaming with pride in her cooking, prepared a welcoming feast for the liberated slaves of Chios. She spread an exquisite table with the bounty of her kitchen. There were golden brown chickpea balls called *revitha keftedes*, *horta* or boiled greens, an assortment of savory kabobs of lamb, salads made of eggplant called *melitzana salata*. She filled plate after plate with different sardine dishes, pickled octopus, fish roe salads, and other seafood delicacies that she had never prepared for Esma Sultan's table, even in the most elaborate of banquets and festive occasions. The slave women swooned over a dish of lamb and potatoes, splendidly flavored with apricots, lemon, and mint.

But it was the almond cookies and baklava whose sugar glazed the smiles of the freed women. Clean, fed, and bewildered, they drank ouzo and rejoiced, crossing themselves so many times, it dizzied the harem to watch their arms whirl and land around their bodies, bobbing in religious devotion.

One woman, Adelpha, spoke for the entire group.

"We cannot believe our good fortune, freed from strange men's groping hands and possession as slaves. We are drunk with joy and your spellbinding hospitality, O blessed Esma Sultan, may God hear your name. Esma Sultan speaks of freedom—surely a Greek cannot truly be alive without liberty, we would rather die. But more than a few of us marvel at the world Esma Sultan has created within the walls of this palace. Many of us have no home or family to whom we can return and beg that we might live amongst the women here."

And so more voices were added to the female orchestra, and kayiks soon crowded the shores of the Bosphorus to hear the women sing at night.

Those who listened closely could hear hymns with a distinct accent—clearly Greek and clearly joyful.

Ivan Postivich insisted a boy shave him the next night in the hamam, as Emerald stood by his shoulder. The young barber's hand was unsteady, trembling at being watched by a Topkapi Palace eunuch.

"You will not allow me to shave your face, Corbaci. Why?" asked Emerald, his hands clenched.

"It is good to allow a boy to practice his trade. How else will he progress?"

"Boy, put the knife closer to his skin—at a steeper angle, you are missing patches," Emerald scolded.

When the boy nicked the corbaci's skin, Emerald smiled broadly.

"You deserve a more skilled hand, Corbaci. A hand that is steady and sure."

"I do not know what I deserve anymore," muttered Postivich and wiped his bleeding face with a towel.

Esma Sultan again summoned the janissary early. She asked him to sup with her in the palace. They drank fine wines from France in cut crystal goblets and ate delicacies from Maria's kitchen, served to them on trays by Leyla and Nazip.

Ivan Postivich relaxed as the wine rose to his head and coursed through his veins with sweet warmth. He reclined against the cushions and admired the exquisite profile of his hostess as she poured him tea. He realized it was a face he had come to know quite well. Its lines, its moods.

Esma Sultan smiled but did not meet his eyes. She asked for paper and a quill and quickly scribbled a note, dispatching it by hand to Nazip.

"Tonight I will tell you the final chapter of Sophie," she said softly. "You will finally understand a woman's suffering.

"Emerald had become my spy, for he smelled the prestige and privilege that my father had bestowed upon me. He was like one of the wild dogs of the city, sniffing out those who had strength. Later, when my father died, Emerald went running to my cousin Selim's bed, seeking favor with the new sultan. But at this point in my story, Selim was in a cage, as harmless as a beetle.

"Emerald had told me that the Sultan had taken pleasure earlier that afternoon with the Circassian beauty. She had left him exhausted, for he was an old man. That news gave me some hope that Sophie would be spared, but my hopes were dashed when I spied the lantern of the Head Eunuch flickering in the corridors of the Serail as he came for Sophie. I kissed my sister on the lips and hastened for the door.

"'I shall never desert you, kucuk,' I whispered. 'Though I am powerless over your fate.'

"I buttoned my cloak at the neck and slipped out the door. Emerald was right outside.

"'Where are you going, Esma Sultan?'

"I had no time to think up a good lie and even if I did, the eunuch would follow me.

"'I want to take air in the courtyard,' I said. 'You may escort me.'

"Emerald accompanied me past the other eunuchs into the torchlight of the gardens. We walked for several minutes and sat on the mosaic benches under the moonlight.

"'You know that the first thin crescent of the new moon is called "la luna sultana" in the Spanish lands,' said the eunuch, the moonlight making his skin glow the ghastly pale of a deadman. 'That's what Fatima of Cordoba called it, when the Moors ruled Spain.'

" 'Fatima?'

" 'She was a scholar and a Sufi, indulged even more than you are. Men traveled thousands of miles to study mysticism with her. But that was a long time ago, before men claimed the physical and spiritual world as their own and women were excluded from scholarship.'

" 'Where do you collect such knowledge, eunuch?' I asked. 'I have never heard such tales in my studies.'

" 'I study books, your Sultaness.'

" 'You have big dreams for a eunuch,' I replied, annoyed with his impudence.

" 'As you wish,' said the eunuch. 'And you have big wishes for a female. Are we not both slaves of a kind?'

"I whirled around to face him, shaken from my thoughts of Sophie. How dare he utter such insults, talking to me as an equal!

"He saw my anger and spoke quickly. 'Forgive me for my impulsive remark,' he said. 'I forgot my station in life.'

"But his words had not only stirred anger, they had touched something within me.

" 'Go on, eunuch,' I said quietly. 'Tell me how a woman is a slave.'

" 'You know better than I,' he whispered. 'When are you free to do as you wish? Even tonight, I must escort you into the dark of this walled garden, though Solaks crawl the perimeters to see that no one enters the sanctity of the Sultan's harem . . . and that no woman ventures out. A woman cannot be trusted for her own body's natural rhythms are the evil's weapon over her very soul.

" 'Tonight is the Sultan's moon—the most urgent of the sexual responses curse a woman at this mark. The Sultan knows it, and he tries to double his schedule of concubine visits to ride the wave of their urges. This is when a woman is at her ripest.'

"I scowled at him. 'That shows how little you know. My little sister Sophie is being bathed at this very minute to lie in his bed. She is stiff with terror. She has no urge.'

"The eunuch dismissed my remark with a slight flick of his hand, and I again contemplated having him beheaded. How saucy a gesture to make before an Ottoman!

"'Sophie is only a girl,' he said. 'Of course she has no womanly urge. This is an indulgence of the Sultan, for no girl should be taken before her first menses. The Ulema and Mufti look the other way to satisfy the curious urges of a Sultan. It is a sin against Allah.'

"I gasped in spite of myself because his words could easily have cost him his life. But he had said exactly what I had been thinking all night.

"'So, why do you not show me where you were going, Esma Sultan? I shall tell no one of your destination, if you will allow me to accompany you.'

"I realized that he would follow me no matter what.

"'I will show you if you follow me. But if you breathe a word I will say you made improper advances towards me and you will be beheaded.'

"The eunuch drew in his breath at the threat, stretching the fabric of his garment to its capacity. He nodded his head, though his eyes began to gleam with mischief, for surely a Princess who slipped out of her bedchamber at this time of night was up to no good.

"And without a word, I led the eunuch to the thick tangle of bushes and as he held his lantern high, we descended into the depths of the earth."

"I could see my father clearly from the spy hole, and smelled the piquant breath of my companion at my side. Emerald smelled of tumeric and cloves as he breathed heavily after the exertion of scrambling through the dark tunnel.

"I was in time to watch as the Head Eunuch escorted Sophie into my father's chambers. She trembled, but approached the bed and knelt as she had been told.

"'Kucuk,' he said, 'my little one. You do not have to approach my feet. Come to me here to my breast and I will comfort you.'

"Sophie gasped. She had prepared herself for the ritual my mother had described and was ready to obey mindlessly, refusing to think of what she was doing. To have to respond to kindness was too unsettling.

"She stood near him but did not move.

"He lifted the sheets and when she did not approach, the eunuch gently took her arm and led her to the bed.

"'Come, lie next to me and do not tremble so.'

"Sophie could not help herself. She shook as she crept into my father's bed.

"I saw his hands, huge, crusted with rings, mottled brown against her pale skin. The bones beneath her flesh were so delicate, so fine. Then his hands turned her over onto her stomach. She disappeared beneath him, a swimmer drowning beneath a wave, and I heard her whimper. A tiny sound. I can hear it still. I saw the look of pure animal lust on his face as he took her.

"And I hated him.

"I felt the eunuch reach for my hand.

"'See what beasts men can be,' he whispered in my ear. 'Is a woman really freer than a eunuch?' he asked. 'Even a princess?'

"'Never,' I whispered, my voice so hoarse, I had to swallow hard to utter the single word. 'I'll never let a man take me like an animal.'

"Sophie whimpered again and my father laughed. Triumph, not joy.

"'Revenge and to Hades with all men!' I said, biting my hand to keep from screaming.

"'And when the time comes, enlist me to enforce your will,' cooed the eunuch. 'I shall serve you well, for my revenge will find comfort, nestled in yours.'"

In the silence, Postivich studied Esma Sultan's face. And he saw something new there, a new kind of sadness—somehow sweet and vulnerable, yet still angry.

Then she took a deep breath and only the anger remained.

"Sophie was lifted from the Sultan's bed by the eunuch. She was too sore and mortified to move and my father had lost interest in her once he had taken his pleasure.

"'Take her to the harem,' he commanded. 'Have Saliha cleanse her. The girl is not to see any of the harem nor receive their congratulations until she can compose herself.'

"The eunuch craddled her in his arms. She covered her face with the blanket he wrapped about her, sobbing silently into the woolen folds.

"I ran ahead of the stumbling Emerald, making my way back through the darkness to the Serail. My cloak flying behind me, I raced across the courtyard and into the corridor just as the palace eunuch delivered Sophie to my mother's embrace.

"My mother received Sophie from the eunuch's arms.

"'I will prepare the hamam,' he said. 'She is to be cleansed thoroughly. She shall use the private hamam and not the communal baths.'

"I stood behind my mother, who pressed Sophie's face deep into the flesh of her bosom. The girl's face was contorted and deep red. She convulsed in her weeping so that I was certain she was going to choke and die.

"'She will be all right, Esma. Summon the eunuch to carry her to the bathhouse.'

"Within minutes we were in the private hamam, reserved for special ceremonial ablutions. The candles had been lit and the water trickled from the pipes into the pool of water.

"The eunuch set Sophie on the wooden stool and tried to take off the blanket.

"'No,' she screamed. 'NO! NO!'

"'Myrrh,' said my mother to the eunuch. 'Let her keep the blanket about her for now.'

"'But I must witness the ablutions.'

"'NO!' screamed Sophie and she began to choke again.

"'If you remain in her sight, she will wake every woman in the harem and bring shame to the Sultan. I know of what I speak.'

"The eunuch looked anxiously at the sobbing girl and nodded.

"'I will have to inspect her before she returns to the apartments,' he said, moving away. He disappeared into the corridors of the hamam.

"My mother dipped the sponge in the copper bucket and pressed it to the girl's genitals.

"Sophie whispered. 'Not there,

"My mother looked at her incredulously.

"'Not there,' Sophie repeated, her voice trembling.

"My mother gasped, realizing what she meant. 'The demon.'

"With the softest touch, she turned Sophie over, as if she were going to spank her like a toddler. She dabbed the sponge between her buttocks and drew it back again, bloodied.

"'Go instruct the eunuchs to light the brazier and make up a warm divan close to it,' said my mother in a cold voice. 'I need to speak with Sophie alone.'

"My mother carried Sophie to the divan almost an hour later. I could tell by the smell on their clothes that she had given the girl opium and may well have taken some herself. Clutched in Sophie's hands was the toy horse I had given her.

"'Let her sleep, Esma,' said my mother, stroking her hair. 'Let her sleep as long as the angels will allow her rest.'

"The Valide Sultan summoned Sophie the next day. My mother tried to protect her.

"'Please tell the Valide that the girl is not well. She will remain in bed today under my care.'

"'The Valide Sultan instructed me to bring Sophie to her,' said the eunuch. He did not move from the doorway.

"'You will have to make her understand that she is very ill. It would be a mistake to move her.'

"The eunuch reluctantly left and an hour later, the old Valide came to our door, leaning on her cane. She was dressed in midnight-blue silks and looked like an old peacock standing on one leg.

"'I have been told that Sophie is ill. I must see her at once!' she snapped.

"The Valide poked her cane through the doorway and thrashed it vigorously, so that we all staggered clear. She hobbled through the apartment to the small room with the brazier still glowing bright, its fiery coals warming the girl who lay next to it.

"Sophie lifted her head weakly, bewildered by the sudden burst of activity as the Valide and her entourage of eunuchs entered the bedroom. She was recovering from an opium stupor and blinked hard, trying to focus her eyes.

"'What ails you, girl?' the Valide demanded.

"'I—I . . .'

"'Well, what is it?'

"'She is still—unwell—from last night,' said my mother, folding her arms across her chest.

"The Valide Sultane turned on my mother, scowling.

"'This girl has been made a concubine and the praises and congratulations of the entire harem and the city itself are waiting to be received. The women wait in the hamam to comb her hair and braid it with pearls. Their hands are full of petals to strew in the ceremonial baths to welcome their sister as they have already welcomed the newly favored Rushdah, who has been bathed and is now resting. The seamstress waits to make her new clothes appropriate for her status!' said the Valide.

"My mother's face fell as she slowly comprehended. 'She is a concubine, but this ceremony is reserved for—'

"'The Sultan has prepared special apartments for her that are adjacent to his own. Yes, she is declared his "favorite," along with Rushdah and shall receive all special privileges that are befitting! He will see her many nights for apparently she has given him great pleasure.'

"This was a particular jab at my mother, who once had lived in those same apartments when she was the Sultan's favorite. But my mother was stronger than the Valide gave her credit for. She pushed back her auburn hair, now streaked with grey that even the strongest henna couldn't hide.

"'I am sure that Sophie will appreciate this reception more when she has had enough rest. We must tell the women of the harem to expect her when she is ready to accept their congratulations by this evening.'

"'Phhhst—I will tell them what I wish, without any advice from a used-up sponge like you! He means to make her a wife! Though I do not understand how my son could waste his ardor on a girl who is not prepared to give him a child! One night is an indulgence, but to be made a wife before she has become a woman is a blasphemy! Night after night of spilt seed. I have trained so many women to give him pleasure who are ready to conceive sons for the Ottoman Empire. Bah! I cannot stand to look at her, the bewitching little whore!'

"I stood in horror, listening to my grandmother. I could not understand how she could be so blind to a man's wrongs, even if he was her only son and Sultan of the Empire. It was this moment when I realized a man's word could poison woman against innocent woman if she surrendered to its violence, and indeed a woman could be the uglier beast.

"I was aware Sophie was moving now, raising herself out of the divan, her nightclothes clinging to her small frame. Her face was no longer frightened, but contorted in anger, a blind rage I had never seen before in a woman, nor seen since.

"'I see the lazy girl has enough stamina to get out of bed after all,' said the Valide, poking her cane viciously at the girl. 'I want to know—how could my son prefer you to Iris, the Armenian dancer I brought to him last week? You who have no breasts, no hips, no womanhood at all. I cannot abide this decision, yet he insists that you must be moved to the favorite's apartments. His precious seed will fall on a barren womb, night after night'

"'The Sultan's seed has not dampened my womb, Valide Sultan,' Sophie said, her voice growing strong with her fury.

"'What?'

"Sophie straightened, looking the Valide in the eye—which was the most disrespectful gesture I have ever seen in Topkapi. All except the royal family look at the floor when addressing the Sultan or his family.

"Her voice clear and steady, despite her pallor, Sophie said, 'I am still a virgin.'

"'Virgin? What are you saying, you little fool?'

"'Hush, girl,' warned my mother, in a low whisper. 'You do not know what you are saying. She is the fire and you are a stick!'

"'Of course you are not a virgin, you whore!' said the Valide, turning to the eunuch, who nodded affirmatively. 'I've seen the sheets and they were wet with blood.'

"'The Sultan did make me bleed. But it was not where a virgin bleeds. It was where the little boys bleed—the little boys he prefers.'

"The Valide thumped her cane hard on the floor and the Head Eunuch brought her a stool. She collapsed and looked around the room dazed.

"'You accuse my son, the Sultan, of beastly acts?' gasped the Valide. 'You little wretched slave, I will have you strangled for treason!'

"'I am not a boy and I am still a virgin. He who is the protector of the Koran, God's Shadow on Earth, should remember the first suras.'

"'You will be silenced by Allah and the Prophet, I swear it! Eunuch! Silence her!'

"'Madame, I cannot! She has been declared the Sultan's favorite and it is not within my power—'

"'Silence her, I say! Strangle the infidel, a demon possesses her!'

"'I know the first sura. I was forced to learn such suras by heart, Valide Sultan.'

"Sophie opened her mouth and pronounced the words in Arabic as she had been taught by the Iman. Words that forbid exactly the act the Sultan had committed with her.

"'Silence, you little demon!' the Valide screeched. 'I shall have your tongue torn from its roots.'

"'Silence? Yes, a fine Ottoman trait! Silence and peace I shall have!'

"And with that, Sophie tipped over the brazier, hot with coals. My first reaction was to jump back. But my mother lunged forward, understanding in an instant. But the young girl was too quick. She seized a red hot coal and crammed it into her mouth.

"We heard the sizzle of wet flesh and the choking scream—though to this day, I cannot tell you whether it was my mother or Sophie who made the cry of anguish."

And again there was silence in the room.

Esma Sultan stared straight ahead. She did not look at the janissary, but seemed to be watching the last dim vestiges of the memory fade from her mind's eye.

"And it was then that I knew I must create my harem. A home for women where we do not live in fear of men. There is no other sanctuary like this in the world. My father died only a few days later of a paralysis that seized his body and mind. I can only believe it was Allah's punishment for what he had done, and in the vacuum of sorrow that filled the palace, I was free to act, with the blessing of my cousin Selim, the new Sultan. He was the power that set free the women from the Palace of Tears and allowed me to buy the beautiful slaves that were mistreated in the markets. I gave them the chance to reclaim their freedom. Some did and some did not. But Sophie came with me joyfully, for her life was already destroyed. Her beauty was ravaged. Her mother had died and her beloved brother was lost to her.

"And so she stayed on, even when she was given her freedom."

Esma Sultan reached for the little gold bell that stood on a mother-of-pearl table.

"I can see by your expression that you do not believe my words, nor my knowledge of women's hearts. You will be quickly persuaded of my truth."

Her hand shook the bell, making a fine tinkling sound that hung in the air. Saffron instantly appeared.

"Send for Irena."

Saffron looked at Postivich and back at the Sultaness, then turned on his heel and left.

"Irena? Irena is a Serbo-Croatian name. And—"

He started to say more, but Esma Sultan broke in. "Do you think I learn nothing from my subjects?" said the Princess in perfect Serbo-Croatian. "And what language did you think my precious Sophie spoke?"

Ivan Postivich shook his massive head in astonishment as the language of his homeland spilled from the Ottoman Princess's mouth.

But it was the next sight that truly stole his power to speak. For as the fair-haired, veiled woman entered the room, he knew her instantly, if only by her eyes. Even with the years that had passed, he had not a moment's hesitation. These were the eyes of his sister.

"Irena. I know that you and your brother must have time to speak. I shall leave the two of you alone. I will return at dawn, so that you have time to share all that you must."

"Stop!" said Ivan Postivich, as Esma Sultan started for the door. "I beg of you!"

"Yes, my impertinent janissary. What is it?"

"Your story—it was . . . ?"

Esma Sultan smiled. "My story was exactly correct, but for the fact I called her Sophie in my tale, so you would not recognize her. I simply never cared for the name Irena. Irena means peace . . . Bah! You must never let anyone know where she is, *Ivan Postivich*, or you jeopardize her life. She shall remain Bezm-i Alem for the outside world. For if my brother knows for certain her where-abouts, he would give anything to have her in his bed at Topkapi. And I think she would rather kill herself than surrender to masculine hands again."

With that, the Sultaness disappeared in a flutter of handmaidens who escorted her into her exquisite gardens.

Ivan Postivich rushed to embrace his sister. He was not surprised when she removed her veil and revealed the pearl-colored scars that ringed her mouth. He kissed her cheeks over and over again, wetting them with his tears.

"Ivan, my brother," she cried.

For the first time in many years, Bezm-i Alem heard her brother speak her name aloud in Serbo-Croatian.

"Irena," he whispered, his massive body convulsing with emotion. "Irena!"

# Chapter 9

Sister and brother spent the night together in the apartments of Esma Sultan. Ivan Postivich's tears bathed the scarred flesh of his sister's face.

She retraced her life from loss to joy to pain. Esma Sultan had rescued her, sheltered her, and treated her as a sister. And in the end it was the kindness of women that had comforted her after she had traded her physical beauty for the sanctity of being an untouchable, protected by her wounds.

Ivan Postivich smoothed her hair with his great paw of a hand and burrowed his face into the space where her neck met her shoulder. He breathed in the unforgettable scent of his home and family and wept uncontrollably for his dead mother. He confessed his life to her in stages throughout the night, in chapters of recollections that came to him in the hours of darkness.

As dawn approached and the light of the rising sun rendered the flickering candles unnecessary, two Circassian servants silently entered the room to extinguish the flames. The slave girls saw the favorite of Esma Sultan in the arms of Ahmed Kadir and smiled inwardly. That the giant had chosen the most unfortunate of the harem women as his lover spoke of secrets of the soul and not just the lusts of the body. They thanked Allah for the generosity of their mistress who had allowed a man's touch to at last caress the burnt flesh of the Sultaness's favorite companion.

"Praise Allah," they whispered to each other as they silently closed the door on the whispering couple.

Irena and her brother whispered their secrets through the dawn and into the day. They had lost their dear family home, their language, and their religion. Their mother died of grief and hardship, with no one left to help her through the hard Serbian winters.

Brother and sister, they had lost everything, but now they had regained each other. Irena's soul was filled, and like the water that escapes the overflowing lip of a fountain, her spirit spilled over with joy.

As the sun burned higher in the sky, Esma joined them. She refused any gratitude. She didn't let them speak. Instead, she warned them that their secret would be revealed eventually to the Sultan. She reached out her hand to Irena's shoulder, holding it gently.

"It would be best if you told him yourself. Secrets are like air. They disperse and travel freely, no matter how you try to keep them from escaping. Should Emerald learn of our secret, we shall die of suffocation. Better you find the best time to use the information to our advantage than to have the eunuch carry the secret to Topkapi."

She smiled gently, an expression Postivich thought he had never before seen on her face. "Mahmud has never forgotten you, despite the many concubines and wives he has taken."

"But once he sees my face," Irena protested. "No one will ever love this face!"

"I love it," Esma Sultan said, stroking her friend's cheek. Irena watched the intricate patterns of the red henna on the Princess's hand drift past. "It is the face of rebellion and determination. It does not show age, terror, or ennui. It is frozen in time, in a moment when you took a stand against a man who abused you. It is a mark of rebellion against man's dominion, even an Ottoman Sultan. What face could be more beautiful, Kucuk?"

The next night, the janissary was not called to the royal chambers. He sat idly in the courtyard, eating pistachios until long after midnight. A yawning servant boy swept up the shells that fell on the marbled ground.

Out of the darkness, Emerald approached and, with his chin lifted unnaturally high, dismissed him.

"Return to your barracks, Ahmed Kadir," he said, his voice officious and distant. "The Princess rests peacefully on the second night of the new moon. There is no need for your presence now."

Ivan Postivich felt a strange wave of disappointment wash over him. As he made his way out of the courtyard, he turned and saw the eunuch's tight smile sour in the torchlight, his hands crossed over his chest in satisfaction.

How could she banish him now from her harem, when he had learned that his own beloved sister was among the women behind the grille?

After so many long nights awake, the janissary realized he would not fall asleep until sunrise. He chose instead to leave the palace grounds and walk along the Bosphorus.

He gazed out upon the water, black in the new moon's light. In these dark waters, he had drowned more than two dozen men, their watery graves unmarked in the immense cemetery of the enemies of the Sultans.

Lost in his thoughts, Ivan Postivich ignored the first muffled scream, thinking his mind was playing tricks on him. Then the agonized wail of a child broke through his reveries and he shouted across the water, "Who goes there? By the Sultan's Royal Janissary's order, announce your business!"

A woman screamed back to him, her voice pleading and hysterical.

"My child, my child! You murderers, don't touch him!"

Postivich heard a sound he knew far too well. One that haunted his dreams: the splash of a heavy sack and the sudden stillness of the frantic voices.

He struggled to steady his breath and strained his eyes in the dim moonlight to find the murder. A single lantern flickered in the distance.

"Fellow Janissary!" called a voice. A launch rapidly approached. Postivich caught the mooring line.

"It is you, the giant," said a soldier, standing at the prow, his tall sleeved cap fluttering in the night wind. "Oarsman, rest. I must speak to this man."

The oarsman nodded. He kneaded his hands, content with a moment's rest.

"You are Esma Sultan's Solak," said the janissary, climbing out of the boat. He had bright red hair and spoke in Serbo-Croat with an inflection of the northeastern provinces.

"I am no Solak," protested Ivan Postivich, spitting in the dust. "I was assigned duty to the Sultaness, but I do not belong to that orta."

"I did not mean to insult you, brother," said the young soldier. "I only meant—" He looked over at the Turkish oarsman, staring into the night. "To warn you. Go into the barracks and cover your ears, for what you will hear will haunt your mind."

"Say more."

"They say that you have suffered murderous nights under the orders of Esma Sultan. Tonight will be worse by hundreds. I am only the first to commit my sin."

"I heard. A harem woman?"

"And her child, a little prince, son of Mahmud's brother Mustafa. They are only the first. Two hundred will be drowned this night."

Ivan Postivich suddenly spied dozens of lanterns rounding the bend of the Golden Horn and heading for the center of the Bosphorus.

"The Sultan has ordered that all of Mustafa's women shall die by his decree and by our hand—"

As he spoke, the red-haired janissary's voice rose an octave, to the range of a young boy. He choked back tears, his face frightened at the prospect of appearing womanish in front of the legendary Ahmed Kadir.

"I saw your great size and recognized you. The taverns still hum with your conquests and your men sing your praises. You have become a legend."

"If I am a legend, I am dead. Peace be with you, my brother. I need no praise. Let us live to serve Allah."

The young janissary fidgeted with his sash. "I came not to give you false praise, Ahmed Kadir. Moments ago, I stood on that launch, considering throwing myself after the two souls I dispatched. Then I heard you call and recognized your unmistakable stature and judged it as a sign from God.

"Give me words that will soothe my soul for I am tormented by this woman's screams and the tears of the little prince. If I had refused the order, I would have died along with the woman and child. But now I live and I cannot suffer this memory, the Holy Mary forgive me and my filthy soul."

Ivan Postivich could make out the young man's pleading eyes in the darkness. He wore his cap clumsily, his red hair emerging in tufts pulled by the sea breeze. His face was nearly hairless and his lip quivered as he spoke. He rubbed his nose on the sleeve of his tunic.

Now Postivich could hear the distant splashes and the cries of the women from the Bosphorus. Their shrieks of terror tore at his soul. He, like Esma Sultan, was haunted by the deaths in these dark waters.

These women—like the men he had drowned—were innocent.

The drowning guard felt something shift within him.

"I cannot offer you words of comfort, brother," he said. "But having seen the denigration of the Janissary Corps, and above all, the drowning of hundreds of innocent women and children, I am ready to strike the head from the serpent. The only words we can speak now are those of revenge, which will wash this stain from our hands and soul. Revenge and justice are words revered in the Holy Koran. We will make those who command this evil choke on these words."

For the next few hours of darkness and even into the sunrise, the Bosphorus was filled with the screams of women. As Ivan

Postivich returned to the palace of Esma Sultan, he saw the torches lit and heard the mad keening of the women of the Serail.

The Royal Kayik was moored to the dock and servants hurried, preparing for the Sultaness's boarding.

"Where does the Princess go at such an hour?" said Postivich to a servant he recognized from the palace.

"She is said to be visiting her brother, our Sultan. She has heard the rumors of the drownings and is hurrying to plead for a stop."

Just then, the Sultaness ran down the stairs of the palace, her cloak flying, and a flock of handmaidens running to keep up with her.

"To the Topkapi!" she commanded, and a dozen oars struck the water.

By early morning, every woman of Mustafa's harem was dead. Sultan Mahmud delayed audience with his sister until he was sure that the Janissaries had carried out their orders and then finally admitted her to his throne room. He rarely addressed her in these formal chambers, but had insisted that she be received here, rather than the more intimate rooms of Topkapi.

"My sister! What brings you so early to a sleeping household?"

Esma Sultan clenched her fists and beat at her knees, the ancient Turkish gesture of grief. "A broken heart, my brother! The Bosphorus moans from so much carnage at your hand!"

Mahmud looked down upon her from his throne.

"My dear sister, Esma, light of my soul. Remember you are an Ottoman before you shame us both. How could I let these women live when a child of Mustafa might be among them? Any one of them could appear with a boy and claim it was Mustafa's issue. The Janissaries are mutinous and yearn for another Ottoman Sultan, one whom they can control like a leashed dog. Mustafa's women could claim the throne using the issue of their womb!"

"You murdered all of them! You murdered even the barren women, the girls. Even Ayse, the Valide with whom you grew up. Don't you remember the games she taught us in the courtyards, the almond pastries she made for us as children?"

"She was the most dangerous of all. She would love to see my blood stain the courtyard and her own son rule the Empire. Did she not try to have me murdered?"

Esma Sultan stared at her brother incredulously.

"You indulged your righteous revenge with the murder of her son Mustafa, our brother. She is an old crone whose womb dried up years before—no fruit could spring from her."

"It was her long due kismet. She should have died along with our brother."

"What right do you have to murder these women? Did you learn nothing from our father and our childhood?"

"I am the Sultan," said Mahmud, raising his voice. "And you will never be!"

Esma Sultan raised her left hand to her cheek as if she had been slapped.

"How dare you question me?" roared her brother. "It is only with my blessings and good favor that you live the life you do. I could seize your palaces and your Serail and take your women to my own harem. I have kept my promise to our father in every way, and our subjects call you blasphemous!"

"What have I done that you have not? Do I not indulge you? I have brought you fair women," spat the Princess. "I have even brought you fair men!"

"You have brought me only those who have consented to come to me. I have asked thrice for the favors of your handmaiden Nazip and the whore has refused me! Never has a Sultan been refused, and this is your doing."

"She will attend you only if she sees pleasure in it," replied Esma Sultan. "She is among my favorites and my adopted daughter. I will only give permission if she wishes your favors."

"This is the way you talk—as if you have never read the Koran and did not know a woman's obligations to men and their Sultans."

"There is no talk of obligation to the Sultan, only to Allah."

"It is our religious tradition, my sister. Women are to serve men. You have filled the women's ears with blasphemy and rebellion. I heard of your antics in the slave market. The men have complained to the Imams that you have publicly denounced a man's right to examine his property. You rock the very principles and traditions that our forefathers have honored for four hundred years!"

"A pox on men and their property! These are women we speak of, not cattle! You men twist Allah's words to fit your indulgences and vice. Mohammed could not have wished to save half of humanity and throw the rest on the rubbish heap. These woman in the markets are Allah's children, too."

"They are infidels and slaves, sister! They are property of the Empire and your behavior incites treason. I have heard you have brought into your most intimate chambers the janissary who despises the Topkapi and most especially you."

Esma Sultan blinked at her brother. "Go on."

"You entertain a traitor in your bedchambers who would kill both of us in our sleep with a snap of his wrist. They say he is chaste with you, though I cannot believe this for I know your proclivities."

"I have many companions in my palace, brother. They are not all for my pleasure. I enjoy many for their company, their minds, and their adventures."

"This one is a man, and a dangerous one. I banished him from his orta so that he would no longer stir mutiny. They say he is still an influence on men, even though he is isolated in your palace. Where does he go when he is not in your harem?"

"I have no idea. Ahmed Kadir is free to conduct his business without my intrusion."

Sultan Mahmud II raised his hands in a gesture of astonishment.

"This is my same sister, Esma Sultan, who loves men knowing that before dawn they will meet their death?"

"That is your doing, brother, not mine. You send that jackal Emerald smelling at my sheets so that he murders my lovers. The blood is on your hands."

She turned away from the Sultan.

"What has this man, this pagan, done to deserve such liberties at your hand?"

"I trust him."

"You are mad, sister. He will die soon by a Topkapi sword or he will deliver my own death. Can you not see what you harbor in your palace walls? The enemy of the Ottomans—and you call him friend!"

"Enough! By my oath, I would attack you myself for the murder of two hundred women. The waters swell the banks of both Europe and Asia with their bodies, rotting at the floor of the Bosphorus. You carried out this terrible deed without my counsel. You have defiled the memory of our father who made you promise—"

"Enough! Promises are all in the past. Only I know what challenges a sultan must face. Your counsel has been wise, my sister, until the moment you took an enemy to your bosom. I shall henceforth make decisions without your guidance. The women are dead, Esma. Return to your palace and mourn them, comfort your nervous harem. That is work of women and not of a sultan."

Esma Sultan fastened her cloak and turned away, her body trembling with emotion. Never had she hated a man as much as she now hated her own brother.

The news of the drowned women and children snatched the joy of finding her brother from Irena's heart. These women had been her friends and companions. There was not one of the victims she did not know.

She, like the other harem women of Esma Sultan, walked numbly through the gardens of the palace, despising the Sultan and the Bosphorus for taking so many lives. Irena studied the seagulls as traitors, vultures from the sea who would pick the beloved flesh from the women's bones, should they wash up from the depths.

But the real traitor, she knew, was the Sultan, Mahmud. When they were both children, she had seen him only rarely. He was almost always in the princes' cage, locked away with his cousin Selim so that there was no chance of a revolt to overthrow his father.

But Sultan Abdulhamid allowed the young princes to attend special occasions and see his harem dance. Irena noticed him watching her, saw the longing in his gaze.

No one thought of Irena's reaction, for it was not important. But for little Irena, too, it was love at first sight. But now that long-ago love turned to guilt and confusion. To have thought she loved a man capable of murdering two hundred women—and, perhaps worse, to have been loved by him. What in her would attract such a demon? Yet, she remembered him and his inquiries about her after the terrible night with his father and the terrible moment when she—but, no, even now she could not allow herself to think of that searing instant when she scarred herself forever.

But through the cloud of that painful memory, she recalled the young prince with tenderness. Esma Sultan had showed her letters he had written, desperate to find her when she had disappeared from the harem. For years he sought her. Until he became Sultan himself. Upon his coronation he quickly became hardened and cruel—like all the rest, and a childhood love was soon forgotten, replaced by war and ambition.

Or had she imagined tenderness where there was none? Can a heart become so scarred with cruel acts of power that it ceases to be capable of love? Or was love always impossible for one such as Mahmud?

And yet, such was her confusion that a part of her heart still wondered if there was any redemption for the damned. Surely God heard the screams of the women and children as they were dumped in the Bosphorus, clawing frantically at the canvas. She could not forgive. Could God?

Irena feared for the future. Would anything ever staunch the flow of blood after so many centuries and exorcise this monster of a Sultanate? The cruel ambitions of men, who murder their brothers, drown their sisters' children, men who would strangle their own mothers to keep their power.

Nakshidil should have more influence with her son than his viziers and ministers. A mother's counsel was what Mahmud needed now, but his ears might be forever deaf to a woman's voice. Deaf to redemption.

At sunset, Emerald did not meet Ivan Postivich at the bathhouse. Instead, the Head Eunuch, Saffron, handed him his towels.

"What privilege is this to be greeted by the head of the Royal Serail? Where is the eunuch Emerald?" asked the janissary.

"I have sent him to perform some errands that will take time." Ivan Postivich shrugged and accepted the towel.

"Surely you have more important things to do than to wait on a soldier."

"I am not here to bathe you, Ahmed Kadir," the eunuch said, and raised his hand to indicate another young man. "Ali will serve you in that respect. First, however, I must speak with you."

Saffron clapped his hands, dismissing the bath servant. "Wait in the cooling rooms. I will send for you."

The servant bowed and disappeared.

Ivan Postivich sat on the smooth marble bench of the hamam and waited for the Head Eunuch to speak.

"Your life is in danger, janissary."

Postivich looked up at the man's eyes and saw that it was true.

"Such is a janissary's life," replied Postivich.

The eunuch considered his remark, his dark eyes glittering

"When you first arrived at the palace, I did not trust you," he said. "It was so evident that you loathed my mistress that I could only hope for your death. Now I risk my own life to give you this warning."

"You honor me."

The eunuch sat down next to the janissary and whispered. "The man who attends you, Emerald, is a spy for the Sultan. He has told the Sultan of your treasonous talk. He says that you are part of the conspiracy that will bring disgrace upon the Ottoman name. These words insure your death, Kapikulu."

"Emerald is a spy for Mahmud," Postivich said slowly. "Was I a fool not to see it before now?"

Saffron nodded stiffly as if this was quite clear.

"He has brought this story of your collaboration with the Janissary plot as evidence for your arrest. It will be commanded that you be imprisoned and beheaded."

Ivan Postivich nodded and rubbed a towel over his perspiring neck.

"If the Sultan calls for my death, there is nothing I can do."

"You can flee, Ahmed Kadir. Back to your homeland! Sail to Venice or cross the Danube to Vienna where they will protect you from the Ottomans."

Ivan Postivich threw the towel down on the wet tiles of the hamam.

"I am a janissary, whether or not I ever chose to be. A janissary never runs away, especially when his life is threatened. That is all I have learned in my life and all I have ever needed to learn."

Postivich felt the eunuch's eyes steady, studying him.

"And you. Why have you not escaped, Saffron?" said Ivan Postivich. "Surely Esma Sultan would accept it if you were to leave and return to your homeland."

"My homeland is forever lost to me. Not only did I give up my manhood, I gave up my Christian faith. There is no going back home. It is a place that does not exist for the man I have become."

"Then we are brothers," said Ivan Postivich. "For my faith has been scratched from my heart, the host snatched from my open mouth. I miss the compassion of my mother's faith. There was the home I longed to return to, but it lies buried under the embers and ashes of my childhood. Gone."

Ivan Postivich stared down at the floor, his eyes glittering. He slowly raised his head and clenched his fist.

"But I rejoice now in my knowledge of the Koran, for it is with a man's voice and janissary's heart that I answer to Allah and cry blasphemy on the deeds of our Sultan. The words of the Prophet stir my heart and demand revenge."

"Would that you remember the forgiveness and love of our stolen faith," said Saffron quietly, "your kismet would be sweeter than the taste of certain death."

With that, the Head Eunuch turned to leave and give specific instructions to the servant who waited in the tepidarium.

Never had there been a more miserable sound than the mourning wail from Esma Sultan's palace for the drowned women of her dead brother's harem. The Solaks gazed with horror at the walls of the harem, their weapons hanging useless at their sides.

At dusk Esma Sultan led the keening women, her harem of over a hundred, to the banks of the Bosphorus across from the deepest channel where their sisters had been murdered. Each lit a candle to honor the memory and soul of the dead women, and they knelt on their prayer rugs, chanting sura after sura of the Koran in their grief.

When the women finally returned to the palace, Esma Sultan strode to her chambers, and threw herself on the crimson divan, weeping, pounding her fists on the silken cushions. Her eyes were so swollen, she could hardly see the white eunuch who approached her.

"Forgive me, my Sultane. Will you be requiring Ahmed Kadir's presence this evening?"

Esma Sultan pulled herself up from the divan and wiped her eyes with a handkerchief stained black with kohl.

"How dare you approach me in my privacy, eunuch! You were not announced, nor permission granted to enter my chamber. I shall have you flogged."

Emerald did not register any fear but instead drew his short body up as tall as he could and twisted his face in a sneer.

"You seem not to be inclined to see any man this evening. I shall tell him he is to go."

"No, stop! " the Princess commanded. "Tell him—I will see Ahmed Kadir later. I must see him."

Emerald tightened his lips at her remark. Then he opened his small polished hands to her, in invitation.

"You know I can foresee your desires," he whispered urgently. "It is not Ahmed Kadir you seek, for he is untouchable as a Muslim. A new Christian man from Galata would serve your needs better. Shall I fetch the carriage? I have heard of a young man whose hair is as fair as wheat and whose body is hard and taut as rope. His hands are large as a horse's hooves, but with elegant fingers, tapered like French candles."

Esma Sultan sat up, gathering her strength. "I shall not be tempted again, Emerald! I have just cried for my women companions, there in the water just beyond our palace walls. I want no more death on my hands."

"But these would be men, your Sultaness," coaxed the eunuch. "They are the beastly gender. You can have your revenge another night, the moon is still waxing and I know the rhythm of your urges." His voice was hypnotic, as liquid as precious oil. "Think of the wet kisses of those young lips on your restless body, dry from this heat, the weight of him over you, again and again, in pursuit of your love and his life."

"Enough!" screamed the Sultaness, her body involuntarily surging towards the image, like the pull of the tide. "Your venom shall not infect me again. It is your own revenge you seek and you have coaxed my royal hand to murderous deeds.

"I shall not add more carnage to these waters. Your lustful ideas have corrupted my soul!"

She took a deep breath.

"And tell me now what happened to the last one. I begged my brother to spare him. I left him chaste so that he might be released. But the janissary admits he drowned him. And I have heard rumors from the docks that he was covered in bruises and bites before he was sent to Bosphorus. That is your vile indulgence, Emerald! Your vile hatred killed him and poisons my brother's mind to insist on this bloodlust!"

Emerald returned her stare and the corner of his lips quivered, stifling a smile.

Her eyes bore into the eunuch. "You lied, Emerald! The boy was killed, virgin that he was. There was no cause!"

"I serve my master, the Sultan. It was his wish."

"He swore to drown those who had shared my bed. My brother had no right to take this man's life, you had no right! I left him untouched, to return to his village to become a priest."

"And what tales he could have carried to the northlands—the weakness of the Ottomans, a Princess who cannot even seduce a lover from the lowest class. What shame you would bring your brother and the Ottoman name!"

"I allowed him to leave! He told me of his being a priest and I never touched him. There was no seduction by my choice, not his!"

"Your brother commanded the death, my Sultaness. I am put on this earth to follow his orders."

The Princess grabbed a jewel-encrusted hairbrush and hurled it at the eunuch.

"If I could have you murdered, I would sing at your death."

"May my Master Mahmud II live a long life and protect me from your eager hand."

"Send in Ahmed Kadir."

"But, my mistress—"

"Send in the janissary, I say, and trouble me no more with your evil counsel!"

The skin of the eunuch's face pulled tight and he stared at the Sultaness.

"You will still call for me, Esma Sultan. Your appetite will never be satisfied, not even with the help of Ahmed Kadir. And if he should ever become your lover, I shall escort him, like all the others, to his death. And that day shall make me smile."

Ivan Postivich entered the room and saw the red eyes of the Sultaness. Silently, he nodded, to show his understanding.

"There was nothing I could do," she said.

"But why?" he asked. "Why now?"

"My brother suspects another coup. He says the Janissaries are mutinous and he must be sure there is no trace of his brother's seed, no concubine who will suddenly produce a hidden heir that the Janissaries can seize and place on the throne."

"Where is Irena?"

"She is with the other women in the garden. Her grief has consumed her. Let her have this time with the women who can console her."

Ivan Postivich nodded.

"But you must go to my stables in the morning and select your horses for Friday's games."

The janissary looked at her, astonished.

"The celebration, your brother's birthday? This is to come to pass with the air still filled with the dying screams of women and children?"

Esma Sultan smiled savagely. "Do you think I would call off a fête in my palace and disappoint my guests? I have planned for months for this day. My brother shall have to appear on Friday and he will see you compete. Tonight I will mourn my sisters and their children. I will keep vigil with the women of my harem. You must rest and be at the stables early to select your horses for the match. I shall send a servant to alert the head groom of your visit."

"Thank you, Sultaness."

Esma Sultan's mouth hardened. "I have never looked so forward to a cirit game in all my life."

# Part III
# Turkish Horse

# Chapter 10

The next morning, Ivan Postivich walked along the Bosphorus to where the horses of Esma Sultan were kept. Her stable was adjacent the Sultan's own, where he kept more than four thousand horses, with nearly two thousand grooms who scurried about with the dedication of priests.

The Head Groom greeted the janissary.

"Ahmed Kadir! What an honor it is to have you ride the horses of Esma Sultan. I shall help you select the best for tomorrow's game."

The Royal Stables were familiar to Postivich. He had spent many days working there as a boy as part of the apprenticeship to the cavalry. He knew the feel of the pitchfork in his hand, the combs used for grooming the Sultan's horse, the ritual of tacking the horse early in the morning for the Sultan's ride to morning prayers.

At the far end of the stables, there was a special building where the Sultan's ceremonial saddles and jewel-encrusted bridles hung. More than a hundred Solaks stood guard, their yataghans and scimitars glinting in the sun, protecting the priceless trappings.

The grooms all peered out from the stalls to catch a glimpse of the legendary rider.

"Abdul! He is as big as they say! Look at his arms! As thick as the branches of the plane tree."

"Have you not seen him walking the streets or in the Spice Bazaar?"

"I swear by Allah's name, never until today. But the Head Groom has promised me that I can watch the games at the Princess's palace."

The barefooted boys dressed in rags pressed their cheeks against the stable door to peek out at the janissary.

"You boys there! To your duties!" shouted the Head Groom.

The faces vanished into the recesses of the stables.

"Come, Ahmed Kadir. Look at this stallion I have for you. Never have you seen a horse more nimble footed."

Ahmed Kadir pressed his lips together in doubt, but followed the groom to the stall.

"There, look at the mighty brute. He comes from a line of horses from the English, bigger than our Turkish breeds."

Ahmed Kadir entered the paddock and approached the stallion, looking him in the eye.

"Calm yourself," he said in Serbo-Croat, as the horse snorted noisily and backed away. He repeated the phrase, over and over, like a chant, and extended his hand, putting firm pressure on the horses neck. The stallion stood still, but his withers quivered as Ahmed Kadir smoothed his flat palm over the animal's back, counting the vertebrae with his fingers.

"A long-backed horse," said Postivich. "You say he is agile?"

"I have trained him myself. I must do so when the Sultan is not present, or he would add this mount to his stables," laughed the groom. "He was a special present to Esma Sultan from the

British Ambassador, the night after a fête." The groom winked. "I believe he enjoyed himself mightily."

Postivich ignored the comment. His hand continued to inspect the stallion, slipping over the horse's fetlocks and measuring the angle of his leg.

"I shall try him. But I find stallions unpredictable and missing the heart of a mare when a competition requires stamina."

"This horse will not let you down, Ahmed. I can swear to this for I have trained him well."

"Heart is not something that comes with training, but I shall respect your opinion."

"If it is a mare you require, let me show you others. I have acquired many foreign horses as gifts from diplomats. I have crossbred them with our Turkish horses and have many strong, bighearted horses, including mares. But I will tell you now, there is no horse in the Empire who will carry more honor on the cirit field than this stallion—except your own mare, Peri."

The janissary's heart fell when he heard his horse's name.

"This stallion is called, 'Sultan's Choice,'" continued the groom.

"Sultan's Choice? What name is that for a horse?"

The Head Groom spat on the stone floor, leaving a glistening spot in the dust.

"This horse was named before he reached Stamboul. It is a British name, and the Sultane has ordered us to use it so as not to offend the ambassador. Here, come! I shall show you some Turkish horses with more appropriate names, horses you can fight on without shame."

After inspecting over thirty horses, Ivan Postivich settled on three, the stallion Sultan's Choice, and two crossbreed mares as reserves.

"Tack them up," he said. "I shall test their agility and temperament. Send your best grooms to the field and we will set up a practice so that I may put this beast to the test."

The grooms, who stood listening in different corners of the stables, descended upon their master, begging for a chance to ride with or against the giant.

"By all that is good and right under Allah, you should choose me!"

"No, me! I have dreamt of the chance to play with the giant. I have followed all his games since I was a babe in the arms of my mother."

"No, me! Who devotes more time to the horses than I?"

The Head Groom ignored their pleas and chose ten grooms. Six on each team would suffice to test the horses, with Ahmed Kadir being one captain and he the other.

The Head Groom rode the stallion first, in a trot around the stable grounds. With a firm seat and hand he engaged the horse, ensuring that the animal knew that he was expected to perform and not to lose his head to the mares who would accompany him to the field. When the mares and geldings were tacked and also circled the stable field, Ahmed saw the great beast lower a callused black penis at the mares who neighed wildly to him.

"This is the test," he said and watched the horseman's reaction.

The stallion bunched up his neck and kicked out in frustration at the rider's grip on the reins. His nostrils flared and a bellowing snort spreaded wet mucus in a fine spray. He kicked sideways and threw his powerful neck in the direction of the nearest mare who whinnied hysterically in his direction. His penis began to quicken and soon stuck straight out like an iron rod.

Ivan Postivich shouted, "Let me ride him now."

The stallion was quivering with excitement. The Head Groom called to Postivich, "Let me ride him a minute more to settle him down."

"Get down!" shouted the janissary.

The groom nodded and took a deep breath.

"*Kus! Kus!*" he shouted, trying to get the horse to stop. As he dismounted the stallion reared and pulled back, fighting desperately to get to the mares who circled the pasture. His sharp hooves flew out at the men who held him, but they jumped away from the deadly front feet.

"Give me your whip," said Postivich. "Hold this brute long enough for me to throw my leg over him."

The groom handed him the whip and held the reins. The stallion's eyes were ringed in white and he twisted his powerful neck to keep his eye on the mares, ignoring the men who pulled at his head, cursing him as they struggled.

"It is too dangerous when he is in this state," shouted the Head Groom.

"Leave him in my hands," said Postivich. "Stallions are all cursed."

The janissary threw his leg over the horse and the stallion reared straight up. Postivich had to cling to the horse's long mane to pull himself into the saddle.

"Allah curse you," he shouted as the stallion tried to buck. Postivich yanked the reins high in the air, pulling the horse's head up so he could not lift his hindquarters to throw his rider. "This is why I hate stallions!"

Postivich raised his whip high in the air and brought it down hard against the horse's flanks. The stallion bolted. Instead of reining him in, the janissary sliced the whip through the air again, stinging the stallion's rump with the leather cord and giving him his head.

The grooms on the mares watched the stallion fly across the pasture, his rider leaning forward, grinning into the wind, bellowing curses and praising Allah in a mix of Turkish and Serbo-Croat, as he raced the horse faster and faster across the field.

At last Postivich pulled the stallion into small cantering circles and motioned to the others to follow him to the cirit field below the walls of the Topkapi.

"His attention will not be diverted now," he called to the others. "The lustiest mare in the Ottoman Empire could raise her tail to him and his organ would remain as tight in its sheath as a eunuch in winter."

The grooms roared in laughter and reined their horses towards the field, carrying the jereeds in their hands and feigning battle cries. The cypress and plane trees that lined the road were powdered in their dust as they galloped.

By the time they reached the cirit field, the stallion had lathered up so hot from his excitement and the gallop that white stockings laced his black legs in sweaty foam.

The bunched neck and tense muscles were relaxed now, but Postivich took the precaution of riding him to the far end of the green field, away from the mares. He tied the stallion to the branches of a plane tree, the animal still bellowing.

A barefooted groom came running across the immaculate turf, his ragged clothes flapping.

"Ahmed Kadir, I will attend to your horse," he said, gasping for air.

Postivich nodded. He wanted to inspect the grounds on foot. Cirit called for quick turns at a gallop, a rider needed to know the condition of the turf and footing.

The field was clipped and freshly irrigated. The loam would be moist but not wet for tomorrow's games. Servants were walking the field, hunting for holes and hidden stones that might bruise the hoof of a valuable horse.

Postivich walked the perimeter and then made serpentines across the grass, his feet memorizing the turf. It was satisfactory. He had played cirit in all conditions and what was battle except a cirit game with life as a prize and death to the loser?

The janissary remounted the stallion and called for the jereed spears. The teams faced each other, separated by a hundred paces. The youngest rider, a groom named Abdul, rode out past the center of the field and as he neared the opposing side, he threw his jereed at the Head Groom.

The Head Groom dodged the spear, reining his horse sharply to the right at a quick gallop and diving low below the saddle. He immediately straightened as his horse flew down the field in pursuit of Abdul, closing the gap quickly. He flung his blunt-ended spear at the boy, catching him between the shoulder blades.

"Score!" he crowed, but his laugh was cut short as a second groom, older and more experienced, galloped out as soon as Abdul crossed back into his team's territory.

The Head Groom spun his horse around and raced back to his team, the Turkish boy in pursuit. The rider threw his jereed, but it missed narrowly, sliding over the Head Groom's back as he flattened himself against the saddle.

Postivich was the last to ride. He spurred his stallion the instant the jereed left the hand of the opposing rider, and before the player had time to finish his turn towards the safety of his team, the janissary's jereed stuck him hard in the small of his back.

He howled in pain, though the stick was too blunt to pierce his flesh.

"Move more quickly next time," yelled Postivich, and he circled his horse, changing leads in midgallop, racing back to his team before his opponent had time to pursue him.

The grooms nodded to one another, for they had seen how accurate the giant's aim was and the ease with which he commanded his horse. And they could see he was not really trying, but only testing the stallion, running him through his paces.

"I propose another game," said the janissary, reining in the stallion. "My horse and I against all of you using the entire field. You come at me in twos, allow me sanctuary when I cross my line."

"This is a mockery!" cried a swarthy youth whom Postivich had recognized earlier as a skillful rider. "No man can challenge an entire team."

"Consider it my Serbian ignorance," said Postivich. "I want to see how much stamina and intelligence this stallion really has."

The grooms nodded and the Head Groom had them file back into their rows in twos to take on the giant. The Head Groom took the first turn, reining his prancing mare into the ready position.

"Ready?" said Postivich, reining his horse out to the center of the field. His horse charged forward at a gallop and before the grooms could realize what had happened, a jereed slammed against the Head Groom's chest.

Two horsemen raced after Postivich, but the stallion was too quick and he crossed the line into sanctuary and immediately circled his horse, a flying change of leads that gave advantage to the stallion, closing the distance on the retreating players.

Two jereeds hit their mark, squarely between the shoulder blades of the grooms.

After thirty minutes of play, the horses stood quivering and the grooms licked their lips, struggling with the dryness of their mouths.

"Enough!" said Postivich. "I will ride this stallion tomorrow and take the Head Groom's mare as back up. She has an admirable intelligence about her and a sure foot, I can see this without riding her."

The grooms, their faces streaked with dirty sweat, noticed that the giant was dry faced and content, a smile creasing his face. He leaned over and slapped his sweating horse on the chest with the blade of his giant hand, grateful for a chance to compete at cirit once again.

But the cirit play was not unnoticed and within minutes the Sultan knew of the game. He pushed past his guards to the top of the walls and looked down on the players. In less than a second he recognized the huge stature of Ahmed Kadir and cursed him aloud.

The Grand Vizier made his way up the steps, panting hard.

"My Sultan! What is it?"

"That traitor Ahmed Kadir, banished from the Kapikulu Cavalry, has the nerve to appear on the royal cirit fields!"

The Vizier, long accustomed to Mahmud's outbursts, recovered his breath. Then he counseled the Sultan.

"I believe that you banished him from the Kapikulu Orta, Sultan. It was not mentioned that he could never ride a horse or play cirit."

"Whose horses are they, if they are not mine! All the Kapikulus ride my mounts! I will have his head."

The Vizier drew in a breath and strained his eyes towards the field. "I do not know all four thousand of your horses, of course," he said. "But I venture a guess that these are horses of your sister Esma Sultan's stables. Is she not staging the cirit tournament in honor of your birthday tomorrow?"

Mahmud pulled at his beard.

"There is no woman more traitorous than a sister," he said. "Especially when she has her own harem and stable!"

"What a buffoonish crew!" laughed the Vizier, squinting his eyes. "Those are common stable boys playing cirit with the giant! What an insult to a great corbaci of the Kapikulu to have fallen so low!"

Mahmud stopped plucking at his beard and smiled at his Grand Vizier.

"Yes, what a delicious insult, my good Vizier! Now I remember why I chose you as my most trusted consultant."

When he got back to the palace, Ivan Postivich had to pick his way through the wagons and carts full of food and provisions for the celebration the next day. There was a great deal of swearing as the workmen unloaded heavy crates of live fowl that pecked viciously at them when they picked up the cages.

"May Allah curse your gizzards!" growled a Turk, kicking at a hissing goose who had ripped a strip of flesh off his fingers. The rest of the workmen laughed at the bleeding man until they too were pecked and howled curses to Allah in turn.

The bakers and cooks supervised the deliverymen, finding little virtue in their work.

"You are damaging the goods! Look how your dirty peasant hands have crushed that precious head of lettuce! You buffoon, don't you know the price of these provisions? They are worth ten of your lives put together."

"Where is the cream! The sun will ruin it! You must put the cream in the cooling pantry at once before it curdles. We shall never buy another drop of milk from your dairy if my yoghurt is ruined from your laziness."

The gates of the palace were opened wider for a flock of sheep, driven by a dozen barefoot boys. The sheep droppings were immediately swept up by a team of handsome pages. Looking too beautiful to perform such a menial task, they pushed the excrement off the cobblestones and into the gutters and sluiced the courtyard with water from silver buckets.

The deliverymen stopped, despite the curses of the various cooks and eunuchs, to regard the boys, for they were as fine as the harem itself.

As one fair-haired youth bent down with a scrub brush to clean the stones, a burly driver whistled at him from the wagon. The workmen laughed and jeered at the comely youth who straightened up and threw a handful of sheep dung at them.

Another man touched himself, gesturing lewdly at the male servants.

"Stop that vulgarity this instant or we shall never buy again from your master's stall. He and you both shall be bankrupt and begging for soup at Aya Sofya!" shouted a woman's voice, as clear as the muezzin's call. It was Nazip, Esma Sultan's favorite servant, her face uncovered and her freckled cheeks red with indignation.

The men stood still, frozen the second they saw the bare face of the beautiful Nazip. With hands in midair, or geese pecking their numb fingers, they stood immobile before her beauty.

She spat in their direction. Looking them in the eye, she delicately removed the traces of spittle from her lips with a lace handkerchief before returning to the interior of the palace.

"To work, you brutes," shouted the Greek cook Maria through her yasmak. She was a large, fat woman who seemed as wide as the wagons and her voice bellowed through her thin veil.

"You cursed issue of whores, dream of impossibilities on your own time!" she shouted. "Your hands to the task, you have no time to fondle yourselves!"

A boy whispered, "Has a woman ever dared to say something so vulgar to a man?"

The Turk next to him said, "In the privacy of the home, I cannot pretend that such slurs are not heard." He threw down another melon to the boy. "Just pray to Allah that this fat one doesn't remove her yasmak!"

On the other side of the palace, the ice man and his crew were unloading snow and ice from their barge, cold treasures shipped all the way from the mountains of Greece. The sherbets of Esma Sultan's kitchen were held in high regard throughout Asia and Europe; they were flavored with lemon and almond, ripe melons, rhubarb, roses, pistachio essence, and incenses of the Orient. It was whispered that those who visited her privately in her harem were given the ultimate sherbet—a fantasy-inducing concoction of coconut, ambergris, and cream, laced with opium.

There was a fleet of barges on the Bosphorus, full of red and yellow silks, candles, incense, perfumes, and precious spices. A small British ship raised hazardous waves as it pulled close to the docks to deliver crates of French champagne. Curses echoed across the water as the merchants fought for dock space to deliver their wares.

"You spawn of a Greek whore," shouted the British sea captain in passable Turkish. "Move your dung carriers out of the way; we have fine wines to deliver."

"Keep your infidel hands on your own dirty genitals and bide your time!" shouted back the Turks as they moored their boats to the dock and unloaded their goods. "We were here first, you miserable wart on a toad's rump!"

There was a splash as the British ship's first mate dived into the water and swam towards the Turks. Within seconds he was on the dock, still blinking back the saltwater when a Turkish workman took a swing at him. The Englishman ducked, then countered with a punch to the Turk's stomach and followed up by bloodying his nose.

"Teach the dirty Turk a lesson, Charlie," shouted the captain, he and his crew hooting and cheering at the fight.

The Turk had turned to vomit, his stomach convulsing from the hit. But without pausing to wipe the spittle from his mouth, he spun around and came at the first mate with a knife, blade flashing in the morning sun.

The Brit pulled out his own blade and circled the Turk on the splintered boards of the dock. The air filled with roars in a mixture of half a dozen languages, attracting the Solaks who stood guard nearby.

"Put down your knives," shouted the commander, pushing through the crowd that had quickly gathered. He raised his scimitar high. "Put down your weapons or I'll send your heads to Topkapi!"

The Turk understood the threat and threw down his knife, gesturing to his opponent with an open hand to do the same. The Brit stood bewildered, his dagger still tight in his fist.

"What's the bloke say?"

"He says, throw down your knife!" said a sunburnt sailor with a wandering eye. "Throw down the bloody knife, Charlie or the Sultan will put your head on a bloody stake!"

The first mate kept his eyes on the Turk and the Solak.

"If I put down the knife," he shouted over his shoulder, "is 'e coming after me with that crooked sword of' is?"

"If you don't put down the knife they will all come after you, you idiot. Throw down the knife and be done with it."

Charlie looked at them warily and threw his blade down onto the dock, so that it stuck quivering in the warped grey planks.

The Solak retrieved the knife and grunted for the workers to continue their work under his watch and scimitar.

"Bloody Turks," muttered the captain as he moored his boat against Esma Sultan's docks.

The palace was in an uproar. Everywhere Irena looked there were people carrying cases of food and wine, arranging flowers, cleaning the carpets with long rakes. The rich smells from the kitchen wafted over the grounds and made her mouth water.

Esma Sultan strode about, scrutinizing the work, and pointing out faults. It was clear from her imperious tone that she would not accept anything but the highest standard.

"What horse did he choose?" Irena asked her mistress.

"Your favorite, of course," she smiled. "Like sister, like brother."

Irena clasped her hands together like a little girl, thinking that of the hundreds of horses in the stables, Ivan would be riding Sultan's Choice. He rode mares, almost exclusively, but the challenge and potential of the stallion had won him over.

"I knew it," she said.

The servant women were aflutter, quarreling and nervous, energized and jubilant. Men sweated and cursed under heavy loads and the entry hall smelled of cold seawater and fresh oysters, plucked from the Baltic and held in huge metal tanks.

It had been many months since Irena had seen a cirit tournament and now she was more excited than ever. To see her brother finally in his rightful place—on the back of a horse—made her flesh prickle with excitement.

Esma Sultan's face was radiant. There was not even a shadow of the illness she had so recently experienced.

"God be praised," thought Irena. Her brother had restored Esma Sultan's health and given her back her spirit—enough to needle and bait Mahmud, as she always had. Irena had never seen her so jubilant.

# Chapter 11

It was the third night in a row that Ivan Postivich had not been summoned to the chambers of Esma Sultan and he paced the gardens. It was the second night that servants other than Emerald had attended him in the hamam. He had not seen the soft-bodied eunuch at all.

Saffron at last appeared, his white turban atop his black head floating like a disembodied skull in the night.

"Ahmed Kadir, rest for tomorrow's game. The Princess sleeps tranquilly, her face content with gentle dreams. She does not need you tonight."

Ivan Postivich nodded stiffly. The eunuch looked at the janissary's face.

"What's this, janissary? Do I see disappointment in your face?"

Ivan Postivich hardened his mouth.

"Disappointment? To be relieved of my duty so that I can visit the taverns that beckon, the whores who have not seen my face in a month? I will be disappointed not to perform my duty to the Princess when pigs climb poplar trees!"

The eunuch did not smile.

"Do not forget whom you serve, janissary. Any male who sees Esma Sultan as anything other than a noble Ottoman Princess will be condemned to death. I beg you not to forget this even if some night it escapes the Sultane's mind."

Ivan Postivich turned to walk away and called over his shoulder.

"I cannot stop to prattle, Saffron. Excuse me, but there are cups of wine to be drunk and fat whores to caress." He strode off, gritting his teeth.

The ferryman took Postivich across the Golden Horn to Galata, where the lights of the taverns flickered an invitation across the calm water.

The streets reeked of cheap wine, fried oysters, garlic, grilled eggplant, and olive oil. Christians and Jews stood outside each tavern, calling to the passersby in urgent tones, bragging of the quantities and good value of the wines and of the beauty of the boys who danced in veils within.

Most of the customers inside the sordid taverns were Janissaries. The rooms reeked of stale drink and dirty, sweating men.

Ivan Postivich chose an establishment and the bearded men at the doorway eagerly ushered him into the dark. A Greek boy motioned to a table.

"Fetch me a *boza*," said Postivich remembering his cirit match.

The Greek waiter hurried back with a foaming glass of boza, a beer with little or no alcohol. He set a little bowl of pistachios in front of the janissary and then disappeared to serve another customer.

Postivich rarely visited the taverns these days. He had come to find the conduct of the Janissaries bordering on barbarous, making his stomach tighten in revulsion. He frowned upon the boys dressed in women's silks, and scowled as they practiced the art of flirtation, tugging at his tunic sleeves to capture hiseye.

"Away!" he said, shaking one off. He threw up his elbow abruptly, gesturing to the peach-veiled boy to leave him alone.

The boy shrugged but didn't miss a beat, shaking his hips and flat abdomen at a group of Janissaries next to the giant. They were eager to watch his dance and rewarded his long groping fingers with coins.

The beautiful creatures made fools of the drunken soldiers who lusted after them. While he did not find the boys attractive, Postivich understood how the lascivious moves and veiled faces provoked even the women-loving men. But to hear the soldiers call out lewdly and grope another man's genitals in public made him turn away in disgust for their betrayal of the dignity of the Janissary Corps and its old, but threadbare honor.

"It comes from sequestering women from men," said a Bektashi, who had slipped—determined and unnoticed—through the crowd and taken a seat—uninvited—at the janissary's table. "We Sufis believe in the inclusion of women. There will always be men who love men, but the situation is exaggerated when there is no real choice. For a woman to dance like this in public would cause a stoning, but a boy? Nothing. So the hypocritical traditions of the Sunnis and Shi'ites keep women caged like prize dogs in heat."

He took a long draw on his opium pipe. "Come to our tekke lodge and I will show you real women, my friend," winked the dervish. "Ones who know how to love a man without veils and witchery, but with her heart."

The janissary continued to eat his pistachios, considering the dervish's words.

"You are Ahmed Kadir," the dervish said after a minute, not asking a question but stating a fact from the depths of his stupor.

"I am," said Postivich, drinking his boza and cracking another pistachio between his teeth.

"The giant," said the dervish, rocking his head. "The Kapi-kulu cavalryman who no longer rides, by order of the Sultan."

Ivan Postivich turned to spit the shell on the floor, already littered with trash and wet sawdust. He knew better than to waste his breath on another intoxicated Sufi but answered him anyway.

"Tomorrow you can see me ride again, Dervish. I shall play cirit at Topkapi for Esma Sultan with my part of my orta."

"Esma Sultan," cooed the Sufi, his hand raised laconically in the air. "Esma Sultan. She cools her lovers with the midnight waters of the Bosphorus. Are you not her drowning guard, Corbaci?"

Ivan Postivich resisted the urge to strike the dervish.

"I no longer have that honor."

"Oh, yes," said the dervish, his eyes wide, but unfocused. "They say she confesses her sins to you every night. You soothe her soul and she has drowned no one in over a month. Some say you are her priest. Some say you are her lover."

"And who would 'some' be?"

"Those who might know, those who also serve the Sultaness. But understand me, janissary, I have no use for gossip but much use for love. It is in love that we find the godliness within ourselves and others. This is the ultimate act of Sufism, to convene with our god and maker."

Ivan Postivich laughed at the dervish and shook his head. He looked down into the film of boza that clung to the side of his empty glass. He snapped his finger for another.

"Dervish, you are drunk with the godliness of the white poppy."

The dervish focused his eyes with difficulty on Postivich's face.

"Your kismet is to love, Corbaci. That is Allah's truth."

"I am no longer a corbaci, and I only know the five-minute love of a whore in haste."

"You are what you were born to be. That too, is your kismet, your destiny. Play hard tomorrow, fight hard in the days ahead. Your body is meant to fight and your heart is meant to love."

"How do you know so much about me, Dervish? I have no contact with the Bektashi."

The dervish sucked on his pipe. "We Sufis have ears for truth. There is a Greek doctor who begs us to keep the giant from joining a Janissary rebellion. The beat of the pilaf caldrons is imminent and this old physician fears for your life, Corbaci. Christian-born as you are, he counts you as one of his lost sheep."

"The doctor realizes that over two hundred women were drowned, does he not?"

The dervish nodded. "He knows. He agonizes over those souls. But it does not keep him from worrying about your life."

The Greek boy brought another boza, saying, "It is paid for by the men over there." He lifted his chin indicating a group of Janissaries in the dark recesses of the tavern, far from the music and dancing boys. One motioned to Postivich to join them.

"My orta," said the janissary. He smiled for the first time in months. "Boy, bring this good man a coffee, thick and strong enough to stand on the table without a cup," he said, tossing a coin on the table. "I thank you, Dervish, for your fine company and advice. But you judge me too generously. I love to fight, yes, but I love only a fight. That is my only kismet, Sufi."

He slapped the dreaming man on the back, almost knocking him off the wooden stool that wobbled under the unsteady weight.

"Ahmed Kadir, you Serbian swine!" said the first Kapikulu who rose to clasp his hand. "Why has it been so many weeks since we have seen you? Does Esma Sultan wrap you in chains and iron fetters?"

"The Sultaness keeps me busy," he replied.

"So we have heard," said a short Albanian whose thighs bulged with muscles forged in cavalry campaigns. "You know of her treachery," he whispered. "What are you doing? Keep your distance from the witch or you will be murdered like a Christian!"

"I listen to her stories," said Postivich, taking a sip of his boza. "That is all I do."

"What depravities you must hear from that whore!" whispered one.

Postivich's fist clenched and the top rider in the orta, a red-headed Tatar, Altug, noticed it, but said nothing. He reached out and laid his hand on his old corbaci's arm. He saw the big man struggle to relax, feeling the touch of his comrade.

"You know she will kill you to please her brother," said a Turk called Aras. "He wants your head. They say he is murderously jealous of you."

"She and her brother are not close right now. I do not fear her."

"Don't be a fool, Kadir!" said Aras. "They are both Ottomans and would spill your blood just to see what color a janissary bleeds. They say Mahmud is in love with his sister, is it true?"

The Tatar raised his hand to stop the talk. He saw a light in the eyes of Postivich that he did not recognize. "Enough!" he said. "Let us raise our glasses at our reunion!"

Aras raised his glass. "To the cirit game tomorrow: we may play against you, but we are one orta!"

The cavalrymen drank deeply and begged Postivich to do the same. He made to sip from his glass of boza and stopped.

"Against me? Am I not to ride with half of our orta tomorrow against the other half? I was told the Kapikulu cavalry was to play an exhibition game."

The Tatar, Altug, shook his head. "The Sultan saw you practicing at the cirit field today with the grooms and stableboys of Esma Sultan. He was so incensed he has declared you will only play if you keep the same teammates tomorrow."

Ivan Postivich slammed down his glass, making the boza spray all over the fly-spotted table.

"These wretched boys know nothing of cirit! I wager they have never been allowed on the cirit field in their lives, most of them! They have been barely ripped from their mother's suckle, the snot-nosed brats! They are beggar orphan children who muck the stalls to put stale bread in their mouths."

"The Sultan gave his decree this very night," said Altug. "We are to have one of the boys on our team as a token for you. You will play us tomorrow with the children and old men of Esma Sultan's stable, by the Sultan's command."

The Tatar smiled at his corbaci, clapping his shoulder. "You know I will fear you, Ahmed Kadir, no matter whether you had trained monkeys on horseback as your teammates. Come, drink, and let us remember our war campaigns and the honor of the Kapikulu!"

They all drank deeply and then the redheaded cavalryman whispered in his corbaci's ear. "We have more serious thoughts to consider. We need to talk about this traitorous Sultan who means to disband all of us, even the Kapikulu. He will take our horses any day now, just as he has taken yours, to render us helpless against him. I am afraid many of the orta will side with him, for what are we without our horses?"

"Would you really fight against the Sultan?" asked Postivich. "Kapikulu have always been Topkapi guards, the most loyal of the ortas."

Altug looked down into his glass. Two other men muttered but did not answer.

"We will see what path each of us chooses," said Postivich. "Let us talk of cirit, and horses. Good cheer, my brothers."

# Chapter 12

Postivich didn't cross the Golden Horn until long past midnight. Though he drank only boza, he stayed late with his orta. Still, he wondered whether, without his leadership, the Kapikulus would stand shoulder to shoulder with the common soldiers or support the Sultan who owned and stabled their horses and bestowed upon them the honor of belonging to his elite cavalry.

The black water of the Bosphorus glittered like crushed diamonds under the light of the waxing moon. He stared up in the sky and saw how the sliver of a Sultan's scimitar had fattened into a thick crescent, swollen with milky light. He counted the days until it would be full and then weaken, its power waning over tides and women.

It had been a month since he had carried out his hated duty for Esma Sultan. To be out after dark now on the water of the Golden Horn brought back memories of the innocent men he had murdered. He plunged his hands into the water as if to wash them, and the oarsman turned to see what caused the drag. Ivan Postivich raised his hands from the dark water, dripping, and did not meet the ferryman's eyes.

The docks below Topkapi Palace were quiet, except for a few fishermen who were preparing to set out for the early morning catch. The dogs didn't stir, knowing there was nothing in the darkness to eat, and a puppy howled miserably somewhere deep in the alleys when his mother snarled and refused him her teat.

Ivan Postivich jumped up onto the dock, barely rocking the boat. He tossed a coin to the ferryman and grunted a farewell. He strode quickly to the gates of the palace, prayed at the muezzin's call, and took a few hours of rest.

When he awoke and rinsed his face, he saw that the Sultaness had provided him with a clean Kapikulu uniform, new boots that fit well, and a fresh turban for the game. He dressed and ventured into the gardens of the palace to see that everything had been transformed for the birthday celebration.

The slaves had erected tents and brought out silk divans and carpets to put under them. Tables were being set up with fine embroidered cloths and banners were flapping in red and gold. There was a raised platform for performances and another two for musicians. Chests of cedar and ivory, filled with delicate silk shawls and parasols for the ladies, were carried to the shade of the trees.

Inside, the kitchens were bursting with cooks' creations of caviar and roe, sculpted mounds of pâtés and cold meats, and platter upon platter of pickled vegetables. There were stews and cold prawns, lamb kabobs and grilled fish, *yahla corbasi*—a yoghurt and mint soup—kettles upon kettles of different pilafs, eggplant and lentil salads, sardines and mussels swimming in oil. The cooks fussed over their breads and halva, cursing Allah for the uneven heat of their ovens and flavor of the sesame seeds that were clearly inferior because they had been bought at an Armenian's stall.

There were huge vats of *ayran*, a drink made with whipped yoghurt and salt, and French champagnes, barrels of beer and wines—even one made from grapes grown on the Bosphorus.

Ivan Postivich drank in the rich smells of the kitchens and heard the feuding between the two head cooks, a Greek and a Turk.

"You cannot use the big oven! I must roast the lamb."

"Lamb in my pastry oven! The taste will contaminate the baklava! Howling daughter of a mongrel dog, you will do no such thing. Meat and pastry cannot be cooked together, you infidel!"

"There is no time to waste. This lamb must be roasted now. I cannot wait while you recite your suras when there is cooking to be done! Back away, you mother of heathen goats! Esma Sultan brought me from Macedonia for my cooking skills, not to share a kitchen with a Turkish peasant!"

"Dirty whore!"

"Dog of dogs!"

"Allah curse the beard of your father, the pimp!"

"May Allah do the same to your mother who surely has as coarse a beard on her ugly face as you possess!"

There was a crash of crockery and screams in at least two languages. A group of Solaks were stationed just outside the door for this very moment, since it was the third fight in two days.

"May you burn in hell, infidel!"

"Heathen pagan, defiler of all that is sacred!"

Ivan Postivich realized it was highly unlikely that he would be served breakfast on this particular morning. He decided to walk to the Spice Bazaar where he could find a cafe that would serve him some tea and bread.

The Spice Bazaar was not as large as the Grand Bazaar, but it possessed a charm that appealed to Postivich. He loved the beautiful rich colors of the spices: the fiery red of the paprikas, the green and rust of the henna, the speckled yellow-bird brilliance of the saffrons. In the market he could hear a cacophony of languages, like a cage of parrots shrieking at each other. There was Turkish to be sure, and Persian, Arabic, French, Ladino, Serbo-Croat, and dialects of other northern countries.

There was a beauty under the awnings of the spice stalls that honored the land, a mixing of cultures and colors that reflected the Ottoman Empire's rich tapestry of peoples and history.

Still, the predominant color was, and always would be, red. Ottoman red.

Postivich found a little table and sat down. A man approached with a huge metal tea vat strapped on his back. He wiped clean a glass and served the janissary some strong tea and clapped his hands for a boy in the pastry shop to come take his customer's order.

The boy brought a plate of bread, some fresh feta cheese, and a few slices of cucumber—a summer breakfast. The bread was encrusted with sesame seeds, oily and roasted fresh that morning.

Ivan Postivich was aware that the people in the Bazaar were staring at him, and this he was used to because of his size. But there was a certain respect that his Kapikulu uniform afforded him, and his new leather riding boots shone under the little cafe table. He felt proud once more to be a Kapikulu, the elite corps selected from among the Janissary.

As he sipped his tea, he watched two Janissaries patrolling the market, swaggering and scowling at the public, their dark looks as hostile as jungle beasts. Both carried bastinados that they swung savagely at anything that crossed their path.

The bigger of the two, a short, thick man with a thick mustache, stopped next to the spice stalls and grabbed a merchant by the arm.

"Jew! Do you have the money you owe us?"

The man widened his eyes. "I told you, I cannot pay you any more. I must feed my family and care for my sick child."

"You will pay me or I will pay you with a beating for your disgusting presence."

Taking his short bow, a *falaka*, from his shoulder, he tied the string tightly around the Jew's feet.

"Don't beat me, sir," cried the man. "I cannot pay you any more this week! My pockets are empty!"

The janissary sneered at him and yanked the bow so the man fell to the ground. He signaled to his companion who took his bastinado and began to club the victim's feet until he shrieked in pain.

"Stop this!" cried Ivan Postivich leaping to his feet and overturning the little table and his breakfast. "What has this man done?"

The two Janissaries drew a collective breath when they saw Postivich approach them, but the first soldier recovered his composure quickly and said, "Stay out of this, Ahmed Kadir. This is our district to patrol, you have no business here. This man owes us money and refused to give it. He is a Jewish scoundrel, a pox on the earth."

The man struggled on the ground his feet red from the beating.

"In Allah's name, I do not owe the men money."

"Release him," growled Postivich, the sound crawling up from deep in his throat.

"I told you to stay out of this, Kapikulu. Go back to your own guard."

"Release him now," repeated Postivich. "You bring dishonor to the Janissary Corps with your demand for baksheesh! Collect your money from the Sultan on payday honestly and refrain from stealing from the citizens!"

"We protect this man and his dirty litter of Jews. He owes us for our work."

"A baksheesh is a baksheesh and no citizen of Constantinople should have to pay a bribe for protection."

"Don't provoke them," howled the man writhing in pain on the dirty tiles of the Bazaar. "I cannot stand another beating! Persuade them to accept payment next week and you will have done Allah's will."

"Listen to this citizen," said the man wielding the bastinado. "He pleads for you to leave him in peace and us to our duty. Go back to Esma Sultan and entertain the harem, giant."

The Jew on the ground suddenly felt the tension of the falaka release as Postivich slammed his fist against the janissary's skull. The soldier's head snapped back like a broken doll's and he fell unconscious next to the cafe's hot grill.

The metal scorched his cheek, and the searing pain brought him back to consciousness.

"Allah, help me!" he cried. The restaurant owner reluctantly threw a pan of soapy dishwater over his head, regretting the waste of perfectly good suds.

The soldier who held the bastinado pulled out a knife and crouched in a defensive stance.

"You would pull a knife on a fellow member of the Corps?" said Postivich, assuming the same pose. "You are no better than a dung beetle!"

The man thrust the blade at Postivich who dodged as quickly as if he were on the cirit field. He pulled out his own dagger and feinted a reply.

The janissary appeared terrified at the Kapikulu's great stature and reputation and jumped back, falling into a stall of spices. A huge multicolored cloud erupted over his head as he scrambled to his feet, choking as he tried to recover his knife. The paprika, saffrons, and henna covered his face and his eyes stung and teared as he coughed and floundered in the choking dust.

Ivan Postivich kicked away the knife and the boy who had brought him breakfast surreptiously grabbed it from under a counter and ran off into the recesses of the Bazaar to peddle it for a good price.

"Do you still want to fight, you dog of dogs?" screamed Postivich.

"Peace, Corbaci," the janissary choked. "Peace!"

"There will never be peace for the Janissaries when there are rotten entrails in its Corps such as you," spat the giant. He looked down at his clean clothes and realized they were stained red and green and brown with spices.

He clenched his teeth and kicked the janissary who lay wheezing in the paprika.

"Now I shall have to play cirit looking like a beggar," he said, rubbing at his ripped tunic.

"That is how the Sultan wants you to play," said a voice.

It was an old man, once fine of stature, now bent and crippled. But Ivan Postivich knew him at once.

"Aga!" he cried, gazing at the old Horse Master. "Are you a ghost?"

"I am not as near to death as the Sultan wished, Allah be praised. Come, let us sit. I never could stand well after spending my life on a horse's back, but at this age it is simply impossible."

They watched together as the spice-blinded janissary staggered away.

"It has been many years now, Ahmed Kadir. But I follow your adventures."

Ivan Postivich hung his head. "Then I am embarrassed to meet your honored eyes. You must know I have been stripped of my position as corbaci of the cavalry."

"Yes, my son. I know of that and much more, I fear."

"Where have you been these years? We thought you were missing and dead in Macedonia. They said they searched for your body for days when your horse came back without you."

"I have spent many years in Macedonia, but I was not dead, only banished from the Imperial City. Were you really told this?"

"It was rumored. No one recovered the body."

"That is because this body, aged as it is, was banished from Topkapi and the Kapikulu. When Mahmud became Sultan, he made it known that I was no longer useful in the Corps and he would not provide me horses. I did leave, after an audience with him, and on the eve of the campaign found it too painful to confess. Forgive an old man his vanity."

Postivich shook his head. He still could not believe that the Master of the Horse sat across from him, alive.

"Today you will have the opportunity to see me play cirit. This you know."

"I know more than I can tell, else my tongue be sliced from the back of my throat."

"What can I do, Aga? I have a ragged team of beggar children—gypsies, Anatolian Turks, all untrained. They are children of the orphanage who work in the stables of Esma Sultan."

"What better horsemen can you find in this world, Ahmed? A team of beggar children—who ride bareback like our ancient tribes—and an aged Turkish head groom who has devoted his life horses. Perfect. As long as they have heart, you can win or at least lose honorably. Cast back to when you were a boy. Think how much you wanted the honor of riding on the cirit field. These children from hovels have the same pure hope, and they haven't seen enough of the world to be disillusioned."

The Master of the Horses pointed to Postivich's stained clothes. "Remember your roots, Ahmed," he said, his old hands shaking. "Remember your tears, for they were pure from the heart. That pureness resides only in the hearts of children."

Postivich looked over at the spice vendor's stall and heard his wife crying over the lost merchandise. Her keening rose to a level that caused the wild dogs in the alleys to howl.

She bent over, filling wooden boxes with precious herbs. Much they could salvage, but some spices were mixed with the filth from the floor, stained and useless.

"Woman," said Postivich. "I would like to buy all that you sweep off the floor."

The vendor's wife gaped openmouthed at the janissary, unable to speak. She waved her brilliantly powdered hands at her husband, urging him to pursue the offer.

The vendor opened his eyes wide and then squinted them again.

"Are you drunk so early in the day? We have paid our bribes, you Janissaries must leave us alone to scratch out a living."

"No, sir, I do not jest," Ivan Postivich said, pulling out coins and dropping them on the small counter of the stall. "Put the spices into a bag, mixed as they be, and I will take them for this price."

The vendor's wife muttered a sura and made a temple of her hands.

Postivich returned to his Aga.

"Bring us both coffee," said Postivich to the boy who hovered near. He turned to the Horse Master and said, "We have some planning to do."

# Chapter 13

When Ivan Postivich arrived at Esma Sultan's stables, the boys ran out to greet him and the old Head Groom wrung his wrinkled hands.

"The game will start in less than an hour!"

"Perfect!" exclaimed Postivich. "And look at the fine clothes our warriors wear."

It was true. The untidy, ragged boys were transformed by new white tunics and leather boots, not as fine as the Kapikulu's, but still garments that made the boys' faces shine with pride.

The boys exclaimed when they saw the disheveled look of Postivich.

"What has happened to you?" they shouted. "You look like you have been in a brawl, Corbaci."

"You look beggarly. What rags you wear!" said the Serbian boy Nicolas, his chin jutting out in disgust.

"Shut your mouth," said the littlest one, the Gypsy, through his teeth. "This is Ahmed Kadir you address!"

"I am not insulted," said Postivich. "In fact, I am honored. Because it is the Sultan's wish that I look beggarly. Torn pants, torn shirt colored in filth—colorful, like a Gypsy."

"Why does he insult me?" whispered the Gypsy boy.

Postivich overheard him, stretched out his big hand and tousled the matted curls of the boy.

"No, this is an honor. We will all look like Gypsies, like Mongols, like Turks, like Serbs, Bosnians, and Tatars, who have conquered and been conquered in this Empire and given it the iron spine the world envies. I have a plan for today, my young cavalry. Come close, and we shall see how a team of mongrels can have victory over the Sultan's elite cavalry."

The drums pounded to signal the beginning of the cirit game as a crowd of several thousand lined the field. Those who were not permitted entry hung from the branches of the plane trees or scaled the cirit field walls every time the Solaks and mounted Sipahis turned their backs.

Esma Sultan looked through the peephole of her carriage, seeing no sign of Postivich or his team.

"Where is he?" she whispered to the veiled Irena.

The eyes above the veil shone bright to meet the Sultane's worried look.

"He will appear," she said.

The Sultan and the Grand Vizier sat on divans under the shade of the billowing tents set up at the midline of the field. They sipped champagne from crystal flutes made in Vienna, the city they had laid siege to twice.

"Descend from your carriage, darling sister, heart of my heart," the Sultan called. "Or is it that you wish to make a quick departure since your drowning guard has not appeared?"

"Do not call him that, brother," snapped Esma Sultan, leaning out of the carriage. "He shall never drown another man again by my oath. And he will appear!"

The Sultan chuckled and nodded to the page to pour more champagne. "Perhaps he does not have the courage to face his old orta. He knows the legend of the living giant is only that—a legend that little children like to tell."

Esma Sultan squinted against the sun, making her fine skin wrinkle around her temples. She extended her hand to her footman who helped her out of the carriage.

"Children's legend?" she said, suddenly smiling. "Yes, quite right. And here are the children who accompany him!"

The crowds parted as Ahmed Kadir rode onto the field at a full gallop on a black stallion. A thousand voices murmured as Constantinople took in his ripped tunic and rainbow splotched uniform.

'"What in the name of Allah is he wearing?" said the Sultan.

The boys and aged Head Groom followed him, whipping their horses and flattening their chests against the steeds' manes as they galloped into the Hippodrome. They did not ride as trained cavalrymen, erect and schooled in fine equestrian technique; they galloped as passionate children who have ridden horses all their short lives.

The crowd roared with cheers at the barefooted boys in rags, who circled the field like wild savages, free and classless warriors on the backs of Esma Sultan's fine horses.

"Did you not even give them boots, Esma?" asked her brother. "How can they play without footwear? I told you to outfit them properly. This is a disgrace! The ambassadors and dignitaries of

Europe sit under the canopies—they shall think the Ottoman Empire is a rabble. These boys look like barbarian Huns!"

She shook her head in astonishment.

"I gave them boots and new white tunics. And starched turbans."

She brought her hand to her cheek.

"A pack of wild beggars," exclaimed the Sultan. "Look at their clothes. What the devil do they have on their tunics? What is this colored soot?"

The drums beat so loudly now that the crowd could feel it in the pit of their bellies. Ivan Postivich motioned for his boys to line up, a first line, second, and third. He took the first line.

"What strategy is that?" said the Sultan, waving his hand in disgust. "The weakest players should lead the front file. Has he lost his senses?"

Esma Sultan looked down. A ghost of a smile flickered on her lips.

"He's mad!" said the Sultan. "Have you fed him opium? What conduct is this?"

The *cavus* rode out to the center of the field and announced the Kapikulu Orta first. It was his job to ensure that all the proud honors of each player were pronounced in front of the crowd.

One by one, he recognized each Kapikulu officer and cited battles and victories, honors and prizes each had won, from Macedonia to Egypt to the gates of Vienna.

When he turned to announce Ahmed Kadir, he hesitated.

"Ahmed Kadir is the honorable Corbaci of the Sultan's Elite Kapikulu Cavalry," he said, his voice wavering.

"Stop him!" shouted the Sultan, rising to his feet. He nodded to one of the Sipahis horsemen. "This man is not a member of our Kapikulu! Make him retract this statement!"

The horseman galloped onto the field.

"Why must you embarrass him this way?" said Esma Sultan, shutting her eyes.

"Because he—" Mahmud looked at her, his mouth twitching. "He is a traitor, a janissary dog!"

Again the crowd raised a bewildered buzz as the cavus was interrupted by the Sultan's guard.

The Sipahi officer whispered to the cavus, who nodded uneasily.

"The Sultan wishes me to correct my statement. Ahmed Kadir is a janissary only, he is no longer part of the elite Kapikulu. I regret my mistake and beg the Sultan's indulgence of my ignorance."

The cavus looked unhappily over at the giant. Ivan Postivich smiled grimly.

"You do not dishonor me, cavus," he said. "Only let me speak."

Ivan Postivich raised his voice, he said to the crowd, "Because these are special circumstances and because the honorable cavus knows nothing of the repute of my teammates, I shall have the honor of introducing them to all Constantinople."

Postivich gestured to his players, lined up on their prancing horses, as nervous as their mounts.

"First, of Gypsy blood and light fingers—"

The Gypsy boy's jaw dropped.

"—excuse me, of *lightest* fingers on the reins and an innate sense of the horse's nature, I introduce Abdul."

The crowd roared as the boy galloped a circle around Postivich and his team, waving his whip in the air.

"Hamid—of mongrel descent—will play second in line."

The boy froze, stunned. "I shall murder him," he murmured, "and stab his dead corpse again and again in revenge!"

"Did I say 'mongrel'?" shouted Postivich. "No, by Allah's word, a noble *Mongol*, the fiercest of the horse warriors and the blood stock from which Ottomans thrive! Hamid!"

The boy smiled uncertainly as the other riders clapped him on his back. He shouted "Allah!" and raced down the front line of the crowd on one side of the field and then back along the other side. Raising his fist in the air, he stood up on the horse's back like a circus performer.

The crowd, who by this time had realized that they were spectators to far more than a simple cirit game, waved kerchiefs and hooted to the rider.

"And who can forget the Anatolian horsemen of legend who gave their blood for our Sultan's pleasures!"

Mahmud stood up in anger. "What is he doing, Esma? What is this drivel?"

Esma Sultan smiled but did not answer, her eyes fixed on the giant.

"And the aged one?" Postivich said. "Does a warrior stop dreaming of war and the cirit field when he has more wrinkles than an elephant's trunk? Not if he has an honorable heart and is a Turk!"

The crowd erupted into a roar. The Head Groom rode at a canter to the centerline, stopped his horse, and bowed deeply.

The Kapikulu team waited, eager to compete but proud of their corbaci's courage. Their faces creased with smiles and they, too, cheered the motley team.

"Start the games!" commanded the Sultan. "Start the games!" He wiped his brow with the embroidered handkerchief of a new concubine. "The man intends to make a fool out of his Sultan. I'll have his head on a stake before this day is out!"

"No, you will not."

"I will do as I wish, Esma. I am the Sultan of the Ottoman Empire and it pleases me to see it so, I shall feed the bloody strips of his flesh to the dogs of Constantinople!"

She leaned close and hissed, "Then I shall have to defy you in the name of our forefathers and Ottoman honor and we will see whom the Janissaries choose, dear little brother. You know they are searching for a sultan who will support them."

"The Turks would never take a woman as their Sultan!"

"No. But they would if she were married," she said. "No matter whom she married. I have as much Ottoman blood as you."

"You wouldn't dare!"

"Shall we see? Shall we see if our father's favorite daughter and her husband are considered fit to rule—just as the Shi'ites chose Ali, the husband of Mohammed's daughter, Fatima, as the Prophet's successor. Shall we see if you are strangled, just as our brother and cousin were? Shall we see, dearest brother?"

"Start the games!" he shouted, turning away from her gaze.

"Start the games," echoed the cavus.

The Gypsy boy, Abdul, rode out and threw the first spear at the cavalryman's chest. Altug the Tatar ducked easily and laughed in disdain at the weak effort. He spurred his horse and galloped after the boy.

But the Gypsy had learned from Postivich's instruction and hung over the right side of the horse like a monkey. The jereed flew over the horse's head and landed with a thud.

Out galloped Ivan Postivich, his horse's hooves pounding the turf. He threw his jereed so fast that the retreating rider was stunned by its blow.

The crowd cheered as the referees indicated a point.

A Kapikulu player—the Albanian—galloped out to pursue the giant. Postivich reined his horse up in midstride and ducked, then switched leads as he crossed back over the line, safe from his opponent's spear.

The Kapikulu player turned to gallop for safety, but he had scarcely taken a complete two-beat at the gallop when he was jolted by the jereed spear striking his left shoulder blade.

Postivich, who had unexpectedly returned to the attack, turned again, galloped back over the centerline and raced back to his teammates.

"Foul! Stop the game!" shouted the Sultan. "Egregious foul!"

The referee blew a horn to stop the game.

"Give me my horse," commanded the Sultan. He pushed the stirrup bearers out of the way and pulled himself up on his horse, galloping to the center of the field.

"What treachery is this?" demanded the Sultan. "These are not the rules of cirit! You dishonor the sport with your cheat!"

He turned to see another horse galloping out to the midfield, the rider enveloped in billowing silks that furled and unfurled over her like heavenly wings.

"Esma," said the Sultan.

She reined her horse and held up her hand, crying out for all to hear.

"My Angel brother has misspoken."

A stunned silence met her words. She raised her chin in defiance and spoke clearly to the crowd.

"The rules of cirit state only that one player advances, throws his jereed, and changes roles to become the defensive player as soon as his spear is thrown. My father, Sultan Abdulhamid explained this to me, and he let me learn even more from the Master of the Horse, sitting on his knee," she said. "This is an unusual strategy, but not against the rules."

She reined her horse around to face more of the crowd. The horse pranced in excitement.

"I would not correct my brother the Sultan, if any mistake did not dishonor the memory of my father, the great Abdulhamid I who honored the Janissaries and the people of Constantinople!"

"Get off that horse, immediately," hissed Mahmud to his sister. "It is a sin against Allah for a woman to be astride a horse!"

"I have indulged you enough, my brother," she whispered, her teeth clenched. "You promised me a cirit game today. You burdened Ahmed Kadir with this ragtag team in order to ridicule him and I indulged you in that. You will look the fool if you do not let the game proceed. It is a leader, a ruler, they crave. Not a coward!"

Then she raised her voice again and called out to the crowd. "My brother the Sultan did not truly mean to question the game. Long live the Sultan and his love of the noble sport!"

She reined her horse back to the Sultan's tent, the crowd speechless at seeing a woman, an Ottoman princess astride a horse.

"She looks just like Sultan Abdulhamid, Allah save his soul!" said an old pasha in the crowd. "The ghost of her father lives in that one."

"It is Sultan Abdulhamid incarnate!"

"Allah, be praised."

Sultan Mahmud II raised his chin, his aquiline nose drawn at the nostrils in disdain.

"Let the game continue!" he announced. He hissed to the cavus, "See that the giant crosses the line each time or he is disqualified immediately and forfeits the game!"

The teams reformed and the game began again.

The Kapikulu team realized that indeed their skill would be judged by the outcome of this game, and they hardened their jaws as the giant scored point after point.

"Charge more quickly," yelled the Tatar corbaci to his squad. "Watch his hand!"

Ivan Postivich circled around and around, throwing the jereed and retreating. His stallion was lathered with sweat and Postivich tasted its salt in his mouth as he slid down the horse's neck from side to side, evading the whistling spears.

Suddenly the girth slipped on the horse's saddle, and the giant hung precariously sideways, unable to right the saddle again.

"Let me take your turn," cried the Serbian boy Nicolas who had been so contemptuous. "By Allah's name! I'll ride the point, I swear!"

"Go, then, countryman!" Postivich shouted.

In a flash of hooves, the Serb raced out to pursue the retreating rider. He stood up so tall in his stirrups, he mimicked the giant, and threw his jereed spear in a high trajectory. It whistled through the air and struck the Kapikulu rider.

Postivich was on the ground now, repositioning the saddle and tightening the girth. He kept the game in the corner of his eye as the Serbian boy flattened himself against his horse's back, avoiding his opponent's spear.

The giant vaulted onto his horse, back into the game.

Esma Sultan could not remain in her seat. She stood at the edge of the tent, tightening her fists each time her team won a point and gasped in suspense each time Postivich avoided a jereed. The Sultan's face grew hard and deep grooves formed down his cheeks as he watch the pure joy in his sister's eyes.

As the giant's team scored point after point, the crowd roared, and the plane trees shook with waving arms of common Turks who clung to their branches like a swarm of cicadas. The horn sounded to signal the end of the game and the cavus rode out and announced that the ragtag team of beggars had defeated the

Sultan's own Kapikulu. The Sultaness gave them a nod as they raced to the royal tent and bowed in unison.

"A disgrace," said the Sultan audibly, but Esma Sultan ignored him.

"We honor you, dear brother," she whispered, with a broad smile. "Now let us go in peace to my palace and enjoy this special day."

# Chapter 14

Ivan Postivich smelled the kitchens in the dark. He heard the thunderings of the British ambassador beyond the courtyard walls and wished he understood what the Englishman was saying.

Postivich had slept fitfully during the early evening, listening to the sounds of the fête. As a janissary and a servant, he was, of course, not allowed to attend, but he heard laughter and cries of delight from beyond the walls of the gardens and he was curious about the extent to which the tales of excess were true. As sleep evaded him, he decided to spy on the partygoers.

Avoiding the circling guards, Postivich heaved himself up into the limbs of a tree just beyond the wall. He scaled the great cypress, making the branches shake and tremble under his weight.

From this vantage point, just a few feet outside the walls, he could survey the lawns, kiosk, and gardens, lit by hanging lanterns and blazing torches.

Harem women walked arm in arm, their hair braided in pearls or drawn up in jeweled ribbons or ivory combs. They sipped champagne as if they were European royalty, comfortable with the ministers and with their wives. While none of them could speak English, many could converse in French, which delighted the Europeans who knew little or nothing about harems except for the lascivious tales that circulated about the embassies.

"Of course we do not share the Sultan's bed!" cried one of Esma's harem in horror, being asked to confirm a preposterous rumor. "We are Esma Sultan's harem. We are in her protection as adopted daughters."

"But does not the Sultan visit you—all of you—and share the pleasure?" asked a particularly drunken Russian.

"A husband having two wives in his bed at once! Is that what is done in Europe?" said Nazip, her hand flying to cover her mouth, and her laugh piercing the air. "Do tell us of your strange customs, for if a man behaved this way to us, under Islamic law we could renounce and divorce him. What rare customs do you practice in Europe? Your habits intrigue me!"

The British ambassador's wife, as dignified as she was fat, answered. "But of course, my dear, we don't take two lovers to our bed at once! Mercy, how you have misunderstood. We are inquiring about your customs, my dear. We are *Christians*, if you please!"

The Sultan himself was holding court under a large red tent, open to the summer air and scintillating with hundreds of chandeliers and candelabras. He smoked a pipe and received few if any visitors. No one approached the Sultan without being summoned first.

The Ottoman ruler sipped peevishly from his crystal goblet and nibbled reluctantly at the Beluga caviar sent to him packed in snow from the Russian frontiers. He watched his sister Esma move from one group to another, gracefully accepting praise from her guests for the day's festivities. She insisted that the British Ambassador dance with her and the harem, which delighted the audience as he removed his jacket and tied up his shirttails to expose his enormous white belly, making the guests double over in laughter. The Russian attaché, who had consumed far too much opium and vodka, took one astonished look and exploded in mirth as spittle dribbled from his lips.

The guests then played harem games, which Esma explained in fluent French and English. One such game was "Beauty or Ugliness," where a "judge" covers her eyes and calls out for all the players to freeze in ridiculous poses—demanding either grace and loveliness or horror or dementia.

Even the stuffiest of ambassadors was dragged into the game, and after consuming vast seas of champagne and wine, they were not so difficult to coax. Men and women froze like beautiful statues of Greek goddesses or in fiendish postures of gargoyles, their contorted features drawing gales of laughter from the spectators.

The Sultan held his goblet out for more champagne, never taking his eyes off his sister.

"I should ask her to sign a pact with the French and British ambassadors this very night," he muttered. "Look at those men, lusting after her like old bulls. She would seduce them into signing away their sons' inheritance for just a glimpse inside her harem walls!"

His fist grasped the crystal goblet so fiercely the stem snapped.

"Sultan! Are you injured?" cried the Vizier. He shouted to a servant, "Quick, bring a clean napkin and pack it with snow."

Mahmud's hand bled copiously, staining the starched white handkerchief. He glanced at his bloody hand with annoyance and then looked again at his sister and her entourage, as several eunuchs attended him.

It was Nazip's turn at Beauty or Ugliness, and she placed her hands over her freckled face and counted to ten in chirping, Ottoman-inflected French. She recited the numbers in the wrong order and then laughed together with Esma Sultan, who kissed her cheeks and bade her try again. The Sultaness's hand lingered on the young woman's bare shoulders as the two of them counted "*un, deux, trois, quatre . . .*"

"Send for her!" commanded the Sultan, suddenly. "Nazip, my sister's handmaiden. I will have her in my bedchamber this evening. Tell my sister it is—a birthday gift to myself, that I shall undo her ribbon."

A servant approached Esma Sultan who was entertaining the Prince de Joinville with an anecdote about her harem. She threw back her long white neck to laugh, gesturing at Nazip who finally completed her arduous count.

"Jolie!" Nazip shouted, and all the players struck their most graceful or mockingly beautiful pose. The Swedish ambassador locked arms with a dignitary from Egypt, feigning flying angels. The Prince de Joinville smiled but did not laugh, his eyes riveted on Esma Sultan.

Mahmud hardened his face as he watched the prince drink in the beauty of his older sister.

"He could have the beauties of Europe, yet he sets his hungry eyes on an Ottoman woman more than a decade his senior!" said the Sultan to his Grand Vizier.

"Yes, he does seem taken with her and with her harem," replied the Vizier. "They are all quite beautiful tonight, each like a shining star in the night sky."

"It is disrespectful for him to stare at Esma this way, as if she were merely a woman, and not a Sultan's sister."

"He's had quite a bit to drink, I should think," said the Vizier. "I believe everyone has, my Sultan."

At last Esma Sultan finished her story and turned to address the servant who had been waiting patiently. Her face hardened when she heard the Sultan's demand, and she looked over to her brother. In a deliberate motion, she nodded her head "no," in the Turkish fashion.

"Allah curse her!" said the Sultan, still peevishly wiping the blood from his cut hand.

The Vizier looked at him.

"What is it, my Sultan?"

"My sister is my enemy!"

"But good Sultan, look at the fête she has planned for you. It must have cost her a Pasha's fortune!"

"She entertains to entertain herself and her harem. This is no celebration for me, can you not see that? She has made a fool of me the entire day, and now intends to make a fool of me tonight at Topkapi. Am I not the Sultan? Can I not choose any woman in my Empire to take as my concubine?"

He clapped his hands for the guard, wincing briefly as he struck the fresh injury.

"See that Nazip is escorted to Topkapi tonight. Do not allow my sister to defy my order. That woman will be delivered to my bedchamber, prepared with ablutions, ready to serve her Sultan. Summon the carriage, prepare to depart."

The bewildered Vizier stared about the party and drained the last of his punch, sorry to leave before the famous sorbets were served.

Nazip had refused the Sultan's invitation to his bed before, for it was the talk of Esma Sultan's palace. They were proud that their freckled mistress could keep a Sultan waiting for her. She had teased that one day, when she was bored with freedom, she of course would go to his bed so that the son she would conceive might one day be an Ottoman ruler.

"I'm simply not in any hurry to become fat and pregnant," she laughed, for despite all her freedom she still remained a virgin. "Besides, once I lie with the Sultan he will confine me to his harem. How could I abide life locked away in the Topkapi Serail after living in the harem of Esma Sultan?"

Now, as the party continued into the night, floating on gales of laughter, a Topkapi Solak approached Esma Sultan and asked her to speak with him in private. When she heard what he had to say, her eyes darted to the Sultan's crimson tent and saw that indeed the guest of honor had departed.

"You may tell my brother, our Sultan, that Nazip is occupied in helping me entertain tonight and cannot attend him."

The Captain of the Palace Guards raised his chin. He had been prepared for such an answer.

"My humblest apologies to your majesty. The Sultan has given me an order and I must obey."

Esma Sultan's eyes flashed and she put a light hand on the Solak's arm, her jewels sliding coolly against his skin.

"Wait, Solak. Do not embarrass the Sultan, who was drunk on champagne, by causing a scene at his own party. I will speak to Nazip in private and within the next hour, I will accompany her to Topkapi under your guard. Send word to the palace that we will come, though I must first attend my guests."

"Allah has blessed me with your kindness," said the Solak, relieved that he did not have to carry out the command with force.

"Let's change the game!" cried Esma Sultan, returning to the party. "Hide and seek this time. Lady Whortley, would you do the honors of being the seeker? We shall play for thirty minutes and then the sorbets and creams will be served, with more champagne!"

Her guests cheered this idea and she smiled engagingly.

As Nazip walked past her, she snatched at her arm.

"Come with me," Esma Sultan whispered, as Lady Whortley counted in both English and French. "I must talk with you at once."

The Sultan sobered somewhat as the eunuch helped him with his ablutions.

"Has she arrived yet?" he asked, as the man sluiced water over him.

"No, my Sultan."

"I shall have her head on my breakfast plate if she does not appear."

"She will come," said the eunuch. "No woman would deny you, your majesty, as they know the punishment too well."

The Sultan chewed at his lip, wishing the eunuch had not mentioned coercion, rather than honor and passion.

The eunuch dried his master's back and helped him into his bed robes.

"I shall not suffer waiting much longer. Where is she?"

The eunuch twisted his hands, but then a Solak at the door gave a handsign—an essential part of the Ottoman Court vocabulary, since the early Sultans would not abide mundane human speech in their courts.

"My Sultan. Your sister pays you a visit. She waits in the foyer."

"Is she accompanied by the fair Nazip?"

"Yes. But she wishes to speak to you before Nazip is presented."

"Now? As I lie in my bed, prepared to receive a concubine!" roared the Sultan. "What manner is this?"

"I beg your pardon, Royal Highness. Do you wish to speak to her?"

"What matter if I wish to speak to her! She will lie on the edge of my sarcophagus and nag me after I am years dead and my body turned to dust! Send her in, but prepare the maiden as Allah mandates. Bathe her in rosewater and anoint her in sandalwood oil and then bring her to my bed!"

The Solak returned with Esma Sultan, who in contrast to what her brother expected, looked radiant, her braided pearls and lapis glittering in the light.

"My Angel brother, you are impetuous. Look at you," she said, gesturing to his French canopied bed. "Is this how you lie as you wait for a virgin?"

"Why do you toy with me? I shall have fair Nazip this very night, and none of your wiles will prevent me! She has thrice refused me and tonight I lose patience."

Esma sat on the edge of his bed and fingered the heavy red brocade of the spread.

"Yes, this is comfortable. It is European, though. Not at all Ottoman."

"My first mother had it sent from Paris. I inherited it upon her death."

"Not as fine a playing field as a divan for taking a maidenhead. Perhaps acceptable if your woman will lie under you and not move around too much, but I should think a Sultan would grow bored making love on such a high pedestal. There is no room for mistakes or you should both tumble out—and how undignified to have an Ottoman ruler injure himself falling from bed with a virgin. Better to move about on the cushions of a divan, as our ancestors have done. The Europeans are timid in their lovemaking—you can see it so well in this narrow bed."

"What have you to say, oh sister?" said the Sultan. "You did not come here to discuss my furniture."

"Indeed. You do know me well, Angel brother." She took his hand and stroked it with the two fingertips she reserved for eating. He shivered at her touch despite himself.

"I shall indeed give you my favorite from my own harem, but with conditions."

"Conditions!"

"Nazip is my own slave whom I share with you, darling brother. She is my property, for whom I have paid good money. I could consult the Ulema and cause gossip throughout the city, but you know that she is mine. And being my own, she is therefore free to make her own decision as my adopted daughter."

She met her brother's eyes.

"Nazip, the virgin, will lie with you on one condition—you must let her return to my harem tomorrow and every night you do not call for her."

The Sultan laughed in astonishment.

"I cannot do this! You know that once she has lain with me, her seed is sacred. She must be guarded by eunuchs to protect her womb from other than me."

"My dear brother—I have no male organs and am no rival for yours. Nor are the ladies of my harem."

"If she should bear a child and it be a son, the Ottoman Empire must be assured there is no bastard, that she has not cuckolded the Sultan!"

"You will send your most vigilant eunuch to attend her in your name. He will accompany her everywhere until she gives birth and the great Ottoman Empire will give a sigh of relief to know that she is chaste and lies with no other man but you. But I will not condemn her to the Topkapi harem, where she will live a life of isolation and male domination. It is paradise to those who do not know better, but she has lived with me. I cannot let her live out her days in desolation, even if she one day becomes Valide Sultane."

The Sultan rubbed his temples, trying to assuage the headache his once favorite sister had given him.

"And she will, dear brother, give you pleasure no virgin on earth can. I know my Nazip," she said, raising an arched eyebrow. "You will be a most fortunate man this night. But only if you agree to my terms."

"Once again you toy with me, Esma," said Mahmud, feeling his penis grow and push up under his white tunic. "Does it give you pleasure, my Angel sister?"

"Dearest brother," said Esma Sultan, smiling and rising from the bed. "Consider our pact. You will have a night of passion. But Nazip remains with me after this night. Consider," she said, tugging playfully on the sheet to uncover him. "I shall wait outside your chamber door to either escort Nazip joyfully to your bed or to accompany her back to my palace."

Mahmud felt the cool air on his exposed skin as his sister drew down the sheets. He drank in her beauty, aged as she was now, and felt himself shiver with arousal.

"Send in Nazip immediately," he murmured to Esma Sultan. "I must have a woman in my bed this night, this minute!"

"Then you agree, my Angel brother. By Islamic law, she became my adopted daughter when I took her as my slave. Only I can consent to your taking her to bed, you know this by the law of the Sheriat."

The Sultan laid his hand on his sister's arm. "She shall return to you tomorrow, and as I take her to my bed, I will remember her as your personal gift. We shall share her, dear sister."

Esma removed her arm slowly from her brother's grasp and stood, bowing to him. As she turned to leave she said, "Do not worry about Nazip tumbling out of your French bed. She has practiced in my own English one and is quite nimble, with a good sense of balance and grace. Enjoy, little brother, and return her to me joyful and full of stories of your prowess to share with the harem."

As she left Nazip, she kissed her cheeks four times and whispered in her ear. Nazip laughed and the sound of birds filled the silent corridors of Topkapi.

Irena had noticed the abrupt departure of Mahmud, as did most of the guests who were not imbibing heavily or smoking opium. The clatter of the horses' hooves on the cobblestones in the court-yard suggested the Imperial carriage was drawing away at a thunderous pace. Could there be some emergency—a declaration of war or rebellion—that would provoke such a hasty retreat from the Sultan's own birthday party?

A short time later Irena noticed the absence of Nazip—and the tinkle of her constant laugh. She thought at first that Nazip was with the Prince de Joinville, but it seemed he was already being entertained by Leyla and other women in the harem.

Even Esma was absent for a while, although she did reappear at the party before the sorbets were served. Her face was unperturbed and regal, without a ripple of consternation. She engaged her guests in conversation and insisted they drink more of the fine French champagne. The French ambassador was giddy with pride as crate after crate was pried open and everyone toasted the health and prosperity of France, a country that could produce such a magnificent beverage.

Nakshidil smiled, too, at the gracious praise for her home country and said she would pass the compliments to her cousin the Empress Josephine of France and her husband, Napoleon. This sent a wave of murmurs through the crowd who hadn't realized her family connections, and another toast was proposed to the health of Nakshidil.

A warm gust of wind ruffled through the leaves of the plane trees and tugged at the women's soft garments. Irena clutched her veil to keep it from rising.

When Esma turned to make her way through the garden, Irena took her hand and pulled her apart from the crowd, into the shadows of the vines.

"Pardon me, O Sultane. Where is Mahmud?" she asked.

Esma Sultan started to say something and then bit her lip. Then she saw her companion's expectant face, waiting for an answer.

"He has taken Nazip to his bed," Esma Sultan said simply.

Irena had grown up in a harem and this should have been no surprise. Mahmud had thrice been refused Nazip's company, and she knew sooner or later, he would have her.

"I see," she said, dismayed dispite herself. She knew too much to feel this way—but she still harbored a spark of love for that young boy, the great love of her youth, who was now Sultan Mahmud II. And it pained her to think of him with Nazip.

Esma Sultan took her companion's chin in her hand.

"Look at me," she commanded, her voice cold.

Irena's eyes were full of confusion. She squirmed but her mistress squeezed her chin tight, the way she used to when Irena was a little girl and the Ottoman Princess wanted her attention.

"My brother is a murderer," Esma Sultan said. "You must realize this and forget about him. Any affection that he showed you at an early age has vanished with his childhood, just as your name Irena has vanished. These are all childish memories, swept away. He is not a little boy any longer but a man who is poisoned with power.

"It happens to them all."

Irena drew back. "There was once tenderness in his boy's heart."

Esma let out a gasp in exasperation.

"That heart no longer exists. He drowned over two hundred women. He wants to kill your own brother! You are a fool to harbor any feelings but hatred for him."

A different voice spoke, Ottoman accented with French. "If only we could preserve the innocence and compassion of a boy's heart."

Nakshidil stood above them on the steps, emerging from the shadows.

"I have always loved my son, but your father would not allow me to interfere," she said to Esma Sultan. "If I could have spent more time with him, if he were not condemned to the princes' caged apartments, I could have preserved some of that goodness,

I swear on all that is holy. He was a good boy. I remember his tenderness just as Bezm-i Alem does."

Esma Sultan approached Nakshidil and took her hand, for the Sultan's mother was trembling on the top marble step. The Valide Sultane's knees suddenly buckled under her and she sat unceremoniously with a thump on the hard stone.

"Are you all right, Valide Sultane?" Irena asked, rushing to her side.

"Age and illness do not allow anyone dignity, not even a Sultan's mother," she said, rubbing her hip and sighing deeply. "I should never want my cousin Josephine to see me so old and infirm."

"I will have the cook make you some coffee laced with amber to cleanse your blood and render you more alert," said Irena.

"Oh, my no! I am making peace with this dizziness and I should not want to destroy the lovely taste in my mouth of French champagne. These spells pass," she said, patting Irena's hand.

Esma Sultan noticed the gesture.

The Sultan's adopted mother looked at Esma Sultan in the flickering light of the torches.

"Do you not believe, Esma Sultan, that a man is capable of compassion, that there might be a small part that is woman in his male heart?"

Esma Sultan's face turned as hard as the marble that surrounded them.

"No! Male and female cannot coexist! Men will always be rotted with corruption and power—they cannot resist the temptation. Not even a woman's hand can change their kismet."

"You are wrong, Esma Sultan," Irena said. "You have always been wrong about this!"

Nakshidil gasped that a harem girl would admonish a princess, the sister of Mahmud. Esma Sultan's eyes widened in surprise.

"Not all is moon, not all is sun," said Irena, her eyes glittering in the darkness. "They both exist in a human heart, be it male or female. Should I ever have sons, I swear I shall teach them compassion above all things."

"You are a fool," said Esma Sultan. "How can you forgive men after what you suffered at my father's hand?"

"I have suffered at the hand of your exalted family, but I know forgiveness. Should I have children—though who would give me a baby with my face burned and twisted?—I shall teach them with all my heart what compassion and forgiveness are."

"You do not understand power," Esma Sultan said. "No one can change men. You speak like a child, not a woman. What do you know of men and their ambitions?"

"I do understand men, power and especially Ottomans," Irena protested. "Much better than you, Esma Sultan—your face is still beautiful. Mine is hideous!"

"Dear girl!" exclaimed Nakshidil.

"And yet I can still forgive, though you cannot," said Irena, her gaze steady on Esma Sultan. "I do not drown a man as if he had no soul!"

The Princess's jaw loosened in shock. Irena was close enough for Esma to strike her face, but the Sultan's sister was too stunned to move.

Nakshidil's face warmed, her old teeth glinting in the moonlight. Her voice rang out as Irena stormed away.

"That one should be the Valide Sultan, Esma. Then there would be hope for the Ottoman Empire . . . and men's souls."

# Chapter 15

The belly of the moon had swollen, fully pregnant with light, flooding the Imperial city of Constantinople with its ghostly aura.

Ivan Postivich could not sleep. Although he still bathed in the evening, he had not been summoned to the harem of Esma Sultan for a week. He could hear her laughter and her parties in the gardens, see the procession of trays carried from the kitchens and hear the cooks argue over the food preparation.

It seemed to Postivich that he had been forgotten and he became increasingly uncomfortable with his post.

One morning, after a fitful night, a knock at the door brought an unexpected visitor.

"The Sultan's doctor, Stephane Karatheodory, would like to have the honor of your company," announced a page. He bowed and backed away from the door, revealing an aged man, turbaned and leaning on a cane.

"Ahmed," said the doctor. He smiled, exposing false teeth of pure ivory, a present from the Sultan. "Will you offer an old man a cushion to rest his bones?"

"I will indeed, but pray, come with me honorable physician. We will converse in the gardens." Postivich saw no need to add that the fountains there would confound the ears of spies. The doctor was no fool.

Postivich took a few cushions from the barracks and escorted the old doctor to the gardens, where a small fountain stood in the shade of the cypress tress.

"I have heard that you have cured Esma Sultan," said the doctor. He groaned as he lowered his aching hips to the ground and settled onto the cushion. "She has declared this to me and shared the confidence that you were her confessor, if I am to have it correct."

"If this is what the Princess told you, so be it," said Postivich. "Am I one to argue with the Ottomans? Still, I only sat in her company and listened, nothing more. I am not a doctor, nor am I a priest."

The doctor nodded his head and studied the flowers of the garden, sucking in the aroma of the honeysuckle on the palace wall. Then he said, "I doubt she told you everything. Did she speak of the murders?"

Ivan Postivich was already inclined to like the doctor, but this abrupt question made his face muscles harden.

"Why should I tell you, Greek?"

"Oh, it is 'Greek,' now," retorted Stephane Karatheodory. "Do not forget you are Serbian and hardly a Turk yourself, Kapikulu. I am old so you must forgive me—I prefer to go directly to the point, like a jereed spear. I came here to give you advice, you hardheaded Serb. Show me respect or show me the gate!"

Ivan Postivich drew a breath and released it in a rush.

"Advice is often wasted on me, doctor. Please forgive my manners and my hard head."

"Well," said the physician, "I jostled my old bones in a carriage from Topkapi to come to speak to you so I shan't give up so soon. I am not eager to ride back up the hill without a little rest."

The doctor drew in a deep breath.

"Let us try an analogy, Ahmed Kadir. Perhaps you can recognize the quiet before a raging winter storm that dashes the docks with walls of water and tears trees up by the roots. Just so, this hush from Esma Sultan will not last."

Postivich looked at the doctor, waiting to hear more.

"The Princess is joyful, more content than I have seen her in years. She runs madly from one fête to another, showering money on her slaves, guests, and hosts. I saw her last night at Topkapi. She sat beside the Sultan, stroking his hand, and feeding him golden dates."

"She and the Sultan are brother and sister," muttered Postivich. "They are fond of one another."

"So they are, my son. So they are," the doctor said, looking at the splashing fountain. He turned back to the janissary. "You've been in the bedchamber of Esma Sultan—one of the only uncastrated males who has been there and lived to speak of it. We are in a small fraternity, my friend."

"Why do you speak of this?" said Postivich, his shoulders tightening.

"Because you may have had the opportunity to see the beautiful calligraphy of our Sultan Mahmud there by the Sultaness's bedside."

"I have never been near her bed, doctor. She converses with me reclining on the cushions of the divan. That European contraption is far from where she receives me, veiled behind drapes of gauze."

"Of course. Well, it is a pity that you haven't seen it. It is a magnificent piece of work and devotion."

"Devotion?"

"To Allah. The Sultan wrote out the entire Koran in the most exquisite calligraphy. It must have taken him many months—perhaps two years of dedication."

Ivan Postivich shrugged. An elaborate gift to give his sister, but the gesture was not so extraordinary.

He said, "The Koran is a long document and I know something of fine calligraphy from my years of tutelage at Topkapi. But two years to copy? Perhaps you exaggerate, my good doctor, the affection and gifts the Sultan has bestowed upon his sister."

The doctor shook his head, as vigorously as his old bones would allow.

"No, Ahmed Kadir, I do not think so. Had he finished it too quickly, it would have killed him. It is written in the Sultan's own blood."

The janissary flinched and turned his back on the doctor.

"So you see, I do know something about the Ottomans." The doctor leaned forward and lowered his voice. "And I know that you may be in grave danger . . . Ivan Postivich."

At the sound of his name, Postivich whirled around and faced the doctor. "How do you know my Christian name?"

"You forget that I have been at Topkapi for many, many years. I have served three Sultans and my father served two before me. I was there when you were brought to Topkapi. It was I who examined you for disease before you were presented to the Sultan. I examined you before and after your circumcision. You told me your name in Serbo-Croatian, and I promised to pray for you and your soul in the Mother Church. I remember each Christian name and mark them in my Bible. Many I have lost track of but not you, Ivan. I continue to pray for your soul in the Holy Church of God."

"Enough! I do not need your prayers, physician. Our Christian God deserted me the day they ripped me from my mother's arms and subjected me to such humiliation."

"God never deserts his followers, my son, though your kismet is guided by his hand. Never mind this theological debate—I come to warn you and save your life."

"Speak then."

"I will be brief and serve God quickly. If the Princess has truly not spoken of the murders of her lovers, she is not 'cured' as she pretends to be. The murders may have been at her brother's command, but she is complicit in sin. Her guilt must be confessed to Allah, but if she hides it, Satan will possess her soul and torment her. Watch the moon. Tonight it has waxed to fullness. I predict that the weakening of light will frighten her with its darkness and she will find that she has only fooled herself into believing all is well. The face of Allah will not turn to her and shall be deaf to her cries.

"If she has not confessed the murders, if she has not spoken to you openly and fully about them, do not go near her now, for I fear it is too late. As much as she might plead and coerce you, do not enter her harem. There lies disaster. The Sultan wishes to fulfill her every need and will grow wildly jealous if you attend her. Let her find another to speak to!"

"She says that no one else can listen to her for no one hates her the way I do."

The physician stroked his temples, his dim eyes looking sad and hollow at the janissary.

"As the moon changes, so do we. Do you indeed hate her, the way you profess, or are these words just echoes of the past?"

A small pinecone fell at their feet and Ivan Postivich looked up into the branches of the trees, swaying in the breeze off the Bosphorus. He thought of the old doctor who sat on the ground next to him, risking his life to warn him of pending disaster. He thought of his Christian name written in European letters in the pages of the old man's Bible, the only place it still remained on earth.

"Tell me, physician," said Postivich, "what world is this that makes me turn my heart away from the God of my fathers and makes me ache for the arms of my enemy?"

He turned now and knelt by the old man.

"I believed in the Christian God and that same God sent me to the hands of another faith in another land. I believed in Allah and the honor of the Janissary Corps and I saw corruption and sinners, honor smeared with the filth of men's sins. I believed in the sacred commandments carried down from the mountaintop by Moses, and I am mesmerized by a sorceress who murders her lovers. I don't really know what I believe anymore—whenever I believe with my heart, I am made the fool."

The Greek physician laid a shaking hand on the giant's head and with a slow motion of his thumb, made the sign of the cross.

"You are not a fool, my son. You are a man who has been tested far more than most. When you die, you will be received into the arms of God the Almighty, be he addressed as Allah or Jehovah. Whatever you call him, he shall know your voice and give you comfort.

"Be at peace, my son."

Ivan Postivich helped the old man to his feet and escorted him to the gates of the palace.

Ivan Postivich strode into the palace towards the Serail, the soles of his boots scuffing on the Persian rugs.

"Who goes there?" demanded the Solak, as Postivich approached the harem door.

"Ahmed Kadir."

"Kadir? The Head Eunuch has not summoned you," said the Solak.

"I wish to speak with Esma Sultan," said Postivich. "Inform her of my presence."

The Solak moved closer, squinting at him. Ivan Postivich smelt the guard's breath, redolent of meat.

"Do as I say, Solak," Postivich ordered. "Esma Sultan will be angry if she knows I am kept waiting here."

The Solak curled his lip, his eyes burning with hatred. He moved past the janissary, opening the door to the harem, closing it quietly behind him.

Ivan Postivich imagined the surprise on Esma Sultan's face. He had sent no message, no prior announcement. Even the Sultan himself would send an emissary before appearing at the door of the harem.

The door opened, releasing a waft of perfumed air, gentle as the women within. The Solak had a sprig of mint in his hand. He chewed at it sullenly.

"Her Highness Esma Sultan will see you, now," the Solak announced.

"She could not stand your stinking breath, could she?" said Ivan Postivich.

As Ivan Postivich pushed past the Solak, the man hissed in his ear. "Who would think the great Ahmed Kadir would spend his nights in the Sultaness's harem? You will die like all the rest them, drowned in a sack."

Postivich shoved the man aside.

"A whole field of mint could not wash clean your filthy mouth," he said, entering the harem and closing the door with a thud.

Esma Sultan was supping on fruit and tea. She arched one brow.

"What has brought you here, janissary?" she asked, reaching for a slice of peeled fig. "I did not summon you."

Ivan Postivich watched her mouth work over the piece of fruit. He said nothing.

"Yes? Why are you here?"

His eyes, stormy blue, focused on her face. "Your nightmares, Sultaness. Do they no longer haunt you?"

Esma Sultan swallowed hard, her mouth tightening.

"My dreams?" Esma Sultan said, dabbing her mouth with a napkin. "This is the emergency that makes a janissary break all Ottoman palace protocol?"

"Yes," said Ivan Postivich, his eyes boring into hers. "It does."

He saw a slight tremor shake her chin. Her left hand touched her lips, wiping away traces of the fig's juice.

"They do not," she said sharply. She looked away. "My nights are peaceful. I enjoy dreamless sleep now."

Ivan Postivich was certain she was lying.

"You have cured me, I think. I thank you. You shall be rewarded."

"I do not require gratitude," growled Postivich. "Or rewards."

He saw her back tense as she straightened her posture.

"I did not summon you," repeated Esma Sultan. She flicked

her wrist, returning her attention to her fruit. "You may leave now."

"No, Esma Sultan," said Postivich in a low voice. "I will not leave."

Her eyes flashed at him in anger.

"No?" she said. "You dare to say 'no' to me, janissary?"

"There is something I must know."

"Must? What 'must' is there for you that occurs in my world, Ahmed Kadir?"

Postivich flinched at his Islamic name for the first time since he was a boy. He stepped closer. Her skin was flawless, fresh from the hamam with the glow of health. Her hair shone with tints of henna, her eyes penciled in kohl. Her bearing was erect and noble, befitting an Ottoman princess.

He took another step.

"You have told me of the cruelty of men towards women in your childhood," he said, voice low. "Now you must tell me of your own guilt."

Esma Sultan pulled back like a cobra.

"Do not dare use that word with me!"

"Guilt!" repeated Ivan Postivich. "You weave night stories of your childhood, yet you speak not a single word of your own hand in men's deaths!"

Esma Sultan's mouth opened in astonishment.

"You told me of men's cruelty in your childhood, of your suffering. Of my sister's sacrifice. But what of your own murderous deeds?"

"Do not speak further," said Esma Sultan, her voice venomous. "You are dismissed, Ahmed Kadir. Leave at once!"

"You know my real name," he said, coming closer. He felt the warmth of her body, the scented oils of the hamam fresh on her skin. "Use it!"

"How dare you!" she said rising.

Ivan Postivich caught her by her wrist, his massive hand closing over her fine bones.

"You know my secrets, I know yours," he said pulling her close. His breath spilt warm over her neck, as he whispered hoarsely into her ear.

"You seduce young men like a whore in a brothel. Perhaps it is the Sultan's order they drown in the Bosphorus, but you condemn them. You bring them to your bed, you sorceress."

"I shall scream if you do not release me," spat Esma Sultan. "The Solak will slit your throat."

Ivan Postivich pulled her close to his face. His fierce eyes burned into hers, amber meeting blue. He felt his instinct surge, akin to a racing pulse on the battlefield. For a second he could taste the tang of dust and sweat, a roar drumming in his ears.

"Scream, then!" he said, and hooking her head into his arm, he covered her mouth with a savage kiss.

Esma Sultan struggled, but the kiss endured despite muffled screams, the furious twists of her body. He tasted fruit deep in her mouth, smelt the spicy sweetness of her skin.

Then he felt something give way, just as ice in a frozen river breaks invisibly underfoot. He sensed an unseen fissure travel far beyond them both.

He stroked back her hair as his mouth moved down her neck.

"The men," he whispered to her, as she gasped for breath.

"Yes," she said, her neck thrown back under his hand. "I am guilty. But I cannot live without love, Ivan Postivich."

"Love? You have never known love, Esma Sultan," he said, his breath hot on her throat. "And your brother cannot wash clean your sins in the Bosphorus."

They heard a knock on the door.

Esma Sultan pushed Ivan Postivich away. She combed her fingers through her hair, where his fingers had tangled the strands.

"Enter," she said, her eyes steady on Ivan Postich's own. She motioned for him to step away.

Saffron walked in, stopping abruptly when he saw Ivan Postivich.

"Forgive me. I did not know that the janissary had been summoned," he said, staring at Postivich.

Esma Sultan's fingertips touched her face, flushed red and rubbed raw from Postivich's stubble.

"Ahmed Kadir was just leaving," said the Princess, recovering her imperious bearing. "Please escort him from the palace to the servant barracks where he belongs."

# Chapter 16

The next night, Saffron announced to Ivan Postivich that he could leave the palace grounds for the evening. Postivich hesitated to leave the gardens, longing to see Esma Sultan again. The scent of the opening jasmine reminded him of the night he had touched her cheek.

But the Head Eunuch kept a wary eye on him, urging the drowning guard to leave. Postivich was unsure of whether the man wanted him to go for his own safety or because Saffron could not bear his presence because it reminded the eunuch too keenly of the drownings.

Ivan Postivich walked to the exterior courtyard and out the palace gate. He stood on the cobblestone road and listened to the cicadas that clung tightly to the leaves above him. Through the branches he could see the moon begin to rise, the first day of its waning. It was about an hour after sunset and there were still streaks of weary pink in the darkening sky.

Postivich thought about the words of the Greek physician. He was an old man, but learned; perhaps he understood the mind as he understood the body. If he was correct, Ivan Postivich would soon be summoned to Esma Sultan's chambers. A smile crept around the corners of the giant's mouth as he welcomed the thought of seeing the Ottoman Princess once more—despite the danger.

*To see the curve of her high cheekbones like a kilij, a Turkish sword.*

The clatter of horses' hooves pulled Postivich's attention from his reverie. A carriage was approaching from the east.

As the moon emerged from behind a cloud, he recognized the horses and the jingle of their jeweled harnesses. It was Esma Sultan's black coach, returning from a late-night foray. He stood in the shadow of a plane tree and watched as the driver negotiated the turn into the palace. In the darkness, the curtains of the Sultaness's compartment were open, a lantern illuminated her profile.

She inclined her head towards a young man, blond and most certainly a Christian. In her hand was a piece of fruit that she offered him.

The driver cursed quietly as his lead horse kicked in his traces and the other horses balked. The abrupt stop jostled the fruit from Esma Sultan's hand. It rolled on the coach floor.

Her head emerged from the window, and Ivan Postivich could see that her eyes were darkened with heavy lines of kohl and her mouth shone in the moonlight.

"You fool," she called to the driver. "Can you not drive these horses?"

"Forgive me, Princess," said the driver, flicking the whip to the lead horse's flanks. "This beast is in need of castration."

Again the stallion kicked, and the other horses reared in their harness.

"He may not be the only one," she retorted. "See that you do not jostle me or my companion again, or I will perform the task on you myself, by Allah's word!"

Ivan Postivich watched the coach disappear into the palace gates. He felt a pain burn in his chest and his throat constricted.

There was no summons for the janissary that night, and the next morning came much as the others had in the last month. There was a soft dew on the grass and the flowers in the garden. If someone had drowned Esma Sultan's lover that night, it had not been Ivan Postivich. He had stayed awake the entire night, waiting for the knock on the door. But no servant had come to send him to the docks and he heard no screams in the night, though he imagined the hard splash of a body, over and over again.

When he went to the kitchens to take his breakfast, he saw a fair-headed man barely past adolescence being escorted to the hamam by two of Esma Sultan's handmaidens. The young man was dressed in a tunic of crimson and gold and he smiled sleepily at the girls who laughed at his side. The Head Eunuch followed, snapping orders to two pages who scurried ahead, toting towels and soaps and urns of oil.

Ivan Postivich strode over to Saffron, and, putting a hand on his shoulder, stopped him in midstride.

"Is this a new lover of Esma Sultan? And if so, why does he smile?"

Saffron's eyes flashed at Postivich, and he motioned to the rest of the entourage to enter the hamam.

"What business is this of yours, Kadir?"

Postivich looked at the eunuch's face and curled his lip. "Am I not Esma Sultan's servant, her drowning guard? I do not choose to perform such foul sins in the light of day where I can see the tears of the condemned as they cry for mercy."

"You are not called upon to perform any service, Ahmed Kadir, except that of keeping your abominable lips sealed and adopting the proper silence of an Ottoman servant. This man is a guest of Esma Sultan and will remain with her for as many nights as she chooses. Her brother, the Sultan, has granted him life as long as he may please our Sultaness and remain within the confines of the palace. And if last night was any indication," added the eunuch, "he shall have a long and happy term indeed."

Ivan Postivich swallowed hard.

"Has any man visited her harem more than once and lived?"

"Of course, Corbaci. You forget that *you* have had that very pleasure. I suspect this is expressly why the Sultan has granted this young man life, so that he will be your competition."

Ivan Postivich cursed under his breath and spat on the marble walkway. Within seconds, a young servant came running, wiping at the spittle with a scented rag.

Postivich turned and looked back at the palace, where the thick velvet curtains were still drawn, shutting out all light.

"A man whose passions possess him lives a short life," hissed Saffron. "Don't be a fool, Ahmed Kadir. Esma Sultan loves no man and unless she marries, no man will live who has loved her. Pray to Allah that she will not tire of this pretty boy for many moons, for if he leaves her palace walls, he will be condemned by the Sultan's decree. He is mercilessly jealous of anyone who entertains his sister, even for one night. God have mercy on this Greek boy, for my mistress is never long satisfied."

The harem women stood outside the hamam, laughing. Nazip climbed up another woman's strong back to peek in through the perforations of the bathhouse, and through her laughter, conveyed the scene of the ablutions.

"He lies on the stone, on his back, Leyla. Ah, that all the riches of the Ottomans could be as sweet as what I see before my very eyes. Surely, our mistress has ridden the divine chariot to heaven, for I have seen no other who is so well endowed."

"You have seen no other but the Sultan, Nazip. Your imagination is limited to one night with a man and you shall have no other," teased a blond handmaiden, who steadied Nazip's legs as she climbed higher for a better look.

"You do not know my secrets, Leyla. Esma Sultan has let me gaze upon her lovers, even touch them, on occasion. She guarded my virginity for her brother, but I have had the pleasure of witnessing several who were aroused. This is the finest specimen I have seen in her court and he is most relaxed, I might add!"

The Sultan's eunuch, who was in charge of Nazip's every move, came racing across the gardens.

"Mistress Nazip! Descend at once!"

Nazip sighed and took the hand that he insistently offered to help her descend. Her hearty companion groaned and rubbed her back.

"What could I see, good eunuch," said Nazip, her eyes dancing, "but the clouds of mist that rise from the baths? There is nothing to report but that the man within was shrouded in vapor, an invisible ghost to mortal eye."

She smiled at her harem companions and whispered, "Ah, to have the freedom of a virgin! How dull and tiresome to be the concubine of a Sultan, where all my fun is spoiled in his honor!"

As the eunuch escorted her back to the harem, Nazip caught sight of the giant. She tried to smile, but her lips abandoned the effort and she looked at him with compassion.

"Oh gentle giant, do not grieve," she said to him. "Esma Sultan has been cured by your company. Rejoice in her health that Allah sent you to restore!"

Postivich stared at her, but remained silent.

She turned towards the harem entrance and vanished into the walls of the Serail.

# Chapter 17

Ivan Postivich left the palace of Esma Sultan, cursing all within its walls. What could he have expected? Of course she would not send for him unless it was advantageous to her. He was a fool to think otherwise, and he cursed himself to Allah that he should be weak enough to hope for more.

*What strange djinn possesses me to crave the love of an Ottoman?* he thought.

Beyond the walls of the palace, he was assaulted by the foul stench of the teeming city. The day was hot, without a breath of air, and the dust lay thick as velvet on the curled leaves of the chestnut trees withering in the pounding heat of the Turkish sun. In the markets, the savage heat ravaged the vendors' fruits and meats, their rotting odors mingling with the stink of the dogs' warm dung. The vendors used moist towels to protect the raw meat, coloring brown despite their efforts, and festooned with swarms of fat black flies.

On the docks, fishermen sluiced cool saltwater over their catch. Dogs barked and snapped at the legions of seagulls that swarmed to the stench, as the fishmongers wiped their brows and cursed the breathless day.

Postivich strode to the edge of the Bosphorus and paid an old fisherman a coin to take him up the Golden Horn towards the River Lycus where he could spy on the horses tethered in the meadows and perhaps catch a glimpse of his beloved mare, Peri.

When the boat neared the banks, Postivich could see the Kapikulus in the fields, carrying out training drills—not cirit or polo, but military routines created by the European cavalries. In the distance, he could make out the members of his orta training in what the Europeans called "precision riding." They worked their horses at an extended trot, a disgraceful gait for Turkish warriors, making serpentines across the trampled grass. The sight made his belly knot as if he had witnessed his orta receiving dance lessons.

"May their beards be cursed!" said the giant at the sight. "What in the name of Allah are they wearing?"

Ivan Postivich squinted against the cruel sun to examine the Kapikulu regiment's new costume: Cossack trousers, black boots, and blue cloaks—the uniforms of European armies. Instead of turbans, they wore small red caps that looked like boxes perched on their heads. He cursed again and spit.

This was the Sultan's "new order," the Eskenji. This was his plan to destroy the Janissaries in the name of "reform." He had stolen their tradition, their pride, even their uniforms. He was murdering the Corps.

The fisherman shaded his wrinkled face with his scarred hands, deep mahogany from the sun and saltwater.

"Blasphemy!" he cried, his loose teeth slurring the word. "They dress like the infidels!"

Postivich shook his head angrily. The fisherman grunted and scratched his testicles.

"Damn the infidels! What use do we have for their ways?" the janissary said. "Like trained dogs—pets for our Sultan. Trotting in circles, bleeding the passion from their veins. No Turkish horse should lose its spirit in the dust of a parade ground. Those horses were bred to gallop straight to the heart of the enemy, proud and brave to their deaths!"

"They say the Europeans feed them on hot bran mash from buckets," the fisherman said, spitting into the sea. "My cousin himself delivered a dozen bags of it to the Royal Stables from a British ship."

"Just because the Europeans are constipated fools does not mean our horses share their weakness!" said Postivich. "Keep their pabulum for their squalling brats and old men. Our horses will shit on their boots without any imported inducements!"

The fisherman howled in laughter, slapping the tattered knees of his pants. His light brown eyes were tinged with the creeping veil of cataracts that would one day blind him and send him begging at the steps of the Aya Sofya for food. But for now, this was a Turk who had the honor of rowing the great corbaci Ahmed Kadir up the Golden Horn—and he had shared a joke at the infidels' expense.

The fisherman raised his oars in the blazing sun and swung the bow out towards the mouth of the Bosphorus, nodding his thanks to Allah for the fine day, and a profession that kept him on the water in the heat.

"Keep him out of my sight!" screamed her voice.

Ivan Postivich craned his neck towards the harem. The perfo-rated walls let the cool breezes in—and the sounds and secrets out.

"I will not have him approach me. Do not accept any tokens from him, and send this kerchief back to him. I shall not touch it!"

"But your Sultaness. He begs to see you and will not take food or drink until you agree to have audience with him."

"Let the infidel starve, then! I should send him from the pal-ace, but that would be his death. Is it not enough that I spare his life by letting him inhabit my court? You must smuggle him back to Galata, Saffron."

"Your brother, our honored Sultan, would hunt him down and kill him on the spot. He has sworn no man who has known your bed will live outside this sanctuary."

The Princess turned away from him and beat her temples.

"Shall I always be haunted by my brother's decree? Cursed man who cannot let me love and be loved without murder?"

Saffron remained silent.

"I cannot abide this infidel's presence any longer!" said Esma Sultan. "The nightmares have returned. And I smell the Christian flesh of this swine-eating Greek on my sheets and in my hair. My harem girls have washed it thrice and I cannot rid myself of his stench. Burn all that he has touched.

"You must take him from this place, Saffron. Ferry him across the Bosphorus. Smuggle him to the White Sea where he can breed with his own kind. We shall tell my brother that we were taking a midnight sail when the boat capsized and he was drowned."

"But my Princess, surely he will return to Galata and the Sul-tan will send his Solaks to murder him."

The Princess leapt to her feet and clenched her hands. She shook her fists at her servant, like a child in a tirade.

"That would be his own kismet! Am I not the daughter of Sultan Abdulhamid? Will I not have the right to decide who resides within my palace walls or will we harbor a man whom I loathe? See that he is dispatched tonight! What happens to him is in Allah's hands. Send for the drowning guard, and see that the Greek is dispatched to another shore, I command you!"

"Yes, Your Highness."

"Leave me. I must rest. I have not slept a minute in three nights."

When the eunuch emerged from the harem, he found Postivich and a Solak on the edge of violence.

"You! Ahmed Kadir—move on!" the Solak shouted. "You are no longer needed here."

"Since when does a Solak give me orders!" the janissary shouted back. "You miserable dog, you forget yourself."

"I give you orders because we have no need for you! Should I see you near the entrance of the harem again, I shall slice your throat."

Ivan Postivich made a lewd sign with his hand, gesturing towards his genitals. "You should try now to see if that is wise, you cowardly Albanian. Come, let's have that discussion now so that I might wring your wretched neck like a sick pullet!"

"Ahmed Kadir!" shouted Saffron. "Stop! You, Solak! You take your orders from me. You, Corbaci. Wait for me at your quarters. I bring a message from the Sultaness for your ears only."

That night, a blue-painted boat sliced through the Bosphorus, a single lantern swinging from the bow. A dark figure towered above the light as the vessel pulled silently to the docks of Esma Sultan's palace.

Two Solaks and a turbaned eunuch stood by a golden-haired youth who was dressed in fine clothes, staring nervously at the dark figure that stood motionless at the bow.

"You are the first man to escape the Sultan's wrath," whispered Saffron. "Praise Allah for your delivery. It is the good will of Her Highness, Esma Sultan, that spares your life. She risks her brother's anger in doing so."

"But—the Sultan's Solaks. They will find me and drag me from my father's house!"

"If you return to Galata, you will be butchered before the cock crows. Seek refuge in your Greek homeland or the outer territories of the Empire, where no one will know your history."

"But—I have pleased the Sultaness in all ways! Night after night I performed to the limits of my manhood. Why does she banish me from Constantinople, the only home I have known?"

The Head Eunuch raised his chin in the torchlight, motioning to the boat that thumped its wooden hull against the dock. As the pages inclined their torches to light the Greek's way into the boat, the burning rags illuminated the giant's face, tight with rage.

"She banishes you to save your wretched life, Greek. Board the boat, you fool, and say a prayer for my mistress's benevolence." Then, pulling the Greek close, the eunuch whispered, "Say no more in the presence of the giant. He will murder you as easily as the Sultan, for his anger is aroused at the mention of the Sultane's name."

The fair-haired youth trembled as he looked at the rocking boat and saw the face of the corbaci in the flickering light of the torches. The giant's upper lip curled and the Greek recognized the bloodlust of the Serb, a people as ferocious as the Turks themselves.

"The drowning guard?" the Greek breathed in horror. "You send me to my death!"

Saffron pushed him forward at these words and he stumbled and fell on the dock, inches from the edge of the water. Ivan Postivich did not move to help him, and the Greek crawled onto the boat.

In the commotion, no one noticed another boat, a royal caïque slipping through the water upcurrent from Esma Sultan's docks. The ghostly white skin of a little man in a crimson tunic would have been visible in the lantern light had there not been such a distraction. He motioned to the boatman, who feathered his oars in silence, drifting close to the reeds that grew along the shore of the Bosphorus.

The boatman, Ahmed, the same man who had so often and so unhappily taken Ivan Postivich out on these same waters on voyages too much like this one—rowed hard across the mouth of the Golden Horn. He then pointed the bow towards the Asian side of the Bosphorus, where the Greek could hide until he could secure passage on one of the ships returning to the White Sea.

The Princess had given the Greek youth gold to make arrangements; gold that was sewn into the hem of his heavily embroidered tunic. He fingered his wealth nervously as the Sultaness's drowning guard stood over him in silence.

As they reached the depths of the Bosphorus, midway between Europe and Asia, Ivan Postivich motioned for the oarsman to stop. The giant took a long look at the spot where he had drowned so many men.

"Why do we stop?" asked the Greek, nervously. He stood up and his movement rocked the boat. "Were you not instructed to take me to the Asian side?" His voice rose in the night air.

Ivan Postivich shifted his gaze from the dark waters to the man, and back again to the water.

"Do as the Sultaness commands, janissary!" pleaded the Greek. "The eunuch guaranteed me safe passage to the Asian shore!"

The oarsman looked at the giant who towered above them both.

"Shall I row on, Ahmed Kadir, or do you wish to pause here a moment longer?"

Postivich nodded his head. "A few more minutes, Ahmed," he said. "I wish to ask the prisoner a few questions."

The Greek swallowed hard. "I am no prisoner. I am the guest of Esma Sultan."

"I have entertained her night guests before," growled the giant. "I am not sure how you are any different."

The youth looked around wildly.

"She has given me gold for passage," he said, his voice rising, "and bids me well."

"I did not see her accompany you to the docks to wish you a good voyage."

The passenger tore at the hem of his tunic with a small dagger that he had tucked in his waistband.

"Here"—he held out a coin—"I will give you gold, but I beg of you, do not defy the Sultaness's command. Row for the shore, boatsman, and there shall be gold for you as well."

The gold caught the light of the lantern, glittering in the night. Ivan Postivich struck the passenger's hand and sent the precious metal flying. It landed with a distant splash in the water.

"That was a small fortune!" shouted the Greek in astonishment. "Are you mad?"

"Look me in the eye, you dog! Tell me what you did with the Sultaness."

"Ahmed Kadir," whispered the oarsman. "What matter is this?"

The great corbaci did not answer. Instead he seized the Greek by the neck.

"Pity on me, Ahmed Kadir," the youth pleaded.

"Tell me how you came to lie in Esma Sultan's bed or you shall die this very minute!"

The Greek's breath came in rasps as the giant closed his fingers tight around his neck.

"Release me and I will tell you all!"

The giant loosened his grip and sent the man flying against the hull of the boat. The oarsman stabbed at the water to keep the boat from tipping. He steadied the vessel once more, but said nothing to the corbaci who remained standing despite the rocking boat.

"Then tell, Greek," said Postivich. "From the beginning."

The passenger rubbed his neck, his throat raw from the grip of the giant.

"I was approached one night in Galata by an envoy of the Sultaness."

"His name?"

"I do not remember. He was a white eunuch, fat and greedy, with lavender lips as swollen as sausages, but he wore the royal tunic with crimson and gold threads. He said that the Princess had heard tales of my—" Here he hesitated.

"Your what?"

"My beauty and my prowess," he said, staring at the giant's muddy boots. "Those were the words he used. He said that the Princess needed a consort, that she was widowed and had finally seen that she could not live without the love of a man."

"Are you so deaf that you have not heard of the men Esma Sultan has drowned! Have you not heard the wails of the Christian families in Galata and Pera who have lost their men to the water's depths?"

"The eunuch promised me that this was not what she sought. She had been cured and only sought the love of one man. He assured me that I would be cared for and protected under the Banner of the Prophet and Sultan Mahmud II."

"Since when does the Banner of the Prophet protect infidels who lie with Ottoman royalty?"

The passenger tried to answer but his mouth was too dry. A high crackling noise was the only sound that he uttered.

"Tell me, then. Was she waiting for you in the coach?"

The Greek nodded, swallowed hard, and found his voice again. "I was instructed to approach the carriage with my eyes lowered. The eunuch told me to walk back and forth beside it, where she could see me. Then he ordered me to retire to my family's home where he could bathe me."

"And did you not become frightened?"

"Frightened? No. No woman has ever tired of my love," he said with an anger born of pride. "Why should an Ottoman princess be any different? Besides, I had the promise of the eunuch, sealed with this—"

He removed something from his pocket. It was an emerald ring with the crest of the waning moon, a diamond star at its side.

"The eunuch gave it to me as the Sultan's promise of safety if I were to remain faithful to his sister and not leave the palace walls. The eunuch said the Princess had become too absorbed with another who was not worthy to clean the filth from her shoes and that I might provide distraction. I served the Sultan himself!"

Ivan Postivich's ears hummed with hot blood.

"The eunuch acted the pimp for the Sultan's own sister!"

The Greek swallowed hard at these words, knowing the giant must be mad to speak such treason.

"I was promised gold and property. I have only done what I was told, what I was commanded to do!"

The giant lunged for the man and caught him by the throat as the boat rocked to one side, taking in water before the oarsman could right it again.

"Tell me. How did you seduce her?"

"I had no need to, by the Savior's honor! It was she who seduced me."

"Tell me, you vile dog!"

The oarsman spoke, "Ahmed Kadir! I beg of you, do not torture the man. I have heard the stories of the Sultaness's seductions. There is no honor here to defend! Let us take the man to safety and forget this night!"

The corbaci did not answer but tightened his grip on the struggling Greek. He whispered, "That first night. Did she—did she speak in her ecstasy?"

His victim's head was now just inches from the terrifying water. His scream carried across the waters and the wild dogs began to bark and howl.

"Tell me or die by these waters!"

"Yes! She called out for another."

"What? You mock me. Smell the saltwater for it shall be your grave."

The man screamed, "No, I do not mock you! She called out, 'Ivan!' and tears coursed down her cheeks, like a wounded girl. 'Ivan.' I swear that was the name. A Russian lover. I don't know." He sobbed.

Postivich pushed the terrified man away and slumped against the bow of the boat, his lungs heaving for breath.

"Row, oarsman," he said, his voice hoarse. "Make haste for the Asian shore."

The blue boat reached the shore in less than an hour. No one spoke again until the wooden hull knocked against the pilings of the dock, waking the sleeping Anatolian guard.

"Who goes there?"

"The servants of Esma Sultan. We have a passenger to deliver safely to your watch. Help him to shore."

The Greek leapt from the boat. As soon as his slippered feet touched land, he ran as fast as he could away from the docks. He scrambled straight up the hill that rose from the water, loosening rocks that rattled down onto the dock.

"What conduct is this?" asked the guard. "Why does he run?"

Ivan Postivich pushed off. "He does not have the stomach for the sea," he said. "Most likely he needed to purge in the bushes."

"A Greek," muttered the guard, wrinkling his mouth in disgust. He yawned a farewell to the departing boat and squatted next to a mulberry tree to drink his tea. He did not see the two figures that slipped through the darkness and followed the fair-haired man, their daggers flashing silver in the moonlight.

The oarsman waited until the boat was well out onto the water before he spoke.

"What spell has she cast on you, my friend? You have behaved as a madman."

Ivan Postivich shrugged and looked out over the moving water.

"I cannot blame my behavior on Esma Sultan," he answered at last.

"Ahmed Kadir, do not forget how we have heard the last words of the condemned men who by our labor have been drowned. I thank Allah we were not to murder this fair-headed man tonight."

"I almost killed him."

"I saw his death written in your face. What demon possessed you?"

"I am not sure, oarsman. I only know that it is more powerful than I."

Then a cry pierced the air from the heavy mist of the Asian shoreline. Ivan Postivich and the oarsman turned, straining their ears to hear more, but there was only the lapping waters of the Bosphorus.

Irena had seen her brother dispatched directly from the palace in the night. She had seen the Esma Sultan's young Greek lover spirited out of the palace, neither tied nor gagged.

She ran to Saffron, her slippers slapping on the smooth marble floors.

"What is this?" she begged him, gasping for breath. "Does the drowning guard return to his occupation of murderer?"

He turned with resignation in his eyes.

"That depends solely on Ahmed Kadir and his conscience. If his pride is stronger than his soul, he will murder again. But this time, the blood will stain his hands only, not Esma Sultan's."

Irena waited late into the night for Postivich to return, listening to the fast-moving water of the Bosphorus from the garden walls. At last when she saw the swaying light of a lantern, she bade a page to run to the docks and summoned the janissary to meet her in the garden in haste.

The night was hot, but after midnight puffs of wet breeze lifted off the Bosphorus and stirred the air. Overhead, the broad leaves of the plane trees rustled in the wind.

Irena sat on a bench near one of Esma's favorite fountains: a high fluted column with a series of graduated marble pools, overflowing with cascades of water.

She saw the silhouette enter the garden from the west gate. Only one man in the Ottoman Empire could cast such a colossal figure in the moonlight.

"Irena, why do you bid me come so late?" he said, his voice hoarse with exhaustion.

"Did you murder the Greek?" Her voice was cold as marble.

"I did not. I left him safely to travel back to his homeland."

Irena did not argue that the Greek's homeland was here, in Constantinople, in Galata, where he had been born, as had been generations of his forebears. Instead she studied her brother's face, ravaged with emotion, not physical exhaustion. He sat down next to her, his massive shoulders crumpling.

"You love her," Irena said simply, stroking his brown hair, matted with the salt air of the sea. His heavy torso sagged into her arms and she heard the sound of tearless sobs.

"I cannot allow myself to love a murderess. And see how she casts me aside, now that she is well?"

"She is not as well as you think. The Greek was a diversion. Her crimes haunt her. But she cannot trust herself to speak to you again."

There was a silence and Irena felt a shift of emotion as subtle as the first wave to change the tide and move the sea out away from shore.

"May her guilty corpse rot in hell!" He stood up, heaving air into his lungs and straightening his back. "I have become soft as a woman from lack of war! I shall not let a woman wither my manhood!

"She is an Ottoman and her brother is my enemy. He shall pay with his life for his deceit and cunning. I shall revenge the humiliation of the Janissary Corps. And the deaths of over two hundred women and children drowned! And the foul deeds I have commited in the Sultan's name!"

"No!" Irena's hand flew to her throat. "Do not continue this bloody way! Follow the Bektashi way and let live! Make peace with the Sultan and stop this bloodshed."

"There is no making peace! He has gone too far in his vile ways. The Janissaries boil in rage."

He pulled his sister to her feet and held her close, his embrace so tight she could not draw a breath.

"Pray for me. The time has come."

"No!" she shouted and a dog barked.

Immediately a Solak called. "Who goes there?"

"I must go," he whispered hoarsely. "Pray to the Blessed Mary on my behalf, sister. Pray to our dead mother."

Irena sunk to her knees, her hands clasped imploring, but her brother did not stop.

"It is I, Ahmed Kadir," he shouted to the anxious guard. "I have asked Bezm-i Alem to deliver a message to Esma Sultan, and the content startled her."

The Solak lifted a lantern as Irena struggled to her feet, the wet grass staining her harem pants.

"Are you all right, Bezm-i Alem?"

"Yes," she cried. "Go with God."

Alone in the garden again, Irena sat down on the bench and stared up at cold stars above her, thinking of the Bektashi Sufis as they lifted their faces to the heavens, swaying like stalks of wheat.

# Part IV
# The Janissaries' Revenge

# Chapter 18

"**K**adir!" shouted a Solak, whistling the name through his rotten teeth as if it were a curse. "You are summoned. Saffron will speak with you. Come with me at once."

Ivan Postivich ached to seize the pompous Macedonian guard and snap his neck. Instead, he followed in sullen silence. He knew that when the Head Eunuch summoned him, it concerned direct orders from Esma Sultan.

Saffron was speaking to three eunuchs about their duties for that evening. He saw the giant enter and waved him forward, dismissing the others with a flick of his hand.

"I have been told by the Princess Esma Sultan that your presence is no longer needed. She has pronounced herself cured. She has given me this purse of gold to pay you for your services."

Saffron reached out, placing the small bag on the giant's palm.

Ivan Postivich stared at the purse. It was crimson with a gold tassel and from the weight, he knew there was a fair sum of money inside. He felt winded as if he had been dealt a mighty blow to his chest.

"Will I not see the Princess before I leave?"

"No. She did not summon you. She is entertaining another guest and will not be disturbed. You are to return to Et Meydan, where you will be assigned new duties as a janissary. She has told me that she will continue to work to persuade her brother, our glorious Sultan, to find a place for you once more as a cavalry guard. But there is little hope of that, I am afraid."

"Am I not to remain here as her—drowning guard?"

Saffron's face hardened. He waved away the eunuchs who hovered near and he pulled Ivan Postivich close.

"Did you not understand what I have said? You are free to leave for the barracks and fight for the Empire. You will never have to drown an innocent man again! Praise Allah, you have been released from your duties here. Forget you have ever met Esma Sultan. Beg for a post in the far reaches of the Empire where you can find peace!"

Ivan Postivich raised his chin in defiance, although he knew the eunuch spoke wisdom.

"I cannot ever forget that I have met her," he said. "She has poisoned my blood."

With that, he nodded a farewell to the eunuch and turned to leave the palace of Esma Sultan.

Postivich strode towards Et Meydan. He wound his way through the streets of Constantinople, surprised to see torches burning in the night, and a curfew commanded by the Sultan blatantly ignored. Wagons rattled up the streets, loaded with provisions. The drivers wore tight expressions, their eyes moving, alert in the darkness.

Meat Square hummed with activity. Thousands of Janissaries met in their ortas, with messengers running from one to the next.

"We will stand brother to brother against the infidel Sultan and his reforms!"

"Death to the New Order. Death to their pagan officers!"

Ivan Postivich pushed his way through the crowd, until he came to where his orta should have been.

The spot was empty, the huge copper kettle gone.

"Ahmed Kadir!" shouted a soldier who saw him standing alone. "You have come to join us! Your cowardly orta has joined our enemies. They have stolen away from Et Meydan and the Honorable Corps to fight with the Sultan."

Ivan Postivich smelled their sweat. He knew the taste and odor of battle and saw the bellicose glitter in their eyes.

"So the day has come," he said.

"The giant comes to lead us!" shouted an artilleryman. "The only cavalryman faithful to the Corps!"

Suddenly the eyes of thousands were on him, as if they had been waiting all along. Soldiers climbed the rooftops of the wooden barracks and scaled the meat stalls to see him better.

Ivan Postivich stood uncertain amidst the throng of soldiers, their dirty faces looking up to him, anxious for leadership. He recognized faces from his boyhood, men who had been proud to join the ranks of the Janissaries, who had fought on foot while he rode astride his horse. He saw another face, the janissary who had beaten the Jew in the Bazaar, his mouth twisting as he looked at the giant with hatred.

These were the men, both good and evil, with whom he would fight against the Sultan.

Postivich's mind was clear. His decision was made. He spoke to the men.

"Reform! Ha! When the Sultan speaks of reform, he speaks of annihilation! We can have no reform with a Sultan who despises us! There may be corruption in our ranks, yes, but it is corruption that has been forced upon us by a Sultan who corrupts everything he touches. The honor and spirit of the Janissary Corps lie in battle—not in the drills of the Europeans who come to tame our Empire so they can swallow it whole for their own pleasure!"

He took a deep breath and his voice boomed across the square.

"If there is corruption, the fish rots from the head down! Sever the head and save the Corps!"

A roar of approval filled Et Meydan Square and the night birds were shaken from their roosts. They flew blindly about the marketplace in confusion.

"May Allah bless Ahmed Kadir, the only true janissary of the cavalry!"

Another cheer went up and men embraced him, stinking with the lust of battle. As they cheered and rallied around the giant, a man in a crimson tunic embroidered in gold thread slipped out the gates of Et Meydan to tell the Sultan of the rebellion and its leader, Ahmed Kadir.

"I must have my horse," Postivich shouted. "Send to the stables and fetch my mare."

A young runner broke from the crowd and sprinted to his side.

"I will return with your Peri, Corbaci," he said, bowing quickly, "if I am not captured by the traitorous members of your orta."

"Tell me boy," Postivich said. "When did they decide not to stand with us?"

"The Sultan took away their horses, and unless they swore a blood oath, they could not ride. The Kapikulus would never willingly fight on foot! They cast their lot with the Sultan to ensure their safety and position."

"Go with Allah, boy," he said. "Do not try to rein in Peri. Let her gallop and she will find her way to the Meydan gates."

The corbaci of the artillery pushed through the crowd and embraced the giant.

"Ahmed Kadir! You come with the benediction of Allah—the men's hearts are eager for the Sultan's blood."

Another roar went up in the center of the square as the Janissaries listened to impassioned speeches from other rebels. Ivan Postivich knew that the Corps fed on the stirring words of all soldiers, not just the commanders. He pressed into the heart of the mob.

"The Eskenji infidels drilled here—on this very ground!" Postivich shouted. He scooped up a handful of dirt from his feet and vaulted onto the platform above the heads of the troops. "This ground that we Janissaries hold sacred was defiled by the Sultan with the parade of infidels! It is here that the Eskenjis shed their janissary uniforms, like serpents shedding their skins, taking on the pagan cloth of the New Order."

The mob shouted, "Death to the infidel serpents!"

Postivich's voice boomed across the square. "The Ulema blessed their pagan rifles! What corruption leads our Sultan to persuade our holy men to his cause! The Bektashi Dervishes stand with us to the death, incorruptible!"

One after another, soldiers took their turn on the platform, shouting as loud as they could so that they might be heard. The voices rose, eager for violence and revenge, and the collective heartbeat of the Janissaries pounded hard, ready for battle.

Soon, the boy who had gone to fetch Peri returned, racing through the Et Meydan gates, riding bareback on the galloping mare. Reaching the mob, the boy reined in the horse and she reared, her hooves slashing at the air. He tried in vain to cling to her mane but she shook him off and he tumbled into the dust.

"Good work, boy!" shouted Ivan Postivich, grabbing her rope. "Settle down, mare, settle down. We will need your spirit for battle."

"There is no saddle," called a corbaci. "The Kapikulus have taken all the tack."

"I need no saddle to fight!" shouted Ivan Postivich, slinging his long leg over the mare and righting himself on her back. "Bring me spears and I will fight the way I was trained as a boy."

An artilleryman ran up with a pouch of spears. Postivich slung it across his chest and reined his horse to the gates.

"To Topkapi!"

The Sultan needed no spy to know the Janissaries were on the march. He heard their cries and shouted to his Vizier.

"Are the bombardiers ready?"

"Yes, sire."

"How many are we?"

"Perhaps nine thousand, matched against perhaps twenty thousand Janissaries, though the Aga thinks many will desert before the battle."

The Sultan pinched his beard with his immaculate fingernails.

"Are you certain of what you heard?"

"Yes. It is the Kapikulu giant Ahmed Kadir who leads the revolt."

"May my sister be damned to hell. I warned her of his treachery! Now the serpent sinks his fangs into our very flesh!"

The Sultan paced the length of the room, his yellow tunic whipping behind him.

"The citizens have long cried out under the extortion and brutality of the Corps. They lust for revenge. Throw open the arsenals. Hand out swords, rifles, and cartridges to the faithful."

"Yes, my Sultan. I shall send runners through the streets to spread the word."

"Let the Sacred Banner unfurl in the pulpit of the Sultan Ahmed Mosque! We shall defend the honor of the Ottomans under the Holy Roof of Allah!" The Sultan's voice rose to a shriek. *"Either the Janissaries will be destroyed or cats will walk over the ruins of Constantinople!"*

Sultan Mahmud II was ready to gamble the destruction of the Imperial City and its people to defeat the Janissaries.

The streets were teeming with citizens—some who had chosen loyalty to the Sultan, some who had cast their lot with the Corps. As the Janissaries left Et Meydan to charge Topkapi, the cry went up, "Mohammed and Haci Betash!" honoring the Prophet and the dervish patron whose spiritual guidance bolstered the Janissary Corps.

But their way to the palace was blocked by Loyalists—Greeks, Jews, and loyal Muslim citizens eager to spill Janissary blood and exact revenge. Their cry also echoed through the narrow streets. "Mohammed and Mahmud!"

At the head of the Janissary army, slashing his way through the Loyalists, was Ivan Postivich. His sword cut across the throats of his enemies and as he galloped forward, he slashed at those who fled before him.

But the thousands of soldiers behind him were soon entangled in hand-to-hand combat. As Postivich reached the Imperial Gate, the mob of fighting men moved slowly, warm blood washing over the cobblestone.

At the top of the hill at Topkapi, the Sultan commanded the forces from an apartment above the Imperial Gate. He saw the giant astride the dappled-grey mare and cursed him.

The Sultan put a hand on his sword and turned to descend to the streets.

"My Sultan! What do we do?" asked the Royal Solak.

"I shall kill this scorpion with my own sting!"

"Please, I beg of you. We cannot protect you if you engage in the battle. The Ottoman lineage will be endangered."

The Sultan's right fist pounded his heart.

"That would please my Angel sister! See what a fiendish enemy she has coddled in her palace!"

"Sire, you must remain in command here at the Imperial Gate. If you should be wounded or killed, there is no hope for victory. Our enemies would rejoice."

Mahmud walked back to the window and stared down at the giant, who was engaged in battle with two Solaks.

"He must die! And it must be by my hand. Capture the traitor infidel—I shall have the delight of beheading him myself."

Ivan Postivich slashed the Solak's neck and the blood sprayed his horse, making her whinny and flare her nostrils. A second Solak was fatally wounded by a tremendous blow that left him shaking uncontrollably until he crumpled to the ground in agony.

"Death to the Sultan!"

The Janissary troops had reached Topkapi, although the assault on the palace was stopped by Loyalists, who fought savagely to keep the rebels from the gates.

"You will not enter the Imperial Gates!" the Sultan roared from his post far above the battle.

The giant pressed forward as a volley of gunfire roared from the palace walls. The bullets flew around him and his horse. Peri threw her head up and whinnied, a roaring neigh. He urged her into a gallop around the walls of the palace, temporarily out of range of the artillery.

He felt dampness on his left leg and looked down. His pants were soaked in blood from where a bullet had torn through his thigh and into the belly of his horse. Her dapples were now blood red.

He pulled the mare into the shadows and leapt down to examine her.

"Peri," he cried. She shuddered and lay down, groaning. He placed his big hand on her red-stained belly. Her breath rattled in her lungs, her nostrils flared wide to take in air.

Ivan Postivich raised his sword and, with a wild cry, charged the gates of Topkapi, in a rage that erased any pain from his wound.

The Janissaries had underestimated the Loyalists. Many men were eager to take up arms against the army that had abused them, demanding bribes and beating them, often savagely, if they refused. The streets were stained red with blood and within a day, the Loyalists had pushed the Janissaries back into Et Meydan and were poised to overrun the square.

With the Janissary camp surrounded by the Sultan's artillery, the gunners—Janissaries themselves—hesitated. Their cannons were loaded with incendiary rounds that would touch off an inferno in the wooden barracks and shops of Meat Square, dry tinder to the hungry flames. Despite choosing loyalty to the Sultan, they could not bring themselves to rain such a hideous death down on their brothers of the Corps, with whom they had shared victory and defeat on the battlefield, fighting shoulder to shoulder.

"Halt!" cried out one of the corbacis, his eyes ringed in soot and dirt. "Send in an emissary to reason with them! We cannot slaughter our brothers!"

But the Sultan wanted no reasoning. Mahmud had waited years for this moment's reckoning and he wanted nothing less than the total annihilation of the Janissaries—he was determined that this was to be the end of the Corps. Even those who had chosen loyalty to the Sultan would never fight as Janissaries again.

As the gunners hesitated, one of the Sultan's men, Kara Gehennem, pushed through the ranks and lit a cannon's fuse. With a roar, the cannon sent a flaming ball into the heart of Et Meydan, setting fire to the barracks. Gehennem raced to another cannon, then another, lighting fuse after fuse, setting off a one-man barrage—and touching off an inferno.

Within minutes, the flames leapt to the sky and the Janissaries, trapped in the square that had been their home, died by the thousands. Among the roaring fire, the explosions of ammunition and the screams of the dying, no one noticed the lone soldier who had crept up behind the ranks of cannons. As quick as the silver flash of his blade, he yanked the head of Kara Gehennem tight against his massive chest and slit the traitor's throat with a jewel-studded dagger, a gift from the Ottoman Princess. Then he disappeared again into the confusion, moving swiftly, despite the bloody wound on his leg.

By dawn, the city of Constantinople was black with smoke. The air was filled with the ashes of the barracks and the dead. Twenty thousand Janissaries had died, most in the inferno of Et Meydan. The stench of death made the inhabitants of the Imperial City gag and cover their faces in damp rags.

There was refuge at the water's edge, where the sea breezes cleansed Constantinople's air. The sea wall of Topkapi was washed pink with the blood of Janissaries, their bloated bodies floating white and half submerged in the saltwater.

Mahmud looked down from the parapets, surveying the carnage. He had sent out scouts to scour Constantinople for Ahmed Kadir, while the fishermen of the Bosphorus were offered a rich reward for recovering his body from water.

It was rumored that his mare, Peri, had been wounded in battle and that the giant had attacked on foot, just as he had done in Macedonia. Mahmud had offered a reward for the mare as well, but no one could find her.

"Conspirators still choke the streets!" he screamed to his Vizier.

"My Sultan. The Janissaries are defeated. Constantinople mourns the dead of both sides and the seabirds pick at the corpses in the Bosphorus. You are victorious. Rejoice in the fidelity of your people and their sacrifice. Do not become obsessed with a single man who can no longer oppose you or give you reason to fear him."

"I will not rest until I have Ahmed Kadir's head on a stake on Topkapi's walls! This is a solemn oath to Allah, by the blood of my forefathers and the Prophet's holy word!"

The Vizier closed his weary eyes and breathed deeply. Somehow, after the horror and fatigue of the battle, he no longer feared the Sultan as he once had.

"One man cannot mean more than these all these dead souls, my Sultan. You have won your battle, Praise Allah. Let us welcome peace."

The Sultan's face writhed in anger and he dismissed his Vizier abruptly. Alone in the Royal Reception Room, Mahmud paced the floor, his slippered feet rasping over the intricately woven carpets.

Ivan Postivich awoke, his right leg in a fire of pain. The festering wound sent hot pulses up the leg and into his groin.

He opened his crusted eyes and saw he was swathed in imperial sheets. He shivered nevertheless and wondered why it was so cold and dank in the middle of July.

He could hear whispering in the far reaches of the room, but the voices echoed as if he were in a cavernous tomb. Perhaps he had been mistaken for dead and brought to a vault, he thought. He smelled the humidity, the coolness of the grave, and heard the drip of water somewhere in the distance.

A rustle of linens and footsteps approached him. A Greek-accented voice spoke in Serbo-Croat.

"You are safe, Ivan Postivich. Your sister has sent you here to Esma Sultan's private cisterns where I can care for you in secrecy."

The Sultan's doctor, Stephane Karatheodory, lifted up the sheets and probed the wound.

"You are lucky that the blood loss was not more," he said, his fingers unwinding the dressing.

A woman's gentle hand reached behind Postivich's neck and tilted his head towards a silver cup of water. He drank greedily and did not look up until he had drained every drop.

"More, I beg of you," he whispered and only then did he realize that his sister, Irena, was already refilling the cup. As he turned to watch her, he felt something around his neck shift and slip against his chest.

It was the golden cross of the Greek Orthodox Church.

"You were brought to me by the dervishes," said the doctor, as he continued to attend to the wound. "They found you at the gates of Et Meydan, shot through the leg with a burning timber across your back. The Sultan has put a high price on your head as if the reward of thousands upon thousands of dead Janissaries weren't enough to sate his bloodlust."

"Good doctor, I beg you, say no more," whispered Irena. "You risk your life and that of your family by attending to my brother. Even the cistern may have ears."

The doctor nodded and with his trembling hands pulled the last of the dressing from the wound.

Ivan Postivich winced as the blood-soaked rag tore away, pulling at the flesh.

"My mare, Peri," he croaked. "Does she still live?"

Irena bent close to his ear. "Do not speak. The effort costs too dearly."

But even as she spoke, Postivich screamed in pain. The doctor had forced a hot poker against his flesh to cauterize the wound. As his cry reverberated, he lost consciousness. His scream faded to silence and the dripping stream of water was once more the only sound that broke the silence.

Ivan Postivich did not know how much time passed as he lay in the deep chambers of Esma Sultan's palace, delirious from the fever of the infection in his wound.

He heard voices and saw visions and fought enemies he couldn't see. One night—though night was no different from day deep in the cavern—he sat up, thrashing against the sheets, wet with his perspiration. He was still caught in the memory of a dream. He had been surrounded by dancing women who moved softly and seductively, laughing at him. Then their steps became heavy, impossibly loud, like the roll of thunder overhead. It was that thunder that had awakened him.

Awake, he found that he was dressed in a palace tunic, embroidered with the Ottoman crimson and gold. He felt his face and knew that he had been shaved while he slept and he marveled that he had not awakened.

At his side were a jug of water and cup. He drained the cup five times before he had slaked his thirst.

Now he looked around, seeing that the candles lit only a small part of the vast palace cistern. There were torches scattered through the darkness that must have lighted a passageway to the palace. Shifting spears of green light clashed on the vaulted walls, reflecting off the deep pools of water.

Again, he heard the thundering. This time he was not dreaming. A bat zigzagged overhead, startled at the vibration.

An old voice cursed in Turkish and from the darkness came a man he recognized, a stooped old gardener from the palace. The gardener walked laboriously towards him, muttering.

"You are awake at last," he said. "How soundly sleeps the giant, how fecund are his dreams!"

"What is that roar overhead? It sounds as if elephants move above us!"

"The cave exaggerates sounds," said the old man, his eyes bleary with age. "For surely they are not elephants. Ha!"

With that, the gardener turned away and stomped off again.

"Stop!" commanded Ivan Postivich. "Where do you go?"

"Follow me and you shall see the secret of the thunder."

Ivan Postivich thought the man must be touched with madness, but he followed him anyway. The stones bit into his bare feet, tender from bedrest. His thigh was stiff and sore, almost beyond bearing, but still he was able to drag himself at almost the same pace as the gardener. Together they limped and shuffled through the flickering torchlight.

At last they came to a ladder, rough-hewn rungs lashed to two oak logs. The gardener climbed awkwardly up the creaking rungs to the top and pushed with one hand on a trapdoor.

The door groaned open and moonlight spilled into the darkness like molten silver. Ivan Postivich struggled up the ladder, wrinkling his nose at the stench of the old man's breath that lingered in the stale air.

The full moon shone fiercely and Postivich blinked and shaded his eyes from the moonbeams.

The gardener gestured from the shadows of the immense jasmines.

Postivich followed the gesture and saw the flowing white garb of riders on horseback. They swung long graceful mallets that swept elegantly through the air and sent a small white ball down the grassy field with a sharp click that resounded in the night.

"Polo?" he said, wondering if he was still under the spell of his fever.

As he sucked in the sweet mingled aromas of the blooming gardenia and jasmine, he heard the gardener's laugh, ringing with a tone of certain madness.

"You see!" he said, bringing his dirty fingers to his toothless mouth in joy. He limped away to the shed where he kept his tools and began raking the grounds as if it were early morning.

Ivan Postivich sunk to the ground, his leg too tired to support him any longer. He focused on one player, graceful and tall in the saddle, riding with an agility that sparked a dim memory. He tried to force his mind to focus and remember.

But it wasn't until he heard the unforgettable laugh as the white ball flew through the upright posts, that he realized it was his sister, who reined her horse with such innate skill and gentle hands.

And in that same moment, he recognized the litheness of all the riders and the high, ringing tone of their laughter and shouts. They were all women. And then, one more voice, lower and rougher in tone. It was the old Turkish Horse Master, applauding Irena's goal, the only male among the eight women riders.

Another rider rode up next to Irena, reached out and caressed her cheek. Esma Sultan leaned over kissed Ivan Postivich's sister in joy.

# Chapter 19

Ivan Postivich grew stronger each day. The greenish light of the cistern was unearthly, reflected through a filter of algae and lingering on patches of moss that lined the cavern walls. Its constancy and silence brought healing peace, for no one would search the palace of an Ottoman princess, not even the Sultan himself.

Those who cared for him brought news of the failed revolt and carnage. Thousands upon thousands of Janissaries had died in the Et Meydan inferno, their charred remains left for the ever-ravenous dogs. Any who escaped the flames had been hunted down and brought to the Hippodrome to be hanged. It was rumored that the Sultan was so murderous in his rage and so greedy in his revenge, delivering prisoner after prisoner to Allah, that the executioners were not allowed to carry off the corpses from the field of death. Hundreds of bodies, in various stages of decay, lay mounded on the ground and the Sultan inspected each one from his horse, red with fury that none was the man whose death he coveted.

"We cannot go on until the bodies have been carried off," whispered an executioner to the Vizier, wiping his brow. "You see how deep the ground is in corpses! The next prisoner could stand on the backs of his dead brothers and never feel the noose!"

"Seek more wagons, then, to cart off their blasphemous flesh," ordered the Vizier. "Find men with stronger backs and quicker hands. The Sultan's rage cannot be quenched until it has seen the dead eyes of the giant, Ahmed Kadir."

Ivan Postivich heard the tales with a heavy heart. He walked about the pools of the cistern, contemplating not just his own future, but that of all Constantinople.

"The Sultan has decreed that the Janissaries and all those who joined them shall die," said a young servant boy who stripped the sheets each day and served Postivich in a makeshift hamam. He stood over a large kettle of water heating over a fire.

"You alone are blessed by Allah," the boy said, his eyes red from the stinging smoke. "The Sultan's New Order has ransacked the houses of Constantinople and even searched the wells and cellars. They have found scores of hidden soldiers and all have been dragged to the Hippodrome to be slaughtered—along with those who had given them shelter," said the boy dipping a bucket in the steaming kettle to bathe the corbaci.

"The Sultan has announced from the pulpit of Sultan Ahmed Mosque that the very word 'janissary' is never to be uttered on pain of death as it is forever cursed by Allah."

Concentrating on his story, the boy did not test the temperature of the water before he poured it on the bather's back.

Ivan Postivich screamed as the scalding water cascaded over his still-tender flesh.

"Forgive me, Corbaci!"

The eunuch, Poppy, who supervised the ablutions swiftly boxed the ears of the servant boy.

"You stupid boy! The Head Eunuch himself has requested the finest care for the royal prisoner and you burn him like the ignorant peasant you are!"

Ivan Postivich whirled around, forgetting his pain.

"Prisoner?"

Poppy straightened his spine, standing as tall as his stunted frame would allow.

"You are a house prisoner," Poppy said stiffly. "And you receive the hospitality of the Ottomans. Yet there are some who think your blood should have already mingled with that of the other traitors in the mud of the Hippodrome."

Ivan Postivich realized by the stiff shoulders and twitching mouth that Poppy had spoken on impulse and was distressed to have done so. The little man tightened his lips as if making a silent pledge not to speak again and turned away.

The young servant, on the other hand, looked as though he had much more to say. Ivan Postivich could see his eyes glittering in the firelight. Still, he only nodded quickly to the giant, gathered up his towels and buckets and walked off into the darkness.

When Dede Mustafa entered the audience chamber, Irena rushed to him and fell to her knees. She clasped his hand and kissed it and he pressed his finger against her forehead.

"Rise, Bezm-i Alem," he said softly. "You never have to kneel to anyone, and certainly not me."

"You saved Ahmed Kadir," she whispered. "You put your own life in danger. And that of the Bektashi!"

He helped her to her feet and gazed into her eyes.

"We are already condemned," he said. "The Sultan has banished us from the Ottoman kingdom, as we are considered accessories to the revolution, since we are affiliated with the Janissaries."

"Banished? Where will you go?"

"Some suggest the northern provinces—Serbia or even the mountains of Albania—where we can practice our religion in peace." He smiled wearily, still cradling her hands in his.

Irena did not remember her father. Dede Mustafa's presence challenged her to think of what it would have been like to have a father's love. She wondered if her father would have been a peaceful man had he been allowed to live, and not murdered by the Ottomans while defending their farm.

*It is possible for men to love and honor peace*, she thought. *Esma Sultan is wrong.*

The Dede asked her about Ahmed Kadir and how he fared. He said that he was unable to speak now with the Greek doctor, as it risked Stephane Karatheodory's life to be seen with a Bektashi.

Irena told him about the illness returning to Esma Sultan and he shook his head. "She will not ever be rid of the ghosts that haunt her if she does not repent. Redemption is her only escape from the fevers and djinns that haunt her. She must beg Allah's forgiveness."

He told her the Sufis were packing their wagons as quickly as possible. Were they to be seen in the city after Sunday, they would be killed by the Sultan's Solaks.

The order of Bektashi would travel at night, so as not to agitate those who lusted yet for the Janissaries' blood.

"They might take ours as a substitute," he said. "Better we travel to the edges of the Ottoman frontier under the cover of darkness and navigate by the stars."

He gave her a blessing.

"May Allah grant you peace and health," he said turning towards the door. Then he called out, "And may your children have the same pure soul as their mother and seek peace and the love of humankind."

That was the last Irena saw of Dede Mustafa, although she would seek his intervention one more time before the Bektashi Sufis left Constantinople forever.

# Chapter 20

As the giant's body healed, drawing on the hard core of strength from a lifetime of work and training, each night of sleep faded into the next. That smooth succession was broken late one night when a scream somehow penetrated deep into the cavern, so terrifying in its desperation that Ivan Postivich's eyes flew open. He frantically looked around, his heart pounding hard in his ears. He saw only the leaping flames of the torches, their tongues of light licking the rough walls. There was no human movement—and now no sound but the drip of the weeping water into the green pools.

Again the scream came, a cry from the depths of a terrified soul. Then again and again.

Postivich's muscles tightened and he looked up to the ceiling. Algae and hanging mosses softened the rock face, where rivulets of water trickled towards the cistern's pools.

The scream came again and Postivich knew it was Esma Sultan.

He called for water. The young boy who had bathed him days ago appeared and hurried to the edge of the pool with a hollow gourd that he filled and brought to the giant.

Ivan Postivich stared at him and remembered their conversations. The boy spoke with a Slavic intonation that tortured the lilting syllables of Ottoman.

"Two Serbs in the bowels of the earth," said Postivich in his native tongue. "Surely Allah means this as a joke before I die!"

The boy smiled. "I am honored to serve you, Ahmed Kadir."

The giant sipped, then drained the gourd. He motioned the boy close to him.

"How long have I been here?"

"It is weeks since the Janissaries' revolt and slaughter."

The scream came again, from above, perhaps weaker now.

"Weeks of sleep," said the giant. "And I waken to that."

"The cries of Esma Sultan," said the boy.

"Has she cried out before this?"

"Many nights. They say she has 'lunacy,' the moon has stolen her wits. The screams only cease when the Sultan's eunuch brings her opium."

Ivan Postivich was silent for a long moment, until the scream came again, definitely weaker this time.

"Perhaps it is not the moon's pale light that has leached out her wit."

The boy widened his eyes and whispered, "It is said that the eunuch Emerald tempts her with men the way the animal keepers throw bloody meat to her pet tigers. He has tried everything to persuade her to take a lover."

Ivan Postivich ran his tongue over his cracked lips.

"I am prisoner here, by Esma Sultan's decree, am I not?"

"You are a prisoner by the Head Eunuch Saffron's mercy. Neither Princess nor Sultan knows of your fate. They both offer gold and jewels for news of you: one for your life and one for your death. It is rumored that when the demons leave her, the

Head Eunuch will give Esma Sultan the great news of your recovery. Now he fears that in her delirious state, your name will spill from her lips, sealing your fate with her rage-possessed brother."

"I must get out of here."

"Were you to try to leave, it would mean both our deaths, Corbaci."

"There must be a way. Tell me everything you know about where we are and how I am guarded."

The boy, like Postivich, had been captured to serve the Ottomans, but his heart and soul remained faithful to his countryman. He could not help but dream of his homeland, of the cool mountains and sweet apples of the fall. The strange customs of the Muslims made his head swirl and his Turkish was slow and clumsy. The giant's words in Serbo-Croatian were a delicious intoxicant to him, and he eagerly obeyed.

The Solak emerged from the shadowed recesses of the cistern, carrying a tray. He blinked and rubbed his eyes still adjusting to the dark of the cavern.

He approached his prisoner with a burning torch, examining the sleeping giant's face for a flicker of his eye, or a waking yawn.

The prisoner snored loudly.

"Has the giant awakened at all, boy?"

"Only long enough to call for a draught of boza, sir."

The Solak laughed and spat on the ground.

"See what a drunkard your countryman is! All Serbs are brutes! He cannot even hold a child's drink like boza. How he could inspire the bloodthirsty Janissaries, Allah curse their name, I cannot understand. We will wake him now and feed him like the weak-chinned baby he is."

The page drew in his breath as the Solak kicked the giant's hip.

"Wake, O great Ahmed Kadir!" the Solak shouted. "The cook sends your meal!"

Ivan Postivich rubbed his eyes and turned his head to avoid the Solak's sour breath. He pulled himself up to a sitting position, imitating a struggle against weakness and the torpor of too many days spent asleep.

The Solak set the tray down and uncovered the plates. The scent of rosemary lamb and minted yoghurt filled the damp air.

"Page! Serve the Corbaci!"

"I find myself overcome with sleep, Solak," said Postivich.

With a snort of impatience, the Solak reached down to grab the janissary to set him upright. As his face neared the giant's, Ivan Postivich's eyes flew open and he wrestled the Solak to the ground, punching him hard in the face. An instant later, the Solak lay unconscious on the rock floor of the cistern.

Postivich had torn a blanket into strips in preparation for this moment and they were tying the guard when they heard the scrape and creak of a door opening somewhere distant in the darkness.

"They will see the Solak!" the page whispered. "I will be murdered for taking your side."

Postivich eyed the boy and gripped his shoulder.

"Every man takes a stand, else he is not a man at all. You have cast your lot; stand by your bet. And by Allah's spit, do not shake with fear or I shall never believe you are a Serb!"

The steps of the unseen visitor faltered and paused and soon a curse rang through the darkness. "May the mother's milk fall untasted from the lips of the eldest son of the swine who carved this path!"

The page watched a smile break across Postivich's face.

"It is the old Greek doctor. Go. Take a lantern and help him! I'll drag this pig of a Solak into the shadows."

The boy took a lantern and ran into the darkness towards the source of the Greek oaths.

The guard disposed of, Postivich made his way to the edge of the pool where he knelt and submerged his head in the icy water. At the third dunking he felt his scalp draw tight against his skull with cold and his cheeks flush as the blood coursed through his veins.

"Ah, there you are, Corbaci! You look more of a drowned rat than a fighting man."

Ivan Postivich stood. His eyes stared red at the Greek physician.

"I am trying to rinse the stupor from my mind. You have kept me here too long, doctor. The lethargy is eating my soul."

The doctor motioned to the page to bring him a cushion. He sat heavily. "The Princess's disease has returned," he said. "I knew it would. She sees ghosts at windows and grasping hands in her pillows that drag her to drown in the goose down. The clean air from the Bosphorus carries nothing to her but the stench of rotting corpses, her former lovers joining with the Janissaries whose blood is mixed in the salty waters."

"And the two hundred women and children the Sultan condemned to death," said Ivan Postivich.

"Such is the Ottoman rule. Indeed, blessed be your confinement in the bowels of the earth, for there is no heaven above you, Ivan Postivich."

The giant rubbed his eyes. "Yes. The deaths of so many drowned men haunt her."

"She swears she will send no more lovers to their death. But she must fight the sexual appetites she has inherited from her Sultan ancestors. And the eunuch Emerald cultivates his power over her, tempting her with pretty boys, like a serpent. But she resists. There is no cure for her ailment but the hand of God."

"Why does the eunuch tempt her with lovers?"

"The devil Emerald so enjoys the murder of men."

The doctor looked away at the torchlight reflected off the pool with a heavenly shimmer that belied the tormented hell above the rocky ceiling.

"And the Corps?" Postivich yearned to hear that what he already knew was somehow not true.

"Gone. No one dares to remember them or speak their name for fear of losing his head.

"And that is why I am here. The Bektashi Sufis are also condemned, though their punishment must still be decided by the mullahs as they are Muslims. They have decided to flee Constantinople. One convoy has offered to carry you to freedom in the northern provinces. They will leave tomorrow night and begged that I carry this message to you.

"When the hour comes, you are to be waiting in the limbs of the plane tree at the west end of the palace. The page will take you there. You will wait until the next to last wagon passes, then descend and climb onto its bed. They will conceal you there and carry you to the Western provinces. From there you will have to make your own way further northwest towards Vienna."

"Vienna?"

"You have no safety anywhere in the Ottoman Empire. The Sultan will not rest until your head is perched on a pike on the walls of Topkapi."

A distant wail pierced the tomb-like silence of the cavern.

"And what will become of her?"

"She will survive. She is an Ottoman."

Ivan Postivich watched the drooping eyes of the old Greek.

"I must see her once before I go."

The physician cursed in a low growl. "You are as hardheaded as any of your countrymen. You will never leave the Ottoman Empire alive, you fool!"

Some water dripped from the giant's matted hair, meandering in a rivulet that trickled into his eye. He wiped at it with a knuckle.

"What does it matter? A Kapikulu warrior cannot die in Europe of old age on a featherbed. I will die on Ottoman soil, where my soul can burn its way to Hades. But first I must see her—though not for the last time, for she shall meet me there in the fire."

Postivich listened for her screams but heard only the water splashing from rock to pool.

The Greek eyed the giant like an ancient reptile looking up into the flickering light.

"I thought once you could save her. I did not realize the power she would have over you."

"Do not speak, physician. It is too late for words to turn me."

"The eunuch Emerald will delight in your folly. He serves the Sultan with keen joy. Will you give him the gift of your own death? One more for him to savor. Drawn into his trap by the beauty of Esma Sultan, to die for the pleasure of the eunuch. Like her last lover, that poor Greek boy."

The doctor bent his neck, the loose skin relaxing in folds around his tunic collar.

Ivan Postivich stared, bewildered. "No, physician. He didn't die. I delivered him safe to the Asian side. He was on his way to Greece."

"He whom you spared was murdered nonetheless, just paces from the Bosphorus. Emerald will not spare anyone who has laid eyes on the Sultaness. The boy's body was found facedown in the mud. Mutilated in Emerald's special fashion. I have seen it too often not to know."

Postivich shook his head. "Mutilation—by the eunuch's own hand?"

"He has his own disease. What was done to him, the theft his manhood, has poisoned his mind. His hatred fuels his revenge, his insanity. He hates all men. And all women too. He is the real villain of Topkapi," the old Greek said, closing his eyes.

When he opened them again, he spoke more gently. "Tell me now, Ivan Postivich. What will you do?"

"I must see her. After that, I do not know where I will go or how. That part of my future does not concern me."

The old physician rose unsteadily and beckoned to the page.

"Then I will wish you farewell. You know how I feel about the Princess. She is an Ottoman. She is incapable of true feelings—her veins are full of jagged glass, her heart is a cold stone."

"How can you be so sure?"

"Because my father, my grandfather, and my grandfather's father were all court physicians to the Ottoman Sultans. They are a special breed, raised in cages because they pose such great danger as pretenders to the Sultanate. You cannot expect them to love like the rest of us do; their souls are made of different metal. It has always been that way."

Postivich looked into the old Greek's eyes. His chest lifted and he shut his eyes, then opened them once more.

"I will consider your generous offer of safe passage. I know how dangerous it was to arrange."

"My wife is dead and my children have their own families. What else is there to risk now but my life, tired and worn as it is? I only wish you to not throw away your only chance to leave Constantinople."

With that the physician waved the page forward and the two began to climb into the shadows, the old man grunting with exertion every step of the way.

Postivich quickly checked the guard and tightened the bindings. He searched the man's pockets and under his tunic, stripping him of two daggers and a gold coin. He pulled off the Solak's boots and wedged his own huge feet into them.

Then he made his way in the dark, following the heavy breaths of the doctor and the *toc-toc-toc* of his walking stick.

# Part V
# The Bektashi Sufis

# Chapter 21

Every page and servant in Esma Sultan's palace was called out to unload the flowers from the oxcarts. Thousands of delicate blossoms were packed between sheets of parchment, layered in precious shaved ice from the mountains of Greece. The oxen bellowed and shook their heads in a desperate attempt to rid themselves of the ever-present flies.

The boys' bare arms overflowed with thick green stalks, the blooms obscuring their vision. The bees of summer buzzed in erratic circles, unwilling to leave the fragrant nectar.

Esma Sultan sat on a cushion, her face drawn tight, her cheekbones almost biting through her skin. She wrinkled her nose in disgust.

This time, the smell was not all in her mind and her harem shared her suffering and revulsion. Hundreds of rotting corpses—the bodies of dead Janissaries—had floated into the eddies of the Bosphorus outside her palace, bobbing in the current.

Nazip wore a green silk kerchief over her nose. Despite her attempts to thwart conception, her belly had begun to bulge with the sultan's child and the noxious smell of rotting flesh sent her into yet another a spasm of vomiting.

"Help me, Bezm-i Alem," she said feebly, pulling the kerchief off her face.

The blond woman contorted her forehead in sympathy as she held her friend's face over the fine porcelain bowl. Her scarred lips sagged in dismay as Nazip brought up yellow bile but nothing else.

"You have nothing left to purge," Irena said quietly dabbing Nazip's face with a cool wet towel.

"How wretched it is to be with child in the depths of August," Nazip said, "in this a stinking cesspool of heat and putrid flesh."

Overhearing, the Princess stirred and leaned forward to rise.

"Where are you going?" asked Saffron. "Lie down and let the servants bring you a soothing tea or ice."

"I am going to look for him," Esma Sultan said, staggering to her feet. "He must be among the corpses clogging our docks."

"Oh, Princess! You must not see the carnage! Let the men untangle the bodies from the timbers and tow them offshore. Rest, I implore you!"

"What sight do you save me from? I have seen it night after night in my dreams—do you think to see it once more will be any more horrifying?"

By this time Esma Sultan had pushed open her garden gate and begun to descend to the grassy garden at the shoreline. Her maids and harem girls followed, though with great reluctance, knowing the specter that awaited them.

"You must stop her, Saffron!" shouted the head Solak.

But it was too late.

The Princess's eyes flew open, the dark irises ringed in stark white. For there, in the water just below her, rocked the bloated corpses of dozens of men, only partially visible under the white fluttering wings of the feasting seagulls. She recognized now the harsh cries and screeches of the birds as the sounds that awakened her in the morning.

"You see, Princess," said the eunuch gently, pulling her away. "There is no 'recognizing' to be done. These men are with Allah, and their souls have been counted in heaven."

"But he could be one of them!" she cried. "Ahmed Kadir could be floating in the Bosphorus without a grave or burial prayer."

Irena closed her eyes.

"Do not suffer," Saffron quickly said. "The giant lives, I am certain."

Esma Sultan lifted her head, provoked by the conviction in his voice.

"What do you know, eunuch? Tell me what you know!" she screamed.

Saffron looked about, twisting his head to see whose ear might seek his voice. Perhaps now was the time—perhaps waiting for her strength and sanity to return was fruitless.

"He lives, Sultaness. He lives."

Her eyes, glazed with delirium, stared unblinking into his.

"Show me his living face," said Esma Sultan. "If he lives, my strength will return." Then she collapsed into her eunuch's arms, unconscious.

The Princess was still unconscious as Saffron motioned the eunuch boys to make up the velvet divan. The small hands of the boys worked swiftly to tuck the corners of the sheets and smooth out any wrinkle or fold that might disturb the rest of Esma Sultan.

Flowers were arranged by the armful around the room, and harem girls stirred the air with huge palm fronds.

Saffron mopped his brow and stared at the Princess, though it was a great breach of etiquette. When the Princess woke, if she had any memory at all, she would demand to know the whereabouts of her drowning guard. He could possibly claim that he had said nothing, that she had fabricated a memory in her delirium. But even in her delirium, she was still an Ottoman and could not be denied.

Why had he said anything?

Then he remembered the dead men, their backs moving restlessly with the flapping of wings, as if the sea itself was trying to rise into the air.

He had wanted to spare her, spare himself, the sight of each body being turned over, its bloated face inspected, the gulls rushing to peck at the newly exposed flesh.

Now she lay on the divan, her dark hair loosened by the gentle hands of the harem girls. She seemed almost peaceful.

"See that the Princess is given proper air so that she may sleep and not be troubled by the stench from the docks," said the eunuch. "You who fan her—some must lift the fragrance of the flowers to her bed, the others fan away any odors from the Bosphorus."

Then, nodding to Nazip and Irena, he turned to leave, quickly making his way to the kitchens where he could send a message to depths of the cistern.

# Chapter 22

The Sultan refused to meet with his ministers and was content with only the company of his eunuch Emerald who clucked in delight over the carnage and demise of the Janissary Corps.

"You are brilliant, my Sultan. You have managed to put an end to the Janissaries and the Bektashi Sufis in one magnificent stroke. Your courage and power will be revered by all your subjects . . . and even more by your enemies. The world respects power and you have used it mightily! Men shall sing your praises!"

The Sultan turned from the eunuch and squinted into the sun.

"What is that infernal noise? Have we yet more rebellions to quell?"

"Those are the women of the city, my son," said Nakshidil, her voice trembling. For days she had taken to her bed, ill at the murders.

"Glorious mother! How is it you came unannounced?" said Mahmud, motioning to a eunuch to bring a chair.

"I asked not to be. I am pleased there is still some power left to a woman in this cursed corner of the world." She struggled with her cane and dropped heavily into the chair, gasping for breath.

Mahmud flicked his hand, dismissing the eunuch.

"Whatever do you mean, Mother? We have been victorious over the enemy—the traitors who challenge our rule have been defeated."

"Victorious! Listen to the wails in the street. Is that the sound of victory? That, my son, is the wailing of widows, of mothers who cry for their sons, wives for their husbands, and sisters for their brothers."

"They were traitors!"

"They were men who were loved by the subjects you rule! Is there never any solution to conflict other than murder and destruction? The streets are streaked in red, the holy Bektashi Sufis flee the city, even the Jewish street sweep will not come out of hiding. What has happened to our Imperial City that provided safe haven for all sects and tolerance for all?"

Mahmud leaned out the window of Topkapi and saw a mother trying to pry her son's head from the palace gates.

"You there! That is property of the Ottoman Empire and your Sultan," snarled a guard.

"It is the property of the womb that carried it," said the woman, wrapping the bloody head in the folds of her apron. Her tears streaked her dirty face.

"Replace it or your head will be next."

"Let her have it, Solak!" shouted the Sultan. "Set her free."

"May you answer to Allah," shouted back the woman from the street. "You monster!"

Mahmud's eyes widened at her audacity and blue veins stood out under the white skin of his neck.

Nakshidil struggled from her chair and plucked at her son's sleeve.

"Do what they ask," she said. "In the name of God and mercy, do as they ask."

Mahmud raised his arm as if to strike his mother, then stared at his hand in bewilderment.

"Forgive me, Mother," he whispered.

"When did you forsake your gentle nature and compassion for such brutal hatred and aggression, my son?"

"When I became an Ottoman Sultan," he answered, turning away from her and looking out at the Bosphorus.

# Chapter 23

"I shall send the kitchen page to the cistern with the message," whispered the Greek cook, Maria, to Saffron. She had been a member of the Orthodox Church of the Greek physician and shared his confidences. "He is a good Christian boy and shares the homeland of the giant. He is still faithful to his religion and our people. He would sooner die than deceive us."

"When does he report?"

"Before evening prayers, I prepare the supper for the Princess and her harem. From that meal, I set aside a bit for Ahmed Kadir. The boy should be here in an hour. What exactly should I say?"

"That the hour has come for him to see the Princess and then leave the Empire forever," he said. "Tell him to meet me at the dockside of the harem wall."

The cook nodded, her eyes closing for a second as if she were learning a recipe and must not miss an ingredient.

"All right, then. Dockside of the harem wall."

"I will be there when I can. He should have patience."

"Patience."

"That is all," he said, raising his chin as he saw a hungry Solak enter the vast kitchen. "Esma Sultan needs proper attention to her diet and I will ask you to consult with the Topkapi doctor to see that her food is properly prepared—flavor her yoghurt with fresh mint," he said, addressing her officiously.

Then he turned on the Solak. "Have I not made it clear that this is the Royal Kitchen? You will not be begging Esma Sultan's cook to delay her duties in order to indulge your stomach."

The Solak ducked his head in submission and backed out of the kitchen. Saffron darted a quick glance to the cook who nodded that the task was understood.

But the boy did not come. The cook had prepared the breads, yoghurts, fish, and a pickled salad for the prisoner and set them in a side pantry out of sight. When the hour came to send the food to the harem, she found her forehead beaded with sweat, so much that a harem servant remarked that the heat and oppressive odor surely had affected her—but not her cooking, mercy to Allah. She should lie down on the divan at the end of the corridor, where the cool of the fountains might bring her some relief.

The cook agreed, thinking that this would be excuse enough for her to take action herself. She promised the harem girl she would lie down or perhaps even walk in the interior gardens to regain her strength.

She instructed three scullery maids to take care of any additional requests, pleasing them no end with the sudden responsibility entrusted to them.

In the shadows of the cypress trees that purred with buzzing insects, the cook found the old gardener sharpening his tools. He looked up at her with a toothless grin.

"What have you brought me to eat, woman?"

She looked both ways, and, seeing no one, took out a greasy sausage of mutton, fresh oregano, and mint that she had rolled in a towel. She kept such pieces of meat and sweets to bribe the pages for gossip, peddlers for extra trifles, and butchers for the best cuts of meat.

The gardener's tongue moistened his lips; the woman was known for her sorcery in the kitchen and especially for her art in sausage making. The minced lamb spiced the air with its meaty aroma and the hungry man reached out.

"Not yet, gardener," said Maria, snatching away the sausage. "This is made from the prize sheep from the hills of Anatolia. You will never again taste a sausage as savory as this, no matter if you live another hundred years."

"You will not give it to me?" said the gardener, his voice dumb with misery.

"I did not say that," she hissed, once again looking around to make certain no one had spied them. "But first you must do me one small favor."

"Speak, woman."

"Show me the garden entrance to the cistern and take me there at once."

The old man's eyes wandered to the cook's sweating neck and dropped his gnarled hands to his groin with a leer.

"Do not insult me, you old fool!" snapped the cook. "You think I would trade my cooking for so limp a noodle? You are mad, just as they say."

"What do you want then?"

"The old entrance to the cistern, you fool. I know there is one here, where the aqueducts carry water to the fountains."

The gardener finally engaged the thought and laughed to himself, licking his lips.

"For that, you will give me the sausage, by Allah's word?"

"I have no time to waste on your Allah. Where is it?"

The gardener led her around the edge of the toolshed into the deep shade of the cypresses.

"Just there," he said, kicking the dry needles from the wooden door.

"Good," she said and shoved the sausage into his greedy hands. "Now go into the kitchens and tell the scullery maids to feed you some yoghurt and honey from the larder. I have sesame biscuits made yesterday to accompany them. Tell them that I am resting and not to be disturbed, else no one will eat tonight. Go, now!"

The gardener smiled at her and plunged the sausage into his mouth, his lips smacking in delight, and hobbled off towards the palace with a sigh of contentment.

The cook lifted the wooden trapdoor. The cool air greeted her like a cat, curling around her ankles and making her sigh with relief from the heat. She lit a candlestick, descended the ladder, walked a few paces, and then stopped suddenly when she heard a man howl with rage.

"What do you mean, he escaped? Where were you? You drooling fool!"

"He caught me by surprise," wailed a second man. "I thought he was asleep. He hadn't moved more than a step or two in days."

"Hopeless drunken fool," she heard the first man say. It was a voice she could almost place, high and irritating, but superior. A man of education. She searched her mind, wondering what person of rank could have found his way to this dark place without the help and consent of Esma Sultan.

"You shall die for your treason, Solak, but first you will live in torture for your complete incompetence."

By this time, the cook had crept to the end of the damp corridor. She held her candle behind her and looked around the corner where the flickering torches illuminated the enormous pool, a makeshift bed, and three men.

The pleading victim, now on his knees, wailed, "I swear I wasn't drinking."

"You lie," said the small man with the educated voice, and battered him with hilt of a sword. As his hand rose, she saw the paleness of his skin and at last placed the voice.

"Emerald," the cook whispered to herself.

The man on his knees fell back as the sword hit its mark. He collapsed onto the uneven stone.

"Seize him and take him to Topkapi," shouted the eunuch to the third man, a Solak like the one who now lay unconscious on the floor. "But as he reaches the Gates of Bliss, see that his ridiculous head parts ways with his neck. This much respect he can show to his Sultan!"

Moments later, standing alone in the chamber, the eunuch stared at the empty bed and tangled sheets. His voice suddenly small in the darkness he said, "I should have known. I should have found him. I should have."

# Chapter 24

The eunuch Emerald lost no time in reaching Topkapi. He demanded to see the Sultan at once.

Mahmud was paying a scheduled visit to one of his wives when the message was delivered. He excused himself from her apartments, refusing her offer of tea and pastries.

"What news do you bring that interrupts my pleasure?"

"The giant lives, Sultan."

"Where? What traitorous beast harbors him?"

"He—he has been hidden in the cistern of your sister, Esma Sultan."

Mahmud wiped his face with his pale white hands.

"I cannot believe this! They say she is ill! She has waking nightmares! She hides the giant—I will give her a nightmare she shall never forget!"

"There must be a conspiracy, my Sultan. I have never seen her consort with him and I watch her night and day."

"Saddle my horse! I shall pay my sick sister a visit at once!"

By the time the Sultan and his personal guards arrived at Esma Sultan's palace, the cook had told Saffron what had happened and sent word to the Greek doctor through an Armenian Christian kitchen boy.

Once inside the palace walls, the Sultan and his guards bent over the soft ground leading away from the cobblestone entrance. When the Sultan arose, his mouth was twisted in a snarl that allowed a glimpse of his white teeth against his glossy black beard.

But though they searched fiercely, no one could find Ahmed Kadir. The surviving Serbian servant boy was already on his way to lands far from the Imperial City. He was aboard a Russian trade ship before sundown, with gold enough to begin a new life—and the knowledge that, unlike so many others, he still had a life to live.

The Sultan bellowed through the corridors of the palace.

"Esma! You have betrayed me!"

He ran escorted by Topkapi Solaks to the door of his sister's Royal Harem and demanded she receive him at once.

Esma Sultan rose from her divan, pushing her auburn hair from her eyes. She had lost weight in the weeks since he had last seen her and looked almost childlike in her white linen tunic.

"I demand to know where he is!"

"What, dear brother, is the meaning of this?" she said, ignoring his demand. "Since when do you barge into my palace, given to me by our glorious sultan father when you were still cutting your teeth?"

"I have been told you conceal the traitor Ahmed Kadir in this palace!"

"Ahmed Kadir? My Angel brother, I have not seen the giant since I dismissed him a day before the rebellion, and that I swear in the Prophet's name."

"I have seen horse dung in the interior of your palace gates."

"What of it? My carriages have been standing ready to transport me to Galata to choose a lover for the night. But I have been so ill—"

"Don't try my patience! There are hoofprints, dozens upon dozens of them that lead towards your interior gardens. Are you harboring a legion of Janissaries?"

"Oh, my brother!" she smiled slowly. "You must refer to the tracks of the polo ponies."

"Polo? What men do you have here to play? Do your eunuchs play polo?"

"No men whatsoever. It is a pastime for the ladies of my harem."

Mahmud strode towards his sister. He grabbed her shoulder so roughly that Saffron instinctively moved to defend her, but she held up a hand to stop him.

"Do not jest with me," said the Sultan, his eyes inches from her. "A man who meant to kill me has been seen in your palace. You nurse a serpent at your bosom and call it entertainment!"

Esma Sultan raised her chin to look over her brother's head. She wrinkled her nose in disdain at the sight of Emerald, who awaited the Sultan's orders.

"You certainly know more about his whereabouts than I do," she replied calmly. "I swear I have not seen him nor spoken to him since before the rebellion. I paid him his wages and dismissed him, long before what you term the 'blessed event'—if a sea of drowned men and rivers of blood could ever amount to 'blessed' in Allah's eyes."

"Then you have a traitor in this house," said the Sultan.

"Oh, most certainly. At least one," she said. "But Ottomans are used to treachery. How they deal with it in a regal manner is the question."

"Tell me about the horses," commanded the Sultan. "How is it that I know nothing about your supposed polo games?"

"I have my secrets, brother," she replied, brushing her hair calmly out of her eyes. "We play at night. Come this evening after dark and bring your own players with you. We shall have a match and you shall see how we play. I shall not be at my best, but my harem women shall perform for you."

Mahmud's eyes scanned her face. He saw only her clear brown eyes mocking him and he loosened his hold on her shoulder.

"Thank you brother, for that. Your grip was becoming tiresome. I hope you don't embrace your lovers with such ferocity, as it would certainly interfere with your lovemaking and give the woman bruises to remember you by. Poor manners and worse memories."

Just then, a white-sheathed harem girl fluttered by.

"You boast how your women eschew the veil," said Mahmud. "All except one."

"And who is she? Why is she alone hidden behind the veil?"

Esma Sultan tilted her head, then gave a small shrug.

"Well, my Angel brother, that was your first love—that was little Irena."

The Sultan was struck speechless. His eyes wandered about his sister's face in amazement.

"Irena?" he whispered.

"Yes. My adopted daughter now. She is untouchable under my protection. Her name is Bezm-i Alem now. Her veil is to cover her scars—"

"I must see her! I don't care about any scars," he said, opening wide the fists he had clenched only seconds before. "I must talk to her!"

"What luck. She is the captain of our polo squad. You will play against her tonight."

"You are joking."

"She is a very adept rider. As skillful as her brother."

"Her brother?"

"The man whose blood you lust for. Ahmed Kadir is her brother, just as you are mine."

Mahmud's jaw dropped open.

"Come, kucuk," clucked Esma Sultan. "Do not act the fool in front of our servants. Does she not have the same fire and pride as her brother? You should see her on her horse. Then you will know for certain."

"I cannot believe that wonderful woman and that murderous cur are brother and sister."

"Oh? And does not all Constaninople say the same about the two of us?"

"Esma—"

Her laugh was alive, as if her sickness has fled. "Come play polo with us tonight. Perhaps her equestrian talent will convince you of the truth."

"I cannot play against women!"

"Why not? There is nothing forbidding it in the Koran."

"Men against women?"

"Are you afraid we will defeat you?"

The Sultan managed a laugh. "I am afraid you ladies might be injured. What nonsense you imagine, sister!"

Esma Sultan lifted her chin. "Come tonight, little brother. Leave your spies at home. Just you and your Kapikulu squad, no Topkapi Solaks. We will play by the light of the full moon."

"So be it. In the meantime, I demand permission to search your grounds."

"Most certainly. I will have Saffron issue the orders and accompany you, if need be. But have that savage brute of a eunuch, Emerald, off my palace grounds within the next five minutes, or I shall have my own Solaks slit his throat."

Mahmud caught sight of the fluttering of a yasmak behind a screen. "Until tonight, Esma."

"We will be ready for the match, my Sultan."

As Mahmud turned to leave, he spied the Persian painting on the wall of harem women playing polo. He examined it closely and saw his sister smiling from the divan.

"A treasure like this belongs in the Topkapi."

"Our father bequeathed it to me. It will not return to Topkapi until my death. If you wish to visit it, you know where it hangs."

The Sultan snorted and left his sister's harem.

Ivan Postivich had overheard the entire conversation. His sister Irena had clothed him in tunics and veils, imploring him to sit rather than stand, as his height would surely draw the attention of Emerald, should he enter the harem.

The women of the Serail conspired to hide the giant, giggling as they dressed him in flowing robes and jewels.

"I shall escort him to the hamam myself!" whispered Nazip.

"Inappropriate talk for the expectant mother of a prince."

"There is nothing more tedious than being pregnant," protested the freckled maid, who had grown quite plump and even more beautiful. "Except to be pregnant with Ottoman royalty."

"Irena, you must get me away from here," whispered Postivich. "I cannot endure these women's caresses without losing control of myself."

"Perhaps you are more suited for cisterns than for a Royal Harem," mused his sister. "They are harmless. Let them fuss over you."

"They are harmless, but I am not. I have not had a woman in months!"

"Poor little brother. Learn abstinence and restraint. It will strengthen your character."

"It is not my character that is strengthening."

Irena looked down below his waist where he gestured.

"Put that away! It is most unbecoming under such fine silks. This is the only way the Sultan will not find you—he is forbidden to touch Esma Sultan's women without express permission. Even I have been saved by this promise."

"If he should ever touch you, I shall cut off his hand and his head."

"Fine boasting for a fugitive who wears a woman's veil."

Once they had searched the palace and its grounds, Mahmud and his men galloped off to Topkapi. There were men in hiding along the way who barked insults from the shadows.

"Murderer! Traitor!"

"Blood on the hands of our Sultan!"

"Long live Ahmed Kadir!"

The Sultan sent two horsemen to locate the source of the shouts, but in the tight warren of alleyways and corridors, he knew the insults would never be punished. A pack of dogs snarled and bit at the horses' hooves, making them bolt.

"We cannot murder every soul who hates the Sultan," said one of the riders. He had already beheaded a dervish who had insulted the Sultan as he rode along the Golden Horn.

"Infidel Sultan!" the dervish had shouted. "You will have to answer to Allah for your crimes!"

"You must be mad, dervish, to insult your Sultan."

"Mad? I mad? It is you who have lost your reason! You shall answer to Allah! Hail the Janissaries! Their desperate spirits clamor for justice!"

The man was executed at once, but the poor dervish was hailed as a martyr. Soon after he was buried, a legend grew of a shining light over his grave.

"Ahmed Kadir must be found and must die." Mahmud's orders were clear and insistent. He understood all too well how dangerous legends could be.

Sultan Mahmud's day of misfortune had not ended. His mother, Nakshidil, had been consulting the Greek Orthodox priest again. She had openly returned to the religion of her birth and demanded the services of a priest at Topkapi.

"Mother! You are worshipping like an infidel under the Top-kapi roof! Our people note your absence in the mosque."

"Let them! I shall die soon and it will be with the blessing of a priest, you must promise me this."

"I can deny you nothing, Mother. But you must not speak of dying. Let me tell you the news from Esma Sultan."

At this Nakshidil smiled, for there was always something interesting and uncommon at Esma Sultan's palace.

"How is the dear young girl?"

"She remains a painful thorn in my side and it is rumored that she harbors Ahmed Kadir somewhere in her palace."

"The giant of the cirit field?"

"My mortal enemy, mother."

"Is there more?"

"Esma has told me that our dear Irena is his own sister!"

"No! The fair Irena?"

"She is in Esma's harem. She alone among the women is veiled."

"The woman they call Bezm-i Alem?" said Nakshidil laughing. She clapped her hands together. "I know her! The giant's sister no less! How delicious!"

"They were taken in the devshirme in the same day."

"And how fares the sweet Irena?"

"She is not permitted to speak to me as she is one of my sister's harem."

"So was Nazip, who is now big with your child."

"Irena remains protected."

The Sultan's mother nodded her head, suddenly quiet.

"I recall her injuries. I was one of the few who were allowed to inspect the burns. The poor child."

"Was she really that disfigured, Mother?"

"Horribly so."

Mahmud gazed at his mother.

"She showed more courage than all of us. I remember the determination, the spite in her eyes, that she was born free and would never surrender her spirit. The scars twisted her mouth into a perpetual smirk, as if she were scorning your father and the Ottomans for eternity." Nakshidil sought her son's hand and held it in hers.

"Her spirit is indomitable," she said. "She was quite a brave girl. And woman."

"I should love to look into her eyes again, but Esma will not permit me."

"I understand. I am sure Irena would prefer not to be reminded of men, especially the son of the Sultan who tormented her."

Mahmud stared at the brazier, contemplating the embers.

"I loved her, Mother."

"Bah! You were at that tender age when even a future Sultan thinks he can love. It was very sweet, but fleeting."

"No, you do not understand. I still love her."

"Impossible. You do not know her. You think you love the woman you imagine she was. It is all a child's fantasy. Besides, an Ottoman does not have the luxury of loving anyone or anything but his Empire. Leave her to your sister who can care for an injured woman, one who has known nothing but pain from men. That is the most love you can show in your position."

"I am going to play polo with her tonight. Under the full moon."

Nakshidil raised her head. "Polo?"

"Yes, Esma has arranged a match between her harem and my squad. I promise I will be gentle with them. It is only for a chance to glimpse Irena."

His mother laughed, as if the tragedy of Irena had fled her mind once again. "Oh, you must go visit your sister more often! You always amuse me with the news from Esma's palaces. How divine! A polo game with the harem, just like the Persian princesses! I must write to my cousin Josephine—surely there is nothing so splendid as this for women in the Courts of Paris. She shall be green with envy! I shall include your pledge to allow a priest to give me my last rites when I die." She added that thought, as if carelessly, but she gave her son a sharp look, making certain he knew his promise was being reported far and wide. Then she was carelessly gay again. "Josephine shall be so jealous she has such a bore as Napoleon for a husband when there are such goings-on in Constantinople. A harem playing polo!"

With that, Nakshidil excused herself and went back to her apartments to compose a letter to her cousin. Mahmud chewed the end of his mustache, wondering how he would approach his long-lost love Irena, and whether he could abide seeing her self-inflicted deformities.

Esma Sultan inspected the terrariums where ornamental plants for her gardens were grown. The gardeners maintained a fine stock of earthworms there to improve the soil. She selected some of the earthworms and gave careful instructions to the boy who tended them.

"Do you know where the willow balls for polo are kept?"

"Yes, my Sultane."

"You must whitewash them and set them to dry in the sun. As we begin the match you must crush a worm and work the slime over the ball. Repeat this every few minutes so there is always a fresh supply of balls on the sidelines. You must keep the arbitrator supplied with new balls, and have him relinquish the old ones. Are my instructions understood quite clearly?"

"Yes, Sultane."

"Good. Keep the earthworms in moist soil until they are to be sacrificed. Make certain the polo ball is slippery with the slime."

"Yes, my Sultane."

At ten o'clock, the torches were lit around the polo field and Esma Sultan's horses were tacked. The head groom and the orphan boys rode them across the goal lines and weaved in and out of the torches to accustom them to the flames and the smell of burning oil. Since this was the routine every full moon, the horses only snorted once or twice and relaxed their ears and necks, drinking in the cool air of the summer night.

The Sultan arrived late, his horses rearing in the courtyard. The three Kapikulus—all former companions of Ivan Postich's cavalry orta—who accompanied him were scornful of the prospect of playing against women and spat on the cobblestones.

"Come this way," motioned Nazip, atop a sturdy mare.

"Nazip, you will not play!" ordered the Sultan. "You carry my child in your womb."

"I will not play because I choose not to, with all grace and respect my Sultan," answered Nazip. "Esma Sultan has already chosen her teammates and I am but a timekeeper. May you enjoy the match. I so regret that I will not play against you."

The Kapikulus groaned at her insubordination but admired her beautiful face and full figure, which was not obscured by a veil or the cumbersome clothing required at Topkapi.

"Come," said Nazip. "Follow Saffron to the field. I shall remain in the stands and cheer you on."

With that, Nazip turned and disappeared into the darkness. Saffron appeared and opened a gate to allow the mounted Kapikulus, their spare horses, and their grooms to enter the gardens.

Mahmud had not seen these interior gardens since he was a small boy. When they were both children, Esma had invited him for visits when her cousin Sultan Selim allowed him outings from the princes' cage under the careful watch of the guards. He wondered now at the perfect polo field she had cultivated, the spectator stands for her harem and female orchestra, and the officials' stand that rose at the edge of the field like a colossal gazebo.

The sidelines were marked in a chalk solution concocted in Esma Sultan's laboratories. They reflected the moon and torchlight with an incandescent glow.

The Sultan's horses snorted at the leaping flames of the torches, rearing on the soft manicured turf.

"*Kus!*" shouted Mahmud. "Our horses are not accustomed to fire."

The horses' nostrils flared and quivered, taking in the strange surroundings. Their flanks trembled and they pawed the ground, eager to break loose from the riders' grip on the reins.

"Ah, this is to your disadvantage, I fear," said the turbaned Esma, atop her stallion. She dropped a polo ball on the turf and struck it with her mallet. The ball exploded in a blue light.

The Kapikulus' horses reared and backed away from the field.

"My God! What witchcraft is this?" said one, trying to rein in his horse.

A veiled woman rode up to them. "You will have to make your horses behave better or you will be disqualified. Is that not right, arbitrator?"

Another woman in a red tunic approached them.

"Absolutely. Your horses pose a danger to both teams—you must get them under control. I suggest you calm them down by riding them about the field."

"But the light—"

"It is one of Esma Sultan's discoveries. A combination of material from our own Turkish earthworms and a solution of coral from the sea. When you strike the ball, it glows with blue fire. Quite beautiful, really."

The cavalrymen looked at each other, uttering a quick prayer against sorcery and begging the protection of Allah against such strange women.

"You should not be so terrorized by knowledge," the veiled woman said. "Come, accustom your horses. We are eager for a match."

"Do as she says," Mahmud commanded. He himself was the first male player to gallop onto the field, demonstrating the horsemanship he had learned many years ago from the Horse Master.

The Kapikulu followed, though their horses bucked madly at the strange sights and smells, shying away from the glowing white sidelines and leaping into the air at the smell of camphor and burning oil.

"Line up," shouted yet another umpire. She, like Irena, was veiled, and her voice was deep.

The red-haired Tatar Altug urged his horse against the shoulder of a horse ridden by a raven-tressed woman, her dark hair escaping from her turban in tendrils. He could smell the scent of jasmine in her hair and was so distracted he missed the moment when the umpire tossed the ball into play.

The dark-haired woman did not. She tapped the ball clear of the milling horses and smacked it across the field. The veiled player deftly controlled the ball with a quick tap of her mallet and sent it flying towards the goal.

Esma Sultan had already fought off her opposing player and was in position to follow the pass. Her turban and flowing tunic cut through the night air as she galloped unopposed and smacked the ball through the uprights.

"Esma Sultan 1!" shouted the referee.

"Play, men!" roared the Sultan. "You disgrace me with your performance."

Within seconds, Esma Sultan's team was ready in the midfield lineup, even as the Kapikulu were sorting themselves out.

"Play!" shouted the referee. The ball was thrown into play while the Kapikulus were still in confusion. Esma Sultan rapped the ball with her mallet, passing it towards her veiled teammate. As the ball was struck, it glittered with the eerie blue light.

Mahmud drove his horse's shoulder hard against his veiled opponent as she raced for the ball. Though shaken by the impact, Irena gave her mare its rein and they slipped past the Sultan's horse. She stood up out of the saddle and leaned far up the horse's neck, striking the ball into the goal before Mahmud could reach it.

As she cantered around the uprights, Irena let loose a cry that the Sultan had only heard on the battlefield when ambushed by Serbian rebels.

"She rides like a goddess," he muttered.

Again, Esma Sultan's team beat the Kapikulus back to midfield when the referee called, "Time! First period!"

The women rode off the field, and without dismounting, vaulted from one horse to another, as the grooms held the reins.

The referee blew the whistle.

As Mahmud galloped back onto the field with his fresh mount, he chastised his teammates. "You are playing women, Kapikulu! What excuses do you have?"

"My horse leaps at each torch!"

"The referee throws in the ball too hastily."

"The ball glows white, then blue," shouted the bandy-legged Albanian. "I cannot rein my horse close enough to strike it!"

Mahmud heard a muffled chuckle from beneath the veil of the woman who rode beside him.

"And you, Irena? Are you enjoying this?"

"Most certainly, my Sultan."

He gazed at her eyes as the torch illuminated their beauty—green with sparks that mocked him, just as they had as a little girl. There, reflected in those eyes, lay the power to mesmerize and defy a sultan, his own father. He held their gaze as long as he could, but was the first to look away, as if the enchantment would sear his eyes.

"Sultan!" shouted one of his men, shattering the spell.

The ball was thrown in and Mahmud reined his horse into his veiled opponent's shoulder. Each rider fought for the advantage, pushing and grunting, trying to get an edge. The ball lay on the turf between them and they bent over their horses' necks, their turbans pressed together and they breathed each other's exhaled air as they fought for the ball.

With a surge, Irena controlled the ball, driving it down the field and following at a gallop. Mahmud cast an angry, but admiring, look in her direction. He tried desperately to ride past her far enough to gain position and force her away from the ball, but could not gallop his horse fast enough. Instead, riding beside her, he watched the wind pick up her veil and pull it away from her face. There in the torchlight he saw the sneering smile that permanently contorted her face—the injury she had inflected on her own beauty to protect her from men's admiration for all time.

And with that glance he fell in love with her again—fell in love with her scars, with her disfigured face. He had hundreds of women in his harem, all beautiful and perfectly formed. But in the twisted smile of Irena was the mark of their common hatred for his father—and . . . ? Courage. It was the sign of the rebellious girl who had been his first love and who possessed more courage than all the sultans he had ever known.

"Great Sultan! Hook her!"

"Hook her!"

They were closing on the goal and she was ready for a fierce shot that would drive the ball through the uprights. Mahmud came to his senses and thrust out his mallet to hook hers and block the shot. Her flexible mallet bent around his in a "U" and slammed in a hammerblow against the side of the Sultan's head.

He tumbled from his horse, unconscious.

The game was stopped as Irena jumped off her mount, calling to him as he lay on the turf.

"Mahmud! Oh, Mahmud, do not die!"

Esma Sultan rode over to her brother. "Rise, oh great Sultan! Surely a slight knock on your royal head by a woman will not be the death of you. It is hardly befitting an Ottoman."

Mahmud's eyes flickered open at the insult. He reached up and pulled the veil from Irena's face. He could not help himself. He blurted, "You are still beautiful, Irena. Your eyes are stars of beauty, your face a map of courage."

"We are not here to discuss beauty, my brother," snapped Esma Sultan. "Mount your horse and let us finish our match."

The Kapikulus and the Sultan were disgraced that night. They lost the match 4-2, though there were no witnesses other than the players and the amused Horse Master, who had been the umpire, dressed in a woman's guise. Ivan Postivich watched from the observation tower, scowling as he watched his sister bend over his mortal enemy in worry.

"I shall kill him before he has the chance to take her to his bed," he swore aloud. The ladies of the harem exchanged looks and hastened to warn Esma Sultan.

"You are to jump onto the cart an hour before dawn," said Saffron. He stood looking almost eye to eye with the giant, his great ebony arms folded across his chest. "You have endangered Esma Sultan and this household long enough. The dervishes shall convey you out of Constantinople to the sea, where you can find passage to another country."

"Constantinople is my home now. I will not leave the Empire."

"Oh, yes, you will, Ahmed Kadir. If you do not leave this morning, I will personally report your whereabouts to Topkapi. I will not risk my Sultane's life with your selfish whims."

"I must see her."

"She is still entertaining her brother, the Sultan."

"Find a way that I might see her and I will do what you ask."

"Swear it so."

"I swear on my mother's holy grave. Only give me time with the Sultaness."

Saffron exhaled nosily and disappeared down the corridor. Ivan Postivich could hear the singing of the harem girls and the accompaniment of the female orchestra. The strong scent of sandalwood wafted out from the harem, where the women lay on their pillows eating dried fruits and smoking opium.

The eunuch returned.

"She will see you. But you must wait until her brother leaves."

Ivan Postivich knelt at his feet. "May Allah reward you for your kindness."

"You have your sister and the Bektashi to thank," he said. Then Saffron nodded and turned to leave, his white robes billowing as he strode down the corridor.

The clock struck two when Saffron returned. He led Ivan Postivich into the inner chambers of Esma Sultan's apartments. The bed he had once seen through the filmy gauze was unmade and the princess lay naked upon her pillows.

Ivan Postivich found he couldn't breathe. She beckoned him with an outstretched arm and it was then Saffron whispered in his ear.

"The dervishes come in two hours. Remember your oath or you are a dead man."

The janissary stood, gazing at the naked woman. He swallowed hard, taking in the sight he had waited so long to see.

"Now, Biscuit," she murmured. "Come to me."

Postivich stripped off his clothes pulling his tunic over his head and pressing his bare flesh against hers. Out of the corner of his eye he saw the Koran opened, the brown-red suras, written in blood on the parchment.

He reached out to close it.

"Do not touch anything," commanded Esma, "but me, O Corbaci."

He pressed his mouth against hers, sucking at her tongue. His hands wandered to her breasts, the nipples still a rosy pink. His mouth followed where his fingers led.

"Give me pleasure," she sighed.

His mouth moved down to the wet spot between her legs and he sucked its juices. Her harem girls had plucked every hair from her body, save for her head, and the skin in the folds between her legs was soft and scented with rose essence.

He shifted his weight onto his arms, hovering over her, his eyes riveted on hers. She held his gaze, unblinking. His arms trembled—not from lack of strength, but from emotion. She saw the tremor in his arms and smiled.

"Ivan Postivich," she said.

He kissed the lips that whispered his true name. Then he kissed her breast tenderly again, his hand caressing the soft damp skin between her thighs.

He entered her. She closed her eyes in ecstasy.

He arched his back to drive his pelvis against hers and for a moment his eye was caught by the sura written in her brother's blood. *What madness,* he thought.

He thrust against her, making her groan, as his mind turned from the Koran to the woman beneath him.

He closed his eyes and moved his hips against hers, and opened his eyes to see her soft brown eyes seeking his. He rolled her over and pressed against her from behind. His fingers sought her genitals and she guided his penis into the wet spot.

They rocked hard against each other with a ferocity perhaps born of hatred and now transformed into the lust of a coupling too long delayed—and perhaps something more. The rhythm

grew faster and harder until there was an explosion and one of
them screamed as they fell back, exhausted.

The room spun and, again, Ivan Postivich found he couldn't
remember how to breathe.

The drowning guard was drowning.

Time passed and he opened his eyes to see the Koran written
in the Sultan's blood.

The words were delicately smeared, as if a damp finger had
traced their calligraphy often. He read the words, but though he
had studied the suras for many years, these were nothing he had
seen before.

*In the name of Allah, the compassionate, the merciful,*
*By the Star when it setteth,*
*Your companion Mohammed erreth not, nor is he led astray,*
*Neither speaketh he from mere impulse.*
*The Koran is no other than a revelation revealed to him:*

*Do ye see Al-Lat and Al-Uzza,*
*And Manat the third idol besides?*
*These are the exalted Females, sublime cranes,*
*Mounting nearer and nearer to Allah.*
*These are the exalted Females, and verily their intercession is to be*
*hoped for.*

# Chapter 25

The little French clock, a present from Nakshidil, sounded the hour. Ivan Postivich and Esma Sultan still lay as one, moving as one wave upon the sand.

Saffron cleared his throat and rang a little bell made of silver.

"I call on you, Ahmed Kadir, to remember your oath."

The giant pulled his lips from the sweet mouth of Esma Sultan.

"It is the Sultaness I protect, not you," added the eunuch. "You have pledged to protect her too. Come with me."

Ivan Postivich sought his lover's eyes and nodded his head.

"I shall do as I promised. Give me five minutes farewell and I shall be at your side."

Saffron answered. "No more than five minutes. I shall take you at knifepoint if I must, but I will not endanger my mistress's life another second."

With that, he disappeared behind the porphyry screen.

"Those suras in your brother's blood? I have never seen the word of the Prophet in such a fashion."

"They are the 'Forgotten Women's Verses A'—spoken by the Prophet. We hold to those suras, and praise Allah for sharing them with the Prophet. They are as true as any other words he ever spoke."

She turned away from Ivan Postivich and looked at the painting of the Royal Persian Harem playing polo.

"The legend is that Mohammed later said that it was Satan who had spoken such gentle words and that they must be struck forever from the Holy Koran. But we feel it was Man and the politics of Medina that altered the holy words of our Lord, and revoked the Prophet's compassion. Al-ilah was the Moon God, married to the Sun Goddess Diana. Al-Lat, Al-Ozza, and Manat are their daughters. It was so in the days before Mohammed and even if we dare not speak these words, the symbol of the Ottoman Empire embraces the image still.

"The crescent moon always accompanied by the gentle daughter star. What is so demonic about womankind, that men should fear their intercession?"

"What the Holy Prophet and Allah gave in infinite wisdom, should never be erased," said Ivan Postivich, stroking her bare shoulder. "And men who seek to bury these words, know not the infinite compassion of Allah."

Saffron burst into the bedchamber. He grabbed Ivan Postivich by the shoulder, yanking him from the bed.

"Come with me, now!" he insisted. "They are within the palace walls."

But before Postivich had a chance to react, a small white figure in a flowing caftan raced into the room.

"I arrest you in the name of Sultan Mahmud!" shouted a high-pitched voice.

Postivich leapt to his feet at the sound of the voice and found the room filling with Topkapi soldiers, led by the short figure of the eunuch Emerald.

Two Solaks immediately tried to wrestle the giant to the ground. He roared and with a twist of his massive shoulders, pinned the two under him before anyone could intercede. He seized a guard's scimitar and began slashing his way through the troops that stood between him and the door.

"Come, Esma!" he shouted.

"There is no place for me to run. I am an Ottoman Sultane!"

When he realized that she would not follow him, Postivich dropped his arms to his side. He was seized by a Solak and swiftly bound in ropes.

"Put some clothes on the beast," ordered Emerald, his lips curling upward. "And take him to the Sultan for execution."

Mahmud lost no time in commanding that the hanging ground be made ready. He sent his Solaks to spread the word in the taverns, Bazaar, and docks that the traitorous Ahmed Kadir had been captured and would die at sundown in the Hippodrome, as had thousands of other Janissaries. The whole of Constantinople would witness his death.

Esma Sultan curled her fingers around the quill, wincing in pain. Her hands were raw from beating on the Topkapi doors. The sultan had refused to see her.

*Dear Brother Blessed Sultan Mahmud II,*

*If you have ever truly loved me, you will spare Ahmed Kadir's life. The people of Constantinople honor him in their Friday prayers, whisper his praises in the marketplace, streets, and taverns. Let him live, and your subjects will see you as merciful and strong.*

*Your loving sister who shares your father's blood,*

*Esma Sultan*

She pressed the wax seal with her ring and sent the messenger running to speed the letter to Topkapi. He was not to return without a reply.

"He will answer me," Esma Sultan said, speaking to Irena.

Irena shook her head.

"It will not be the answer you hope for. I cannot put faith in a letter. Come, I have another plan."

Irena led her mistress into the gardens.

"Open the taps," Esma Sultan commanded a eunuch. "See that we are not disturbed."

"Hear me out before you speak," began Irena. "What I propose is as fantastic as any game we ever played as children in the Serail of Topkapi. Except we will be playing for lives."

"What have you concocted, sweet Irena?" said Esma Sultan, looking at the young woman sadly. "There is nothing that can negate a Sultan's command."

"Are you truly untouchable?"

Esma Sultan raised her chin proudly.

"My father Sultan Abdulhamid decreed I was his favorite daughter. I am as royal as my brother himself."

"The Sultan would not dare harm you?"

"Of course not. He would kill anyone who did."

Irena smiled. "Then listen to my plan."

An hour later, the messenger returned, his head bowed low.

Esma Sultan rose from a bench where she sat forehead to forehead with Irena, whispering.

"A reply from the Sultan," he announced, looking at the grass under his feet.

He delivered the letter to Esma Sultan's hands, and backed up bowing.

"What does he say? What does he say?" said Irena.

Esma Sultan unfolded the parchment. Her hand flew to her mouth.

*"Be there to see the giant die."*

The Sultan's chief Solak led Ivan Postivich from the stench and darkness of the Topkapi dungeon. The prisoner's hands were bound with rope behind him. Feeling had long since left his arms and fingers.

The helpless giant blinked his eyes against the sunlight. He sucked in the fresh air of the courtyard, like a drowning man. He halted midbreath, detecting a familiar odor, spicy and welcoming.

Horse.

He heard a whinny before he had time to recognize her.

"Peri," he whispered. "Peri, my beauty."

The bridled mare moved towards her master, but was abruptly yanked back by the attendant. Postivich noticed that there was no saddle on the mare.

"The Sultan has decreed that you be hanged from the plane tree," said the Solak. "You will be mounted on your horse. The noose shall be put around your neck. At the Sultan's command, your horse will be whipped forward into a gallop. You will be left hanging."

Ivan Postivich did not answer. He stumbled towards his beloved Peri, his eyes scanning the indentation deep in her shoulder where she had been wounded.

"The Stable Master did well tending her injuries," he said, his hands longing to stroke the newly formed flesh. His eyes brimmed with tears—the first emotion he had shown since the Solaks had taken him prisoner.

The chief Solak jerked his hand upward.

"Place the prisoner atop the horse," he said.

Two men seized Postivich, heaving him onto the mare. They led the prisoner to the Hippodrome and his execution.

When the afternoon dust and heat had settled and the cicadas' buzz was quieted by the Bosphorus breeze, the population of Constantinople gathered in the Hippodrome. A stout rope had been tied in a noose around a branch on the old plane tree, its bark stripped from the weight and friction of so many hangings.

The man Constantinople called Ahmed Kadir was brought into the area, his head, shoulders, and torso covered with a cloth sack, much like the sacks in which he had drowned his victims.

"Look!" said the ropemaker, humiliated his handiwork would be the death of Ahmed Kadir. "The giant rides his own mare, Peri."

"The horse appears to have recovered from her wounds," said man at the ropemaker's elbow. "Now she is pressed into service as her master's executioner."

"How's that?" said another, listening to the conversation.

"Once the noose is around the giant's neck, the Sultan will give the command to whip the mare into a gallop, leaving Ahmed Kadir swinging from the noose."

The New Order of Topkapi, dressed in their European uniforms, watched uncomfortably, for the death of a brave soldier was never the desire of an honorable military man. There were calls from the crowd, and jeers and curses from Sufis who had the courage to shout their insults to the Sultan.

As Peri was led to the plane tree and the sack was removed from Postivich's head, the executioner whispered a prayer to Allah and asked his victim's forgiveness.

"You must serve your Sultan," was the giant's reply. "Go ahead and perform your duty bravely."

The thick rope was placed around Postivich's neck and underneath his chin and gently tightened as if his mother were straightening his collar before sending him off to school.

"Thank you for your kindness," said Postivich.

The Sultan watched the executioner's tenderness, scowling.

*Where was Esma Sultan? Why was she not here to witness the death of this traitor?*

The crowd looked up at the Sultan, waiting for his order to proceed.

*Where is my sister?*

As the Sultan raised his hand to initiate the execution, a murmur rippled through the crowd.

Two veiled women galloped into the Hippodrome, their cloaks flying behind them.

The crowd watched motionless.

One approached the Sultan, grasping his hand in midair and yanking him off his feet before he could signal for the execution. The other raced towards Peri and the groom who held the reins. With a cry from the battlefields of the Serbian plains, she swung a scimitar, the blade slicing through the rope and then sinking deep into the chest of the fat white eunuch, who stood beside the executioner.

"Esma!" the Sultan screamed. "Treason!"

The only answer was her laugh, ringing in the air as the women galloped their horses out of the Hippodrome with Peri in pursuit, her rider swaying, hands tied behind his back.

Mahmud hesitated. The Kapikulu captain spoke, "Your orders, my Sultan?"

"Capture the women and bring them back alive. Do not harm them in any way or you shall be executed. Do not forget for an instant that my sister is an Ottoman Sultane."

"And Ahmed Kadir?"

"Kill him on the spot."

It was nearing sundown, and the women rode hard for the hills east of the city. Their horses' shoes clattered on cobblestones and then thundered on hard-packed dirt. Wild dogs tried to pursue them, but were quickly outrun. The orphan boys cheered as the three riders raced past the stables—and the boys upset a melon cart to slow the Kapikulu who pursued them.

A Serbian boy climbed onto a horse and bade two other boys to do the same. They rode along the riverside and doubled back to the stable, their beardless faces gleaming in the setting sun. The Solaks saw their silhouettes and followed them, while the trio of fugitives plunged into the River Lycus and rode off to the hills beyond.

When the Kapikulu captain finally realized his mistake, he cursed the boys and their heaving steeds, and raised his scimitar over his head.

The old Head Groom rode out, breathless from the chase.

"Sir, we are required to exercise the polo and cirit horses at top speed every day," he said. "Why do you pursue us? Do you have a fatwa for these orphan boys of the charity of Aya Sofya and Esma Sultan?"

Three days later, there was still no sign of the women or Ahmed Kadir. There were many citizens who hated the Sultan for the massacre of the Janissaries and considered it a bad omen. There were humble homes and shepherds' huts that were open to a hero who had escaped the Sultan's wrath.

At Topkapi, as the sun set on the third day, the ailing Valide Sultan, Nakshidil, begged to receive her last rites. The city mourned the imminent loss of a woman who was known for her charity to the poor.

A eunuch accompanied Dr. Stephane Karatheodory and his female assistant into the Valide's room. Once the room was secured and the eunuch sent to guard the entryway, the nurse stripped off her veil to show Nakshidil her pearl-glazed mouth and twisted grin.

"You have returned at last, Bezm-i Alem!"

"Irena. I am your Irena. And you shall rest in the peace of the arms of the Holy Virgin."

"A woman's embrace I would welcome," Nakshidil said. "Forgive my son. He has too much of the Al-ilah in him and not enough of Diana."

"His sons will not," said Irena.

"You will bear his sons?"

"If you wish it so. Perhaps then I can stanch this bloodshed and curse upon Constantinople."

Nakshidil coughed weakly.

"Lie back, Valide Sultane. You tire yourself with such emotion," counseled the physician, signaling Irena to keep silence.

"No, no! Let her speak!" cried the dying woman, her hands clenched in fists of pain. "Where is Esma?"

"She has returned to her palace in Ortakoy. She is meeting with her brother to negotiate peace between them. He cannot forget that they have loved one another all their lives. As part of the agreement, I shall return to Topkapi as his wife and bear his children. And I shall be the Sultan Valide after you pass."

Nakshidil grasped Irena's hand. "Ah, my daughter! My grandsons shall have compassion."

"That much I swear. They shall learn compassion and mercy, and the essence of the Women's Verses."

Nakshidil smiled blindly at the ceiling.

"If only I could write to my cousin Josephine," she whispered.

Irena bent over the dying woman and kissed her forehead tenderly.

"Close your eyes, my Sultane. May you rest in peace."

# Chapter 26

*Pirot, Serbia*
*March 1831*

Five years after the Massacre of the Janissaries, an old friend set out in search of Esma Sultan's drowning guard. The road to the north was hard and frozen and the wind cracked ice from the branches of the plane trees, frightening the horse. The rider whispered soothing words, "*Kus, Kus,*" to his mount, wishing there had been an early spring rather than this hard frost on a strange road at the farthest fringe of the Empire.

There was no one to point out the way, but Ahmed the oarsman, now four years an officer with the Ottoman navy, was skilled at navigation. He blinked up at the North Star, clearly visible in the night of the new moon, and heard again the words the Sufi had spoken in the hushed and hurried conversation that had sent Ahmed riding into the night. Go north, the Sufi had whispered. The giant lives.

And now he was here, on this cold lonely road on the Serbian frontier. In the black of night, he was keenly aware of the breath and heartbeat of his horse, the sweat and warmth beneath his legs as the horse walked mile after mile through the empty countryside.

*The village must be near*, he thought. The Sufi's hastily sketched map was stuffed in his saddlebag, but Ahmed had memorized the route and the landmarks.

The mare, as if she shared his thoughts, broke into a trot and whinnied, the shrill sound startling Ahmed, sending a violent shiver up his spine.

In the same moment, a black coach caught up with him from behind, the clatter of its wheels emerging from the echo of the horse's whinny, its side lanterns illuminating the patchwork of hoarfrost on the trees along the road.

Ahmed saluted, seeing the red crescent and star on the side of the coach, knowing that this was an Ottoman convoy. The turbaned driver didn't acknowledge him, barely reining the horses wide enough to keep from clipping the rider. He sat grimly, eyes straining ahead, weary from the ten-day trip from Constantinople. His turban was grimy, splattered by the frozen mud churned up by the carriage wheels.

As the coach brushed by, the crimson velvet curtains parted and Ahmed saw an aquiline profile of a woman. He pulled his wool cloak around his face with one hand, keeping his horse in check with the other. He had no wish to be recognized.

When the Royal Coach had passed, he urged his horse into a canter, taking care not to follow too closely.

As he crested the hill, Ahmed surveyed the village below. A simple hamlet beside a stream, bordered by an orchard. The trees were bleached skeletons, frosted and glowing in the dancing light from the coach lantern.

Ahmed stopped his horse and watched the coach until it stopped in front of a thatched-roof hut at the edge of the trees. The coachman rubbed his freezing hands hard before descending to help his passengers.

A beam of light broke from the hut's open door, and a giant of a man emerged. He stopped just outside the door and stood erect.

Two women emerged from the coach, the first wore a diaphanous veil. She turned, gazing at the little house, the stream, and the orchard. The huge man met her halfway to the coach, tenderly removing the yasmak and kissing her face, as a brother would. Her face glowed with pearl-like incandescence in the lantern light.

A moment later, the second woman emerged, taking the driver's offered hand. She walked a few steps with imperious elegance towards the man and her traveling companion. Then she broke and ran to her lover and he to her. He swept her up in an embrace that hid them both from Ahmed's view as they merged into a single figure. The coachman and the other woman turned away as well. It was a passionate moment that no other should witness, meant for no eyes but the lovers themselves.

Ahmed smiled down at them, and silently turned his horse back towards Constantinople.

# HISTORICAL NOTES

## TOLERANCE IN TURKEY

Bezm-i Alem did indeed bear Mahmud II two sons, Abdulmecid and Abdulaziz. Abdulmecid became the first Sultan to grant equal status to Christians and to publicly deplore the slave markets.

"It is a shameful and barbarous practice," said Sultan Abdulmecid, " . . . for rational beings to buy and sell their fellow human creatures. Are these poor creatures not our equals before God?"

Sultan Abdulmecid protected the Jews from the persecution of the Christians. He declared that the "Jewish nation will be protected and defended." The Sultan decreed a Kosher kitchen and a Sabbath leave be instituted in the Imperial Medical School so as to encourage Jews to study to become doctors.

Most importantly, he wanted to unite people under the banner of humanity and the Turkish nation. The Sultan pronounced, "In one word . . . to nationalize all these fragments of nations who cover the soil of Turkey, by so much impartiality, gentleness, equality, and tolerance that each one finds its honour, its conscience and its security interested to cooperate in maintaining the empire."

Never had anyone dreamed that such equality and altruism could have been championed by an Ottoman Sultan.

It was whispered in the Bazaar that the unprecedented kindness of the young Sultan was due to his mother and that the bloodshed of the Janissaries had at last dried and faded from the conscience of Topkapi. Bezm-i Alem became one of the most benevolent of all Valides in Ottoman history, aiding the poor and particularly the women of Constantinople.

Esma Sultan retired to her palace outside the Imperial City. On June 29, 1839, Sultan Mahmud II died in Esma Sultan's house in Camlica, at the age of fifty-four. On July 15, only a month after the Sultan's death, Kaptan Pasha Ahmed, a former officer in the Imperial Navy, sailed into the port of Alexandria, leading most of the Ottoman navy over to Muhammed Ali of Egypt. Europe sided with the Ottomans and came to their rescue, though parts of the Empire were lost forever.

And the drowning guard? He is a fictional character, not traceable in the Ottomans' meticulous records of history. But, as the novel would say . . .

Some say he led a rebellion in Serbia that finally freed the territory from the yoke of Ottoman rule. Still others say he lived out his life in a northern village at the edges of the Empire, where he entertained a mysterious veiled woman on the new moon of certain months.

There were many in the Bazaar who swore they had seen a phantom giant riding the seven hills of Constantinople atop a grey-dappled horse every full moon, and that the dogs howl at his presence.

But then everyone loves a legend.

# AN OTTOMAN GLOSSARY

**ABLUTIONS:** In respect to Islam, the ritual bathing of Muslims in preparation for entering a mosque or before seeing the Sultan. The Koran also requires bathing before and after sexual relations.

**AGA:** The master or gentleman; also the head of an organization such as the aga of the Janissaries.

**AKCE:** A silver coin.

**ALLAH:** The word for God among the Muslim people.

**BASTINADO:** Punishment, by beating the soles of the victim's feet with a cudgel or truncheon.

**BEKTASHI:** A liberal order of Sufis who were attached to the Janissary Corps.

**BEZM-I ALEM:** Jewel of the Universe.

**BOSPHORUS:** The strait that divides Europe from Asia, connecting the Black Sea to the Sea of Marmara, which then joins the Mediterranean. The Bosphorus provided Constantinople the sea access that made it the major trade city of the world.

**CAVUS:** The official who starts the cirit game and announces the players and their accomplishments before the start of the match.

**CIRIT:** An equestrian sport used to sharpen cavalrymen's war skills. Two teams line up on opposite sides of the field and one member of Team A throws a javelin or spear (jeered) at a member of Team B, trying to hit the rider. Once the jeered has left the hand of Team A's player, another opposing rider on Team B gallops out with a jeered of his own and tries to hit Team A's player as he wheels around and races back to the safety of his team's line.

**CONSTANTINOPLE:** The ancient capital of Byzantium, and later the home of the Ottoman Empire. The name of the city was officially changed to Istanbul in 1930. During Ottoman times it was also known as Istanbul, Islambol, Stambul, Estambol, Kushta, Tsarigrad, Rumiyya al-kubra, New Rome, New Jerusalem, the City of Saints, the Gate of Happiness, the Eye of the World, the Refuge of the Universe, the Polis, and the City.

**CORBACI:** A janissary title, equivalent to "captain" of a unit or "orta." Corbacis were normally identified by a soup ladle tied to the sash of their tunic, which indicated that they were not only the orta's leader, but saw to it that ample food was provided to their fighting men. Each "kazan" or copper pilaf cauldron was marked with the banner of an individual orta.

**DERVISH:** A member of a Sufi order.

**DEVSHIRME:** The "gathering" of children from Christian families to serve as palace servants and in the Sultan's army.

**DJINN:** An evil spirit, especially associated with still water and death.

**EFENDI:** Title of honor, equivalent to master or sir.

**EFRIT:** A spirit, usually malevolent.

**EUNUCH:** A castrated man and a servant to the harem and to the Sultan himself. Purchased in the Sudan or other parts of North Africa, boys would be castrated by a Copt, as castration was strictly forbidden by the Koran. They were then transported to Constantinople. Some white captives were also castrated and served as eunuchs in the Ottoman Empire.

**FATWA (ALSO FETWA):** A written reply or order by a Mufti concerning Islamic law.

**GOLDEN HORN:** An inlet of the Bosphorus, dividing the city of Constantinople. The ancient walled city of Byzantium is located on the southern shore while the Christian and Jewish settlements of Pera and Galata was located on the northern shore.

**HAMAM:** The bath or bathhouse; often a socially important gathering place for women during idle time, where news is exchanged.

**IMAM:** A leader of prayers and often a teacher.

**JANISSARY:** A member of the Sultan's main army, composed of 196 ortas or divisions. The Janissaries were primarily non-Muslims who either volunteered or were drafted into the corps as young children. They were circumcised and converted to Islam.

**KADIN:** a woman or wife, in the novel used as the wives of the Sultan.

**KADI:** A judge administering the law of the Koran (Sheriat) and Ottoman law.

**KAPIKULU:** The highest echelon of the Janissary soliders, picked by the Agas and Sultan to be educated at Topkapi palace. The best were trained as elite cavalrymen.

**KAYIK:** Boat, usually narrow and streamlined for gliding across the Bosphorus.

**KAYMAK:** Heavy cream.

**KORAN:** The holy book of Islam.

**KUCUK:** Small or little; a term of endearment, "little one."

**LALA:** Tutor.

**MAHMUD II:** The son of Sultan Abulhamid and half brother to both Sultan Mustafa (who tried to murder him) and Esma Sultan. Sultan Selim III was his cousin.

**MEHMED II OR MEHMED THE CONQUEROR:** The Ottoman Sultan whose forces conquered the kingdom of Byzantium and captured Constantinople in 1453.

**MINARET:** A mosque tower from which a muezzin calls the faithful to prayers.

**MUEZZIN:** The man who calls the faithful to prayers five times a day from a minaret.

**MUFTI:** The highest religious official who interprets the Koran and metes out punishment (including fatwas).

**MULLAH:** A title of respect for a man learned in the Koran and Islamic law.

**ORTA:** A unit of the Janissary army, usually approximately one hundred soldiers. There were 196 ortas in the Sultan's army.

**OTTOMAN EMPIRE:** The vast state founded in 1299 by Osman Bey, which became a true Empire in 1453 under Mehmed II. The Empire at its height encompassed the modern states of Romania, Hungary, Egypt, parts of Greece including Macedonia, Anatolia, Syria, Libya, Armenia, Georgia, Ukrania, and Persia. Mehmed the Conqueror captured the prized jewel of Europe and the Orient, Byzantium, and its capital, Constantinople.

**PALACE OF TEARS:** Palace where harem women are retired, either because they are too old or because they belonged to a prior sultan.

**PASHA:** An Ottoman title for officers or governors of high rank. The relative rank of pashas was indicated by horsetails, displayed as a symbol of rank (three horsetails was the highest).

**PERI:** A benign spirit or fairy.

**PERSIA:** The former Empire that now is Iran. Persians were admired for their grace and culture, fine literature, language, poetry, and art.

**SERAIL:** The French word for harem; also *seraglio* in Italian. Both terms used in novel.

**SERBO-CROAT:** A language or dialect that served as a common tongue in communicating among the conquered people of Eastern Europe (especially Croatia and Serbia).

**SHERIAT:** The law of the Koran and Islam as administered by the Kadis (appointed judges by the Sultan).

**SIMIT:** A pretzel-shaped bread.

**SOLAK:** The Topkapi guards (and archers) who formed the 60-63rd ortas of the Janissaries. They served as palace guards and were fiercely loyal to the Ottomans.

**SUFI:** A member of a Muslim order; one who searches for higher level of spirituality. Sufis are sometimes known as "gentle Muslims" and have more tolerant and diverse views on women, prohibitions, etc.

**SULTANE:** An Ottoman princess.

**TOPKAPI:** The Royal Palace of the Ottoman Sultans, located on the shore of the Golden Horn, its eastern walls flanking the shore of the Bosphorus.

**TURSU:** Pickle or pickled vegetables.

**ULEMA:** Muslim legal scholars and learned men of a mosque who are the arbiters of sharia law.

**VALIDE:** The mother of a Sultan.

**WHITE SEA:** The Mediterranean.

**YALI:** A waterside residence.

**YASMAK:** A veil, usually of fine gauze.

# AUTHOR'S NOTES ON
## *The Drowning Guard*

Visiting Istanbul in the summer of 2001, I was swept away by the vibrant history of Constantinople—the rich mix of cultures and religions, and the continuing sense, even now, of the tremendous world influence this city has possessed across the centuries. Constantinople has been referred to as the "Jewel of the Universe" and certainly its location on the Bosphorus at the junction of Europe and Asia, its ancient cathedrals and mosques, its massive walls and soaring towers and bustling Bazaars are beyond compare.

I have woven this tale as a skein of fiction around a core of truth. There was an Ottoman Sultan Mahmud II, who was an extremely handsome and powerful ruler, who had an older half sister named Esma Sultan. She was indulged beyond all others and her father Abdulhamid I gave her a palace when she was only ten. (Visitors to Istanbul can stay in one of her palaces, which has been converted into an elegant hotel.)

And her life was indeed a scandal. Philip Mansel, author of *Constantinople: City of the World's Desire, 1453-1924*, wrote that Esma would haunt the countryside and the Christian neighborhoods looking for lovers. It was rumored that the physically spent young men were subsequently dispatched into the Bosphorus, after she had her way with them. (Drowning was a common way of disposing of enemies and other inconvenient people in the time of the Ottomans.)

Ottoman princes who were in line to the throne were a constant threat to any reigning Sultan—even though he often was their father—and so they were "caged" (in extreme hedonistic luxury) until the Sultan's death and their own ascension to the throne. At that time, the warden would approach the cage and announce the prince's liberty and impending coronation. There is a story of a male pretender who tried to hide and refused to leave the cage when the guard approached him, thinking that surely it was a trick and he was not chosen as the new Sultan, but the next victim of strangling.

Not all Sultans were as deeply paranoid about their progeny usurping the throne and many princes were allowed to spend time outside the cage and attend ceremonies and celebrations. However, they still had to return to the cage when the occasion was finished.

Mahmud II is reported to have drowned over two hundred women from his half brother Mustafa's harem. Drowning, strangulation, and poisonings were common in the Sultans' time.

As to bisexuality, this was a way of life in Constantinople during that era. While Esma Sultan did in fact introduce her brother Mahmud to Nazip and Bezm-i Alem, women from her own harem, she also introduced him to a man, Mustafa Efendi, who became the Sultan's personal secretary and one of Mahmud's many lovers. (And it is true that Nazip, happy living in the palace of Esma Sultan, thrice refused him, as was her right as Esma Sultan's adopted daughter.)

And, yes, Esma Sultan, although a princess, had her own harem—as did many important and powerful eunuchs. A harem was a sign of status and wealth. In Esma Sultan's case, her harem may have been largely a matter of housing slaves, servants, and female companions. She also had a female orchestra.

The massacre of the Janissaries was, regrettably, very true. Many of the aspects of that sad event were as I have portrayed them and the Bektashi Sufis were banished from Constantinople for their affiliation with the Janissary Corps.

Although there is no record of women's polo in Constantinople itself, the neighboring lands in Persia and Armenia did indeed have women polo players in the royal court. Turkey has pre-Islamic legends of strong women riders who challenged men on horseback.

Nakshidil, or Aimée, was a young French girl of Martinique who was captured by the Barbary Pirates and sold into slavery. (She was the protagonist of Janet Wallach's novel, *Seraglio*, Nan A.Talese Books, Doubleday.) Aimée was delivered to the Sultan Abdulhamid and named Nakshidil after his favorite wife, who had recently died and left a young son, Mahmud. The new Nakshidil took the place of the dead mother and raised Mahmud as her own son. She later became Valide Sultan when Mahmud II ascended the throne. (Mahmud himself just narrowly escaped death during the same struggle, when a servant woman threw ashes into the eyes of Mustafa II's men and the young prince hid silently in a pile of laundry.)

Mustafa II was in power for only a few years before the political tide turned against him, and his younger half brother, Mahmud, was installed as the new Sultan.

Nakshidil always maintained that she was Empress Josephine's cousin and she brought French music, language, and culture into the Serail and Topkapi. When she lay on her deathbed, her devoted son Mahmud II allowed a Christian priest to enter Topkapi and administer the last rites to his beloved mother.

The Greek doctor, Stephane Karatheodory, was the Sultan's personal physician during the lifetime of Esma Sultan. Said to be able to read the Bible in eighteen languages, he was an intellectual who began a dynasty of court physicians to Mahmud's sons, grandsons, and great-grandsons.

Research indicates that the people of Mecca did worship the

moon, Al-ilah, before the coming of the Prophet, Mohammed. The passages that are commonly called "the Satanic Verses" are the same benign words that invite the intercession of women— specifically the gentle Al-Lat, the daughter star that borders the crescent moon—into man's decision making. What is so terrible about inviting the feminine into the world? Here is an example of the Yin and Yang of the Near Orient and we realize that there was a time when the male and female—the moon and the sun—played a part in divinity and, arguably, everyday life in the Middle East.

And yet, the term "Satanic Verses" sounds so malevolent— such a misnomer for those few words in the suras, so beautiful and forgiving, so full of hope. The message was, and still is, an urgent prayer for equality and a universe that appreciates the feminine nature, with its gentle intercession and compassion.

The sons of Bezm-i Alem (also named Irena/Sophie in the novel) ascended the Ottoman throne. Abdulmecid (1839-61) became the benevolent Sultan who was known for his reforms of the strict Ottoman rule, his openness and benevolence toward other religions and cultures, and his love of women and wine (which, as alcohol, is forbidden under Islamic law). I believe that his reign may have set the groundwork for the intellectual aspirations and accomplishments of progressive politics to come decades later—specifically for the democratic achievements of the great leader of the Turkish people, Mustafa Kemal or Ataturk.

And the Drowning Guard? When each lover was drowned, there had to be someone—an assassin—to carry out the murderous deed. I began to wonder what kind of man he would have been, the nightmares and regrets he would have endured, and started to write.

My gratitude to Philip Mansel for his exquisite and learned work about the Ottomans, for it was his account of Esma Sultan that inspired this novel.

# ACKNOWLEDGMENTS

Philip Mansel's book *Constantinople, City of the World's Desire 1453-1924* was a major fount of information and inspiration for *The Drowning Guard*. Not only were his sections on the life of Esma Sultan critical to my novel but so were his descriptions of the Janissary Corps and their rebellion against the sultan in 1826.

Thank you to the country and people of Turkey and in particular, Istanbul.

The splendor of the city and the legends of Constantinople dazzled me. How could I not write about such a magical place?

My sister Nancy Elisha has read every page published and unpublished of my novels. Had she not given me early and steady encouragement, I may not have become a writer. I love you, Nancy.

Along the way there were friends who were early readers of this novel, long before it was published. Thanks to Sarah Kennedy Flug, Lucia Caretto, Nancy Kuhn, Ted Diamandopoulos, Anne Fitzgibbon Shusterman, and John and Susan Boslough. Thank you for keeping me afloat when my spirits dipped, enduring so many years without a publisher.

Editor and screenwriter Lindsay Guzzardo discovered my novels and believed in me. Eternal gratitude to you, Lindsay. I'll never forget you.

My agent Deborah Schneider recognized potential in my rough drafts twenty years ago. Thank you, Deborah, for taking me back after such a long absence and jump-starting my writing career. Thanks to Cathy Gleason and Victoria Marini at Gelfman Schneider for their hard work on my behalf.

Terry Goodman oversaw the publication of this novel. Terry, Lindsay was right. You are great. Your sense of humor carries the day. Thanks for stepping in as my acquisition editor and making this happen.

I appreciate my agents in London at Curtis Brown. Thank you Betsy Robbins, Sophie Baker, and Claire Nozieres for helping me connect with readers in other languages.

My editor Melody Guy worked hard with me on the novel, making suggestions throughout the manuscript that greatly improved the read. Thank you for your great patience and expertise, Melody.

My Amazon team—how do I love you? You send me Fran's chocolate caramels, cheery emails, and good news. You help me to connect with readers every day, to my great joy. Thank you, Nikki Sprinkle, Jessica Poore, Gracie Doyle, and all the rest.

My thanks to the production team, including copyeditor Paul Thomason, Jackie Ball, Brent Fattore, and Michael del Rosario. Also, my gratitude to proofreader Elaine Caughlan. What a lot of care and research you put into this, with all the Turkish, Ottoman, and Greek words in my story.

Thanks also to the Amazon art department. You always knock my socks off!

Thanks for the arresting cover design by the BookDesigners.

Marly Rusoff, thank you for your hard work on early versions of this novel, so many years ago. Also thanks to Kim Witherspoon and David Forrer, who also believed in this novel.

Alev Lytle Croutier, Bonnie Kaslan, and Rain Yagmur Archuleta—thank you for your generous offers of help with Turkish, Ottoman, and Greek words. Meltem Sonmez, thank you for helping with pronunciation in reading the Brilliance audio version of the book.

And thanks to the good energy of my yoga instructors, who straightened out the kinks in my mind and body while I worked on the book! Thanks Marlon McGann, Bel Carpenter, and Joanne Connington.

My gratitude to my beloved parents, Betty and Fred Lafferty, who read to us every night as children before we went to sleep. Those Grimm's fairy tales shaped my imagination at a tender age, sending their furling tendrils into my dreams. Is it any wonder I became a writer?

Gratitude to the Aspen Writer's Foundation and director Julie Comins Pickrell for a scholarship awarded in the summer of 2004, where I worked on an early draft of this novel at Aspen Summer Words. Writer Ron Carlson taught me to "stay in the room." As his student I learned to see more, use my senses as I lingered in a moment longer, rather than racing on to the next plot point. (Best writing advice anyone has every given me, Ron . . . and I kept the fig in the story.)

Thank you to Lisa Consiglio for her support through the years.

This book would never have been possible without the help of other authors' research. At one point while researching this book, I had fourteen books marked with sticky notes, all spread out on my bed while writing one single chapter!

Some books that were invaluable—those I returned to time and time again—included: Philip Mansel's *Constantinople: City of the World's Desire (1453-1924)*, St. Martins Press, 1998; *The Imperial Harem of the Sultans, Memoirs of Leyla (Saz) Hanimefendi*, Peva Publications, 1994; *The Imperial Harem, Women and Sovereignty in the Ottoman Empire*, Leslie P. Peirce, Oxford University Press, 1993; *Lords of the Horizons*, Jason Goodwin, Picador, 2003; *The Ottoman Centuries, Lord Kinross*, Harper Perennial, 1979; *The Janissaries*, Godfrey Goodwin, Saqi Books, 1979; *Istanbul*, John Freely, Penguin Books, 1998; *Harem, The World Behind the Veil*, Alev Lytle Croutier, Abbeville Press, 1991; *Istanbul: Memories and the City*,

Orhan Pamuk, Vintage International Editions, 2006. My gratitude to these authors for their expertise that informed my prose.

Finally, thank you Andy Stone. You taught me the craft of writing and pure dedication. You have always been my first editor . . . and the love of my life.

# ABOUT THE AUTHOR

NORAFELLER.COM

The daughter of a naval commander, Linda Lafferty attended fourteen different schools growing up, ultimately graduating from the University of Colorado with a master's degree and a PhD in education. Her peripatetic childhood nourished a lifelong love of travel, and she studied abroad in England, France, Mexico, and Spain. Her uncle introduced her to the sport of polo when she was just ten years old, and she enjoys playing to this day. She also competed on the Lancaster University Riding Team in England in stadium jumping, crosscountry, and dressage. A veteran school educator, she juggled teaching and working polo ponies while writing this book. She lives in Colorado.